RUHE

RUHE

SIXTUS BECKMESSER

Copyright © 2024 Sixtus Beckmesser

The moral right of the author has been asserted.

Apart from any fair dealing for the purposes of research or private study, or criticism or review, as permitted under the Copyright, Designs and Patents Act 1988, this publication may only be reproduced, stored or transmitted, in any form or by any means, with the prior permission in writing of the publishers, or in the case of reprographic reproduction in accordance with the terms of licences issued by the Copyright Licensing Agency. Enquiries concerning reproduction outside those terms should be sent to the publishers.

This is a work of fiction. Names, characters, businesses, places, events and incidents are either the products of the author's imagination or used in a fictitious manner. Any resemblance to actual persons, living or dead, or actual events is purely coincidental.

Troubador Publishing Ltd
Unit E2 Airfield Business Park,
Harrison Road, Market Harborough,
Leicestershire LE16 7UL
Tel: 0116 279 2299
Email: books@troubador.co.uk
Web: www.troubador.co.uk

ISBN 9781805144434

British Library Cataloguing in Publication Data.
A catalogue record for this book is available from the British Library.

Printed and bound in Great Britain by 4edge Limited
Typeset in 12pt Adobe Garamond Pro by Troubador Publishing Ltd, Leicester, UK

Matador is an imprint of Troubador publishing

To the wonderful people of County Kildare and Franconia

CONTENTS

1	Wiegenlied	3
2	Königshof	19
3	Viktor	32
4	Enthronement	48
5	Vienna	62
6	The Fund	68
7	Durch Zauber Zu Dir Kam	81
8	Johannistag	93
9	Champion	106
10	Verlobung	115
11	The Visit	119
12	The Chase	137
13	Tannhäuser	154
14	Tiresias	168
15	The Letter	180
16	The Long Pilgrimage	192
17	Searching	213
18	A Stony Path	232
19	Festspiele	250
20	No Laws but His Own	267

Acknowledgements 277

LIVONIA

PART FOUR

1
WIEGENLIED

Im Schweige der nacht
Nur lacht mir der Quell.[1]

R Wagner *Tristan und Isolde* Act 2

At night, she could just hear the rustling of the trees mixing with the deeper murmur of the stream as it rushed down amid the pinewoods. The water then passed through the broad meadow, skirting the side of the orchard. She sat listening to it at a sleepy three o'clock while her greedy son guzzled at her breast. She would talk to him as he sucked.

'I don't know whether it's down to Franken or Kildare but it's great trencherman, you are.'

Niki would gurgle but whether in agreement or just because of Detty's generous milk supply, she never knew. After burping lavishly, he would give a sigh and go rapidly to sleep. Detty, by now wide awake, would lie listening to the *Bach*.

Autumn was now stretching on, and the apples were nearly ready to be picked from the orchards to begin fermenting. Later the alcoholic

---

1   In the still of the night, it is just the stream that laughs with me.

juice would be distilled into the famous Oberdorf *hausgemacht Apfelbrannt.*

It was an idyllic life. Marc was on temporary secondment from London and was enjoying active soldiering again. He was involved in exercises near Ingoldstadt. He had a good many free days and evenings, so he was often home around at bedtime.

'He's all your son' he would say gazing at Niki, still with a slight air of unbelief, as the scion of the von Ritters made his demands incisively known.

'He's even got your voice.'

'Yes,' retorted Detty 'and your smile, your eyes and your hands.'

Max and Sophie had restored and given them an apartment in the *Altes Herrenhaus*, which was in the middle of the orchard behind the *Schloss*. It had been built as a dower house for the widow of an eighteenth-century *Graf*. It had a modest two stories finished in the local cream rendering surmounted by a small belfry and a grey onion dome. The rooms were generous with high old wooden ceilings and a fabulously attractive but rather impractical kitchen. Detty had the help of Giovanna, the daughter of an Italian family, who had moved locally. Gianna's father, Giovanni, known to everyone as GiGi, was employed at the family timber yard several kilometres away towards Bad Steben. Her mother, Amelia, worked at the *Schloss*. Gianna had returned from Italy, where she had been staying with friends to complete her *maturita* and had some time before she needed to go back to Italy for university. There seemed no urgency about university and in the meanwhile, she was delighted with the chance of helping the young *Contessa* with her *bambino*, which also provided the opportunity of practising her English and learning a bit of German.

On fine days, Niki had his morning sleep in the shade of the fruit trees under Gianna's watchful eye. The pram had to have a net to protect him from the autumnal buzzing wasps and windfalls. But once it was fixed, Detty could then go alone across the drive and lawn to the back terrace and the music room at the *Schloss*. She was studying *Magdalene* and *Elisabeth* hard. As a change she worked on *Sieglinde* which she was learning, speculatively, at the same time as her serious efforts for the roles she was definitely going to sing, including next year's Bayreuth *Tannhäuser*. When the increasing rain of the Franconian late summer poured down, she took Niki with her, covering the short distance between the two houses in the car. He gurgled happily enough on the floor by the piano while his mother did exercises and recited. One morning, just to see how it went, for the first time since he had been born, she sang *Allmächt'ge Jungfrau, hor mein Flehen*[2] in full voice. She was afraid it might frighten him but no – she was enchanted to see her little son looking up at her smiling as she sang. As she finished '*nur anzuflehen für seine Schuld*'[3] the door to the music room opened quietly and her mother-in-law peeped into the room.

'It's still there then, Detti' she said, 'that was wonderful.'

'I think it's coming but I feel quite nervous about it.'

'That's sensible of you. Don't be in too much of a hurry. Some have come unstuck trying to push on too quickly after a baby. I had a cousin who didn't realise that she wasn't ready until she got on stage. Fortunately, it was only *Erfurt*, and they were quite kind to her, but it didn't help her confidence.'

'I know, but I think that it's the anxiety that makes you want to try. Just to see if it's all right, you know.'

Sophie nodded understanding the 'it', the singer's *doppelganger*, the unexplained capricious shadow, the voice.

'Coffee?' she added.

A brief gossip then back to serious work until lunchtime.

Every third day, Detty took a rest from practising to work on, what she proudly called, her project. Behind the *Altes Herrenhaus* on the edge of the pinewood sloping down to the park, was an old summerhouse. Beautifully made from ancient oak, it had seen much better days, the windows were glassless, the pine floorboards rotten and the two doors off their hinges and standing forlornly against the walls. The oak cladding though was sound, for the most part, and the inside was carved lovingly

---

2   Almighty Virgin hear my prayer.
3   Only accept this prayer as his protection

with more than a little of the art that had produced the great *holzschnitten*[4] of Lucas Cranach, born in nearby *Kronach*, and of his contemporaries. She had fallen in love with the summerhouse immediately she saw it and was determined to restore it. In jeans, trainers, and leather gloves, she worked away replacing the old floorboards and cleaning and oiling the ancient panels.

Although she accepted that she was not highly skilled, she thought that she had learnt a bit since her hilarious, but disastrous encounter with the plasterer's craft in the opera house at Königshof. Gianna joined in the fun and with Niki sleeping in his pram, they worked away like a couple of kids on a school project.

Amelia, however, coming over from the *Schloss* with a message from Sophie, was scandalised. At home in Italy, *Contesse* even *Contessine*, behaved as they should and didn't strip wood in jeans and sweaters. At a family discussion in the evening, GiGi pointed out that Detty was Irish and that probably accounted for her unconventional behaviour. *Gli irlandsi*, he said, professing profound world-knowledge, *sono sempre un po' strani a causa della mancanza di pastasciutta e anche per motivo del tempo feroce trovato in Irlanda.* [5]His words of wisdom were greeted by a sniff from his wife and a smirk from his daughter but for the time being the matter was settled.

From time to time, Detty would go towards Bad Steben to the family timber yard for some hinges, other fittings, or a bit of advice from GiGi, who not only had skill as a cabinetmaker but also regarded the proprietor's family as his private domain.

*

One morning a week, she had a further day off and went with Sophie into Bad Steben itself. She had grown very close to her mother-in-law and really enjoyed chatting with her. She had also developed a considerable

---

4 Wood carvings
5 They are always a bit strange because of the lack of pastasciutta and the ferocious climate of Ireland.

admiration for her as a businesswoman. Kind and gentle in the home, as anyone could be, Detty had noticed that she was respected with circumspection at work. She was proud of her profession and amused the local officials when she filled in any document forms, whether related to her work or not, by always signing herself *Sophie von Ritter, Försterin.* The locals smiled. Female foresters were unusual enough, let alone ones who owned one of the biggest forests and forestry businesses in Franconia, to say nothing of being part of the ancient aristocracy. Sophie had a practical eye too. Detty always remembered her expression when Richard, the gardener, brought in a basket of logs for the fire with ivy still clinging to them. *Schrecklich!* She muttered to herself and when her daughter-in-law looked puzzled, she smiled and said: 'They shouldn't have ivy on them in the first place and they certainly shouldn't go out – here or anywhere else like that.'

They usually did a bit of shopping together in Bad Steben and then gorged on *Caffe und Kuchen* at the best *Konditorei* in the little spa town. Detty's other, less regular, trip was to Hof, while Gianna looked after Niki. She loved the small town, the outpost of Franconia. Like a child, she delighted in the ritual of her regular hair appointment in the *Marienstrasse*. The *Friseur* went through a charade of ecstasy over her chestnut-gold mane, remarking frequently that there was little that she needed from him. She was, however, always pleased with the result and there was an extra spring in her step as she left the salon. Then, conscious of her sin of vanity, she would make her way to the *Marienkirche* in the *Altstadt* and after spending some minutes in silent prayer, she would light a candle for Liese.

Once, when the lovely lime wood carvings were shining in a particular soft late summer light, transmitted through the great window, she stood for a long time thinking of her friend. She felt guilty at her own accidental survival and thought repeatedly how much she missed Liese. With her, there had always been laughter, jokes as well as valour and comradeship. Murmuring, as she had murmured after the shock of her violent death, 'We shall not look upon her like again' she roused herself and left the church. She completed a bit more shopping for the things that she couldn't get locally. She drove home deep in thought passing through the woods and open fields, damp with the melted dew of the bright but colder day. After one visit to Hof, she called at the *Schloss* on her way, going in through the kitchen to drop off some shopping for Hildegard.

'There's a friend of yours here, Frau Gräfin. Herr Max said to ask you to go through, if you came in.'

It was unusual for Max, to be at home at that time of day and, puzzled, she went through into the Hall. To her surprise, her father-in law, Max, was standing with Father Dieter in front of the massive stone grate still with its arrangement of summer flowers.

She just had time to wish Father Dieter *'Grüss Gott'* when Max broke in:

'Detti, we have some wonderful news, but sad at the same time.'

She raised her right eyebrow quizzically at him.

'Perhaps Father Dieter had better explain it all himself.'

'To cut it short, the Holy Father has appointed me auxiliary bishop.'

Detty, good Catholic as she was, had only a vague idea of the exact status of an auxiliary bishop, but was, truth to tell, feeling upset by the prospect of losing a friend and the priest who had celebrated her nuptial mass and baptized Niki. She realised this was selfish but looking more sad than delighted, she said: 'Congratulations, of course, but we will miss you terribly. Where are you going?'

'Somewhere you know pretty well, Frau Detti, Bialovsk.'

Detty allowed her generous mouth to drop wide open then break into a broad smile.

'Ah, that's different, so we shan't lose you at all. You mean you will be with Bishop Majorowski. He's lovely but is old and he has been ill. You will be helping him then?'

'Of course, and in the meanwhile, I've got to learn Russian.'

'They mostly speak German round Bialovsk even if Russian is their first language. But if you want some help I'll give it to you – assuming that is that you don't mind my Ziatovian accent.'

'I really would be grateful. I am afraid the Slav population won't be happy with a German. Although, I guess....' he blushed 'if I was known to talk Russian with your accent it would be in order.'

'I'm not used to being flattered by a Bishop – you'll turn my head' she laughed.

'Auxiliary Bishop elect' he corrected solemnly but with a twinkle.

*

Marc looked round the door quietly. There she was at the side of Niki's old-fashioned wooden cradle. Unaware of his presence, she was singing the gentle sibilants of '*ceol a'phiobaire*'[6] to her son. Marc, not understanding a word, stood looking proudly at his wife. It still amazed him that the voice that had clarioned over the Bayreuth *Festspielhaus* could encompass softly this gentle tranquil song. She looked up.

'*Das war wirklich schon,*'[7] he muttered.

'Not really' she said 'I have a poor acquired accent. I love Kildare and we have the greatest horses but you need to be born in Donegal or Galway to make the Gaelic sound as it should.'

'I'll take your word for it. But I do sometimes wonder how many languages our son will have to learn.'

'*Deutsch über Alles!*' she parodied the old words of the National Anthem 'we can't have the heir to the von Ritters speaking fractured German' she laughed.

There was a knock at the door. Marc opened it to find Father Dieter, folder in hand, grinning sheepishly rather more like a schoolboy than a Bishop.

'Is it all right?' he asked anxiously.

'*Natürlich*' Marc answered 'Detti's just finished with Niki and is ready for you. Will you stay to supper? I'm just off to practice my new honed Chef skills with a *Fränkischer Wildschweinbraten* – *Vati* gave us the leg after his last shoot. There is plenty and we won't have many more opportunities to entertain you – at least not here.'

'How could I refuse?' said Dieter 'that would be wonderful.'

Marc rather ostentatiously donned the long Irish butcher's apron,

---

6 Music of the Piper
7 That was beautiful.

which his mother-in-law had given him to celebrate the birth of her grandson. Peggy was rather taken aback when she realised that Marc regarded it as a badge of office symbolising the duties of a new father, rather than a joke.

As Dieter retired into the Study with Detty, Marc began confidently slicing thick rashers off a broad piece of *speck* with a large *couteau de cuisinier*. Once the study door had closed, the professionalism evaporated and Ulla Jacob's *Besten Rezepte von Franken* rapidly appeared. He worked steadily larding the marinated meat, seasoning, searing, then adding the herbs and the onions. The appearance was good and the smell gorgeous. With the roast safely in the oven, he checked everything. The *Klöse* had already been supplied by Hildegard, as had the specially prepared *Rotkohl*. He decided they would need an *aperitif* and put the *Wurzburger Spätlese Trocken* from the family estate to chill and opened the *Cote Rotie 1992*. He found the red currant jelly that was essential for finishing the dish and he just checked that the sour cream was in the fridge. Disaster struck. There was no sour cream. This was ridiculous he said to himself; there had to be, they always had sour cream in the fridge. He checked again. The awful truth dawned. They had all been away. Detty had been in Livonia, with Niki and Gianna; he himself had been on a field exercise. The fridge had been emptied and turned off. Gianna had collected basics from the village before going off for the evening to be with her family but that had not included sour cream.

The man who had led the tanks across the Fojn and had masterminded the assault of Königshof was for a moment non–plussed. Should he suffer the ultimate humiliation of interrupting Detty in the search for the Holy Grail alias sour cream? But what could Detty do? She had saved a nation, rescued her friend from torture and death, sang unrehearsed one of the most difficult roles in the operatic world but even she could not conjure *saure sahne* out of nothing. There was only one thing for it – Hildegard. There was no question of saving face. Hildegard had known him since he was in his cradle so he had no face to preserve. She would have it. If he ran as fast as he could to the *Schloss*, he could collect the precious cream and still be back to serve his *pièce de resistance*. He set out with all the application of a commando on a mission, telephoning the *Schloss* on his

Handy as he went. He brushed his mother, intent on inquiring after Niki, aside and breathlessly demanded Hildegard. The latter came up with a calm assurance that the *saure sahne* would be at his disposal.

The steaming roast was waiting, savoury, in all its glory as teacher and pupil came out of the study. The proud chef presented his dish and just found time to enquire how the lesson had gone before they sat down.

'He's a natural' said Detty 'it's amazing the progress that he has made.'

'Your wife is a flatterer, Marc, it must be, how do you call it? The Blarney? I think that I was at the back of the queue at *Pfingsten*- the gift of tongues didn't reach me' he laughed.

During coffee the phone rang, Marc answered it – bottle of *Birnewasser* in hand.

'Yes, she's here. I'll pass you over.' He put his hand over the receiver automatically but probably uselessly.

'It's Julian,' he said giving the name of her London agent in a conspiratorial voice.

Detty took the receiver wondering what on earth could be the reason for a phone call at ten o'clock – OK – nine o'clock in England, but still late for a call from a business.

'Bernadette, how are you?' Julian was far too proper to go in for diminutives.

'I'm great, thank you,' she grinned at Marc and Dieter 'but I don't imagine that you have called at this time of the evening to enquire after my well-being.'

'Well, no – although, of course, I do care'- humour wasn't his strong point.

Detty waited.

'Well, it's like this. Can you do four *Leonores* in Budapest next month?'

With a growing sense of unreality Detty asked, 'Which one?' she didn't really think it would be *Il Trovatore* or *La Forza del Destino* but she thought that she could gain a few seconds of thinking time by asking.

'Oh *Fidelio*, of course, I didn't think you knew the others.'

'No, but I'm a quick learner.' Detty was beginning to enjoy herself.

'Apparently Izabella Franz, their home-grown dramatic soprano, has had to have her gall bladder out.'

'I'm sorry to hear that.' In fact, Detty wasn't surprised. She did not know Frau Izabella personally but had seen her at Salzburg and knew that she abundantly fulfilled her GP father's old mnemonic of 'fair, fat, female and forty' as a predictor of gall bladder disease. She wondered rather inconsequentially, how with her great girth, even without gall bladder problems, she had intended to manage the trouser role of *Leonore*.

Concentration, however, Julian needed an answer.

'Who is conducting and what about the others?'

'The conductor is Tibor Markowitz, the music director. The tenor is Sandor Nantesz.'

'I know him. He's been *Froh* and *Eric* at Bayreuth – fine voice and good stage presence. He's a definite plus. What about the others?'

'Home grown but topflight – they are producing some excellent voices at present. I'll e-mail you the full cast list. This is a prestige production. It was supposed to be a national *tour de force* but Frau Frantz's operation has rather upset that as they have no other topflight *Leonore*.'

'So, they want to settle for an Irish/ Bavarian/ Livonian substitute?'

Detty was being mischievous and Marc and Dieter were suppressing sniggers.

'Do they know that I have had a baby?'

'I didn't think that I should ask that but they asked whether you had 'resumed your career' so I assume that they did know.'

'What did you say?'

'I said that I knew that you had started singing again but didn't say anything about professional engagements.'

'Very tactful –thank you.'

'Can I think about it?'

'Only until tomorrow. They want an answer.'

'OK, I'll sing the *Abscheulicher* in my bath tomorrow morning and see how it goes. Then I'll ring you or I might send you a video by e-mail.'

'Good night, Bernadette, you will ring, won't you?'

'Of course, I will. Good night.' She rang off.

'Detti, you're impossible!' her husband remonstrated 'the poor man's only trying to do his job.'

'He's a humourless idiot' she replied, 'but unfortunately, he is rather a good agent.'

Marc turned to Dieter.

'Support me, Dieter, you must agree that having to ring up temperamental sopranos late at night can't be an easy job, without being teased rotten.'

'I'm sure he doesn't mind Frau Detti's joking.'

'There you are, the tact of a Bishop – all right, I know – an Auxiliary Bishop Elect.'

Marc, suddenly serious: 'Are you going to do it? Are you all right?'

'The last time you asked me that, it had amazing consequences.'

Marc looked uncomfortable for a moment. Neither of them was prepared to admit to the young priest that the question had preceded the start of their vigorous pre-marital love-life.

Detty, thinking that she shouldn't have made the allusion, went on quickly and seriously: 'Yes, I'm pretty sure that I am. My exercises have been going well. I know the part backwards and it's a good opportunity to start again without the paparazzi. However, I wasn't entirely joking with Julian. I would like to do the *Abscheulicher* in full voice before I give him a definite answer. If you can come Marc, I'll go over to the music room and do it to-morrow morning before I ring him.'

'I've never heard you do it' said Dieter wistfully 'I wish I could come to Budapest but with this new commitment there isn't a chance.'

'You can come over to-morrow morning, if you like.'

'But that will be a private rehearsal' then he added' Are you sure that you wouldn't mind?'

'Of course not. If I can do it in front of two thousand ferocious Magyars all baying for my blood and crying that I'm not a patch on *die Izabella*, then how can I mind one friend? How about nine thirty and we will have a late breakfast back here afterwards? I really had better warm up in the bath then we will go over to the *Schloss*.'

'I will ring *Mutti* just to make sure she hasn't arranged anything.'

In spite of the confidence of the night before, they both felt strangely tense as they set out pushing Niki in his pram over the grass through the welcome but chilly level sunshine of the early Franconian morning. *Fidelio* brought back so many memories. The plane with Mara back from Moltravia, their first row in that very park when Detty had her announced her mad ambition to sing the peon to freedom in the middle of a vicious police state. Finally, the extraordinary night when she had achieved her goal and all Livonia, newly free, had responded to the trumpet call and her voice.

Marc set the score on the Bechstein; he didn't need it but form dictated accompanists had to have scores. He glanced up at Detty whose right hand rested lightly on the side of the piano in a recitalist's stance which contrasted incongruously with her jeans and sweater. He played the agitated introduction and as she tensed, furious and dramatic, before bursting out with the sabre scything '*Abscheulicher*'.[8]

The jeans and sweater became the boy-disguised wife in the Spanish prison. The anger melted to the rainbow colours of remote hope and then determination strengthening in the face of the impossible. Marc at the piano knew, with huge relief, that the voice that had made him fall in love, was still there. Not only was it there but it was also stronger, fuller, more mature, and magnificent. As she finished the high '*Gattenliebe*'[9] Detti realised that there was a little group listening to her. Sophie and Max had been joined by Father Dieter, Amelia, Hildegard and the two *Dienst Mädchen* from Oberdorf. Max started to applaud and the others, feeling that they had been given permission, followed. Detty remarked quietly: 'I really didn't expect a full audience. Thank you so much for listening.'

Father Dieter was speechless for some minutes then said: 'That was truly magnificent, Frau Detti, I have heard you sing Bach wonderfully and everything at the Easter before your marriage but never quite as splendidly as that.'

---

8   Monster
9   Married love

Detty laughed, 'I am afraid it was a bit loud for a drawing room but I shall be in a big theatre next time so I wanted to sing out.'

She turned to Marc 'You're the only one who will tell the truth – was it OK?'

Marc smiled:

'I suspect that you know the answer to that but in case you really have doubts, yes – it was brilliant.'

'OK, Budapest next stop. I had better ring Julian.'

*

She decided to drive. It wasn't that far. Almost by chance she passed through Bratislava on her way from Vienna to Budapest and something made her deviate into the centre. The small city bordering the growing Danube still cast its charm, but the memories kept flooding back. She couldn't forget that this was the place that Liese had taken by storm with a combination of her wit, forcefulness, and charm. The ultimate success of the revolution was in no small part due to the diplomatic offensive that she had mounted so skilfully here. Detty looked at the raucous tourists in the street cafes – many more and more frivolous since she was last there. She wanted to shout at them 'This was a city of a real heroine – bow down, get on your knees and pray to do likewise'. They giggled on, oblivious of the furious but powerless *Valkyrie* who was cursing them silently and irrationally.

Budapest was a relief. It was decorative but older and more serious. She found her hotel, left her luggage, and rang the opera house.

Asked to come round at once, the Intendant was moving from foot to foot looking embarrassed.

'We are so grateful to you, Frau O'Neill. To obtain a singer of your calibre at short notice is so fortunate. I am afraid though that I have some bad news for you. Herr Nantecz has laryngitis and cannot sing. We have indeed had so many problems with this production. However, we have been fortunate enough to obtain the services of Herr Viktor Lobchenko to sing *Florestan*.

'Who is he?' asked Detty, genuinely puzzled and not put off by the management speak.

'He was sent us by our agents. He is Belarussian, of course, I have not had a biography yet but he certainly has a fine tenor.'

'Well, that's all that matters' said Detty cheerfully.

The mystery tenor appeared for the *sitzprobe* looking relaxed in smart jeans and a light grey cable-knit jumper – understated, but expensive, Detty decided. The black shoes were also handmade and Detty was pretty certain that they came from the same London Jermyn Street maker favoured by Marc. There was a paradox in that this unknown Belarussian tenor did not appear to be short of money. The overall impression however was favourable. The slightly wavy fair hair had that very faint copper tinge often found in Russians of all origins. However, his most attractive aspect was the broad smile from the corners of his generous mouth. To cap it all he had the figure of an athlete which was very different from some of the fellow members of his *fach*. Detty realised that being paired off with very large partners, particularly tenors, was part of the job. She also knew full well that many of her soprano colleagues, including the one she was replacing, had what could politely be described as generous figures; nevertheless, she took care to keep fit and in excellent shape and was woman enough to consider it a bonus to have a well- proportioned partner. After all, most leading roles involved a certain amount of close contact and, although she was distinctly wary of green room romances, a good-looking man was an advantage.

The *Generalprobe* went well apart from a most unfortunate horn player who played a viciously split note in the introduction to '*Komm Hoffnung*'. He came up to Detty afterwards and apologised most formally. She was caught in a dilemma. If she said that it didn't matter, it implied that she was one of those unmusical singers who failed to note such things.

She settled for: 'You have an amazingly difficult instrument, *mein Herr*, I would be very proud to play it as you do.'

She hoped that she hadn't overdone it. It seemed to go down well and she was pleased to notice the orchestra members treating her now with respect and almost friendship.

Viktor had a brilliant light dramatic tenor and his *'Gott! Welch Dunkel hier!'*[10] soared round the theatre thrillingly. Their *'Euch werde Lohn'* was a real pleasure. They both gave it their all in *'O, namenlose Freude'* and the act finished with a warm sense of achievement.

Before they left the stage Viktor said in good German with an attractive Russian accent: 'As we are husband and wife, we had better get to know each other, see you in the bar for a coffee.'

Her *'Ja, gern!'* was warm enough although she realised that his invitation, whilst not exactly lecherous, had a slant that could be interpreted as implying more than coffee.

He was standing in front of the fire in the bar warming himself. She got her first chance to have a good look at him without the preoccupations of her role. He was extraordinarily beautiful. Unlike so many of his colleagues, he had a good muscular athletic figure. He was just over medium height with expressive, finely chiselled features and hair fair flecked with old gold. In the theatre café, he smiled and stepped forward to greet her.

'In spite of our recent intimacy we must introduce ourselves – Viktor.'

'Detty.'

'I have heard about your reputation from Königshof. I didn't expect you to be quite so young and ravishing.'

The chat up line was obvious but the smile flashed again and it was all pleasant enough. Detty joined in the fun.

'I expect that they told you that I was an old Irish crone who terrified them all.'

'Not exactly.'

'I see that you've met – other than on stage, I mean.'

The voice of Tibor Markowitz made them turn towards the door.

'I saw you arrive, Frau O'Neill, and came down to introduce you but I was too late.'

'We have already got on well enough on stage.'

'Thank you, *gnädige Gräfin,*' Viktor accompanied this with an ironic bow.

---

10 God! How dark it is!

'*Bitte schon!*' she answered bowing in return.

'When you two have finished shall we go and have lunch.'

'*Jawohl,* Herr Professor Generaldirektor!!' they answered laughing almost in unison.

2
KÖNIGSHOF

*Wenn man nicht weiß wohin mit dem Ball,
dann muss man ihn einfach in's Tor schießen!*[11]

SEPP HERBERGER- GERMAN NATIONAL FOOTBALL COACH

After a brief pause back in Oberdorf, Detty set off for Königshof ten days later with Gianna in tow. There had been quite a struggle with Gianna's parents who were reluctant to see their daughter, even though she was rising nineteen, go away from the family but eventually Detty prevailed. The idea of Giovanna staying in the President's residence was greeted with wide-eyed excitement and finally won the day.

Arriving at Königshof made Detty feel edgy and slightly, unreasonably, resentful. She was on a high after a rapturous reception in Budapest, but which, she realised, was not a little due to her partner who had sung a *Florestan* of passion and drama. Also, she resented that she was having to abandon her autumnal Franconian idyll. She had never felt like this in Livonia before. Even her return there when it was Moltravia, in the days of horror, had been attended by tingling fear and foreboding, but never boredom or resentment.

---

11 If one doesn't know where to pass the ball, one must just put it in the goal!

As always, they were expected at the Presidential penthouse on the fifth and top floor of the Hansehaus. The 'Penthouse' had always been a joke amongst the Oblovs and their intimates. It was indeed the top floor of the Hansehaus but rather than a penthouse in the usual and luxurious sense of the word, it consisted of a series of small attic rooms which had usually been occupied by servants under previous regimes. Low ceilings pierced by dormer windows lay in wait to catch the unsuspecting head of anyone above average height. Mostly men suffered but the tall Irish woman had already encountered, painfully, the protruding joists. The last Fascist government had abandoned the building altogether because of its 'unfortunate' democratic associations and had constructed themselves hideous, but luxurious, apartments in the menacing complex of the now destroyed Winterburg. The spacious and elegant rooms on the floor below the penthouse were, in theory, at the disposal of the President. Nicklaus Oblov was, however, the most self-effacing of men except where his country was concerned. He thought it pretentious to occupy these rooms with a household consisting only of himself and the odd day servant. Sometimes it did include his daughter when she was back from Munich. In practice, therefore, the large salon on the floor underneath with its plush adjoining dining room and ensuite bedrooms together with the kitchen and necessary service rooms, formed a suite that was used only for official functions.

Detty's forebodings were justified. Mara greeted her with the accustomed enthusiasm but it was soon obvious that all was not well. When Detty mildly mentioned that she was intending to watch David Sensky, Liese Zahnsdorf's bereaved partner, play football for Königshof that evening and asked Mara if she was coming, the latter exploded.

'I can't stand another bloody football match.'

She was not usually so outspoken but football seemed always to touch a raw, unstable nerve. It was odd, the subject seldom arose but, particularly when David was playing and Liese was still alive, they were occasionally invited to a match. Sometimes Mara seemed interested and quite keen to go but at others it was a red rag to a bull, if her diminutive and very female friend could be described as a bull. Detty wondered idly if it had some connection to the past. If it was something in the past, it must be the distant past, before they had met because, as far as her friend knew, she had had no recent connection with footballers or their game. At all events Mara now vented her feelings forcefully.

'And this time, I don't have to be there and you're not even singing.'

'I know – but it's only for David. He nearly gave up when Liese was killed and I promised that we would both come if we could. It's his first home match since Liese's death and I feel that I must be there for her sake.'

Detty paused recalling with agonising clarity the evening after Liese's death when she comforted David like a baby cradling his head in her arms.

'OK, but I think you are going gooey over this footballer, I shall tell Marc.'

Mara now laughed, embarrassed at her outburst.

'That's why I need you to chaperone us at dinner so I'm not carried away with lust at his beautiful muscular legs.'

Leaving Niki with Gianna, they set out dressed in kapok lined coats and mufflers through the misty air, now almost wintry. The traffic was dreadful. Their taxi did its best to wind between the road works around the stadium. The stadium itself was finished but the great ceremonial avenue was a sea of rutted mud. Detty who had wanted to walk the kilometre to the *Hansestadion* rather than hang around in a stationary taxi, felt justified but it wasn't a good start to the evening. Finally, they were able to get out into the warm after the bitter frost. Detty felt the cold and thought that she was losing her toughness because of her southern life. Come to think of it, Mara herself had only just returned from the relative warmth of Munich for the weekend. Compared with this chill, even the early Franconian autumn, not famous for its mild climate, was almost tropical.

They were warmly received by the President of FC Königshof and, fortified by a hot coffee, and shown to their seats in the President's box.

Even the greatest enthusiast would have to have reckoned the game dull. It was a local affair against *SV Bialovsk*. The women wore no colours as two Livonian sides were involved and they were both too important for favouritism to pass unnoticed by the media. David

Sensky was solid and scored the only goal in a goalmouth scramble but he would have been the first to admit that, by his own high standards, it was a pedestrian performance. He was smiling but subdued when he came from the changing room, his hair still damp from the shower, to meet the girls in the Concourse. His dark locks, reaching the nape of his neck, and his Mediterranean stubble, which made most of the girls of Königshof go weak at the knees, were in place but the face it surrounded was that of a lost soul. A little boy all at sea amidst a great and irremediable tragedy

The food at Golabki was as good as ever but the ghost of a lively irreverent face and a laughing voice hung over them. It was brave of them all to tackle Liese's favourite restaurant again. Liese had been ambitious, determined, incisive and commanding but always her friendly temperament and sense of humour had shone through. She could give one of her subordinates a dressing down but then point the way ahead and finish with a laugh. She had managed never to leave them humiliated. The three of them at dinner, in their different ways, kept thinking about her. It was an uncomfortable evening. David was kind and courteous and insisted on paying for them both. He formally and correctly thanked Mara for coming, kissing her hand, and said how much he and the team had appreciated her presence. He then kissed Detty goodnight on both cheeks knowing that to her, at least, he need say no more. The women were unusually silent in the taxi ride back to the Hansehaus. Detty was still overwhelmed by the recent tragedy. Mara, who had known Liese well but had not been as close to her as the other two, had an odd, worried look, which Detty never remembered seeing before. She wondered what was going on behind those blue eyes and golden curls.

As she went to bed, she felt lonely. She always missed Marc when he was away on duty but this evening she ached for his calm sympathy and solid good sense. Turning over restlessly she started to think about *Die Meistersinger*. She was amazed at her own foolhardiness. She had, rather stupidly, she now realised, launched a tirade in front of Helge and the Königshof management about some modern *Regietheater* productions of *Die Meistersinger*. She had made the legitimate point that *Meistersinger* does not lend itself to creative director orientated productions and could they please have somebody who would put the *Nürnberg* back into the show. Helge had responded by saying quietly 'How about you, Detti?'. The suggestion was taken up with enthusiasm by the others and, allowing herself to be carried away, she said that she wouldn't mind trying. From then on, the whole thing gained an unstoppable momentum. The outcome was that Detty found herself, totally inexperienced, by general acclamation, directing the Königshof *Die Meistersinger*. This was as well as singing the admittedly relatively undemanding role of *Magdalene* which although technically a mezzo part lay comfortably within her range. Fortunately, the Principal of the *Königshof Kunst Hochschule* not only had experience in set design but knew the theatre itself and was extremely keen that his newly resurrected college should undertake the scenery and costumes for a simple but traditional *Nürnberg*. A huge additional asset was Anna Härtel, a very young, but brilliant choreographer from Berlin. She had been recruited by the Music Director, Helge von Grunstrand, to take imaginative control of the complicated crowd scenes and work with Detty on the production. Nonetheless as she tried to go to sleep, she was appalled by the magnitude of the task that she had set herself. She wanted something inspirational and exciting but true to the work's roots.

*

The flat over the library at the lodge at *Schloss Krenek* had been warmed up with loving care. The Board of Governors had insisted that the joint-founding Presidents of the music school should have the use of the flat when visiting on college business. Marc von Ritter had laughed and insisted: 'But not at the same time!'

He knew that Hank Schliessen, the great American tenor and co-President of the music school, had more than a little admiration for his wife and a reputation with women which was not to be trusted.

This time, however, he need not have worried. Detty was there, accompanied only by Niki and Giovanna. Her sole preoccupation was to help the college staff with the winter competitions and rehearse *Die*

Meistersinger with Helge von Grunstrand. Hank would be appearing but later. In his inimitable way, he had turned up at the planning meeting for the St Nicklaus Fest. It had been held during the previous summer and it was at this meeting that the momentous decision to try to scale the mountain of *Die Meistersinger* had been taken. When it came to casting, late in the day, he had announced that he would like to sing in the production and, if it were allowed, he would choose his role. At that moment, with a twinkle in his eye, he said that it was time for coffee and he needed to phone the Met in New York. The Festival Committee filed out into the Great Hall of *Schloss Krenek* making bets as to whether the great man would sing a mature but vibrant *Walther* or try his hand at *David* which would suit his sense of fun if not his more mature years. Helge believed he should do *David*.

'After all apprentices in Nürnberg in that era could be old age pensioners.'

'Hank will thank you for that.' Detty laughed.

When they re-convened, they were about equally split as to which of the two roles, he would go for. Hank re-entered with a broad grin:

'Will you really let me choose, Helge?'

'Of course, how could I do otherwise? Which one would you like – *Walther* or *David*?'

'Neither I will sing *Kunz Volgesang*.'

This *coup de thèatre* caused general astonishment; even Detty, who thought that she was used to Hank's tricks was taken aback. *Kunz Volgesang*, the furrier master, is a tiny tenor part consisting of a few interjections and some ensemble passages involving all the masters. It is usually the role of a very junior principal or a promoted chorister, certainly not one to be taken by the greatest living Wagner tenor.

Helge, looking disappointed, broke the silence: 'Why, Hank? What's the idea?'

'Simply that it's your show; you have an extremely promising young tenor available already. Lev will make a splendid, lively *David*. You should find another youngster for *Walther*. Neither of the big tenor roles in *Meistersinger* should be sung by an older tenor. In this way, I can be around to give them a bit of advice, if they want, and help Detty with the production, if she wants. Also, it shouldn't matter too much if I am a bit late for rehearsals because of the Paris gala.'

It was typical of the man, thought Detty, to have thought the whole thing through, to help as much as he could, to encourage the whole company and yet not let his star status unbalance the cast. However, despite her admiration, her mind jumped to the next problem and she muttered under her breath 'You don't find good *Walthers* easily.' – fortunately nobody heard her.

*

As dark fell, they set out from the college in their horse drawn sleds. The first one contained four singers, a violinist and accordion player. They began a journey round the district. The female staff and girl students wore furs and finery over white blouses and dark figured skirts in the national tradition. Some also wore the pretty *Karuna*, home-made like the rest of their costumes, round their brows. The boys and men lead the party, dressed in long knee length black coats over tight trousers and thigh length boots which distinguished them from their Russian, Polish and Lithuanian neighbours. At each village in the former *Key*, songs were sung, drinks were produced and toasts drunk.

They arrived at a clearing in the woodland where the forest floor had been made ready for dancing. The spit roasts of boar and venison blazed. The equipment and the expert chefs had been borrowed from the army. Local volunteers made up the numbers. It was a timeless scene but Detty suddenly was reminded of the forest clearing where her life had been saved by the intervention of an angry, fearless forester. Tonight, it was a dark forest full of joy but the memory gave her a frisson of fear.

The dancing accelerated in a great breathless crescendo, the furs were thrown aside and in the frosty evening girls and boys hurled each other around in a fiery frenzy. Detty hadn't a clue what she was supposed to be doing. She was gathered up by swain after swain and tossed in the incisive rhythm, one with the students and the locals. She felt exhilarated and excited. It was the first time since the war that, here in Livonia, she had been treated like a normal girl rather than some sort of icon. Flattering as they were, she was glad for once to shed the Frau Komturin and *Frau Gräfin* labels.

Her Munich training came in useful when, hot and thirsty, she impressed her partner of the moment, a freshman trombonist from Sovils, by downing the large, courteously offered, glass of beer almost in one. Whether he was emboldened by seeing this or by his own large vodka Detty never knew but, shyly, he was able to tell her that he had heard her sing *Simple Gifts* and the *Freiheitslied* at his school in Sovils.

'You were at St Paul's?' Detty asked not knowing quite how to go on, as suddenly the festive dream world was transformed into a hideous image in her mind. He nodded.

'When it happened?' she asked, knowing that she didn't need to say what 'it' was,

'Yes, but I was playing football- out of range- I was one of the lucky ones.

She was whisked away by Kurt Westerhagen, the head of keyboard studies and had no time to ask more. The black image remained.

At the end of the Ball, far into the dark morning, the boys lit torches and returned marking a flaming way, down the forest paths to the *Schloss*. She threw herself into bed at the Lodge. It had been a great evening and she had had fun, but the shadows remained.

*

Snow came early to Munich too that year. The footprints were deep down the pavements of the *Ludwigstrasse* and into the *Max-Josef Platz*. Detty stood confronting a miniature virago. The fierce fury of the small blond before her was so intense that it threatened to melt the snow for metres around. 'Hell hath no fury.'

'It's all right for you to be calm and sympathetic – you have a man in a million all to yourself. They broke the mould when they made him and certainly, God didn't extend the miracle to his brother. He's a sly bastard – he's been two – no three timing me for ages. Well, he can get lost – I've had it.'

Detty had arrived the evening before on a flying visit to discuss singing *Senta* with the *Nationalstheatre direktion*.

'Of course, we are not asking you to audition, Frau O'Neill, after Maestro Doktor Meilin's recommendation that would be ridiculous, but you might just like to come down and get the feel of the stage. We will make sure that the main stage is free'.

An audition by any other name, Detty had thought as she practised the *Senta*'s ballad with Helge von Grunstrand at the College as a break from *Meistersinger*, but no competition yet, she thought, and at least I rate the Main Stage. She knew that even after nearly one hundred and fifty years, a Bayreuth reputation was still, if anything, a negative in Munich. In the event, however, it had gone well and she was pleased to be singing soprano again and soared to the difficult finale of the ballad with skill and zest. She knew that her voice, richer since the baby, was in great shape and the compliments after her ballad were genuine. She was completely honest, too, when she said what a thrill and a privilege it was to sing in the great theatre that she had loved ever since she had first entered it, in a delirium of young love, as part of the audience at *Der Rosenkavalier*. Afterwards the 'non audition', she had walked down the *Leopoldstrasse* on air. She came down to earth with a bang when she met up with the fraught and furious Mara.

'How about a beer?' enquired Detty, not wanting to get too enmeshed in her brother-in-law's misdeeds. Secretly and guiltily, she felt considerably relieved that Mara seemed to be seeing through Bill at last. Marc's younger brother, Graf Wilhelm von Ritter, always known just as Bill, was, as even his sister-in-law had to admit, devastatingly attractive with his cheerful open features, smiling brown eyes and a chat-up line that had been highly honed by much practice. But that was the problem, his conquests made *Leporello's* catalogue song sound like a short shopping list. The only difference was that the *mille tre* were in Germany not Spain. Detty and Marc had both realised that Mara's liaison with Bill, nurtured by the high tension of her escape from the Farm and the beauty of Franconian peace and freedom that followed, would inevitably end badly. Detty was relieved that the break-up was accompanied by spirited fury rather than tears and desolation.

They pushed into a crowded Augustiner Keller full of midday shoppers. Detty ordered two *helles* and they sat in companionable silence. It was broken by Mara:

'I suppose that I always knew that it wouldn't work. After all he's not the sort who would come home in time to bath the baby, is he?'

Detty, conscious that the villain's brother had done exactly that just smiled quietly, trying not to appear smug. She reflected that she had acquired one von Ritter on a peak of high emotion and had fallen precipitously and unguardedly in love with him. He had been a real-life knight in shining armour who had appeared miraculously to save her from gothic horrors. She had had no idea of what he would be like in the cold light of daily normality. Miracle had followed miracle, however, and he had proved himself as a loving and caring partner even with regard to more humdrum, everyday life. Her astonishing luck, as she saw it, made it more difficult to comfort Mara and she was conscious that, for the first time in their close friendship, jealousy was near the surface. The best course was to listen but say as little as possible. After the outburst was over, Mara calmed down, said that she must get some shopping and would see Detty later, back at the *Victualienmarkt*.

Detty returned to the von Ritter flat. For an aristocratic apartment, it was extremely simple and unusually situated overlooking the *Viktualienmarkt*. The little flat had been owned by the family for some time. Recently it had been the *pied a terre* and centre of the bohemian lifestyle of Bill von Ritter during his stay at the University. Now Bill had de-camped to Vienna with his new *inamorata* – an event that had occasioned the outburst from Mara, which Detty had experienced that afternoon. These torrid developments had, however, meant that the flat was now empty and available again for the use of the rest of the family. Detty prepared the *Abendbrot* garnered generously from the massive and exotic choice displayed every morning below their windows. As she laid out the *Kalte braten, Blutwüste,* and other *Aufsnitt,* she hummed the *Jägerchor* from *Der Freischutz* and looked forward to seeing David Sensky play in his big match that evening. Marc was coming down from his army posting at Ingoldstadt the following day and the three of them were going to Oberdorf for the weekend. It was a short break before Mara and Detty returned to Königshof.

Mara came back nearly two hours later letting a blast of icy air from the stair well into the flat. She was silent and thoughtful as she pulled off her snow-covered boots. Detty, looking for a neutral subject, asked:

'Did you get anything interesting?'

'No' came the curt reply then after a pause, obviously realising that you can be rude even to your closest friend.'

'I crossed the *Lüitpoldbrucke* and walked round the *Maximilian Anlagen* for a bit then I crossed the *Ludwigsbrücke* and came back.'

'A bit chilly in this weather,' she tried not to sound surprised but Mara's next question really startled her.

'Can I come to the match this evening?'

Mara claimed to hate football above all things. Detty wondered what was going on but carefully sounded matter of fact.

'Of course, I'll ring Stefan.'

*

Despite the skilled multi-national expertise of *Bayern* and some displays of technical brilliance in mid-field, there was always the towering presence of David Sensky who seemed to have recovered his zest for the game. He was back in defence when needed, which was often, but then on the break, lurking quicksilver, with quiet unostentatious confidence. He always seemed about to make a through run to the edge of the *Bayern* penalty area. It was at once reassuring to the small knot of away supporters and always threatening to the Munich defence. No wonder that *Bayern* wanted to sign him. Detty mentally pinched herself, hardly believing that this self-assured athlete, great in stature and in presence, was the same man who had wept like a baby in her arms a few months before. If he was playing for Liese now, he was making a damned good job of it. As the game, with a nil-nil score line that had clearly unsettled *Bayern's* star-studded team, entered injury time, his chance came. Kaspar, the other hard-working Königshof mid fielder, intercepted an uncharacteristically sloppy, ill-weighted, pass just inside the *Bayern* half. He shaped as if to pass but dragged the ball across behind his standing leg with the inside of his foot and set off clear of his marker with space to pass forward. Sensky, racing through towards the Munich box was ahead of the pass. The tiny Livonian band held their breath as the linesman glared fiercely at the Königshof mid fielder but the flag stayed limply at his side. The big man turned to collect and, in a flash, rolled the ball behind him towards the goal with his right foot. Then he spun like lightning away from the challenging defender. Instantly he thundered the ball inside the other closing full back, a multi-million euro Brazilian, and past the despairing arms of the goalkeeper into the far corner of the net. Total silence in the Allianz Arena, apart from a few hundred spectators in a far stand who dissolved in delirium and two girls in the VIPs stand who joined the chant of 'Sensky, Sensky, Sensky' waving their gold and black scarves.

'That was terrific', Mara was flushed with excitement.

'I thought you hated this game.'

Detty had no sooner said it than she could have bitten her tongue off. Mara, struggling with her bruised ego, didn't need caustic comments from her friend.

'That was different,' she said, 'it reminded me…' she hesitated, 'of something that I had forgotten.'

The hero of the hour looked drained as he came out of the dressing room looking round for the women.

'I've got to go back to the hotel for the Press to have a second go' he said before they could even comment on the match 'but I'll come round as soon as I can – if I may, that is.'

It was after midnight when the taxi finally stopped *im Tal* and an exhausted looking David Lensky rang the bell at the flat.

He recovered with an armchair and a hot coffee. Detty tried to find the right words.

'That must have been great this evening.'

'Yes, it might have been…' His eyes dissolved into a pool of distant misery.

She knew that it had sounded hollow and she cursed herself. But it had been great, even she knew that. Her knowledge of football was scanty to say the least. She remembered, as a tiny girl the glory days when Jackie Charlton took her country into the last eight in the World Cup of 1990 but her patriotic upbringing was with the GAA and horses. Football was, to say the least, a peripheral Saxon sport.

She was aware, however, of the small figure at her side almost vibrating with excitement. Whereas she had been trying to find something appreciative to say, Mara suddenly came out with: 'How on earth did you turn, change your weight and then control the ball to strike inside like that with your weaker foot and all in a flash?'

'It wasn't all me. I had a great assist from Ralf.'

'Yes, it he made a fine Cruyff turn but yours was in a different league – so fast and then the finish! Even after Ralf Kaspar passed it didn't seem that you could make anything of it. The defence seemed to have everything covered.'

It was said not only with enthusiasm but with authority. David and Detty looked at her equally thunderstruck. David recovered first, grinned and looked accusingly at Detty.

'You told me that Frau Mara knew nothing about football and hated it but I think that we need her on the coaching staff at Königshof.'

Mara blushed then laughed 'Don't you think that I've got enough problematic jobs already?'

She didn't offer any further explanation of her sudden show of expertise and after a modest comment by David, food and drink were produced and the conversation changed. Detty went to bed pondering and wondering how little one really knew even about your closest friend.

3
VIKTOR

heil und hehr, laut und hell
wies ihr auf mich

WAGNER *TRISTAN UND ISOLDE* ACT I SCENE 3[12]

She wasn't usually uncertain but this time she did wonder if she had done the right thing. Casually, at the lavish last night dinner that Budapest had arranged for them after the *Fidelios*, she had mentioned the Königshof *Walther* problem to the others. For a time, there was a desultory discussion about the requirements of the role whilst Viktor sat watching intently then he said quietly. 'I am learning it at home.'

Detty suddenly had had a fantasy of that bright, clear tenor singing the *Preislied* and had pricked up her ears but she said nothing. She knew that, even if he was learning the part, he probably wouldn't know it in time for the festival. Anyway, a tenor of his ability would have at least two years engagements already arranged. Casting was not done casually after several glasses of *Belaton* wine. It involved, as she knew well, agents, fees, contracts and most of all, forward thinking. They had made a great

---

12 Glorious and bold, loud and clear, he pointed to me.

mistake, she thought, not nailing this vital role much earlier. She didn't know if Helge had solved the problem, as he was entitled to do, in her absence. She tried to put it out of her mind and join in the general chat.

That night she hadn't slept. It was not surprising that she had been on a high after singing *Leonore*. It was so special and it had been a satisfying and successful performance. Indeed, it had been altogether a superb *Fidelio,* not least due to Viktor. He was so different from Hank. He didn't have Hank's deep feeling and understanding but it was a thrilling voice with a gleaming naturally lyrical high range. He would be a splendid *Walther.*

'Nothing ventured…' she had thought and eventually slept.

At first light she had 'phoned Helge. As always, he was running round the lake accompanied by his faithful short haired pointer bitch, always known as *die Souffleuse*, the prompter, because she almost never left Helge's side. *Sou* as she inevitably became called was so much part of the picture that the wags of the *Königshofer Philharmonica*, before one rehearsal, had fixed up a desk complete with score and her favourite dog blanket. On seeing this, Helge, nothing abashed, poker faced, left the pit, returned leading *Sou* who, good as gold, jumped onto her blanket and remained *tacet* beside the leader throughout the rehearsal. At the end, she earned an ovation from the hard-bitten professionals, one of whom remarked in Detty's hearing, that he wished some sopranos could perform as tactfully. Detty's immediate riposte was that that was rich coming from a horn player. There the matter rested – generally agreed by the hearers at a score of one all.

Helge, catching his breath, heard Detty's dilemma.

'No, we haven't found anybody else. If you think he's all right, try him, Detty, give it a go; there's nothing to lose. Yes', he added, '3,000 thalers per night (€1200) – no more – if he will take a bit less it would help. I know it's not much but he has a limited track record and we can't afford much. I trust you about his voice and if he is on, and thinks he can perfect it in time, ask him to come up here as soon as he can. I know it's irregular but we haven't much time and he certainly seems our best chance. We will talk fees and contracts when he gets here.'

Feeling slightly tense, Detty had gone down to the hotel breakfast room. Viktor was already there and waved her towards his table. She asked for a *café Americano*, collected a *Mákos Kifli,* the Hungarian poppy seed croissant, and some fruit and sat down beside him.

'Did you sleep well?' he asked courteously.

'Yes, fine' she lied 'and you?'

'Like somebody just out of a dungeon,' he smiled.

'Ever thought of entering a singing contest?' she asked and it was his turn to look startled and a bit insulted. She went on: 'As you have heard, we need a competitor to sing in a summer Bavarian meadow in a Baltic winter. Are you, by any chance, free?'

He suddenly looked serious.

'Are you joking?'

'No, all true but you must be booked up.'

'No, Detti, I am taking study leave with a few stand-ins and covers if they come up.'

'But do you know the role?'

'Almost, it needs a bit of polishing. I know most of it already; if I get a chance to sing it, I will learn very fast.'

'Does that mean you are interested? The fee is not high but you can get your agent to talk to Königshof and come to some arrangement. There might be' Detty was thinking of Hank 'an important US endorsement if it goes well. When can you come?'

'I need to go home to Minsk first but I can come by the end of the week.'

'Fine'

*

Detty was already in the Great Hall of the *Schloss*. Helge and Viktor came in almost together.

'This is our music director, Professor Dr Helge von Grunstrand.'

'Helge, meet Herr Viktor Lobchenko, possibly aka *Walther von Stolzing.*'

'I am delighted to meet you, Herr Viktor, you come with a very high recommendation. I gather that your *Florestan* was stunning.'

'Thank you, Herr Meister,' Viktor accompanied this with a low bow. 'It was a great privilege to sing with such a distinguished *Leonore*.'

'As we have finished the introductions, shall we go and see how we get on with *Die Meistersinger?*'

'*Jawohl,* Herr Professor Generaldirektor!!' they answered in unison, smiling.

They crossed to the old library of the *Schloss,* now the main rehearsal room. It was a fine big room with an oak gallery and panelling. The room was big enough for extensive piano rehearsals and had a sympathetic acoustic. The Königshof sound engineers had been round talking about bass traps and optimising the air gap. Detty, as the resident *Regisseurin,* had tried to look wise when she accompanied them but had privately admitted that she had not understood a thing. They had moved a few things and added some panels but they weren't too obtrusive and to her relief the fine old room had been left pretty much in its original state. The new library which adjoined the Presidents' apartment at the Lodge had just received its finishing touches. Mara had agreed to do the official opening later that week but meanwhile the staff and students could use the books and scores which were already in place. As a result, the congestion in the old *Schloss,* which had made any work with the larger ensembles particularly difficult, had been greatly relieved.

'As you are all here and Viktor has to go back to Minsk for a concert the day after to-morrow, I thought we would run through Act 1 Scene 1 and I'll decide what to do later if we have time.'

The opening chorale was sung by the students, as the professional chorus had not been called. Detty, fully occupied as *Magdalene,* in the opening exchanges, had no problems with her colleagues. As Helge stopped playing, she was surprised when a group of students and staff who had gone up to the gallery to listen, applauded spontaneously.

Helge seemed really pleased as he congratulated first the improvised chorus then the principals.

'It's a difficult scene to do really well,' he had added.

When Detty saw the DVD however, she knew why he had been so pleased. There was real vocal acting in the scene. Martina's lovely voice sounded completely right for the teenage *Nürnbergerin,* but the most impressive thing was Viktor's joyful characterisation of the young lovelorn knight. *Walthers* can seem a touch flabby but this was a real masculine knight.

It had been a satisfying day followed by a satisfying evening. The kitchen at Krenek had done them proud. Marc arrived late but had joined them all for the after-dinner chat and the occasional musical interpolation, accompanied by coffee and *Zwetschgenwasser*. Contented, Detty walked with him, hand in hand, down the frosty drive to the Lodge and their apartment behind the new library.

*

As always Detty was out of bed first, Marc still seemed fast asleep. She slipped on her silk dressing gown, faced the cold, undefeated yet by the early morning central heating, and walked over to the window. She looked out down the path through the woods towards the lake. The path wound through the trees which were covered in a delicate tracery of frozen cobwebs, until it disappeared into the misty morning. The wispy light didn't reveal the lake itself but the near trees and grass sparkled in the early sunlight. Gazing at the scene, inattentive, she allowed her untied robe to slip off her shoulders. Oblivious to the cold she stood naked, entranced at the morning view, thinking that the steaming bath to follow would be even better after the cold.

After a long pause she heard a whispered voice behind her: 'You're gorgeous, Detti.'

She turned, smiling to face Marc's star struck gaze.

'I am a wanton – standing in front of a widow with nothing on.'

'There's no one to see you here, except me, and perhaps I am allowed to look.'

'I don't usually display my back view,' she said thoughtfully, 'even to you.'

She looked troubled and pensive. Her back view was always a reminder. She didn't care so much about the puckered AK47 wound high on her otherwise elegant thigh. It was a battle honour and, privately, although it was disfiguring, she was proud of it. The back was different.

Even the swimsuits that she chose always covered as much as possible behind.

Marc knew her thoughts. He knew that she resented terribly the host of small white scars, which though fading, still disfigured her lovely back. These were the marks left when she had been viciously flogged with a birch by Gregor Tushkin, the ferocious Armourer, at the order of the sadistic Stefan Konradin. It had been during the nightmare of her detention at the Farm Camp, long ago, in another life but one that somehow never left her.

'Detti,' he said, with determination 'you should be proud of those marks, those scars – they are your stigmata – the wounds of St Francis.'

'His were on his hands and feet, mine are on my back and bum – not quite the same' she snapped grimly, remembering in every horrid detail her agonising and humiliating ordeal. He immediately regretted his attempt to reassure her. His face showed his own ghastly memories of her loved and lovely form, barely conscious and bloody, half carried, half dragged from her public torture. Seeing his face, she smiled gently:

'I deserved to be punished for my conceited arrogance. I'm sorry, *Schatz*. Take no notice of me. You know I'm OK.'

She threw herself on him and they loved fiercely and passionately as they always did until they lay side by side breathing deeply.

'That is the best balm,' she said at last, 'it always was and is.'

They lay in silence for some minutes gazing at the old, beamed roof above them.

'It's strange, though' she said at last 'While I was waiting after Konradin had told me what they were going to do to me, I thought that the humiliation would be the worst part. It wasn't the pain was. It was excruciating, terrible – there was just time enough to think between strokes and it seemed as if he was tearing my body, searingly, down to the very bone. The first ones weren't too bad and I thought that I could cope. Then it got worse. I tried to take my mind out of my body, to think that it was happening to someone else and I was watching from outside. I had read somewhere that this was a way of withstanding torture. It seemed to work for a time. I could hear the screams from a distance. They didn't seem to be coming from me. Then it was so dreadful that I felt my soul crash in onto my scalding body, like the rafters collapsing in a burning house. After that there was nothing but dreadful pain – no thoughts – just agony and, for a time, I wanted so much to die to stop it. But, afterwards, largely thanks to Mara, the pain went. It went surprisingly quickly, when I think about it, but the dreadful sense of humiliation returned. Even that wasn't the worst thing though. After my kidnap to the Winterburg, I faced the choice of losing my soul or having myself physically destroyed bit by bit – first my femininity, then my voice and finally my brain. I made the choice, as I had to and prayed, and then, as you know, a miracle happened and I was allowed to save myself. Not only that but I was lucky enough, yes, I repeat, lucky enough, to exert the most emphatic revenge and personally kill two of them. I gloried in it. Of course, I confessed after my killings. Three times I had violated The Sixth Commandment. I knew that I should confess but I felt no real remorse so I suppose the sin is still with me. The first confession was in Berlin whilst I was waiting for Mara. The young priest seemed astounded by my confession, told me that the killing was justified but that my revelling in it was a sin. I suppose he was right but I think he was out of his depth. He just gave me a faltering penance and absolution. The second time, I went to Hof. I felt that I couldn't go to Father Dieter in Oberdorf as he was a friend who had joyfully married us. The priest at Hof was older and very thoughtful. He listened to my story and to my feelings. It was more complicated the second time. I had no remorse at shooting Kovacs but the killing of the young NAS girl was different. In a way I did feel some guilt for her. The priest listened to me quietly. In the end he said, and I remember it well, word for word 'You have been through much, my daughter, more than most of us will ever have to face in a lifetime on this earth. I think that your penance is in your thoughts. Go in peace and sin no more.'

'You have never told me because you knew that I blamed myself for what happened to you at The Farm and you wanted to spare me. I saw it; I was there. But I knew in my heart all the time how you felt, loving you, how could I not? I am so glad that this morning you felt that you could talk to me about it and the Winterburg at last. I suppose my revenge was watching that unspeakable building destroyed by the FWL.'

They lay silent again, staring up for a long time.

'I have often wondered about how Mara coped with her ordeal. We only have talked about fragments of it – some bad enough, in all conscience but never her deepest feelings, never in detail. I have not dared' then she added thoughtfully '– perhaps I should have done. After all, she doesn't have you.'

'She is very deep – our friend. She seems so young and still innocent but behind it is grim experience and reality. I don't know what she has hidden but it is there. Close as we are to her, I suspect that there is still a lot that we don't know.'

'Yes, I have thought that too. I wonder if we shall ever know.'

There was another long, thoughtful pause. Then Detty rolled out of bed and walked over to the window again; this time displaying her scarred back without embarrassment. The mist had cleared and she could see the rushes round the lake in the watery autumn sunshine. She heard from below, her son being called a '*bellissimo bambino*' and subsequent chuckles and gurgles.

'Time, we joined Gianna and Niki, they will think we have passed out,' she said, turning to Marc.

'Although she's young, I think Gianna is enough of an *Italiana* to know how a man and a woman who love each other, and see each other all too seldom, spend their late mornings together' he laughed.

*

Detty felt strangely uncomfortable. There she was with the sash of *Komturin* of the order of *Sankt Nicklaus*, her proudest possession, round her shoulder but she still felt out of place. It was a warmer day and pouring with cold Baltic rain. The VIPs, staff and students all struggled in an egalitarian fashion to get into the small reception area and the reading room of the new library itself. It was a day of celebration. The new library was to be officially opened by the President's daughter, the first lady of the Hanseatic Republic of Livonia and her dearest friend. It wasn't the weather or the cheerful disorganisation, which bothered her but Mara herself. Indisputably she had grown into her unofficial office and showed a warm courtesy and a real interest in the various public duties that she undertook. Mara was clever at giving little speeches which never seemed pompous but right for both her age and her position. However, Detty however knew that all was not well. She sensed a deep unhappiness which had become worse since Mara's torrid relationship with her brother-in-law, Bill, had finally hit the rocks. Without doubt Mara wanted and needed a man. Part of the trouble was that her exposed public position made it difficult for her to have the normal casual friendships which a girl still in her early twenties might form and which might lead to something more. But, and this was what puzzled Detty, that was, she was sure, only part of the story. There was something else at the back of Mara's mind which even her closest friend hadn't fathomed.

The formalities over; the Great Hall felt much more relaxed.

Detty had to admit that Mara looked fabulous. She had taken off the smart full three-quarter length black coat that she had worn for the ceremony. She was wearing a cream silk shirt, black bolero jacket and a black skirt to mid-calf where the hem met her smart black winter boots. About her neck was a green foulard flung round with casual elegance. The Livonian motif was there but not overstated. Her fair hair had been carefully done and shone splendidly for the occasion. Her startling blue eyes on the surface were sparkling with life. Detty noticed that she wasn't the only one admiring the guest of honour. Viktor's eyes were out on stalks.

Detty muttered to Marc: 'I hope our newfound tenor can keep his mind on the job. Have you seen the way his fiery Slavonic gaze is devouring Mara?'

After a suitable pause, Viktor gulped the rest of his wine and threaded through the crowd towards Detty. 'I wonder,' he said with uncharacteristic awkwardness, 'if I could ask you a favour?'

Detty raised one eyebrow at him quizzically. She knew what was coming.

'I wonder if you could introduce me to Frau Oblova. I have heard a lot about her and I would so like to meet her.'

'I am sure you would and I think that I could arrange it.' There was only a touch of irony.

*

Die Meistersinger was all consuming for the next weeks and drove everything else out of Detty's head. For a small ensemble, albeit talented, to attempt this great Everest of lyric music was bound to create some problems. There was much that was good. The *Königshofer Philharmonica*, during the orchestra rehearsals, sounded, as always now, wonderful. The chorus, proud of their training under Bernhard Meisl, acknowledged to be one of the great chorus directors, was splendid in their cohesion, musicianship, and spirit. Bernhard came to rehearse them as often as he could but his commitments were world-wide. Even when he wasn't physically present his meticulous enthusiasm encouraged the choristers to even greater things. Martina Schlerova looked charming and sang with increasing assurance as *Eva* and everyone agreed that in Viktor Detty had found a *Walther* to dream about. The Masters inspired by the indefatigable Hank, who spent much more time in Königshof and *Schloss Krenek* than he had initially promised, all sounded good. Detty enjoyed working with Lev Forjela who, she suspected, far from being intimidated, rather enjoyed flirting mildly with his admired Livonian icon, whilst singing his extensive role with brilliant humour. The sets were coming on and Detty's own ideas about the production caused no great problems and were well received.

So far so good, the problem however was in the major role. The *Hans Sachs* was to be Max Hieren the distinguished veteran Königshofer. Unknown to Helge and Detty, he had developed serious vocal problems since the time when he had sung a distinguished *Pizarro* in the legendary liberation *Fidelio*. Further he was clearly finding preparing and memorising the massive role hugely difficult.

Detty and the other principals involved in the production had been assured by Max that he already knew the part. In rehearsal this was clearly not the case. It became starkly obvious to Helge and Detty that, with just over a month left before the production there was no way that Max was going to be able to sing *Hans Sachs*. After a particularly disastrous piano rehearsal of the difficult *Flieder* monologue in act two, Helge was seriously worried. He had decided to take this rehearsal himself. The reason was that a distressed *repetiteur,* Olaf Svenden, who was an experienced member of the voice department at the college, had come to him confessing that Max was 'having great difficulties.' This turned out to be an understatement and a potentially great embarrassment, to say nothing of a threat to the entire production. Max was a distinguished local artist who had survived the revolution with credit and as such was known and admired in Livonian artistic circles. However, even at a supposedly relaxed piano rehearsal, it was apparent that he was a distance away from knowing his lines and singing the music, let alone acting convincingly one of the longest, most difficult, and complex parts in all opera.

Helge had immediately had a private word with Detty, who had suggested that they talked together in her flat after the lunch break.

'I think that it's obvious he will not be able to do it.'

'Is it really that bad?'

'Yes', replied Helge bluntly, 'he's a mile off'.

'What are the options then?'

'I think option is rather more to the point. We have to play the 'indisposed' card and then get an available international bass baritone and the money to pay him. It's a tall order.'

'OK it's going to be very hard to find a singer of calibre, who knows the role, at this late stage and it's going to be expensive. We are in no position to haggle terms. We both have horrible jobs. I suggest that you break it to Max and I will draw the coverts starting with the agencies including Julien but I don't have a lot of hope there, then Hank, Eileen, and Bernhard. By the way, please let me know how it goes with Max as I will meet him and need to know.'

It started badly. Meisl was unavailable as he was touring the Andes after working at the Teatro Colon in Buenos Aires. Hank's secretary said that she didn't know where he was right now but Detty could try his cell phone. It was switched off. Desperate, she rang the helpful secretary again who said that she would be seeing him 'shortly' and would get him to ring back. Was it urgent?' Detty, after a moment's hesitation, said 'yes'. She was worried that poor Hank, knowing her past record, would think that she had been kidnapped again or something of the sort. Julian, her agent, said he would try but he didn't know of anyone free straight off 'Skilled bass baritones who know the part aren't two a penny, Bernadette.'

'Really?' said Detty with heavy sarcasm and rang off. I'm being a bitch again but he does ask for it, she thought to herself. Then I must go to confession and do a penance – but after *Meistersinger* -if there is a *Meistersinger*. She then rang round the other agents with variations on the same response. She was getting desperate.

Eileen, as always, was more help. She had a list of possibles for most roles but *Sachs* was a difficult one. There was a chance. Some were former pupils, some friends and some the products of extensive networking. She rang back an hour later.

'Detty, I have a possible solution and at the same time a problem. Walter Liebig is available and his agent says he would reluctantly accept your fee range. That is a bit surprising in itself as he has an established reputation over many years. He sang the *Hollander* and *Telramund* at Bayreuth and loads of other roles at the top houses including *Wotan* and *Sachs*. The very fact that an artist of that standing would accept a very modest fee at, forgive me, a smaller theatre made me wonder a bit. Then I remembered that he had cried off sick when booked to sing *Barak* at Vienna last year and he doesn't seem to have done much since. I rang a contact that I have at the *Staatsoper* in Vienna for the real story. You've probably guessed it already, but yes – he had voice problems. It was whispered that the problems related to drinking too much although he is said to have produced a medical statement later saying that that was not the cause. Despite his denial, it seems that other managements aren't prepared to take a chance with him. My contact seemed vague about that and apparently there had also been some sort of row with the mighty Maestro Carbonaro, who was conducting, and we all know that he has a very short fuse. The Intendant and particularly the conductor felt that he wasn't up to scratch, at least for Vienna, and arranged a diplomatic sickness. They were a bit tight lipped and I got the impression that I hadn't heard the whole story. In the end my contact said that all may well be OK now. However, it's obviously taking a chance. He's only in his mid-forties. What do you think?'

Detty thought for a long time.

'Are you still there?'

'Yes, sorry,' she said at last. 'It's a difficult one. I'll talk it through aloud. None of it will be new to you but it will help to clarify my thoughts and you can tell me, as always, where I have got it wrong. Like most singers, I obviously have ever sympathy with a fellow artist who is trying to re-establish a career after a problem. There but for the Grace of God... I know Walter Liebig's reputation and have heard him broadcast. It is-was- a great voice. I have never heard him sing *Sachs* but I imagine he would have been superb. Right voice, right temperament in short he is, or was probably, a fine singing actor. Everything else being equal we would have jumped at him. However, I am very worried by your doubts. In spite of Hank's presence as a singer cum coach we are a young inexperienced ensemble, me included, in fact, specially me, tackling one of the highest peaks in the whole repertory. Maybe we shouldn't be doing it but it's too late to have second thoughts now. Helge, my colleagues, and I must have confidence in the keystone of the work- *Sachs*. We have unexpectedly lost one fine artist due to a similar problem. Max Hieren sang a sparkling, spine chilling performance as *Pizarro* two years ago but can't cope, poor chap, now. But we have very little time and it may be a question of Hobson's choice to either take a chance with Walter or cancel the show which would be terrible for morale all round. Can you stall the agent for a day to let me talk it through with Helge?'

'Yes, of course. Sadly, it doesn't sound as if he has other engagements queuing up.'

'I know. It's a worry but he may be OK with other managements running scared. And thanks, by the way, for being a tower of strength, as always, for your loose cannon pupil. I'll ring tomorrow.'

'Didn't they tell you not to mix your metaphors at your Convent? But seriously it's a pleasure to try and help.'

It was nearly eleven o'clock but Detty took a chance to ring Helge at the *Schloss*. He was still up having a coffee after walking the Souffleuse round the moonlit lake. After lengthy discussion, he agreed with Detty's solution and her doubts.

'It's very worrying but I don't see that we have an alternative, Detty, we must go with him or cancel. Ring them in the morning and say yes.'

'How did the discussion with Max go?' she asked.

'Bless him. He's such a sensitive chap and he made it easy for me. He said he really knew the answer in advance and wasn't surprised. He agreed very readily that he couldn't do it. He had said that he had realised it himself sometime before and should have withdrawn earlier. He said he really had thought that he knew the part as he had sung quite a few excerpts at one time or another, it was only when he studied it seriously that he realised how massive it really is.'

'Longer than all three *Wotans*,' Detty interrupted.

'*Genau!* Anyway, he said that he felt dreadful about leaving us in the lurch. It was very sad. He had obviously set his heart on doing the great role and hadn't wanted to admit, even to himself, that he wasn't up to it. He nearly had me in tears at the end when he said that it had always been his great ambition to sing *Sachs* and he supposed that now, he never would.'

'I know how I would have felt if it had been me with *Isolde*. To have the greatest role in your *fach* snatched away at the last minute must be the cruellest thing.'

There was no more to be said except goodnight. It was after midnight and Detty in a sombre mood went to a lonely soldierless bed. Marc had left that day for an exercise and how she missed him when he was away. She tried to sleep but it was useless. Everything went over and over in her mind. It must have been after three in the morning when she finally dropped off.

She was wakened from a deep sleep with her mobile shrieking in her ear from the bedside table. The ring tone was awful at the best of times. She had intended to get it changed for months but hadn't got round to it. Anyway, were any of them any better? Mara, in one of her skittish moods, had suggested that she had Hank singing *Gott, welch Dunkel hier!* and had been rewarded with a clip round the ear from her powerful friend. Mara, unrepentant, had threatened to send for the security police and tell them that the President's daughter was being assaulted by the IRA. This time, the awful noise went on until Detty eventually groped for the phone, feeling frightened. She was a soldier's wife and she knew only too well that soldiering was never safe and this night-time call made her shudder with anxiety. Eventually she grasped the phone and muttered an incoherent 'Hello'.

She instantly recognised the rich American drawl on the line.

'Sorry about the time, baby, but I was told it was urgent.'

Detty struggling to pull her wits together haltingly explained the problem.

'Poor Max,' was Hank's instantaneous response, then, 'Have you talked to Dieter Einsel?'

This seemingly irrelevant question irritated and startled the sleep-drugged Detty.

'No. He's not coming until next week. His wife's just had a baby so he wanted to stay in Freiburg as long as possible. Anyway, he has done *Pogner* before and knows the part well. We have enough to rehearse already anyway, so we agreed willingly enough. He will be here about the time you arrive back. But why do you ask? We know he's OK. He's familiar with the role.'

'But he also knows *Sachs* and wants to sing it.'

Detty was thunderstruck. She could hardly believe that a solution was apparently staring them in the face and neither she nor Helge knew it.

'How do you know?' she stammered

'He told me. He sang *Marke* to my *Tristan* in Paris last year. We've always got on well but we had lunch together between performances and he told me he had learnt *Sachs* on spec and had quite a lot of coaching in it. He now wanted to have a go somewhat out of the limelight. He should be very good. He has a big range, is sympathetic on stage and has a real interest in the period and background. You haven't given him much time but I think he will jump at it.'

'We have to find another *Pogner*,' she mused aloud.

'That should be easier. I'm not sure who knows it. You could offer it to Max but he's probably too shell-shocked having been jocked off *Sachs* and it would be difficult to keep on the 'indisposed' bit if he sings another role. I would be inclined to try Walter Liebig. I am sure he knows it and perhaps we could both fish around for an enthusiastic youngster as a good cover with a reasonable chance of getting on if there are problems. I think it is more than likely that Walter will be OK in a shorter role and it may give him the chance he needs to get some good reviews and more work. It would do him a good turn and dig us out of a hole.'

'You are a miracle, *du bist heil und hehr, laut und hell*', mightily relieved, she teased him with Isolde's sarcastic quotation from *Tristan*.

'Heh, I don't want any sarcasm and I don't want to finish up dead in a ruin in Brittany – not for real – I've done it often enough in the theatre and it's hard. Upon which subject its high time we fell in love again.'

'Now you really make me tremble' she said now very wide awake 'you're on, but we must talk about it. Where might you want to do it, for instance?'

'Why not Königshof? They seem to like us.'

'I have to learn it – I know bits but it will take a lot of Eileen to get it right. We'll talk about it quietly when you're back. '

'*Ciao ciao, bellissima*'

He rang off. There was no more sleep. The problem not yet solved went to the back of her mind as she tossed the final night hours away with *Isolde's* narration and curse flowing, loud and soundless, through her wide-awake brain.

4
ENTHRONEMENT

'Aspetti, signorina,
le dirò con due parole
chi son, che faccio e come vivo. Vuole?

Puccini, Giacosa & Illica- *La Boheme* Act 1 [13]

The Cathedral in Bialovsk was reputed to be the oldest in Livonia and dated back to the days of the first Teutonic knights, some said that a western monk had penetrated up the Fojn by boat even before the marauding knights. The motto of the city *'In pacem, conquisto'*[14] referred to this legend but it had come to be regarded as ironic during the recent war-torn period.

The warm brick of the old church with its stone mullions, seemed to leap out of the lushness of the small green, protected and not yet battered by winter frost and snow. The building was of typical Baltic brick which distinguished it from its sister at Königshof which,

---

13 Wait, Signorina, I will tell you in two words
    who I am, what I do and how I live
14 With peace, I conquer

unusually for that region, had been built of local stone from a quarry, long since gone.

The most remarkable feature of the cathedral, however, was its situation. When the city had been made the seat of a diocese in the fourteenth century, it had been decided to enlarge the existing church to create a cathedral. This had presented a problem as the east end of the church was very close to the Fojn. To have enlarged the west end would have unbalanced the entire design as well as requiring the destruction of the Guildhall. Nothing daunted the intrepid medieval Bialovsoviks set about driving mighty wooden piles into the Fojn which enabled them to push out the apse and the choir substantially into the river. The citizens always maintained that they had had divine help in this mammoth task. There was a strange recent twist to this assertion. During the civil war when Bialovsk had been, for some months, in the front line, the immensely vulnerable cathedral had survived with only minimal damage. This happy, apparently miraculous, phenomenon had confirmed the especially sacred status of their cathedral in the minds of the citizens.

Detty, rather self-consciously, adjusted her green and white silk sash of St Nicklaus so that it lay correctly across her black winter coat and took Marc's arm. She felt strangely nervous again. The occasion reminded her of a visit she had made to Maynooth College, as a teenager, when she was at St Conleth's Convent. Despite her faith, she felt somehow an outsider, in unknown territory.

Inside the building seemed quite warm perhaps because of the throng of people and the multiple richly robed priests. Rather irreverently she wondered about the collective noun for bishops. Was it, like the ceremony, a Consecration? Cardinal Archbishop Kunz from Königshof was officiating. He was tall and gaunt with a pronounced lantern jaw. Imprinted on her mind was his presence officiating at the Thanksgiving and *Te Deum* at Königshof after the liberation. When she had filed past him with Marc at the west door of the *Dom* at the end of that ceremony, after their thanks, he had smiled fleetingly and said simply '*Danke Ihnen, meine kinder- pax vobiscum*' – nothing fulsome, nothing over the top from a man who had withstood the ravages of the Fascists with courage and dignity. He had been helped a little when in the worst days of the 'God is dead' regime when he had been awarded a Cardinal's hat. It could have backfired and Mara had told her that everybody held their breath to see if he would be executed or sent to a Concentration camp. Fortunately, they didn't dare and he survived. Detty thought without any jealousy 'It was fortunate he was more important than me'.

She didn't know Father Dieter's two supporting Bishops or the Papal Nuncio. Then there was old Bishop Majorowski, in a chair to the side, looking shockingly frail and old, world weary, wasted and almost shrinking into his vestments. She remembered him preaching anathema to the Fascists when he knew it would probably cost him torture and death. She made a note that she must go and see the generous old man while there was still time.

Father Dieter looked incredibly young and nervous in his white stole, cope and biretta during the presentation, oath, and examination, but his voice was loud and firm, audible throughout the great church. The ceremony moved on to the Consecration proper with the laying on of hands and the moving "Receive the Holy Ghost". The ritual reminded Detty of the Initiation of Knights in her own Order of St Nicklaus. She wondered if thinking that was blasphemous, probably not, she concluded. After all they were all sworn to serve the same Master. She felt maternal towards Dieter. They had had fun with the Russian lessons and the intimate friendship of the small village of Oberdorf but Detty, devout Catholic as she was, wondered how it felt to face life without a close companion, without the warmth that meant so much to her.

She woke from her musing when the choir, obviously meticulously rehearsed for the great day, sang *Veni, Creator Spiritus* and the great prayer for the faith of the bishop elect. He then received his crosier and the ring was placed on his right index finger. The Gospel bible was closed and presented. The Mass was completed with the enthronement on the faldstool in front of the *predella*, as the *cathedra* proper was still the prerogative of Bishop Majorowski. The bishops processed round the church to bless the people and the *Te Deum* followed. Bishop Dieter, arrayed with Crozier and Mitre then genuflected and intoned '*Ad multos annos*' and with the kiss of peace and the final blessing, it was all over. A reception had been arranged in 'The Woman in Armour' as the Palace, always modest, was still a wreck after the war.

*

Detty drove back. Marc as always made a ritual grumble about the leg room in the little car. He then made some equally ritual racist and sexist remarks about wild Irish girls and their driving skills. Detty was still driving her much-loved silver bullet which, in spite of the carry cot problem, she had refused to give up. Her mother-in-law, tactful as always, had supplied a dilapidated Land Rover from the family forestry department for use when Niki's accoutrements were definitely going to swamp the X4.

After a pause reflecting on the ceremony that they had just witnessed, Marc turned to Detty:

'Did you see Mara?' he asked.

Detty replied, a trifle crossly, 'Of course, I saw her. We were talking to her after the service.'

'I didn't mean that. I meant during the service.'

'No, I was watching what was going on. I was rather moved; he still seems so young.'

'Well, apart from Dieter, it was like the first scene of *Die Meistersinger* in a real church too. She couldn't take her eyes off your tenor and he's obviously been rehearsed well because it was reciprocated.'

'I never took you for a gossip, Marc von Ritter. Isn't your army giving you enough to think about?'

'The army has taught me to be observant. Another thing, I also noticed the score of *Tristan und Isolde* open on your bed this morning when I came back from running round the lake. I assume this has something to do with your own tenor admirer, who I know telephoned the other day and, that being the case you should be learning something about eyes meeting, *schmucke Irin*[15]. With all these gorgeous tenors around, I can't think how you finished up with an amateur baritone.'

---

15   Decorative Irish girl (TristanAct1)

This last speech resulted in the driver slapping the passenger hard on the thigh. It was a shrewd move because there could be no reciprocation. Marc was a gentleman and, more important, he had enough reservations about his wife's *Valkyrie* driving without adding another hazard of his own making.

'Anyway, you're a fine baritone. You could have had a great career if you had spent time on it rather than doing the practical *Siegfried* heroics.'

'If you continue to take corners like that, we will both finish up on a funeral pyre, also for real.'

'I think that's very ungrateful. I satisfied myself at the reception with a glass of revolting pasteurised apple juice whilst I noticed my back seat driver husband tucking into his father's excellent *Sekt*.'

'The market is poor; I have to do something to support the Bavarian economy.'

Detty noticed, not for the first time, that it was not the German economy and smiled. She was proud of being a native of Kildare and Leinster, when it came to football and hurling but even, she never really felt of either having a separate economy.

'Anyway,' Marc interrupted her thoughts. 'I'll tell you another thing. Mara offered him a lift back to Königshof and he, believe it or not, rapidly accepted.

'Hussey!' interjected Detty then a darker thought struck her out of the past.

'Has she got a detective with her?' she said quietly.

'Oh, my God. I don't know.'

The rest of the drive to Krenek was in silence. The fun had gone out of it.

As they entered the Lodge flat, they both said, simultaneously: 'Better find out!'

Mara rarely carried a *Handy*. She maintained, with some truth, that they were usually tapped by the press or some other unsavoury agency. Detty dialled the private number of the Hansehaus penthouse. To their huge relief, Mara herself answered immediately.

'Just wanting to find out that you got back safely' Detty adopted the sort of tense cheerfulness that she remembered her mother copying, with a high-pitched English accent, from the late Joyce Grenville.

'Of course, I've got back OK. We stopped for a drink on the way. By the way, Viktor has asked me to attend his *Preislied* rehearsal next week, if you don't mind, he says.'

'How could I possibly mind?' said the flabbergasted Detty, and then she muttered to herself, 'Talk about fast work!'

They flung themselves into armchairs, exhausted and speechless with relief. Marc stirred: 'You never really loose the anxiety, do you?'

Detty just nodded. He got up, switched on the *cafetera*, then dived into the cupboard producing a bottle of his parents' home grown *Zwetschgenwasser*. Reluctantly Detty shook her head and fetched the demanding Niki and started to feed him. The telephone rang. It was Helge to say that the good news was that he had 'phoned Dieter Einsel who had agreed to do the part of *Hans Sachs* and was obviously hugely flattered and thrilled by the challenge. Dieter had said that they had already decided to call their new daughter *Eva* but the change of role would make it more important to them both, even if a bit less appropriate.

Mara duly appeared the following day only to find that they had had to change the rehearsal schedule, as Dieter couldn't get there from Freiburg until the day after that. She took it all in good heart, knowing that her emotional needs came second when her friend, as co-director, was scaling operatic heights.

Detty drove to the airport at lunchtime the following day to meet Walter Liebig. She was apprehensive as to what she was going to find. Walter's agent in Munich had e-mailed the day before to say yes – he knew *Pogner* and would take the part. Even the fee, more modest still than that proposed for *Sachs* was acceptable. It all seemed too good to be true and Detty was worried. She remembered vividly a story that Eileen had told a year or so ago about a similar situation when a famous baritone who had recently had some time 'resting' was found unexpectedly to be available by a company in a fix. He had been hired at once and with great relief. The only snag appeared to be that he said he didn't drive and could they make sure there was a taxi at the station. That should have been a clue but it seemed unimportant. When he arrived at the station at eleven o'clock in the morning, he stank of alcohol, recent and stale, and could hardly stand up. His speech was slurred and incoherent and his later attempt at singing predictably dreadful. The present situation seemed worryingly similar – but they had got their *Sachs* and they had to take a chance with Walter.

She put the label with '*Herr Walter Liebig*' round her neck and waited by the gate for the passengers from Berlin to appear. He threaded through the crowd with his bushy moustache twitching as he smiled at her. His deep blue eyes wrinkled and twinkled as he held out his hand for a firm handshake. He was stocky for a bass baritone but with broad shoulders, a deep chest and generous mouth. Detty assessed singers in much the same way as she had been taught to assess racehorses by her uncle Christy Lorne. With a slight soft south German accent, he said:

'Frau O'Neill?'

She nodded and welcomed him feeling a surge of relief. At once she was sure he was OK. They walked to the car park chatting about Königshof and the less than welcoming glowering weather. Detty paid, swearing at the newly installed parking machine while Walter laughed, a good belly laugh, with the moustache twitching again. She eventually got her ticket back, found the car and drove off to-wards the city centre and his hotel.

'I expected someone a bit older,' he started as they reached the new main road. 'You are young to be *Eine Regisseurin.*'

'Yes, I got there by a rather strange route,' she smiled thinking his comment was just right; if he had added 'beautiful' as many did, it would have been over the top.

'Yes, I looked you up on the internet. You have certainly had an interesting history. Sometime, I would like to hear the full story.'

'The old Chinese curse. First, tell me about yourself.'

In an accurate *sotto voce basso* he sang:

'Aspetti, signorina,
le dirò con due parole
chi son, che faccio e come vivo. Vuole?
Chi son? Sono un cantante

> *Che cosa faccio? Canto*
> *E come vivo? Vivo*

Detty, giggling, said, 'Thank heaven you didn't sing it as it should be or we would have made a mistake.'

She was beginning to enjoy herself and his company.

'Well, I should know it. I've sung *Colline* enough times and heard the real version of it waiting for my cue from the Courtyard. They get all the good tunes, don't they – tenors, I mean. But you're a soprano, so I suppose you're in the same union.'

'I've never sung *Mimi* but anyway you've got a pretty good tune coming your way. I think *Pogner*'s address is one of the very best passages.'

'Yes, I am looking forward to it. I haven't done it for a while' then in a gentle voice that almost neutralised the resentment 'you wouldn't trust me with *Sachs* then?'

Before she had time to answer, he went on: 'I don't blame you. After Vienna I am extremely grateful for you trusting me with anything. It was a shambles and I handled it badly.'

Detty, feeling that she had been given permission, asked, 'What really happened? I only know bits and that from one side?'

'I will tell you willingly and Meister von Grunstrand but I would ask one favour.'

'Please do.'

'I would like you both to hear me sing first.'

'Agreed. Unless you feel that you want a session with a repetiteur first, I think Helge would like to do Act One Scene Three with piano to-morrow. With your arrival, we've got everybody here apart from *Kunz Vogelgesang* and he arrives at the weekend. We can get one of the students to fill in. No problem.'

'Fine, by the way who is *Kunz Vogelgesang*, it's not a part that usually goes to imported singers?'

'Henry Schliessen,' said Detty, with a straight face and in a matter-of-fact tone of voice.

'*Gott in Himmel!*' exclaimed Walter 'I thought you said to my agent that this was a small-town production with inexperienced singers!

Having the world's most famous *Heldentenor* singing a minor role, doesn't exactly sound like it.'

'It is a small-town production with inexperienced artists. But like, I imagine, the Vienna saga there is an explanation but also like Vienna, I think, that can wait until you've met the team and had a rehearsal. But you're OK for to-morrow?'

'Yes. Can't wait.'

'We are still rehearsing at Krenek as there's more space and most of the cast have sung in the theatre before. We will probably move into town next week. It takes about an hour from your hotel, if we aim to start at eleven to allow us a couple of hours before lunch, is that OK with you?'

'Fine.'

'We could give you a room at Krenek but it's rather overcrowded as there is a lot of building still to do – money permitting, and you will probably be more comfortable in town. Would you like to go out and have something to eat?'

'Thanks, but I had quite a long wait in Berlin and had a meal there. I wouldn't mind an early bed if I've got to prove myself tomorrow.'

She dropped him at the hotel and headed for Krenek starting through the evening rush hour. She was on a high. She always enjoyed the drive once she was out of town into the woods and fields. Even when it was nighttime and she couldn't see the countryside beyond the headlights, it still seemed suddenly peaceful. Meeting with Walter Liebig had pleased and relieved her, like a great weight being lifted off her shoulders. This production, although being staged in a minor centre, had still, for various reasons, been the centre of a good deal of international attention and she was frightened that it would be a fiasco. After meeting Walter this seemed much less likely. She sang as she drove. It was a chaotic mixture of *Magdalene*, *Elisabeth* and *Sieglinde*. She even tried a bit of *La Boheme* after Walter's *improvviso*. She made *Mi chiamo Mimi* sound dreadful. She made a vow to try and sing more lyric parts, but not perhaps *Mimi* but if a bass-baritone could sing *Rodolfo*, why not have a go? But it would need a lot of practice. She remembered singing the great *Messiah* arias at Henley an age ago. She laughed to herself at the idea of her tall, shapely, athletic figure playing a waif dying of consumption. Probably no more incongruous than some of the large *Mimis* of the past, but better to stick to safer roles. It was a mad world but just at that moment it was going OK.

She went straight up to the *Schloss* when she got to Krenek, hoping to be in time for a meal. She hadn't been sure that Walther's plane would be on time and had told Gianna that she probably wouldn't be in that evening. Helge was waiting for her in the great hall.

'How did it go?' he asked anxiously.

She put her finger to her lips and muttered:

'*Shuss*! But I think we're all right. He loves singing and I think there is more to the Vienna story than we have heard. He has also got, as the lonely heart columns say, GSOH.'

'Can you explain?' said a puzzled Helge 'What are lonely hearts columns and what is GSOH?'

Detty demanded a beer and then explained about English newspaper and internet dating columns and the asset/requirement of a Good Sense of Humour.

'I would hardly have thought you needed those things' said a still puzzled Helge looking very serious.

'I don't, *Maestro*, but it doesn't mean to say that I don't know that they exist.'

*

There was a hushed excitement in the old library of the *Schloss* when they gathered there the following morning. To Detty's immense relief, Walter arrived on time in the hired car looking just as keen and spritely as the day before.

Ernst Hellmann, the senior *repetiteur*, took the piano to allow Helge to concentrate on what was happening. In a subdued but true conversational voice, Liebig started the scene to *Beckmesser*:

> *Seid meiner Treue wohl verzehen*
> *Was ich bestimm, in Euch von Nutz*[16]

---

16 Be assured of my good will, my plan will help to assist you.

Fine, thought Detty, very relaxed and not trying to prove anything to anybody. Truly professional.

Hartley Thomas, Detty's fellow student, the wonderful black baritone from Manchester, was enjoying himself as *Beckmesser*. He was pedantic and meticulous but not too much of the fool.

Detty really began to enjoy the glorious music and forget her anxieties. Viktor's splendid tenor announced his presence and the Masters assembled with a student tenor proudly singing *Vogelgesang*'s small interjections. Kevin Scott, the Irish baritone who had impressed as *Don Fernando* in the liberation *Fidelio* called the roll and then announced:

Das habe Ihr, Meister, sprecht![17]

Detty held her breath. This was crunch time.

Walter started in the same conversational manner that he had used for the introduction. Then:

Das schöne Fest, Johannistag,
ihr wisst begehn wir morgen[18]

and it was all right – better than that – fine – a great moving bass poem enchanting them all, flowing over them with melody and serenity. The great bass baritone of former years with his brilliant phrasing and passion was back and back with a vengeance. Detty could understand why he hadn't wanted to talk about his troubles until they had heard him sing. When he finished with:

Eva, mein einzig Kind, zur Eh'[19]

There was a stunned silence followed by a highly improper burst of applause. Helge, rapped his desk:

'Ladies and Gentlemen, I realise that you found that magnificent, so

---

17 You have the floor, Meister, speak!
18 The Feast of St John we will celebrate tomorrow.
19 Eva, my only child, to wed.

did I. Our compliments, Herr Liebig, it is a great privilege to have you here amongst us. But may I remind everybody, that the scene doesn't finish here and we will be late for lunch.'

They all laughed.

'And I would also remind you that we are all on holiday for the weekend which allows the team to prepare the theatre for us to descend on them next week.'

They continued seemingly buoyed up by the exhibition of supreme vocal acting that they had just heard. Everybody was better than usual. Suddenly there was belief. It was going to happen and happen well.

*

The long rehearsal day of October 31st, the eve of *Allerheiligen* finally came to an end. All the cast felt exhausted but satisfied. As well as the normal All Saints holiday, an extra public holiday had been declared that year for *Allerseelen,* November 2nd, in particular memory of the soldiers who had died with Liese Zahnsdorf.

On the Friday evening, they all had dinner at Krenek. Although not officially formal, it had a festive feel about it and everybody dressed up as best they could and the *Sekt* flowed. Marc had arrived back that day still in uniform and hurriedly changed. Walter took Detty on one side.

'You wanted to hear about Vienna and I think that I owe it to you to tell you.'

Detty nodded expectantly. 'The only thing is that I don't want what I have to say to become public knowledge. Is there somewhere that I could go with you and Maestro von Grunstrand where we could talk in private? It is, unfortunately complicated and extremely messy.'

Detty thought for a minute. 'We could go down to Bialovsk to an inn where we would be left alone. There are two problems. I must be back in Königshof the day after tomorrow in the afternoon to sing in a Memorial Service for a very dear friend of mine. Also, would you allow me to bring my husband Marc? He is an officer in the German intelligence corps and extremely discreet. I don't know anything about what you are going to tell us but Marc can be helpful where difficult situations are involved.'

'Of course.'

The memorial service was at eleven in the Cathedral. Marc and Detty stayed the night in the *Hansehaus*. Detty was to sing Strauss's *Allerseelen* after the homily. Diffidently she had asked whether it would be proper wear her formal Captain's uniform. She explained that it had close associations with her service with Liese, who was being honoured. She wanted to wear this rather than the more senior Colonel-in-Chief's regalia which was usual at *Freiwehr Livonia's* passing out parades. In time for the rehearsal earlier in the week she had received a courteous message from the current deputy Commander in Chief saying that Colonel O'Neill could of course wear any uniform and insignia to which she was entitled and that she felt was appropriate.

She felt a thrill and simultaneous sadness when after finishing dressing she put on her service hat with the distinctive green and white cockade and turned to face Marc in his formal uniform as a Major of the *Bundeswehr*.

'Will I do?' she asked.

'*Jawohl*' he said surprisingly curtly adding 'but I have an official duty before we can leave.'

Detty looked at him quizzically. It was a tense occasion but she hadn't expected him to be so abrupt.

'While I was on exercises, I received a message from Brigadegeneral Kramm to the effect that, because of circumstances, deputising for the more usual senior officer, I should invest *Leutnant Bernadette O'Neill (retired)* with *Die Ehrenmedaille der Bundeswehr* for her gallant service with the *Heer* and in recognition of her afterwards serving with distinction with our allies the *Freiwehr Livonias*. He pinned the medal on her chest, stood back and saluted. Detty after a moment's hesitation saluted in return.

The ceremony over, Detty burst into tears. Marc put his arm round her.

'Brigadegeneral Kramm sends his apologies that it has taken so long after he promised it to you. There was a problem about your length of service. It must be seven months and that was a bit difficult to fix. Then I pointed out that the medal can be awarded to soldiers in allied armies and that your service with the FWL would qualify. Finally, there was discussion of whether in that case the citation should be for a FWL officer or a *Bundeswehr* officer. Eventually they decided the *Bundeswehr* rank and citation was in order and appropriate – so here it is.'

Through her tears she looked at Marc's *Ehrenkreuz der Bundeswehr in Silber* and then down at her own chest with the more modest but similar black red and gold ribbon of Germany nestling next to her green and white sash.

She felt an indescribable pride but the only thing she could say was: 'I've ruined my make up.'

'That's a fine response from somebody who has just been decorated as a German heroine.' Marc was back to his teasing self then practically 'We have time for repairs.'

5
VIENNA

Falke! Falke!
Warum weinst du?[20]

STRAUSS/HOFMANNSTAL: *DIE FRAU OHNE SCHATTEN* ACT I

'You see it was a horrible tangle. There were some whispers at the time that the scheming around that production of *Die Frau* would have provided a plot for another Strauss masterpiece, although personally I think it was more suited to Verdi or possibly Alban Berg rather than Strauss. But *'Die Frau'* certainly provided the cast and the backdrop. It didn't have much to do with singing – not mine nor anybody else's – but that wasn't how it appeared afterwards.'

He paused for a moment while the fire at Die Dame in Rüstung crackled and a log crashed onto the wide fire dogs. Detty, Marc and Helge waited intrigued.

'I suppose that it's rather appropriate to discuss it here in Livonia as it all started with the falcon or rather the Voice of the Falcon. This part was being sung by a French lyric soprano called Marie-Paule Lefleuve. Do any of you know her, by the way?'

---

20 Falcon, falcon, why do you cry!

They shook their heads.

'Well, I met her in Munich when she was singing *Musetta* in *La Boheme* and I was *Colline* in the same production. I have been free since my divorce five years ago and we liked each other and began an affair. It didn't have time to progress very far but I was pleased to see that Marie-Paule was singing in *Die Frau* with me at Vienna. What I didn't know was that the conductor of the show, the great Massimo Carbonaro, was one of my predecessors in the affections of Mademoiselle Lefleuve and still regarded her as his personal property. Marie-Paule had never mentioned it to me and anyway she confirmed later that as far as she was concerned the affair had been over months before I met her in Munich. You may wonder what this has to do with my vocal problems but please be patient.'

Kurt Steuermann, the landlord of *Die Frau,* knocked at the door, opened it ajar and coughed discretely. He then asked whether the Frau Komturin would be ordering 'the usual'. Detty had to explain to Walter that 'the usual' was coffee and *Zwetschgenwasser* and that the Frau*'s* plum brandy was regarded very highly. Walter's face lit up and he needed no second invitation. Kurt was used to having confidential and sometimes highly secret meetings in the private rooms of the old inn. His past record as a warrant officer in the *Freiwehr Livonias* made him utterly discreet and the inn ideal for this purpose. After he had served them with their coffee and *digestifs* himself and put more logs on the blaze, they settled to their drinks and Walter continued.

'Well, you know what theatres are. I took Marie-Paule out one evening for a drink as soon as we had both arrived for rehearsals. We went to one of the small *Heurigen* in *Neustift* but although we tried not to be obvious as luck would have it, we had the misfortune to run into one of the stage managers and her husband. Well, of course, by the following day when we arrived for rehearsals, it was all round the theatre that we had been seen together. In due course we learnt that Maestro Massimo had gone purple with rage over our, fairly innocent, assignation and then had gone into overdrive to find out as much as he could about our relationship. When he had discovered what little there was to discover about Munich, he went into an even more evil rage.

It was really *Otello* all over again and there wasn't much more than a handkerchief to provoke it – well, perhaps a bit more.'

He smiled to himself before going on.

'The first rehearsals were extremely tense with Massimo either ignoring me or swearing at me, but I tried to remain calm. It wasn't good but I tried to give my best artistically and ignore the sparks.'

'However, after a few days something very odd happened. I began to start tripping over things, then I had difficulty in swallowing and my singing went to pot. I couldn't articulate properly and soon even had difficulty in speaking. Massimo immediately accused me of attending rehearsals drunk and soon it was all round the theatre that I was on the booze. I was mortified and completely perplexed but when the Intendant called me in I had to agree that I was incapable of singing. I told him that I had had no more than the odd glass of wine with meals but he just smiled and said '*Natürlich*' but obviously he didn't believe me. He was furious at having to find a replacement for a key role at the last minute. He offered to say publicly that I had been taken ill and was unable to sing. It was the usual 'indisposed' line. I had to agree as I knew that I was in no condition to sing.'

'I left Vienna and feeling physically and mentally terrible went home to Bavaria. There I quickly sought medical advice from the *Friedrich-Baur-Institut der Neurolog* back in Munich. After a very extensive examination and a lot of tests, the Professor said that they thought that I had been poisoned by something and mentioned 'post synaptic neuromuscular blockade' which was totally incomprehensible to me. However, they could find nothing specific on the tests and perhaps it had been a temporary thing. They questioned me very closely about what I had eaten and drunk but I could remember nothing out of the ordinary. Then they astounded me by asking if I had by chance suffered any bites. I asked them what sort of bites and they shook me even more by saying snake bites in particular but also insects. They wanted to know as well whether I had been to the USA recently – I hadn't. I had sung *Fiesco* at the Met three years before but they said that that was too long ago. In the end I asked the Professor what they had in mind and after some humming and haring, she said that my symptoms somewhat resembled the effects of a Rattle snake bite. I thought that she was joking at first but she wasn't the joking type. I was flabbergasted.'

'Fortunately, I was already improving quite fast. I was walking and talking normally and the swallowing had returned to normal. The Professor said that she thought that whatever it had been had gone from my system which was why they couldn't find anything in the blood tests despite sending the blood to the toxicology reference laboratory.'

'I called in on my agent and explained that I was having medical investigations and that he should cancel engagements up to three months. After that, I went home to walk in the mountains and have a think. Two things happened then, one good and one very bad. My voice returned almost perfectly. I was sure it had and I got one or two trusted friends to listen at home and to tell me truthfully and they agreed. Obviously, I didn't have the opportunity to sing in a big space but I was ninety per cent sure that I was back to normal which seemed to support the Munich professor's theory that I had been poisoned.'

'The bad news was that I could get no new engagements and even the ones that I had already, cancelled. They paid me cancellation fees if they had to but they were very tight lipped about the reasons. I was, as you can imagine, furious and distressed. My career seemed to have hit the buffers and I was still puzzled as to how this had come about. It may have been paranoia but from the start I suspected it had something to do with that bastard – excuse me Frau Bernadette – Carbonaro. He had been eaten up by fury and jealousy that I had dared interfere with what he regarded as his harem almost his *droit de seigneur*. It was completely irrational but apparently, he was obsessed with compulsive jealousy centred around Marie-Paule and me, although he had no continuing relationship with her and he had no right to interfere in her life, or mine, in any way.'

He paused.

'Is there by any chance any more of the fabulous *Zwetschgenwasser* or will asking for another make you think that Carbonaro was right after all?'

Detty smiled.

'I don't think so. I'll tell Kurt he has yet another convert.'

She got up and went out to find the Landlord. While she was gone Walter said: 'Am I also allowed to say how much I admire your wife, Herr Graf, without being misunderstood, that is.'

'I have had to get used to people admiring my wife over the years' smiled Marc 'I am cuckolded on a regular basis by the whole of this country.'

When Detty came back, he went on: 'The third act' he said with a half-smile once they had their further coffees and *Zwetschgenwasser,*

'*Götterdämmerung.* I made some discreet enquiries. It appeared that Maestro Massimo, either personally or via his agents, had informed almost every theatre and concert management in the world that I was a degenerate lush, far down skid row. Fortunately, either that information did not reach the Royal Northern College of Music or, as I like to believe, Professor Vaughan, for whom I have always had a huge admiration, didn't believe it. So, I am here and I can't tell you how grateful I am to all of you. I will try to give you a *Pogner* to remember. I would like to add that I have been hugely impressed by your young enthusiastic set up and if there are any more roles or teaching that I can do, I would be only too happy.'

'That's very generous and I think that we might well take you up on it but let's get *Die Meistersinger* over first.'

*

Breakfast was a silent affair at *Die Frau.* Walter had drained himself the night before and the other three were still mulling over his ghastly story. Detty had wondered at first whether it was true. After all they had only heard one side and Walter had good reason to find an excuse for Vienna. She rapidly dismissed her doubts. The man exuded honesty and his fine singing critically supported his case. In addition, his Munich hospital notes would be recorded and producible if required. No, the story had to be true, however improbable it might seem.

It was Helge who broke the silence.

'Detti, I'm a bit worried about the Cathedral concert. We settled the programme ages ago and the *Dom* is booked. I have rehearsed the orchestra and Vladimir has done quite a lot of work with the chorus and seems satisfied but they need to get together with the *Domchor* and we haven't done any rehearsing with soloists. Things have changed a bit since we first arranged the soloists.'

'I'd forgotten all about it. *Meistersinger* has driven everything else out of my mind.'

When they had first planned the *Sankt Nicklausfest*, they had decided to have one or more major productions in the fortnight around Advent finishing with a concert in the Cathedral on the second Sunday in Advent which was near to St Nicholas day itself on December 6th. The first part of the concert was to be a complete performance of Berlioz's *L'Enfance du Christ* and then a short festive second half.

Detty quickly reviewed the arrangements: 'Max was going to do *Herod*. I will try and find him and ask him if he still feels able to do it. I know Hartley said he would stay on and do *Joseph*. That should neutralise the racist taunts from *Meistersinger*. I'm *Mary* and Hank is doing the Narrator. We haven't yet cast the two small bass parts and the tenor centurion from the senior voice students at the College. They will need some rehearsals with a repetiteur. I'll talk to Ernst. He's in a very good mood after being promoted to *Musikalicher Supervisor*, Head of Music Staff, and he knows the good performance diploma students well so I am sure there will be no problem. Can we schedule a *Sitzprobe* at Krenek after the last *Meistersinge*r and then we will have time for the *General probe* the day before in the Cathedral? What about the carols and songs in the second half?'

'Is Viktor going to stay around?'

'I think he might have a reason for doing so.'

6
THE FUND

Oh! God! That bread should be so dear,
And flesh and blood so cheap!

Thomas Hood

There had been a partial thaw overnight. The basement steps under the peeling old tower block were wet and stank of wet concrete and tom cat. The flats above were of the terrible grey block sided type once pervasive in Eastern Europe but now thankfully disappearing, except from the very poorest areas on the outskirts of cities. Detty glanced back guiltily at her immaculate Z4. Much as she loved it, not for the first time she wished that she had something less glitzy for these visits. Nothing she could do about it now, she thought, and turned her attention to the slippery steps and, reaching the bottom, knocked at the door.

The door was opened slowly and suspiciously. The face that peered round the edge of the door had once been young. Now it was not exactly old but the waxy taunt skin, fleshless over the bones of the face, spoke of hardship and misery:

'Frau Dötsch?' the girl nodded diffidently *'Ich bin Bernadette von Ritter, ich habe Sie gestern abend telefonieren.'* [21]

The girl smiled. It was as if a weight had fallen from her and she suddenly looked her eighteen years.

'Come in, please.'

She ushered Detty into the room inside which was clean and tidy but cold and almost bare. There was a sink and a single tap and a very old two ring electric stove balanced on a wooden box. An old oil stove provided the room some heat and on one wall was a radiator which seemed to contribute little to the losing battle against the bitter cold. There were two doors at the back of the room. One door was partly open and revealed a lavatory and a tin basin with another single tap. There was no evidence of a shower. The other door was closed and presumably led to the bedroom.

In front of the oil stove an old woman was hunched in a creaking defective wicker chair.

'Mother, this is Frau von Ritter who has come to try and help us.'

The old woman held out her hand and tried to get up. Detty did a quick calculation from the information she had had about the family and, with a shock realised, that 'the old woman' Maria Dötsch's mother Barbara, was not yet forty.

Maria busied herself making tea, found Detty an incongruously elegant Meissen cup and mugs for herself and her mother.

'As I said on the telephone last night, we are doing up a house in the centre which will be divided into apartments, we will probably be able to offer you one before spring if the work is on time. They won't be luxury but…'

'They will be heaven compared with this.' Maria flashed her smile again as she finished the sentence for Detty.

'I can't tell you how grateful we would be, Frau Bernadette.'

'I know it's extremely painful but do you feel up to telling me your story from the beginning. I must write a report and it would be very helpful to hear the whole story.'

---

21 I am Bernadette von Ritter I telephoned you yesterday.

'Of course, I dream about it most nights. It might do us both good to have it out in the open again' she plunged straight in 'my father was a shipwright at *Baltikmarin*. We weren't wealthy but we had enough and a small, but good, apartment near the docks. The job was reasonably secure and important and although we always hated the Fascist government, at first, to be honest, it didn't make a lot of difference to us personally. There was still plenty of work and regular wages. My brother, who was two years older than me, and I went to school where we were fed a lot of propaganda. My dad told us to avoid discussing anything which might get us into trouble and we followed his instructions. My brother, though, gradually got more and more angry about the things that we heard whispered were happening.

'The last straw came when he was coming up to eighteen and he got his call-up papers. The evening later he burst out "I'm never going to fight for those bastards" and the following evening he was gone together with a friend. I heard later that they had joined the autumn revolt down near Solanova. As you probably know all the early revolts were put down savagely and my brother was killed just a few weeks later. However, the NAS didn't wait for him to be killed. There was a crashing at the door of our flat at six o'clock one morning about a week after my brother left. Three NAS thugs came in demanding to know where my brother was. Of course, we genuinely didn't know and said so. Then they turned nasty. They pulled my clothes off and the first brute had me over the kitchen table while the others held me down. I was just short of sixteen and a virgin. He was very rough and it hurt terribly with blood all over me. My dad tried to stop them but they held him back. Then he broke loose and grabbed one of them. The third drew his gun and shot my dad in the back of the head. It was awful he just lay there dead while the second and third one had me. Then they went for my mum and had her. Then they took everything from the flat and, worst of all, burn our ration books. The day after they came back put my dad's body in a truck with some other dead people and then locked us out of the apartment onto the street. We were both in a terrible state, injured, cold and starving. We had not been great churchgoers but in desperation we struggled to the house of the local priest. He got some nursing nuns to care for us and eventually found us this place. We were really lucky because there were so many, so many... and so many died.'

Detty was silent struck dumb by this terrible story although she had heard others almost as bad. As for their being lucky, it was an astonishing idea of luck. Yet again she cursed her talent. What on earth was the use of a soprano voice in the face of this horror? Inadequately she just said:

'We will try and get you the very earliest apartment and meanwhile find you clothes and a better stove until we can get you moved.'

They sat in silence nursing their cold teacups. After a long pause, Maria looked up and spoke shyly, in contrast to the dead pan way she had recounted the horrors.

'We reached the end of our tether and despaired. I was pregnant from the rape. I was growing larger by the day because of being forced by a man who only wanted to hurt me. But for all that my little girl was sweet when she arrived and perhaps his father didn't understand what he was doing. She is here now, a lovely little girl, three years old. She is at nursery school and doing well.

But at that time both of us only wanted to die, only wanted for the misery to end. But one day we heard from the nuns, over the whispering network, that Nicklaus Oblov was back in the south and that this time the partisans hadn't been wiped out and that the revolt was holding. At first, we didn't believe it but the whispers continued and became more detailed and we began to believe and even hope' she lowered her voice and looked at the floor.

'Then we heard something even stranger. The nuns told us that a young foreign hero had been sent by God and was helping Oblov to save what was left of us. There was a stranger part still. A beautiful tall foreign woman with indomitable courage and the voice of an angel was performing miracles in the name of freedom from terror and for justice on behalf of ordinary people.'

Maria stared silently at the floor and her mother, who had been silent while her daughter spoke, at last broke in.

'Maria will not tell you but I will. We had decided to kill ourselves together as there seemed to be no future but when Maria heard the exploits of that young Irish girl, she said to me "Mum, we can't kill ourselves when those people are risking everything to help us and save us." Frau Bernadette, we are so grateful for your promised help but I would like you to know that anything you do for us in the future, cannot compare with what you have done for us in the past.'

And, at last, she too had the ghost of a smile 'we will always remember the day when the heroine of Livonia drank tea under our roof. Bless you.'

'It was very good tea' was all she could think of muttering as she turned to go, grateful that she wasn't wearing eye makeup. It was some minutes before she could see clearly enough to start the Z4 and head back to the Hansehaus.

She returned from the visit moved but gloomy. It was now more than two years after the war and the suffering of some of the survivors was still terrible. She always tried to make three or four trips each year to meet the worst maimed and disabled by the war and the torture that had preceded it. She reached her destination and flashed her zapper and the gate to the auxiliary car park opened. She eased the little sports car into a vacant place. The grandly titled *Hilfsparkplatz* was actually a bomb site behind the Hansehaus, it was designated for shops and flats but the economic problems had had the proposal put back and, in the meanwhile, it had been roughly bulldozed flat, given an electric security fence and called into service for extra parking for the Hansehaus. The President, Nicklaus Oblov, had tried to insist that she parked in the front of the Hansehaus with the official cars but she had firmly but politely refused and smiling, he had muttered to himself 'you can see who really runs this country!' She stared gloomily at the desolation of twisted girders not yet removed at one end. These were punctuated by old plastic bottles with the occasional tuft of grass growing in between. It seemed symbolic of the shattered lives of the people that she had just seen.

She walked round the block to the front entrance of the Hansehaus thinking, not for the first time that they really should get a flat in the city and not keep relying on the Oblovs hospitality. But it was difficult. She knew that both Nicklaus and Mara enjoyed their company and was sure that they would be hurt by any attempt to break the present arrangement. Mara had fussed around with pleasure preparing one of the two Penthouse spare rooms and telling Detty that it was for her and Marc whenever they wanted it. On Niki's arrival she had gone out and got a cot for her Godson. The so-called Penthouse was modest in the extreme with Nicklaus' study, four bedrooms, a kitchen, and a living room. Its only luxury was a small roof garden which in good weather, commanded a glorious view of the city and the Baltic beyond. On a warm summer's night, the shimmering view had an opalescent beauty. Detty remembered the first time that she had seen it soon after the Oblovs moved in. She had stood in the twilight with her arm round Marc uncharacteristically gazing quietly.

He had just murmured: 'It is beautiful now in spite of all the damage.'

'It means so much to me.'

'Don't I know it, *Schatz*, it's my rival and it nearly took you from me – more than once.'

'It's strange' she had said gazing over the rooftops to the sea 'I hated this city so much when I first came here. It seemed the eeriest, saddest, most sinister place that I had ever seen but now it seems part of me, my essence.'

She ran up the steps into the ground floor reception. Falk, the veteran ex FWL Warrant Officer was on duty. Their history went back a long way. Falk had arrested her as a spy after she had crossed the Fojn and he had never forgotten the embarrassment of that moment. At this time, they both had something else on their minds. They had not seen each other for some time, as by coincidence he had not been on duty when she had passed the desk recently. He had been at the military funeral of Liese and her colleagues but they hadn't spoken.

'Welcome back, Frau Hauptmann, *wie geht es Ihnen?*'

She smiled; he always used her rank in the FWL despite his oft spoken prejudice about women in the army. She was secretly rather proud of this modest title. She felt it had made her truly part of the war. She had however gently persuaded him to stop saluting her.

'Fine, thank you, Falk. I saw you at the funeral, I am sorry I didn't speak to you but it was…'

She didn't know how to finish and he spread his hand with his face showing terrible grief. He had admired Liese and adored her like a daughter although for much of the war, she had been his Commanding Officer. He claimed to disapprove heartily of women soldiers, let alone women COs, but Liese could do no wrong.

'*Shrecklich!*' he said under his breath and Detty nodded.

She asked about his wife and two sons and allowed him to open the lift door for her.

Gianna was still out. Mara had begged to be allowed to look after Niki for the afternoon and was jogging him on her knee when she got out of the lift. She kissed Mara, took Niki and flung herself into an armchair.

'Has he been OK?'

'Good as gold. We discussed Goethe and the European economic situation,' she joked.

'He's not Thomas Carlyle, you know.'

'How was your day?'

'Terribly depressing. Some of these stories are unbelievably horrible.'

'Perhaps this is not the moment but I have had an idea that I need to discuss with you about helping the war casualties and there is also a favour I want to ask from you.'

Detty looked at her quizzically and then asked rather inconsequentially: 'Have you got any of that Jameson left?'

Mara nodded,

'OK let's both have one and then I'll be ready for anything.'

Mara poured the whisky with the reverence due to communion wine, passed a glass to Detty. They clinked glasses.

'Well, the idea is that we could start a proper charity to help the relief of victims of the regime and the war. I mean, what you do is great but...'

'You're right it's not great – it's far too piecemeal, far too little, and not properly organised. An official charity would be much better.'

'You would have to be President of it of course.'

Detty thought for a moment. 'I think that I've got a better idea. I am President of much too much already. You would be a much better choice but I have another suggestion.'

She thought again for a moment then made up her mind and said, with decision,

'We dedicate it to Liese and ask David Sensky if he would be President. I don't know whether he would do it but he's a national icon and obviously was very close to Liese.'

'Brilliant – if he would do it. I am afraid you will have to ask him. I can't think anyone else could – General Zahnsdorf perhaps.'

'No, I'll do it – it's the least I can do. It's late tonight but I'll ask him to have lunch with me later this week and ask him face to face – better than telephoning. Would it be OK if I suggest that we could serve as Vice Presidents?'

'I think we ought to ask a serviceman to serve as one. Ulrich Zahnsdorf would be an obvious choice,' Mara said thoughtfully.

'Or Kurt Steuermann, the Landlord at Bialovsk' added Detty 'or your splendid receptionist, Falk Jurowski.'

She was thinking of the conversation that they had just had in the hall downstairs and of how he would value being associated with his dead heroine.

'Room for all of them on the Committee.' Mara adopted her decisive 'First Lady' tone, 'But we had better sort out David first.'

'OK I'll see to it ASAP, *gnädige Frau,*' she teased. 'What was the other thing, by the way?'

Mara suddenly looked uncomfortable, 'I've been asked to unveil a memorial at Solanova and I wondered whether you could do it instead.'

Detty was puzzled. She knew Mara took her President's daughter and First Lady duties very seriously and had performed hundreds of ceremonies including openings, unveilings – all sorts in fact. She wondered why this one was different.'

'Of course, I'll do it if you want. Does it clash with something?'

'No.'

Detty waited but nothing more came then: 'I just don't want to do it, that's all!' Mara's voice pitch climbed until she almost screeched the 'that's all 'then she looked embarrassed and muttered 'I'm sorry'.

Detty, very puzzled, said calmly, 'Of course, I'll do it – no problem. Who do I contact for the details?'

'Ivan Kovacs, he's the *Haupt Bürgermeister* of Solanova. I'll write to and apologise and say that I have asked you to do it'.

Her calm had returned.

'No relation, I trust?' said Detty. Frederick Kovacs had been the sadistic medical officer at the Farm Camp who had later become chief of the notorious NAS under the former fascist regime.

'No,' laughed Mara, now entirely composed. 'It's a very common name in the southeast.'

It was late and they said goodnight. Detty went to bed beside her sleeping son still pondering Mara's strange outburst. Was it something to do with Solanova? It was a small market town, in the southeast and seemed to have made a profound impression on her friend. Could it be something in Mara's past? But it seemed hardly likely. Mara had still been a convent schoolgirl when they had first met and surely, she had not had much of a chance to have a 'past'. Of course, though, she had lived through disturbed times and Detty had always realised that, close as they were, Mara did not talk about it. She wondered whether what the *Bürgermeister* had to say when he contacted her would provide an explanation. She gave up the puzzle and slept.

*

Ivan Kovacs, the *Bürgermeister,* was as kind and courteous as his namesake had been brutal. At lunch before the Ceremony, he told Detty the strange story of the young NAS officer whose heroism they were celebrating. He related how Stefan Moser had, late in the day, realised the nature of the dreadful regime that he was serving. One day he was part of an escort taking captured partisans to public execution by hanging in Solanova. He had planned very carefully how he might save his prisoners. The complicated plan had worked but he had been killed in the attempt. He had given his own life but had saved all the prisoners. It was this act of great courage that the memorial was to celebrate.

Kovacs went on: 'There was then a lot of argument about the nature of the memorial. We decided that a statue of Moser himself was the only proper thing. There were however two problems. What did he look like? We tried to get a photo from captured NAS records only to discover that Stefan's file had been destroyed in the Winterburg inferno during the liberation of Königshof. Then an odd thing happened. Through the post to the *Rathaus* at Solanova came a good copy photo of a young man in civilian clothes. It was addressed to me personally and included an anonymous cryptic note reading "This may help you".'

'We had to be sure that it was of Moser. Fortunately, Andreas Weber, the leader of the partisan brigade whose members were saved, still lives here running a sawmill. He was the last person to see Moser alive, so we showed it to him. He said that it was indeed a good likeness of Moser. He also added that he thought that he knew where it might have come from in which case it would certainly be genuine. I waited for him to explain but he said no more. I pressed him. Then he answered very calmly. "I was sworn to secrecy. You will understand, under the circumstances, it was a sacred oath so I shall say no more but trust the likeness" so we had solved one problem.'

'The other problem was tricky. How should we portray Moser? His heroism related to the fact that he was a member of the NAS but could we really put that hated uniform on a public monument. There was a lot of furious argument but finally the uniform was accepted. The monument has him, hatless in NAS uniform but reaching towards the Livonian chalice and falcon. It's a fine statue.'

Detty was very moved and thoughtful as she left the *Rathaus* to walk the few meters to the shrouded statue standing on the spot where the partisans were to have been hanged. The story and the solemn mood of the luncheon had fired her up enough for her to give an impassioned speech for a few minutes. She reached for the shroud over the statue and gently drew it aside revealing the lifelike handsome young man his face grimly determined, his arm stretching out towards the Chalice and Falcon of Livonia. Andreas Weber laid the first wreath signed by all the survivors then the *Bürgermeister* laid one on behalf of the town. Then there were other flowers from relatives, the services and well-wishers.

The *Bürgermeister* gave his speech of gratitude to Stefan and thanks to Detty for her role in the war and performing the unveiling. They shook hands and Detty smiled her thanks and, thoughtfully, got into the car for the drive back to town.

*

The frozen mist settled on the pine trees, there was moonlight and the stars sparkled above the frost in the jet-black sky. The little car drove into the deserted square quietly. It was past two in the morning. A small figure, apparently female, in a long coat down to her winter boots, her hair covered with a dark scarf, got out and reached behind the seat to pick up a bunch of flowers. She left the door of the small saloon open and the engine running quietly. She walked over to the statue and stood looking at it for a moment. Then she bent down and lifted the *Bürgermeister's* wreath, placing the red roses, dark in the moonlight, carefully half underneath it. She then stood gazing at the statue again for some seconds before, stifling a silent sob, she turned quickly on her heel and walked back to the car. She got in pulling the door quietly to on the first latch and drove off into the forest night, pausing only on the edge of the town to slam the door firmly shut and wipe another tear from her eyes.

She then set off towards *Schloss Krenek*.

*

The council man arrived in the morning and set about his task of making sure that any litter left round the monument after the ceremony was collected. He tidied the flowers carefully but paid no particular attention to the half-hidden bunch of red roses with a small plain card, neatly handwritten with the words:

"*Stefan, einmal, jetz und für immer, deine Tamaruska*"[22]

Detty was shovelling a rather mushy banana into Niki when Mara rang.

'Can I come and have breakfast with you?'

---

22 Stefan, once, now and forever your Tamaruska

'Of course, we have a full orchestra rehearsal of Act I at eleven at the theatre. If you're free you can join us.'

Mara arrived looking tired with bags under her eyes. There was an unusually awkward silence at breakfast. At last Mara broke it.

'Thanks, Detty, very much for doing the ceremony.'

'It was a very moving experience. I was privileged to do it.'

She spoke carefully trying to find the right words. After another long silence, Mara looked up and straight at her friend.

'You know, don't you?' was all she said.

'Some of it and a bit I have guessed. Do you want to tell me the rest?'

'I felt that I had let him down by not doing it. I was terribly ashamed but I couldn't, couldn't… I couldn't have done it without breaking down and I am so grateful to you. Afterwards I felt so guilty, after you did the ceremony yesterday, I drove down to Solanova in the middle of last night and put flowers at the foot of the statue and a card with my love. I don't care who knows now.'

'You have just driven all the way to Solanova and back alone in the middle of the night?' expostulated Detty.

'I had to,' she said simply and there was a long pause until finally she went on: 'It's strange, isn't it? I bet you never realised when you met the little schoolgirl on that dreadful journey to The Farm that I had already had the great love of my life. I have never really got over it. With the others and Bill, the sex was fun and I was jealous of him two timing me but it wasn't like Stefan – that was different, completely different. But I know what he would say now 'Go out and have a life, do it for me, I want you to'. He was never selfish – well I suppose his death showed that if anyone needed proof.'

'I'll say' said Detty quietly 'You talk about the little schoolgirl but somehow you always had a strength, perhaps *zähligkeit,* resilience is a better word that I admired but couldn't quite understand. Sometimes, even then, you seemed so much wiser than me although you were so young. Perhaps now I am beginning to understand. When you are ready tell me the whole story. I have learnt enough about Stefan to know that he was a remarkable and fine man.'

Mara nodded slowly.

'If we don't set off, we are going to be late for the rehearsal. After everything do you really want to come?'

'Yes, I think I do,' said Mara firmly.

They drove to Königshof in silence and went their separate ways at the theatre, Detty backstage and Mara into the first circle. Helge wearing jeans and a thick sweater against the cold, appeared in the pit, and said 'Hi' to everyone in the orchestra and auditorium. He then had a quick chat with the second cello whose wife had just had a baby before climbing onto the podium.

'Bar one, ladies and gentlemen, please.'

He then gave his incisive downbeat and sent his fine orchestra into the grand C major chord which launches *Die Meistersinger*. It was the right end to twenty-four hours which had torn her soul apart. Silently Mara dedicated the music to her lost love and to life.

7
DURCH ZAUBER ZU DIR KAM

An open foe may prove a curse,
But a pretended friend is worse.

JOHN GAY: FABLES: *THE SHEPHEARD'S DOG AND THE WOLF*

Mara slept late and awoke to find the apartment already deserted. Her father was downstairs in his official office and the von Ritter entourage had left for the theatre. She made herself a cheese and gherkin sandwich and turned on the coffee maker. Detty had been converted to Italian coffee by the influence of her friend *Totti* at the *Maggio Musicale* in Florence and had bought a small machine as a present for the Presidential household. She had had a little difficulty persuading the security staff at Pisa Airport that the *cafetera* was, as it appeared, rather than some fiendish component of an Improvised Explosive Device. However, the security man was eventually satisfied on the, to Detty, dubious grounds that the case bore the name of a well-known Italian make. The machine had become a prized Hansehaus institution which spluttered its way to various types of coffee throughout the day.

She was refreshed after a sound night's sleep and was now able to muse on the events at Solanova with sadness but without the heart-wrenching distress that had dogged her quiet moments for years past. The statue couldn't bring Stefan back but at least his heroism had been publicly acknowledged. She felt now he was at peace. She was immensely grateful to Detty for taking her place with the minimum of fuss and without asking searching questions. She knew that she could not have delivered a eulogy to Stefan without breaking down and displaying their very secret intimacy for all to see. She had found her relationship with Bill frustrating and she had blamed his perpetually roving eye but she now had to acknowledge to herself that since Stefan she had felt that she had to keep men emotionally, if not sexually, at arm's length. She had had several affairs in the intervals of her on and off relationship with Bill. She acknowledged to herself that she was highly sexed and needed the physical pleasure of Bill and the others. She knew she was very attractive to men as she was elfin, pretty and flirtatious. She also knew that she was good, and perhaps too willing, in bed. But she realised now that she had been unfair herself and that her boy friends had perhaps sensed that they were getting only half the story, only a strictly rationed part of Mara. She had thought that, because she knew that she was sexually uninhibited, they should be satisfied and not expect more. She had always frankly recognised that in some ways she had behaved like a tart but had thought that she didn't care. Unconsciously she had justified her promiscuity by preserving her soul for the dead Stefan. She now questioned that attitude and began to recognise it as sophistry. She could not be faithful to Stefan by giving her body without commitment. She had been reminded on several occasions in the confessional that whoring could exist without payment and was just as much of a sin. She had done her penance but had always been ready to sin again. Somehow her close friendship with Detty had made her more cynical. Detty had confessed to her, and she believed it implicitly, that Marc had been her only partner but that hadn't prevented her friend being exhibited and punished horribly, ostensibly for a sexual sin that she hadn't committed. In a strange paradoxical way, Mara had said to herself that this injustice had cheapened the whole tangled web of sexual morality. If society and men could behave like that towards women then they deserved her private distrust and she had been justified in keeping her love for Stefan apart whilst taking what she could get physically elsewhere.

But it was a tangled web and belatedly she had now begun to realise that she herself had perhaps been the cause of her unsatisfactory relationships, at least in part, Perhaps, in her attempt to separate her deeper feelings from her physical appetite, she had, instead of protecting herself, caused herself more hurt. This was a different view from the conventional morals of the confessional but it struck her with much more force. She also began to see that perhaps, even without knowing about Stefan, Detty had seen her dilemma but had felt that it was too sensitive a subject to broach directly.

But there was another dimension now. The new regime in Livonia had always claimed to be open and without caucuses of 'top people', those who saw themselves as being as being aside and different from the ways of the general population. However, she realised that the young President's daughter, the popularly styled first lady of Livonia, couldn't be seen out and about in the company of young men without it causing comment. It had been different in Munich where she had been one student amongst many but here in Königshof she was in the limelight.

What of Viktor? At that moment almost on cue, the private phone rang.

Very properly, the voice said: 'Frau Oblova?'

'*Ich bin am apparat,*' she answered with the slightest uncontrollable tingle.

'I am not needed for the rehearsal this morning. Could we meet for coffee?'

'Great! Where and when?'

'How about the Café Daina in an hour?'

'I'll be there.'

She wondered whether she was again being disloyal to Stefan then she wondered whether her position as the President's daughter and hostess would be compromised by appearing in public with a young foreigner. She considered the first question seriously. Her trip to Solanova had somehow exorcised her guilt. The memory of Stefan was still sweet and precious but it was time to move on. With regard to her public position, she felt that neither her father nor any reasonable Livonian should take exception to her trying to lead the life of a normal young woman in her twenties. After all there was nothing disreputable about Viktor, was there? He was a fine singer taking a leading role in a benchmark production here in the city. He hadn't even tried to seduce her yet and that made a change from those who had regarded sex as the normal recompense, on a first date, for a *Achtel* of wine and a couple of *Bratwüste*. If the paparazzi wanted to photograph them together, what the hell did it matter? She was used to them. To be seen out with Viktor was, at least to her, less of a problem than being described as 'a schoolgirl princess' a couple of years back.

He met her with his broad warm smile, '*Hallo, wie geht's dir?*' and then kissed her hand. It was just right, warm and admiring without being intrusive. They chatted easily over coffee and *Kuchen*. She told him about Munich and her degree. Then she asked about his home and family.

'I am now an orphan. I was born in 1980 and am the only child of a very young couple who lived southeast of Mozyr on the Pripyat River in the south of Belarus.'

He broke off but after a moment went on: 'I don't suppose you have ever heard of the place or the river, have you?'

She shook her head pushing a rogue wisp of her fair hair back over her ear and gazing at him intently.

'Well, not many people have, but it is very near a place that you will probably have heard of.'

He paused again waiting and looked seriously at her. For the moment the smile had gone. She said nothing and looked at him expectantly.

'Chernobyl,' he said quietly at last.

Her face puckered in horror.

'I was lucky. I was six years old and was away from home staying with my aunt in a suburb of Minsk – out of the immediate danger area but my father was a fireman and my mother a doctor. They both went south at once to the disaster. They survived and came to stay with my aunt in Minsk. They couldn't go home – nobody went home. A little over year later, almost at the same time they both got ill with leukaemia. They were treated in Minsk but it was no good. My father died quickly. My mother was very brave and struggled on for three years but then she died too.

I was brought up by my aunt. I did well at school and went into the Belarussian civil service. I sang in the unit choir. The choirmaster spotted my voice and worked hard to get me a scholarship to the Minsk Conservatoire. I had some wonderful teachers there and prospered. I went on to the Division of Opera Training at the Belarusian State Academy of Music where again I had fantastic teaching. After that I found it relatively easy to get local work but it's harder getting accepted in the international field. Growing up is hard with no parents.'

Mara found it hard to say anything after this final bald statement and they sat in silence for some minutes.

Viktor broke it at last: 'I think that you know about losing parents' he said with a sad smile 'I know that life here has been terrible as well. Can you talk about it? I know you have lost your mother and your father was important in the revolution but do you have any other family? The civil war must have been horrible.'

She shook herself.

'It's a bit difficult to know where to start. You asked about my family. My mother just disappeared. She had been very outspoken and forceful in the free government and after the fascist coup they just took her. We know that she was executed but we don't know where. Hundreds were just taken off into the woods or the *Winterburg* and shot in the back of the neck. Then they were buried in mass graves. Since the civil war we have uncovered some of them but it is very hard to identify anybody. A few scared woodmen and villagers saw some of it happening but it took them a long time to say anything at all about it. Slowly now it comes out.

'My father you will meet. He had had important, no very important, ministerial positions in the free government but had not been as outspoken as my mother and initially Travsky thought he could use him particularly when he took me as a hostage and sent me to The Farm. Travsky was wrong. Still waters run deep and from the outset he hated the fascists with a burning hatred. Travsky began to realise that he had made a mistake and that made it a bit tough for me.'

Viktor looked at her quizzically. He wondered just what 'a bit tough' really meant but he said nothing.

She went on: 'Like many daughters, I adore my father but especially for his simplicity and marvellous way of getting things done without fuss. He was hugely damaged by the loss of life in the early suicidal partisan revolts against the Fascists…'

Her eyes filled with tears but after a pause she continued: 'In fact, he did his best to restrain them during the first, hopeless, attempts but that didn't stop him taking charge when he knew that we really had a chance.'

'It must have been touch and go even then, wasn't it?'

'Sure, and there was a time when I was certain that we were going to be wiped out like the others.'

'But you weren't?'

'No, and perhaps you should know why that was. We had better planning and some, not much, more in the way of resources. Above everything else it was due to a small group of people who were truly extraordinary. Liese Zahnsdorf who tragically died last year was one. But there were two others who were even more important, and you know both of them, Bernadette and Marc von Ritter. I met Detty when she was a student teacher at my Convent, The Sacred Heart, she was very young, very talented and very beautiful. We girls saw her as a role model not much older than ourselves but we never realised what lay submerged in her character.'

'But returning for the moment to my family. There were only three of us. I was an only child. Both my parents were involved in politics and diplomacy. Both my mother and father had been ministers in the pre – Fascist government. We think that my mother was almost certainly shot in the Winterberg but there are no records. They cremated the bodies and destroyed the records. She was a good mother, always around when I was hurt or sad. Never too busy. My father escaped for the moment under house arrest as he was too important as a pawn in their game – so he lived. But I think what happened to my mother was a warning to my father as to what might happen to him ..or me. As it was, I was sent to the Farm.'

'What was that?'

'It was a form of concentration camp for women – although there was a men's version nearby. We were really hostages as well. It was horrible, they didn't kill us or rape us but they did almost everything else to produce a living hell. I don't think that I can describe the things that went on. But there were good things too. I really met Detty there although I had seen her as a student teacher at the Convent. She was from Ireland of course, but also from Oxford University. I can't think what she made of the horrors that had suddenly ensnared her on a simple teaching assignment; at least I had had warning of type of people who now controlled our country and us.'

'She was sent to the Farm with me. Travsky was obsessed with hostages and had some sort of muddled idea that she could be used as a bargaining counter with the EU or at the very least maltreated to demonstrate his power and independence from world opinion. You should realise that everybody feared him because he had uranium and the potential to make home-made nuclear war heads or at least sell materials to other rogue states.'

'But to return to Detty, he, Travsky, had made the biggest mistake of his dreadful career. Travsky was a male chauvinist writ large. He hated and despised women and couldn't conceive what the young Irish student teacher could do. To be fair to Travsky, which is hard, neither could the rest of us. It all appeared to start as Travsky had intended. Detty met Marc von Ritter who, as an undercover agent for German intelligence, had succeeded in getting himself enlisted in the Moltravian army and was attached to the punishment regiment next to the camp. That in itself is a story for another day. Marc got Detty to copy some vital information about the Farm detainees. When she was handing it over to Marc they were discovered. Marc's quick thinking made it appear that they were *in flagrante*. Come to think of it there may, in the light of after events, have been a lot of wishful thinking there.' Mara smiled 'Anyway it saved their lives but gave Konradin, the Governor of the Farm and Kovacs the dreadful medical officer, the opportunity they were awaiting.

They virtually ignored Marc's role and he was given some very minor punishment. For Detty however it was quite different. Konradin had dug up some medieval statute from the days of the original Hansa town which dictated that unlicensed prostitutes should be flogged through the town. A not uncommon punishment everywhere at that time. Anyway, Konradin amused himself by adopting this as he hated The Hansa and its principles and thought it would be a ghastly joke to adopt one of their statutes for his own ends. He decided to punish Detty as an 'unlicensed prostitute' and have her publicly flogged as a publicity stunt. The politics gave him the excuse but at heart it was just sadism. He was the sort of man who enjoyed torturing women and the more attractive they were the better.'

'The punishment was carried out by the third member of this ghastly trio, the so-called armourer, Gregor Tushkin, a huge powerful double-dyed sadist. In front of a lot of so-called dignitaries he birched Detty until her back was a bloody mass from her shoulders to her knees. It took me three days to get the birch splinters out of her back. I thought that she was going to die from shock or blood poisoning. I tried everything I could to save her. I am not sure how much difference I made but she's tough and she recovered. Then they turned on me. They didn't flog me but it wasn't very nice either.'

Viktor wondered again what 'not very nice' meant but said nothing as Mara went on.

'Anyway, as I said they misjudged Marc and Detty. Marc first got Detty out – in a garbage truck – by the way. Then they got back to his unit and they got a bit of help. In the event however Detty rescued me almost single-handed shooting dead the dreadful Tushkin in the process. She admits that that was a great moment and she enjoyed the look of panic on his face when he faced the girl that he had tortured holding a gun.'

'But it didn't end there. Detty married Marc. It was lovely. I was *ihre Brautjunfer* at the wedding. It was the first really joyous occasion that I had ever had' for a moment she looked wistful 'then Detty was kidnapped from England and taken back to Moltravia apparently to satisfy the lust of Konradin who, although he had had her tortured, had some sort of twisted crush on her. She escaped again, killing the unspeakable Doctor Kovacs in the process then she wanted to join me with the new revolt in the *Interfluss*. Marc argued with her but she won and he told me later that her main reason was that she wanted to sing *Leonore* in Königshof when it was liberated – can you beat it?'

He shook his head in unbelief.

'Anyway, she then wrote the National Anthem, got herself deliberately captured to pinpoint the fascists' HQ. She was nearly murdered again but escaped as Marc led a 'borrowed' squadron of tanks across the Fojn in a brilliant manoeuvre and advanced on Königshof. But that wasn't enough for Detty. She got herself shot by a sniper whilst deciding that *Schloss Krenek* would do as a music school – I can show you the spot by the lake. The advance was stalled at the *Zehnheiligenweg* so Detty went through the drains into the city to liase with the partisans and organise the final assault. I am virtually a pacifist but I still thrill when I remember the roar of Marc's final barrage against the defence line and realised that this time after all that we had been through, the thunder was ours. They were heady days but now you know why Bernadette Niamh O'Neill is a Commander of the Order of Sankt Nicklaus.'

'That explains a lot. I know now why this country regards a *Dramatischesopranistin* – although I suppose it's appropriate in a way – as a guardian angel. I thought it was a bit strange but now I understand. But what about the rest of your family?'

'I have no extended family that I know of. There were only the three of us and I think that I've really told you all there is.'

'You haven't really told me what happened to you.'

She shrugged. Clearly, she didn't want to talk about it anymore. He took the hint and then there was another pause until, hesitating, he said;

'It's getting late. I wonder if you are ready for lunch.'

'Sure,' she said smiling and, after the dark moments, looking beautiful and extremely young.

This was the first time of many. They were inseparable and of course it was noted. At first the Media were generous. After all, young love between a handsome talented foreigner and the beautiful and extremely popular daughter of the President was the stuff that gossip columns adore. Mara had become adept at getting the paparazzi on her side and, in return for some arranged interviews, they were generous enough not to be too intrusive. To the repeated and obvious question: 'Are you going to marry Viktor, Tamara?'

She always replied putting her head on one side coquettishly and giving only a winning enigmatic smile.

'What puts that idea into your head?' she would counter.

'Well, you seem to be seeing a lot of him.'

'Of course, we like to encourage talented artists to come to Livonia.'

'But he seems a bit special.'

'Certainly, he is working with Maestro von Grunstrand and Komturin O'Neill on an extremely prestigious production of *Die Meistersinger*. You could ask me about Herr Liebig, Herr Thomas and Herr Einsel and Herr Forjela to say nothing of Frau Schlerova. They are all very interesting artists. I am sure the Hoftheatre Press Office will give you full information.'

They knew that they were being teased but it was done charmingly. Once they were sure that they would not get any further they gave up and concentrated on getting shots of Mara with Viktor which wasn't particularly difficult.

It was difficult to keep Mara away from rehearsals. Obviously given her VIP status she could always get in and anyway Detty would hardly have wished to keep her out.

It was obvious that the principal tenor was the main reason for her attendance. Detty was happy for Mara and was woman enough to know that Viktor was very attractive. She always felt, however, that Mara was too keen to throw herself into relationships and she worried about her. She tried not to mention her anxieties. Anyway, she felt, with her history, who was she to talk?

Once she did ask how Mara really felt about Viktor. She tried to make it matter of fact but they knew each other too well.

'But he is gorgeous!' said Mara with her eyes shining. 'He is everything I could wish for. *Lohengrin*, with shining armour. Honest, brave, and caring.'

Detty didn't know if it was deliberate but she was stunned by Mara's reference to *Lohengrin* which had formed such a significant moment in her relationship with Marc. Privately Detty wondered if *Lohengrin* himself or Viktor, as his portrayer, was any of these things that Mara attributed to him but she only said to herself, rather inconsequentially:

'But we don't know his name.'

'What do you mean? You're not jealous, are you?' Mara was angry and disbelieving.

'No, I'm not jealous.'

She nearly added, 'I've got what I want,' but at the last moment remembered that it would probably still rub salt into a half-healed wound.

'It's just that he is a bit like *Lohengrin*. He has come to us out of nowhere and without much baggage.'

'You're getting middle aged, Frau von Ritter, what has happened to the heroine of Livonia who would risk everything for an idea and a principle?'

This barb hit home. Was she? She had to admit that perhaps she was a becoming a bit more cautious. The real problem was that she cared hugely about Mara and realised how vulnerable she was to hurt. However, she knew that this was a no-go area. For her part she thought that perhaps Frau Oblova was getting a bit mature to be sitting at every rehearsal gazing at Viktor with cow eyes like a teenager about to swoon at her pop idol. That too was better left unsaid. She had never had a catty row with Mara and this wasn't the time to start, nevertheless she had a vague feeling of disquiet.

In any case Detty had enough to keep her occupied. Although things were going well, the workload of directing and performing was crushing. There were all manner of issues major and minor to consider. Above all her concern was keeping her cast fit, both physically in the depths of a Baltic winter, and psychologically. So far there had been no major problems after the initial casting difficulties and so it remained until the all- important dress rehearsal. Anna Härtel, unfailingly good humoured, had the chorus throwing themselves into the Act 2 riot chivvied along by jokes about Bavarian bumpkins delivered with her Berlin accent accentuated to make the point. She announced to the laughter of all that she was only a *Boulette* and didn't understand anything far from the Spree. As well as the riot scene, she then produced very lively but beautiful dancing tableaux for the final *Festweise* scene. Detty was hugely impressed and very grateful to have these complicated crowd scenarios taken off her hands. Anna even proposed a modification to the *Katharinenkirche* opening scene, keeping the traditional atmosphere but making it much livelier.

The *Generalprobe* had started at nine o'clock. As soon as the rehearsal had finished there was a press conference and by the time Detty had changed and removed her make-up, it was getting very late. She looked at her watch anxiously. She had arranged to have a late lunch with Lev Forjela, Hartley Thomas and Anna but now lunch was almost turning into dinner. She was on a high. The great work would happen. Helge had the orchestra playing with thrilling beauty. The cast were fine and had melded into a great team. Detty had asked Viktor to join her party for lunch. He looked embarrassed and muttered how sad he was that he had a previous engagement. At that moment Mara had arrived from the Grand circle just in time to hear Detty mutter 'I bet'. This was greeted by a ferocious glance from her tiny friend before she went off prancing at Viktor's side. Detty sighed and turned to leave the stage door with the waiting Hartley and Lev who were exchanging smirks at their tenor colleague's amorous preoccupation. Then they left in search of the late lunch at Golabki which the long suffering Mandek had been keeping ever since two o'clock.

8
JOHANNISTAG

Das schöne Fest, Johannis-Tag,
ihr wisst, begeh'n wir Morgen.

WAGNER: *DIE MEISTERSINGER* I AUFZUG[23]

'If we are going to get Dottoressa Maria Angela Spinelli here, we must do something about the coffee.'

Detty stared at the grey, brown liquid, pooling lugubriously in the bottom of her plastic disposable cup. Anna Härtel, the delightful *Berlinerin* choreographer looked puzzled.

'*Wer, bitte?*' she said while Marc and Hank burst out laughing. Clearly there was an 'in' joke and Anna was not a party to it.

Marc was on a short leave and was having a great time acting as assistant to his wife and Anna. He was filled with small boy enthusiasm and pleasure and Detty had to admit that his attachment to Anna made her just a bit jealous.

'Maria Angela Spinelli is a gorgeous lyric soprano who is the toast of Italy and a dear friend of my wife's.'

---

23 The great St John's Day midsummer feast, we celebrate tomorrow

Detty clocked that yet another woman was being described by her husband as *prächtige*.

'You are developing a roving eye, Herr Graf. You must be learning from your brother,' she said.

'Heaven forbid!' he said.

'Nevertheless, I shall vet my friends carefully before I introduce them to you in future. But if we are to get *Totti* here, we do have to get the coffee put right. To call this substance coffee would mortify her Sienese soul.'

She stared again at the muddy amalgam, then sighed and shrugged her shoulders:

'However, *Die Meistersinger* first.'

The coffee was indeed an approximation in the improvised artists bar, but, however dreadful, it was socially necessary. Detty made a mental note to try tactfully to get it improved.

Despite the coffee problem, to her surprise she felt quite relaxed, considering that it was the afternoon before an important first night. She was enjoying singing *Magdalene* hugely and had been pleased with the Final Dress Rehearsal, *die Generalprobe*. The complicated choreography had gone with verve and skill thanks largely to Anna and the invited audience had responded enthusiastically. Detty had made a big effort to get the Conservatoire students and music pupils from the High Schools into the theatre in as many numbers as possible. It hadn't been easy as the stalls were taken up with staff, relatives of the cast, photographers, and media people. The capacity higher in the house had been very limited but at least everybody present had seemed to enjoy it. As a result, as the first night approached, Detty felt fairly confident. She was even enjoying her dreadful coffee and wondering if a cream cake would drown the flavour and whether it would be wise so close to a show.

Several other members of the cast had dropped by for a coffee and a word before going off to change and warm up. Just as she had finally decided against the cream cake, a flustered Lisa, one of the young Assistant Stage Managers, rushed in looking worried.

'Frau O'Neill, they have just phoned from the hospital to say Manfred Kolkov has just been admitted after a road traffic accident with a broken left hip.'

'Oh, poor Manfred – how did it happen?'

'Apparently, he stepped off the curb and a van hit him. It isn't clear whose fault it was.'

'We haven't got a cover for the *Nachtwächter*, have we, Lisa?'

'No, Frau O'Neill, it is such a small part that we thought that we didn't need one. I could go round the choristers and find out if anyone knows it and could sing. After all it's very short.'

'You'll have to, I think, Lisa and when you've found somebody you will have to do the fore curtain announcement as I shall be in costume.'

'Very good, Frau O'Neill, but most of the choristers won't be in yet. You know them; they always arrive at the last moment.'

'Yes, I know. As you say, it's a very short part but it is important and prominent and needs to be well done and must be in costume or else it loses the whole point. I hate leaving it to the last minute – it would be a disaster if we couldn't find anybody.'

'Wait a moment' said a voice from the chair opposite 'I could sing it if you would let me. It's straightforward. I can get the range and I know it already.'

'Marc, you're a genius. You'll have to do it in costume – it loses all point otherwise. Go and see about your costume at once. From what I can visualise Manfred is about your height and build so it should be OK.'

'*Jawohl*, Frau Regisseurin' Marc said, already getting up and grinning excitedly from ear to ear, as Detty went on.

'And you, Lisa, find Elena from costumes and get her to standby in case Marc needs some costume adjustments. You will make the fore curtain announcement, no need to go into detail, just say 'Unfortunately Herr Kolkov has met with an accident and is unable to sing the role of the *Nachtwächter* in to-night's performance of *Die Meistersinger* but we are extremely fortunate to have obtained the services of Herr Marc von Ritter to sing the role at extremely short notice.'

Marc was nearly out of the bar before he turned to see his wife smiling broadly.

'You're loving this, aren't you?' she said.

'You bet' he answered in English 'it's a huge privilege. I never thought that I'd get to sing a professional part.'

The audience assembled with the murmur of excitement which, worldwide, anticipates an important first night. The lights dimmed and the young Lisa neatly dressed in her black trouser suit duly appeared through the opened curtain in a spotlight. There was a momentary groan. This drama always heralds a substitution. In a clear voice, with just a hint of the *platdeutsch* of her native land, she gave the announcement. She was almost thrown into confusion however when, after a moment to allow the message to sink in, a burst of applause started slowly then rose to a crescendo round the theatre followed by loud cheers. A minute later, almost unnoticed, Helge climbed onto the podium and, with just a moment's glance round to see that everybody was ready. He gave his vigorous downbeat and the orchestra burst into the massive first chord of the overture. Detty, almost subconsciously, thrilled to the fine playing that Helge was getting from his cherished orchestra but was now feeling huge first night nerves. She glanced sideways at the radiant looking Martina, who made a truly beautiful *Eva*.

'*Toi, toi, toi*', she whispered and got the whisper back from Martina. '*Gleichfalls!*'

She felt for her hand and squeezed it as they took their place at the back of the shadow- sketched church and waited for the chorale to finish. When she had got the comforting squeeze back but she wasn't sure who was encouraging who. Then Viktor's clear tenor launched into his stuttering question and they were off, involved in the badinage of the first scene. Suddenly it was all great fun. And it got better. Lev gave the performance of his life revelling in the intricacies of the *Tabulatur*. As he had promised, Walter Liebig produced a sonorous and beautiful narration, making Detty momentarily regret that he wasn't singing *Sachs*.

After leaving the stage at the end of the first scene, she hadn't been able to resist going round to the broadcasting box and peeking at the audience, The theatre was not fully restored but a great deal of work had been done. Even when it snowed now, the roof didn't leak and tarpaulins were no longer, on view. Somehow this was reflected in the audience. The fashions were still a bit self-conscious and uncertain, but they were more modern and less redolent of the pre-war mothballs.

The *Sachs* himself, Dieter, dispelled any of her doubts with a fine portrayal of the wise and affectionate widower, still young enough to have to struggle hard to banish his own love of *Eva*. The complicated second act worked well. Detty enjoyed herself trying to restrain her stage lover from taking revenge on the rather sympathetic *Beckmesser* of Hartley Thomas, whilst Anna's beautifully contrived melée of apprentices and neighbours made excellent use of the old theatre's creaky stage space. A tall but appropriately diffident night watchman confidently brought the act to a close.

In no time it seemed to Detty she was following Martina into the quintet and then, her vocal work done, she just enjoyed the chorus and the authoritative Dieter in the final *Festwiese* scene.

In the instant after the curtain fell, Detty turned to the assembling chorus and principals and said quietly '*Herzlichen dank zu Jedermann*'. The curtain went up to a satisfying roar from the house.

'It's your job you're the leading lady' Detty learnt across to Martina.

'No, you,' she said.

'Do as you're told – at once.' Martina took one look at Detty's stern expression and skipped off to collect a beaming Helge to the sound of re-echoing cheers.

The most satisfying moment for Detty came next when she was able to lead her very young and inexperienced production team on stage also to generous applause. She wickedly muttered to Anna beside her.

'If this was Bayreuth, this would mean the show was a flop, but I reckon that they are a bit more generous here.'

The other three performances passed in a flash enlivened only by Marc trying to insist that he relinquished his impromptu role to a professional chorister. Fortunately, Helge was within ear-shot.

'Herr Marc, you may be a General but I am Music Director here and if you imagine we are going to change one of the star performers at this stage. You are completely mistaken. Why, it would bring bad luck to the whole show!'

This was unanswerable and Detty was mightily relieved that she was saved from deciding.

Afterwards she could not remember ever having enjoyed performances so much. The singing was great, the orchestra fantastic and, modestly, she felt her production team had done them proud. Nuremberg was there, but not a pompous still less a Nazi Nuremberg. It was a city where there was art and joy, elegance, and fun – and where life, old or new, was lived to the full. Detty had put her love for Franconia and its *Kreis Haupstadt* into it and it showed. Not surprisingly the German critics who had bothered to make the journey to this intriguing but, in the final analysis, small scale production, had loved it. There was a bit of muttering from some of the British press about racism and the black *Beckmesser*. This was countered by a longish article in the *New York Times* praising the enterprise and making a particular point about the quality and dignity of Hartley Thomas's performance which, as they concluded, 'gave something new and well thought out to this magnificent but often abused opera'.

To Detty's relief, Sir Henry Knight, the doyen of London critics, hadn't made the trip. He contented himself by adding a footnote to an article on the influence of Hindu rhythms in late Messiaen to the effect that he was sorry to have missed the Königshof *Meistersinger* but it had to be a mad world when the most distinguished current *Heldentenor* confined himself to a bit part and our most promising young dramatic soprano chose to sing a second line mezzo role.

'He's saving himself for Bayreuth' Marc said to Detty over breakfast. She pulled a face:

'I am afraid that you are probably right.'

There were only three days after the last *Meistersinger* to prepare for the second part of the *Sankt Nicklaus Fest*. This was to be a concert in the Cathedral. The first part was Berlioz's *Enfance du Christ* complete and the second a medley of seasonal music. Fortunately, the choir, mainly from the Cathedral and local schools was separate from the *Die Meistersinger* production and had been able to rehearse for some weeks. Helge, with his normal meticulous planning, had rehearsed the orchestra in between *Die Meistersinger* work. The principals, however, had had little time to work on the Berlioz aside from the opera.

'You haven't forgotten the Cathedral concert?' enquired Detty anxiously of Hank who, to make up for his miniscule role in *Die Meistersinger,* had agreed to sing *Le Rècitant* in the performance.'

'Oh heck, it had quite slipped my mind! Can I sight read it?'

'I think that you're winding me up – again.'

He just smiled. Fortunately, Dieter had already been booked as *Hérode* and Hartley had agreed to stay on to sing *Joseph* with Detty as *Marie*. Walter Liebig, full of pleasure and gratitude after his triumph as Pogner said that he would be delighted to sing the two smaller bass roles if he was permitted and it seemed churlish not to let him. He would throw in *Zerbinetta* if required.

'Flexible as your voice is, Herr Liebig, I think you might have a few problems as a coloratura soprano' said Detty. She had a great holiday feeling after *Die Meistersinger* and was thoroughly enjoying the pre-Christmas fun. 'And I think that your performance as *Zerbinetta* might rival mine as *Sarastro* which, I might add, my esteemed voice teacher once suggested. After all there are male sopranos but not many female basses.'

'At least it can be done nowadays with a full set of gear. I don't fancy the previous customary modification.'

It was the eighth of December, the nearest Sunday after the feast of *Sankt Nicklaus* itself on the sixth. The cathedral was brightly lit with chandeliers and the choir stall lights. Hank soared into the first recitative and no one would have believed that he had said to Detty beforehand 'The *tessitura* of this will kill me. I think that you are trying to assassinate me.' The choirs of shepherds, angels and Romans were dispersed all round the choir and the apse. They were all in costume and it presented a very colourful picture. The great moment, however, was when Mary and Joseph were finally welcomed into the Ishmailite home and the electric lights were dimmed. Then columns of young children from all the Königshof junior schools appeared from the sacristy. They carried little tea light lanterns and plates of smoked fish pirogies and blinis together with sweet cakes and ginger biscuits. They passed down through the naves and the transepts distributing their goodies to the congregation. This marvellous moment was a complete surprise to Detty and the cast who joined in the wild applause. It took some enquiries to discover that Anna Härtel had taken time out from her *Die Meistersinger* work to contact all the head teachers at junior schools and the clergy at the Cathedral not forgetting the head of the Lutheran church to see if it would be allowed. The matter was finally settled by the Cardinal Archbishop himself who muttered something about 'suffer the little children' after which there could be no argument. Detty made a point of specially thanking Anna who said, laughing: 'Just a case of Prussian efficiency but I was very relieved that they didn't set fire to the Cathedral.'

The brief second half was all popular Christmas songs with the congregation joining in. The start was *Veni, Veni, Emmanuel* then Detty sang a solo of the *Confessio* from Pergolesi's Psalm 110 *Confitebor*. Then a *Stille Nacht* and finishing with a resounding *Adeste fideles*.

Despite the approach of Christmas Detty felt a bit flat.

How do you follow *Die Meistersinger*? The feeling of deflation was ubiquitous. Yes, they had had a success. The press of Europe had noticed. Many had come to Königshof to be present. But now?

There was, in the back of Detty's mind an idea. A celebration of the spring even if it was to be next winter. A joyful work full of life and, she had to admit, she dreamed of singing the leading role. *Agathe* had haunted her since her life in Kildare, now she thought it was possible.

She awoke not knowing where she was then she heard the sound of the *Bach* and knew that she was at home in Oberdorf. She had dreamt of making love and now she felt Marc next to her. Wickedly she woke him and whispered: 'I'm feeling wanton.'

He didn't seem to mind. He played her like the piano he played so well. Gradually he skimmed over the notes of her body with a sensuous arpeggio. Then he caressed her breasts gently tonguing over her taut nipples. He knew instinctively what she wanted, to arouse her, to send little darts of pleasure through her, at first she was drugged with sleep then she awakened and responded, reaching a pulsating crescendo that yearned and vibrated within her until at the moment when she felt she could stand it no longer her entered her and together they boiled to a climax that came and came again for her. As they lay exhausted she whispered:

> 'Mein Mann, mein Mann, an meiner Brust!
> O dank dir, Gott, für diese Lust!'

and he answered her softly:

> 'Wer ein holdes Weib errungen,
> Stimm' in unsern Jubel ein!'[24]

Fidelio had been so much part of their lives; it was now almost a creed. They knew that, after all, the great Wilhelm Fürtwangler had said that it was more of a mass than an opera.

After a long pause she smiled at him and said: 'I know two lies – that northern men don't understand lovemaking and that marriage kills romance.'

'Have you got much experience of southern men?' he asked with a twinkle in his eye and was rewarded by a slapped thigh.

Marc returned alone to Königshof in mid-January. It was the first time he had been there without Detty. Leaving her with Niki at Oberdorf felt strange but he had been invited by the *Freiwehr Livonias* veterans as guest of honour at their annual dinner and he felt that he couldn't refuse. He was touched by the warmth and affection of the men that he had briefly commanded but at the same time felt embarrassed. Although he had enjoyed the tacit support of his German superiors for his Livonian interlude, it had been a delicate balancing act. He felt now that this episode in his career should be laid to rest so that he could get on with his day job as an officer in the *Militärischer Abschirmdienst.* The latter carried, to the English speakers, the unfortunate acronym of *MAD* which was singularly inappropriate for the sober and hard-working German intelligence service.

He had had to think hard about the tricky diplomacy of his speech. He began by thanking them for the invitation and made a few jokes about Night Watchmen and the poor performance of *Bayern* against Königshof in the recent Champions League match. Officially as a Franconian,

---

24   All who have gained a lovely wife, let them join our rejoicing.

he supported Nuremberg in their yo-yo between the first and second division of the *Bundesliga* and, like almost everybody outside Munich itself and the vociferous supporters of *TSV 1860* in it, hated *Bayern*. In practice his support consisted only of reading the result in the morning paper after a match. In his speech he went on to produce some anodyne, non-contentious remarks about European unity and co-operation in the difficult economic situation. He ended by sending Detty's heartfelt good wishes to everyone present. This produced vigorous and prolonged applause. At the end he was relieved to find that he seemed to be the only one who thought that his speech had been boring.

He collected his coat from the cloakroom and was off to find the taxi that had been ordered for him when he heard a voice behind him.

'Thank you so much for coming and for mentioning the team.'

He turned round to the tall young man who had spoken. His face was very familiar but for an instant Marc couldn't place him. Then he remembered; it was David Sensky who he had met briefly with Detty at the Memorial Service for Liese and her dead colleagues but apart from that he knew the face only from the TV screen. He had been put off the scent because he had never seen David in formal clothes and he was fairly sure that David had not been in the FWL.

'You look surprised to see me here, Herr von Ritter, and that's natural so perhaps I should explain that I was invited because of Liese. I was not in the FWL during the war although I have joined the reserves since – the medical corps – the training is fascinating and I'm learning a lot. I just feel that I want to have another interest besides football-particularly now after Liese. No, I stopped you because I just wanted to tell you how much I appreciated Frau Bernadette's help and support after Liese was killed.'

'Detti was very close to Liese and felt dreadful that she wasn't there when she died. Although, obviously, I was, selfishly, very glad. I know that she was so pleased to be able to at least do something after Liese was killed.'

There was an awkward pause. Marc was sure that there was more to be said but neither of them seemed to know how to go on. Eventually David broke the silence.

'I must go home. I have a match to-morrow and I need to get to bed. Not that there is much to go home for and sleeping is a bit of a problem. I don't know why I am moaning to you. I ought to be ashamed of myself.'

Marc had never seen himself as a counsellor but he supposed commanding men and trying to understand their worries and problems came close to counselling at times. He realised that this young man was not 'moaning'-he was deeply miserable. There was something that came from the back of Marc's mind that puzzled him. He knew that Detty and Mara had seen David in Munich and that he had seemed much more composed and had played really well. So why had this desperate gloom come back now? Perhaps this was delayed bereavement but he felt it wasn't only that -there was something more.

On an impulse he said: 'Look, I'm here for three days for a meeting at the Defence Ministry as well as the dinner this evening. Could I come to the match tomorrow and then perhaps we could go out to dinner afterwards and talk a bit more?'

David's face lit up. 'That would be great. I'll get you a ticket for the President's Box.'

'That's very kind but do you think I could go in the Cathedral stand. I would really like to mix with the fans.'

'As you wish but you'll probably be recognised and mobbed – with enthusiasm, I mean.' At last he smiled. 'I'll get the ticket sent round. Are you at the Hansehaus?'

'No, the Veterans booked me in at the Hansehof Hotel and I thought it was courteous to accept.'

'Very well. The Hansehof it is. I'll see you after the match. Oh, and by the way I'll send you a pass for the Main Entrance – not that I can see anyone turning you away.'

'You never know.'

He had once heard that you were a football fan if you understood the offside rule. Marc did, so he must count himself as a fan but that was about it. The match was a domestic affair against Sovils and clearly the team from the capital had too much fire power for the stoutly defending provincials. Marc followed it with half his attention and two nil seemed a fair result. David threatened from midfield but his only benchmark through run was foiled by a good save from the visitors' keeper. The other half of his attention tried to work out the meaning of his talk with David the night before. He got nowhere and was just as puzzled when the final whistle went as he had been at the start.

'Congratulations! How do you feel about Golabki?' Marc enquired when they met in the main concourse.

'Golabki would be fine. I like it there despite the memories and it's reasonably peaceful.'

And private, thought Marc, but said nothing but, 'OK'.

They talked through the meal about their history. David explained that he had been taken on 'as a baby' by the *Roma FC* Academy and was there when the fascist coup had occurred in Moltravia. He had tried to join the partisans but, when he made contact, he was told that as a young footballer in Rome he could be much more use in an undercover intelligence role.

Marc nodded. 'We have quite a lot in common then.'

'That was how I met Liese. I went to Bratislava to play in a match and liase with an agent from the FWL. I didn't know who my contact was but it turned out to be this fantastic girl and I loved her at once.'

His eyes filled with tears. 'She took a bit longer but to cut a long story short we soon became an item. And now she's gone.'

Marc allowed a long silence.

'You must always live with and love her memory but...' he paused thinking that he was about to be the gauche soldier and put his foot in it, '...I am sure, Liese wouldn't have wanted you to become a monk.'

'You mean that in time I may find somebody else who I can love who is different?'

Marc nodded. David's next words shattered him.

'Yes, that's the problem. I already have. I have been disloyal to Liese's memory but it's much, much more difficult than that. I cannot tell you who she is. It wouldn't be right.'

He stopped. Marc looked shattered. He thought that he knew what was coming and didn't know how he could respond. David suddenly realised what he was thinking and helped him.

'No, no, I am sorry. My God, I shouldn't have said it like that. No, I am not in love with Frau Bernadette… at least I am but so is every man in Livonia. She is a saint but no, I didn't mean her. I can assure you that but it still wouldn't be right to tell even you who the girl is that I think about all the time when I'm awake and try to dream about when I'm asleep. It wouldn't be right at all. It's too complicated.'

Marc had composed himself but felt that he couldn't push David any further.

'I think we had better have coffee and *Zwetschge*,' he said summoning Mandek.

They shared a taxi to David's apartment in silence. Then Marc went on alone to the Hansehof. He puzzled about who it could be that David couldn't mention. If it wasn't his wife – and he was sure that it wasn't – David's shock had been too genuine then there was only one person that he could think was possible and he could understand David's distress 'Oh my God what a mess,' he thought to himself.

9
CHAMPION

You can become a winner.
only if you are willing to walk over the edge.

Damon Runyan

From the first week or so of March, they all held their breath. There had been important recent races at Ascot, Leopardstown and elsewhere but everybody knew that these would fade into insignificance in a couple of weeks' time. The main work was over; it had been completed at Cheltenham, Newbury and Punchestown in December, January, and February. Firebrand, the winter favourite after her spectacular show in the December Cheltenham and Punchestown meetings, had dropped behind the English star, Mulligatawny, who had run away with the Newbury race under a big weight. Firebrand had slipped in the mud at Leopardstown, recovered well but managed only third. They were all mightily relieved when she was sound and ate up in her stall.

It had been one of the wettest winters on record and many said that the Leopardstown meeting should have been abandoned. Nevertheless, Firebrand's less than spectacular performance was enough to demote her to second in the ante post market for the Champion Hurdle behind the lightning-fast Mulligatawny with several other West Country trained English horses creeping up on her in the betting. The run up to Cheltenham was, as ever, a buzz of excitement.

Marc and Detty had returned to England together and were enjoying being in Henley. Marc was working from home on an elaborate NATO intelligence co-ordination plan which kept him sequestered over the computer in the gabled attic room that Detty had used in whilst at Oxford. This left the piano in the old bar for Detty who was working hard perfecting *Elisabeth*. She had been booked for *Agathe* in *Der Freischutz* at Covent Garden in three years' time which had been a feather in the cap of the dreadful Julian. She hadn't done much about it but she still had the idea that a more domestic *Agathe* would be useful first. There was also the terrifying prospect of the Königshof *Tristan* although this was still a secret matter between Hank and herself, plus, of course, her observant intelligence officer husband.

From Henley she was able to fly to Manchester easily to work with Eileen Vaughan, which she did regularly one day a week also Marc could get to London or Shrivenham, when the need arose. In the mornings they ran together before they started work. The Thames Valley spring weather was, as always, variable but even the rain and the mud didn't stop them running to Temple Island and on a good day it was bliss. If possible, after work, they liked to spend as much time as possible in the open air, back along the river or in the hills. This depended also on the capricious English spring weather but there were more possibilities as the evenings got lighter. When the wind and rain closed in, there was the compensation of meals together by the fire and a trip across the road to the pub. Marc had fallen in love with the local pub and enjoyed gossiping as a regular. He had developed a serious Teutonic enthusiasm for real ale and a discriminating palate. Landlords would be left wondering about this smiling but severe German who enthused about the importance of the regular cleaning of cellar lines.

One evening on a pub visit, there were some new people in the bar when they went in.

Detty pricked up her ears when she heard:

'Triumph stars almost never win the Champion Hurdle, Five-year-olds have a dreadful record in the race' declaimed by one of the local pundits.

'They've done better recently' said another of the group.

She noticed a gentle Irish accent when somebody that she didn't recognise chipped in:

'She didn't win the Triumph, and anyway she's special. She's the sort that eats records, not one that's frightened by them.'

Detty overheard this as they searched for a seat after they had collected their beer. She looked up, showing a flash of interest for a moment and glanced at Marc who was inspecting his pint. She returned her gaze to the cold, grey Thames. The speaker had seen her flash of interested reaction. He obviously had no clue that the tall young woman who started talking quietly, to her foreign companion was the owner of this special horse. Her accent and interest, however, had been spotted.

'I'm right, aren't I?' the Irishman said, looking to Detty for support.

'I very much hope so – tell you what – if Firebrand wins the Champion Hurdle, I will take you to Kildare to meet her trainer.'

'You're having me on but I would like to meet her owner?' the Irish enthusiast said with a twinkle 'I'm told she's a good looker.'

'Now that would be an exaggeration' Detty said while Marc tried to control his laughter.

The young Irishman looked suddenly abashed and was wondering what he had said to cause this reaction. Marc, who felt he had been rude, and was sorry for his laughter, took pity on him.

'We have been very rude' he said, 'but I would like you to know that my wife, here, is the owner of Firebrand and I am sure that she meant what she said.'

'You're still having me on.'

'No, seriously, I am her owner.'

'I am honoured to meet you, ma'am' he said now not abashed, but with the natural courtesy of his race.

'I meant more than the invitation to visit Firebrand at home. We need you to come with us to Cheltenham and give her a bit more support. But tell me first, what are you doing in Henley when it's hardly out of winter?'

'I work at the weather centre at Reading but I prefer to live here, it's more peaceful.'

'Where do you come from?'

'Kilkenny – like the cats – Steve Flannery.'

'It's a wild part down there – so I've been told' said Detty grinning.

'And yourself, ma'am, you don't sound like a Dub?'

'I should think not, but too close for comfort – near Athy, County Kildare.'

'Bernadette von Ritter and this is my husband, Marc.'

'The same Countess von Ritter who appears on the race cards?'

'Yes, but that doesn't stop me being a village girl from outside Athy. My husband's the aristocrat' said Detty – a touch tetchily indicating Marc who said with mock solemnity and an exaggerated German accent.

'I married, how do you say, underneath myself.'

Detty, by this time, knew Marc's trick of playing the solemn Teuton making funny gaffs in English but she still found it amusing. She laughed uproariously with the others, at first puzzled, joining in. Before she had stopped laughing Marc added:

'I think we should be shouting. What will you all have?'

Detty recovered and said to the Irishman.

'You'd better give me your address so you can come to Kildare.'

'You're that confident, are you?'

'Let's just say hopeful.'

*

Prestbury Park was shrouded in cold mist. They could see several furlongs from the stands down the hill to where the courses join but there was no sign of Cleeve Hill or the far side of the track. Christy was sure that there would be no problem with racing and anyway they were early and the mist would burn off.

The Firebrand supporters club had swollen. Mara and Viktor had flown in the day before. Brian and Peggy had crossed from Ireland with Christy and Deirdre. Mara was like an over-excited child and kept talking about how thrilled she had been to visit Christy's stable at the

Curragh. Viktor seemed pleasantly puzzled by the whole scenario but was too polite to admit that he couldn't see why there was all this fuss about a horse race. Gianna had her hands full with Niki but seemed at home at the races. She admitted to Marc that her father, GiGi, always had an annual date with the Easter meeting at San Siro. Also, he could be seen slipping into the *ricevitoria* for a few combinations on *il Tris*. Completing the party were Steve Flannery and his girlfriend, Abbie, who were regular race goers but couldn't believe their luck at being entertained as 'connections' of the Irish Champion Hurdle heroine because of a casual conversation in a pub with a girl who turned out to be Firebrand's owner. Detty had been as good as her word and, win or lose to-day, Steve and Abbie were coming to Kildare the following week to visit Christy Lorne's stables.

They went for coffee and as they came out, as if by magic, the top of Cleeve Hill glinted in the sunlight sparkling in the improbable glory of an early English spring, although the lower slopes were still obscured by the chilly mist. Detty, suddenly, thought of the time, seemingly long ago, that, in desperation, she had been comforted by a sudden, unexpected, ray of sunlight streaking across the bleak toilet room at the Farm camp. That's blasphemous, she thought to herself, the first time had been about her friend's survival and this, surely, is only a horse race. But it did matter, it mattered achingly.

She had slept badly, eaten no breakfast which she knew was foolish, particularly as she had to sit and watch Marc tuck into bacon. eggs and sausages followed by generous portion of toast and marmalade. Then she had absentmindedly fed Niki and found that her usual gossip to her son had dried up. To be truthful, she was guiltily relieved to hand him over to Gianna for the day. It had been arranged in advance that Gianna was to bring Niki to the Races. Detty had realised that it would be best to be unencumbered and had arranged for her parents, son, and Gianna to be an independent supporting party. Then she had turned to the Racing Post over a coffee. Reviewing the prospects for the Champion Hurdle, the paper was pompously scathing:

'*The Irish mare, Firebrand, undoubtedly has some ability but she has shown herself accident prone and seemed over-rated in the winter market. In addition, it must be remembered that five-year-olds have an uninspiring record in the Champion Hurdle. This mare, although well placed when suffering interference in last year's Triumph Hurdle, did not, in the event get into the frame. Her decent Irish form is too thin for this contest and others have more appeal and should prove too good for her. Manysthetime and Oxymandrias have solid claims and may chase MULLIGATAWNY (nap) home.'*

The critical remarks had caused Firebrand to slip further in the betting until she was relatively friendless at thirteen to two with four horses shorter and the fancied Mulligatawny at seven to four.

Detty felt impotently furious. Firebrand had slipped over once in a quagmire at Leopardstown. How did that make her accident prone? As for the Triumph Hurdle last year, even her brilliant filly could hardly get into the frame when she had been knocked over through no fault of either horse or rider.

'It really doesn't matter' she said to a patient Marc 'It's this afternoon that counts.'

When they gathered in the parade ring, she was still furious.

'The Saxons don't think much of her apparently' she muttered to Jess.

'The Saxons don't know her – yet. They will learn. She's enough speed to make the rest of them look like a bunch of gee-eyed Jackeens. Given a clear round this time, she will go close. It will take a good one to beat her.'

Detty had heard Jess's colourful language before but he was a very professional jockey and she had never heard him speak with so much passion.

The last bit of waiting at last was over. Firebrand had been a picture in the paddock and several friends and acquaintances commented on how lovely she looked. Detty had not intended to bet but was so furious at the disparaging remarks that she went to her rails bookie and backed her filly with enough money to make him startled and wipe her electronic price rapidly off the board. When she next looked Firebrand was back to second favourite with her price halved. Afterwards she felt guilty. She had never backed any horse with that sort of money before. She whispered to Marc.

'If she loses, I shall have to go to the Met to pay the bookmaker.'

He had murmured 'Is it that bad?' and just squeezed her hand. As they got back into the stand, she felt the usual tense hush of the crowd before the start of a big race. When the big screen showed other horses, she kept flitting back to the real-life view through her binoculars far down to her left at the two mile plus start.

'They're off.'

As they took the first hurdle up the hill and passed the Grandstands it was obviously a fast pace with one of the front runners, improbably named Idolatry, out on his own and cracking on. Detty was pleased. She knew that Firebrand had speed and stamina and the last thing she needed was a false run race. Jess had her tucked in towards the front of mid division. So far so good. She flew the three hurdles up to the top of the course with Jess settling her between the jumps to stop her hitting the front too soon. She noticed the third from home on the neighbouring New Course with a shudder of dreadful memory as Firebrand edged up into sixth place. Down the hill towards the second from home she was tracking Oxymandrias and Ancient Fable. Mulligatawny was tucked in behind the two leaders, Souwesternboy and Manysthetime. Then it happened. As they came to the second last, it was almost like a re-run of the previous year's Triumph Hurdle. Inexplicably, Oxymandrias cannoned flat footed into the hurdle and came down sprawling Ancient Fable with him. Both lay right under the feet of Firebrand. Detty sobbed in horror, whispering 'not again'.

She saw the pile of men and horses right under the hooves of her mare and shut her distraught eyes. Her eyes were tight shut for several moments. Then she opened them clutching Marc's hand. A blue and white quartered cap with green starred jacket was leaving Mulligatawny, the favourite, for dead and devouring the ground towards Manysthetime, the solitary leader. Regally, she swept past, into the lead and sprinted up the dreaded Cheltenham hill, putting lengths of turf between her and her failing rivals with every stride, to the roar of the Festival crowd. Jess appeared still to have a double handful and said afterwards that he never had her off the bit until he set her alight in the last furlong.

It wasn't until she looked at the replay that Detty realised that Jess and Firebrand had had to do an Olympic slalom to survive at all. *The Racing Post*, the following morning, forgetting its previous disparaging remarks, said that O'Donoghue had performed one of the most remarkable feats of jockeyship ever seen at Cheltenham. Firebrand, despite the difficulties, had decimated a quality field in the Champion Hurdle and appeared to be in a different class to her rivals. She had given the greatest display since Istabraq and was still only five years old.

For now, Detty was only barely aware of Marc urging her down from the third floor of the stand amid a mass of well-wishers, in order to lead in the winner amid the swelling Irish Cheltenham roar. Once she had got to the horse, she said just the one word 'brilliant!' to Jess, kissed Christy and then kissed Firebrand on the neck providing pictures for the following day's racing pages. The royal progress followed with Christy and Deidre on one side and Detty and Marc on the other. Detty whispering repeatedly in the mare's unconcerned ear 'You've just won the Champion Hurdle and you're still only a baby!

In the winners' enclosure to more applause Jess slipped from the saddle and a delighted owner hugged him.

'I'll do it all again for that but it wasn't me anyway. It was all the mare. She's not only game and fast but she's a ballerina. I don't know how she got round those fallers. It was nothing to do with me. She's the best that I've ever ridden.'

'Don't believe him' said Christy 'It was a savage ride.'

After 'Horses away', they reluctantly left their heroine to Sam the girl who did her, whose broad cheeks and broader smile said everything as she led the unconcerned mare back to the stable.

'She looks so calm it's almost arrogant she's saying to us "What's all the fuss about? Not much in beating that lot!" even if they are the best in the world.'

Detty whispered her thoughts to Christy as the mare was taken away to the stable. Christy nodded:

'It's been a grand day.'

They crossed to Ireland the following day. The heroine of the moment had eaten up well that evening as the feted guest in her Gloucestershire stable. After a lengthy breakfast, Detty, Marc, with Gianna and Niki collected Mara and a bemused Viktor. Later they were joined by an ecstatic Steve and Abbie and drove to the high-speed ferry. There they met up with Christy, Ken the travelling head lad and Sam with, of course, the mare looking as calm as ever.

'She travels well' mused Christy.

'You mean that we can plunder the Saxons again,' laughed her owner.

'Sure can. I understand that her owner had a sizeable bet on her.'

'Anything JP McManus can do; I can do better.'

'I am not so sure about that but a little bird told me it was his sort of size of wager'.

'I was just cross about what the pundits said about her.'

Christy smiled.

'You're the one.'

There was a small postlude to the Champion Hurdle which Detty treasured almost as much as her trophy. One day it arrived at Henley and waited there rather a long time until they got back. When Detty finally opened it she was overcome. It was a beautiful Irish silver salver engraved 'To two great ladies and a great gentleman, Firebrand, Bernadette, and Marc for a day we shall never forget. With love Abbie and Steve.' Detty supposed that it was that Firebrand came first that really made it special. She replied immediately saying that she was so sorry to have been so long in thanking them for their moving and lovely gift but she had been away. 'See you next year – one is not enough, love Detty'.

10
VERLOBUNG

I am to be married within these three days:
married past redemption,

Dryden: Mariage a la Mode I I

'Viktor has asked me to marry him and I have said yes.'

Detty was stunned. She had picked up the telephone at Oberdorf totally unprepared. She wondered what to say. She needed to say something happy and positive and for goodness's sake why not? But somehow.... somehow...

Eventually she settled for:

'That's very exciting news, Mara. Tell me all about it.'

But she knew that she had blown it. The pause had been too long and they knew each other well enough to know when enthusiasm was muted. Even Detty herself didn't understand the reason for her vague sense of foreboding.

It was now Mara's turn to pause. When she continued her voice was a bit flatter. The high spark of enthusiasm had gone and she sounded like a wilful small girl half demanding and half pleading for acceptance.

'He took me to dinner at Golabki last night and proposed. I said 'yes' at once and we had Champagne. He produced a yellow diamond ring from Russia which he said would match my hair.'

'That sounds wonderfully romantic.'

Detty was trying hard but knew that it sounded false.

'Can I still come next week and can I bring Viktor?'

'Of course, you can. You know that you don't even have to ask. This is your Bavarian home.'

At last, she was able to say something genuinely positive and she felt mightily relieved. She was aware that Marc had come in silently and was standing behind her.

'Mara and Viktor have got engaged and they are coming to stay next week.'

Detty watched her husband to see if he showed any signs her own doubt. He didn't. He burst into a broad smile:

'That's wonderful. Are they going to stay here or at the *Schloss*? I assume that it's one room.'

'What do you think? The spare room's a bit primitive here but we do at least have another bathroom now.'

'I am sure that it will disappoint my father who would love to have Mara as a guest but I think you are right, they should be here. Perhaps we can have my parents to dinner to introduce Viktor and have a bit of a re-union.'

They really fitted in very well. Viktor was a tower of strength at Summerhouse restoration and the project advanced by leaps and bounds. Beautifully neat oak joints and skilfully joined planks seemed to flourish in his hands. One day Viktor asked if it would be possible to borrow a hand router for some jointing that was going to take too long by with hand tools. Detty obediently rang Gigi at the timber yard. Predictably he seemed very dubious even when it was explained that it wouldn't be his daughter or her boss who would be handling this potentially lethal tool. Eventually he insisted on bringing the router up to the *Schloss* himself.

Once he saw Viktor in charge, he had to admit that the router was in good hands even if the operator was a Greek or an Egyptian or something like that. Geography was not GiGi's strong point.

Mara seemed gradually to relax and return to her old fun-loving self. Detty began to think that she had been wrong and that all was well. After all she had turned up in Moltravia with nothing but a recommendation from Oxford and from her Convent in Ireland. If her why not Viktor?

The return of Trudi from Munich and a session in the *Adler* produced plans for a new Oberdorf Easter Festival. The programme took shape quickly. It turned out well even if it didn't have the high romantic gloss of the first Easter. Trudi played the Chopin B flat minor Sonata followed by the four Ballades. She was indefatigable and she then accompanied Detty singing the Wesendonk lieder.

They broke for wine and cakes and then resumed for Viktor to sing Glinka's 'Doubt' and 'Alone I Pass along the Lonely Road.' This was followed by a spirited if not always accurate rendering of the Haydn Opus 76 no 5 Quartet. By popular demand there was an encore of Marc and Detty singing and this time they offered *Bei Männern*. This was followed by a lot more eating and drinking.

*

Sergei Mikhailovitc Zanedin thought that he was making progress. It hadn't been easy and he had had a good many setbacks but he thought that he was now on course. He sat down contently in the Aurora café on Nevsky and ordered an espresso *doppio ristretto*. He stirred in excessive amounts of sugar and picked up *The International Herald Tribune*. Nothing to worry about there, just the usual. French farmers were protesting and tipping artichokes into Breton streets, the American Secretary of State was buzzing round Libya, Egypt and Jordan, Japan was in recession and the European Union was going bankrupt. Various soccer and baseball teams were performing their usual boring antics. He put the paper down and began to review his own position.

At least he was in charge now and could control things up to a point. But trade had certainly had its problems. He had had to make a massive diversification. Weapons were becoming very difficult. The old USSR weapon systems were virtually obsolete and other countries were producing better and newer alternatives which could be relatively easily obtained by the well heeled powers. Fortunately, the market for girls and drugs was holding up well. Of course, the unit price was lower and there was a bit more groundwork involved but the profit was still there for the asking. But he did need to re-open Moltravia – he refused to use the stupid old-fashioned name that the present idiotic government had re-adopted.

The old regime had been a huge asset. It had had free ports, open frontiers, storage space that nobody queried and a compliant monolithic regime which responded well to favours and a greased palm. Anybody asking awkward questions was disposed of quickly and the general population had been too fearful to make indiscreet investigations or ask too many awkward questions. It was so useful and he couldn't believe that it had gone for good. It wasn't that he hadn't tried to get it back. He had been on hand in his cover job in Moltravia wasting his life. He hadn't enjoyed it. It seemed so ridiculous helping Travsky with his fantasy of breeding a super-race whose only mission was to serve him personally. Travsky had got the idea from Hitler but it hadn't worked for him either. It was a long-term project anyway and both should have known that they weren't going to last long enough to see the fruits of their megalomania. But it had been a complete waste of time.

11
THE VISIT

Be thou as chaste as ice, as pure as snow,
Thou shalt not escape calumny.

SHAKESPEARE: *HAMLET* ACT 3 SC 1

'I've no close family as you know but I would like you to meet my aunt and show you Minsk, our capital, and our country. After all, when we are married it will be your country, at least in part, as well as mine.'

'I'd love to. It would be great to see it with you. But I will have to ask my father, it's boring I know but, although I am an adult, I don't have normal freedom. I am sure that you understand.'

He looked sulky and clearly didn't understand at all. Mara found that his inability to treat her as in any way special was refreshing. She was getting fed up with the first lady status and the semi-regal deference that most people in Livonia accorded to her. However, there were snags as at present when she was caught between a rock and a hard place. She knew the interview with her father was going to be stormy and it was.

'I've lost you once to a fascist concentration camp then I lost you in Russia to a group of white slave traders. If it hadn't been for Detty and Marc I would have lost you for good.'

'I got myself out of Russia. Detty and Liese only fetched me when I had already got free. I can look after myself and anyway I have Viktor now.'

'You don't know what you are saying. Viktor is an operatic tenor. Marc von Ritter is a highly skilled special forces soldier.'

'Bernadette von Ritter is an operatic soprano but it doesn't seem to hinder her resourcefulness.'

'That's not the point and anyway Detti is a once off. They don't make many like her.'

'Her soldier husband let her face the most appalling risks for the good of this country and you are trying to stop me visiting the peaceful homeland of the man I love and am going to marry.'

'Mara, be sensible. I know that we are at peace but you must realise that Belarus is not without its problems and you are a high-risk kidnap victim. You have had problems in Russia once and now you want to go back to an unstable adjacent country with a man who has no family and who you hardly know.'

'He's my fiancé and I've known him for eight months. You yourself said you liked him.'

'I did and I do but that isn't the point. In the last analysis I can't stop you. You are an adult and this is a free country but if you go like Jacob you will bring down my grey hairs with sorrow to the grave'.

'Jacob got his children back.'

'As I say, let me think about it for a couple of days. I can't and will not stop you but I would like to have time to mull it over for a day or so. It is no good asking you to take a detective, is it?'

She shook her head and stared out of the window over the spring Baltic.

'They wouldn't let him in and anyway the last one, poor chap, didn't do me or himself, much good.'

She nearly missed the connection at Riga and found herself wishing that she had taken the longer but more straightforward journey via Berlin.

Minsk wasn't as she had imagined it. The airport was sparklingly modern and in fact rather impressive. Viktor was all smiles and rather like an excited schoolboy. He kissed her passionately and chatted rapidly.

The taxi ride gave her an idea of the city. It was much smarter than she had imagined. Even the old Soviet housing blocks had been smartened up and many of the buildings were obviously new.

She took stock over her breakfast *Kefir* and thought, again, about the final agreement that she had eventually wrenched out of her father. Wearily he had said:

'I didn't mastermind the struggle to set this country free to finish up over controlling my own daughter. If you must go, you must but I am not happy about it. Belarus has contained most of the elements devoted to de-stabilising this country since the fall of Travsky and I'm not convinced, will never be convinced that we have heard the last of them. Winston Churchill, that wise old English reactionary, once said that the price of freedom is eternal vigilance and for once he was right.'

She didn't explode, though the discussion had been fiery enough up to then. Instead, she just put her arms round his neck and said

'But I love him, *Vati*.'

I'm trying to convince myself a little voice in her head said:

'He's my fiancé and everything to me.'

The little voice sighed 'We are only going to visit what remains of his family, little enough in all conscience, and his city. Surely you can't mind that. It really is reasonable enough, after all we are engaged to be married. I'll be incognito. It's only for a week. Nobody will know me.'

'That, Mara, is half the problem. I would much rather you went with me on a State Visit. There's safety in that.'

For a moment she looked agonised then she had stuck out her jaw just a bit.

'I must go, *Vati*, unless you absolutely forbid me, otherwise he will think that I don't trust him.' That's the truth the disturbing little voice whispered.

'Very well, my darling, As I said I cannot stop you. I would have preferred you to have a detective' he repeated 'but we would have to get diplomatic permission for that and it would make it semi-official.'

'No -for God's sake – no. Not after what happened last time. They are an added responsibility and no protection.'

'In that, at least, I think you are right.'

*

Viktor needed to talk to his home agent about a Gala Concert to celebrate his increasing international reputation here in his home city. He had met his agent in the bar of the hotel downstairs. She wasn't needed and had stayed in their room, looking at the pictures she had taken.

The trip had gone well. Viktor's aunt had entertained them royally and was full of apologies that her tiny apartment wouldn't allow them to stay. Viktor with some pride had shown her the sights of the improving city. Privately Mara thought that it still had a way to go to rival Königshof to say nothing of Berlin or Munich but tactfully kept her opinion to herself. She flicked the photos over on the tiny screen of the camera. The two of them together. Their meals in the best restaurants that Viktor knew, the shopping trips, the sights and the country walks they had taken after a drive in their hire car. They didn't go south towards the border. It was still dangerous and anyway Viktor had no ties with that region now. She had rung her father every day to allay his fears and the last night he had seemed reassured and more relaxed.

'I told you it would be OK. What could be more normal than a girl visiting her fiancé's hometown? I'll be back safe and sound the day after to-morrow.'

'I'll be very glad.'

She put the camera back in her handbag and got out a book. Viktor should be finished soon and they were going out to dinner in the best restaurant of the city. Viktor had saved it for their last night. She looked forward to the love making that would follow more than the dinner. Their sex had been good and she thought a touch smugly, that it was marvellous to have a lover who was great in bed and reliable. She need no longer envy Detti. The house 'phone rang:

'We've finished and Andris will be going but he would like to meet you so come down and have a drink at the bar before he goes.'

'I'll be down.'

She checked her hair and her make up. Locked the room and went to the lift. They were in the bar. Andris was older than Viktor but probably not by much. He seemed older by virtue of his steel grey hair tied in a ponytail at the back and reaching the shoulders where it met his expensively cut suit. The bright black shoes and silk tie finished the picture of a prosperous businessman. Definitely not the Bohemian type of agent but none the worse for that. He leapt to his feet as they were introduced and kissed her hand. They chatted for a moment until the barman brought the drinks. The men had whisky and Mara had ordered a vodka and tonic. Andris toasted them and wished them every happiness.

'I hope that you will be as happy as them.'

He pointed to a genre painting of a country wedding behind Mara. She got up to have a closer look. It was a happy picture. No great talent, but it added a touch of comfortable local atmosphere to the otherwise rather sterile surroundings of a modern hotel bar. The bride was a pretty fair girl in a local country dress rather like a more modest version of a *dirndl* with its low but not too low neckline and full- aproned skirt. It reminded Mara of *Les Noces,* the Stravinsky ballet that she had once seen in Munich with Bill.

'I'd like to wear a dress like that for the wedding. It would bring in a bit of your homeland.'

'I'd be very touched if you did.'

Andris cut in.

'There is a couturier here in town who still specialises in traditional dresses for weddings and other ceremonies. The dresses are lovely and look really special. If you have time before you get the plane back to Königshof, I'll get him to come to the hotel and show you some patterns.'

'We don't leave until the day after to-morrow in the afternoon although we must get to the airport so this is really our last night in town. That will be fine.'

'That's settled then. Here's to the most beautiful Belarussian bride ever.'

She just smiled as they raised their glasses. She sat back contented.

'It was a pleasure to meet you. I must now go back to my room and change before we go out.'

'OK, I've just got a couple of things to sign with Andris then I'll be up.'

She went to the lift and turned to wave but felt dizzy and clutched the lift door holding it open. She pulled herself together with an effort and got into the lift and pressed the button. As she got out and fumbled in her bag for the room key, she felt strange. Then everything floated and got misty. She was sure that she had left the men downstairs but as reality faded. She thought that she had heard Andris voice saying something very odd 'Just a short visit and she'll be back – young and beautiful and free as before. You might even still want to marry her but she will be destroyed inside and with her, our friends hope, her father, his government, and their wretched so-called democracy. Then they can get on with things.' Viktor seemed to be distressed and protesting in some way. Whether she heard it right or not didn't matter. She remembered nothing afterwards. Not even looking at the bride's dress in the picture.

The next thing she did remember was being on the plane back to Berlin – alone. She couldn't think what had happened. She couldn't remember how she got to the plane and sensed that something was not right. Worst of all what had happened to Viktor? He should have been with her. She felt OK but bit muzzy. She checked the date on the newspaper her neighbour was reading. No mistake there but she really didn't know what had happened to Viktor or why she could remember nothing of the last thirty-six hours. She felt anxious and worried but apart from the inexplicable absence of her fiancé nothing seemed amiss. She felt sure that she hadn't been injured or raped. Nothing like that could have happened without her feeling some pain or unusual discomfort at the least. She knew that sometimes drugs were used to rape women but surely, she would know. For sure she had had a hectic love life for the last week and perhaps her nether regions gave witness to it. Nothing unusual, however. She was sexually mature. One of the things she admired about Viktor was that he was passionate but never hurt her. He did not go in for rough stuff like some of her other lovers. She was always ready for him and damp with expectation. Perhaps of the two of them, she was the more forceful.

She thought for a moment about 'phoning her father. No, that wouldn't do. She was OK. She didn't want the humiliation of explaining to him that something had gone wrong. Anyway, what could he do? She could certainly manage to wait the two hours for the Königshof plane. She found her way to the transit lounge. She needed to go to the Ladies which was normal enough after a flight. But to her relief there was no stinging. She took out her handbag mirror and just to be sure inspected her body thoroughly. Finally, she examined her lower regions with the handbag mirror and there still seemed nothing amiss. She finished her inspection and was telling herself that she had become obsessional. Then she noticed it. Her pubic hair smelt of soap or shampoo. Nice soap not coarse or unpleasant but expensive and strongly scented. It was a famous make and she recognised it because Detty used it. For a moment she tried to persuade herself that she had taken some of Detty's by mistake but she knew she hadn't.

The normally short flight to Königshof and equally short taxi trip from the airport to the Hansehaus seemed to take an age. She got her key out, opened the door of the apartment and flung herself into a chair. To her great relief, Detty was there but her father was out.

'Mara, what on earth's the matter? You look as if you have seen a ghost and where's Viktor?'

'I don't know' her voice was strangled and after a terrible pause she burst into tears and the story, as she knew it, came tumbling out.

'You're sure about the soap or shampoo?'

'Yes, certain. I have always used the same Givenchy range after you bought it for me in Berlin but I know you use the Carvin. I'm sorry to ask you but would you mind awfully having a look for yourself. I think you will recognise the perfume but I don't want to make a fool of myself.'

'Of course, if you don't mind.'

Mara slipped her jeans off and her briefs down and lay on the sofa. Detty looked and sniffed carefully. After a pause she said:

'Unfortunately, I think you are right. I hoped that you weren't. Mara, I know what you must do now and it's not very nice. You need to see a discreet gynaecologist with forensic experience and have full examination as soon as possible. I think you know why. It looks as if you have been drugged then interfered with in some way. But you have been cleaned up very carefully, possibly by the same person or people – probably a man or men who interfered with you in the first place.'

'Why do you say that?'

'Apart from the obvious reason because no woman would have made that mistake. Women generally are used to perfume and wouldn't use a scented shampoo, or more likely body lotion, which happened to be about if they were trying to hide their activities. Men probably wouldn't think of it as important. Now, do you know of a suitable gynaecologist here in town? Almost certainly, if what we fear is true, there will be DNA or semen remnants inside you or around you in spite of the clean-up. Does Viktor use a condom?'

'No'

'Probably doesn't matter because we can eliminate his DNA.'

'If we can find him. I am fearful for him too.'

'I'll ring Tanya Lopokova in Liese's old unit. She is discreet and will know the answer. I've got her home number. I hope she's in. Is this line scrambled?'

'Yes', came the whispered reply.

Detty found Tanya and got the answer at once. In a few minutes she was ringing Professor Hoffmann's private emergency number. Without giving a name, Detty described the problem to the listening doctor. At last, the doctor asked the patient's name. Detty looked at Mara who nodded.

'Tamara Nicolaevna Oblova'

The was a long silence over the 'phone then:

'I can see her at home. Can she come round straight away? I could come to you but sometimes I am recognised so better not. I have the gear here – poor girl –what an ordeal.'

'We will be straight round.'

Then after she had rung off

'Better take my car. We don't want taxi drivers involved.'

Mara roused herself.

'I'll get a pool car for you or me to drive; that will be safest of all. Your silver car is well known here.'

'You're not fit to drive anywhere' said Detty firmly.

Professor Hoffman was her grey haired but only in her forties. She was neat, kindly, and smiling but not effusive. She ushered Mara in and said to Detty;

'Take a seat, Frau von Ritter, we may be some time.'

Detty was confirmed in her knowledge that security was going to be a nightmare. She hadn't given her name on the phone but she was immediately recognised. She wore the Waiting Room carpet out pacing up and down for a seeming age. Eventually a pale Mara emerged with a wan lost look that shocked Detty. She had never seen that look before even in the resourceful youngster that she had first met.

'Do you mind me talking in front of Frau von Ritter?'

'No, I would prefer that you do. It would help me to remember what you say. She is my oldest and dearest friend.'

'I have done a full examination and taken blood, urine and vaginal specimens for infection and DNA. I will not be able to tell you anything definite until the tests are back but, and it is only the urgency and sensitivity of the situation that makes me speculate before the facts. You have evidence of' she smiled 'vigorous recent sexual activity' but from what you have told me that would be entirely normal. There is no evidence of damage to your inside so if you have been raped you have been raped extremely gently which, as of course you will realise, is unusual. That may be significant. There is some slight crusting around your anus. Again, if and I say if, anyone interfered with you in that region, it must have been done very gently. Women and men who are anally raped usually have moderate or extensive tearing, unless they have regular anal sex. There is normally other damage but you have almost nothing. This slight crusting may not therefore be significant but I have taken samples just in case. You have told me two things which are very important. First, that Herr Lobchenko has been your only consenting sexual partner for over six months and that you have never engaged in anal intercourse with him. I am assuming for the moment that Herr Lobchenko himself didn't perpetrate this crime. If he did of course then we will only have one source of DNA.'

Mara burst out in disconsolate sobbing. After all she had survived something had snapped. Detty knew her toughness but even toughness is limited. The doctor put her arm round Mara's shoulder and went on 'I know that this is very painful for you but please confirm absolutely that these two statements are completely correct.'

'They are.'

'OK, I'll have the most important answers by this time tomorrow. If you will forgive me, however, there is something else I would like to share with you which isn't strictly medical. I have read in the press and specialist literature cases where important people with powerful enemies who are usually organised criminals, are kidnapped, and drugged. Then when the victim is either unconscious or in an automaton state, he or more usually she, is made to perform acts that are criminal, obscenely pornographic or in some other way destructive of their character and reputation. An investigative Italian journalist has written extensively about this phenomenon which he calls 'delegitimisation' – a bit of a mouthful. Of course, Saviani has written mainly about investigative journalists like himself being victimised and quotes extensively the case of Anna Politkovskaya, the Russian investigator, who was threatened with just such a fate before being killed. It occurs to me, and I am far ahead of the facts, that this may be what has happened to you, Frau Tamara. I know that you are a popular and valued public figure in Livonia. I don't want to quiz you about your father's possible criminal enemies, here or elsewhere. But do you think it possible that criminal groups have obtained material of this sort with a view to damaging the government and your father by leaking it to the gutter press or the internet?'

'Only too possible' said Mara flatly.

'You came here via Frau Hauptman Lobokova. I would suggest that you go back to her and seek out any other people who may help to investigate if this material exists and if so, how it may be countered. It's not going to be easy.'

'You have been hugely helpful and I will contact you in person for the results tomorrow' said Detty 'and may I ask you to send your account for all the time, expertise, and trouble you have taken to me at The *Musikschule* at *Schloss Krenek* for services rendered to me personally. You have my permission to think up any gynaecological ailment to which young women are subjected to cover the situation.'

Professor Hoffmann replied somewhat stiffly:

'Frau Komturin' Detty noticed the use of her formal title for the first time 'I love this country and I love the family that has done so much for it. The *Deinung* is a privilege to try and give something back. There will be no fee only a fervent prayer that we can find a solution or that I may be wrong. Good night.'

'Good night, Frau Professor, and again our thanks.'

As they went the few steps to the car, Detty said quietly 'Tanya and Lawri'.

She knew Tanya started work early, so at first light she presented herself at the Intelligence Unit Headquarters. The Desk Sergeant didn't know her, so eventually she had to rummage for her moth eaten FWL pass to gain admission.

Tanya had been confirmed as the new commanding officer of the FWL intelligence unit quite recently. After Liese Zahnsdorf had been killed Tanya had assumed the job temporarily as the next most senior officer in line. She had performed so brilliantly that, despite her disability, it was inevitable that she was confirmed in the post and promoted Captain and in view of the increasing size and importance of the unit. It was rumoured that a further promotion to Major was in the pipeline, When Detty entered she was there dashing around in her wheelchair as always. Her excuse for her early hours was that she needed twice the time to do things because of her wheelchair. Those who knew her reckoned that she did things twice as fast as those with both legs. Detty rapidly brought her up to date with Professor Hoffmann's theory and information: 'I think we need the official and the unofficial if we are going to get anywhere' Detty finished '*Licht Alberich* and *Schwarz Alberich*.'

'Hang on. Which one am I?'

'*Licht Alberich*'

'I may have a defective under carriage but I'm not sure I like being called a dwarf.'

'Brush up on your *Ring*, Frau Hauptmann, *Licht Alberich* is *Wotan*, the half wise Chief of the Gods.'

'Right but I think that I would rather be *Pallas Athene*. I know *Wotan* fathered a lot of children but I bet even he didn't have any. I might be one up on him there.'

Unusually Detty was struck dumb and involuntarily glanced at Tanya's trim, though wheelchair bound, stomach.

'You're not – are you?'

'Sure am. You may wonder how I knew Professor Hoffmann so well. She is doubly qualified as a specialist pathologist and gynaecologist. She likes looking after difficult mums, like for example mums without undercarriages.'

Detty rushed over and hugged Tanya.

'I'm so pleased. Who's the lucky dad?'

'Jurgen Müller, he's a *Feldwebel* in my unit. You probably met him on the way in.'

'Yes, He's good at his job. He nearly threw me out. But isn't it insubordination to impregnate your CO?'

Tanya laughed.

'Not in this man's army or this woman's unit. Anyway, we are going to get married. Might have to be put off while we try to sort out your mess.'

Detty thought it was unkind to point out that it wasn't her mess so just said:

'Where do we start?'

'OK' Tanya said: 'We need to know, first what material they have, if anything, second who they are, third how they intend to use it and last why they think that they need it in the first place.'

'I think that, assuming that they haven't gone public with it already, Black *Alberich*, Lawri, may be best placed to find out who they are and what they have got. I'll talk to him as soon as possible. The security situation is so damnably tricky that I may have to go to Lübeck in person rather than 'phone or e-m. I might send him an enquiry in general terms over a scrambled phone first.'

'OK, I'll get down to threats to national security. Who wants to bring the Oblovs down and what they stand to gain from it.'

'I'll let you know as soon as we have Mara's tests. Meanwhile look after yourself. I don't need to tell you that COs of this Unit don't have a great track record. We were dead lucky when we replaced one but sure as hell, we don't want to do it again.'

'You don't have to tell me that. I would much rather still be number two and have Liese. How we all miss her.'

*

Lawri, the rock-like Holsteiner, was, as always, massively reassuring. It made Detty proud to be German until she realised with a start that she wasn't. She had known nothing about this country until a fateful day when as a prisoner, almost a slave at her lowest ebb, Marc had come into her life and with him his country with its doom-laden history and its huge powers of recovery. Perhaps, as a foreigner, as a German by marriage, she could acknowledge the virtues of Germany in a way that its natives, overwhelmed by their chequered history still found difficult. Marc had come up to Königshof when he heard of the crisis and had rung Lawri with a coded outline of the problem.

Now that Niki was weaned and Gianna seemed to have delayed her return to Italy indefinitely, Gianna could take Niki back to Oberdorf with a driver/detective whilst Detty interrupted her rehearsals to go to Lübeck. She could even stay there until Lawri had either found out something or drawn a blank. With a flash of inspiration Detty suggested that Mara came with her. It would get her out of Königshof where her distress might give her away and perhaps it would also convince her that something positive was being done.

Despite his shock, Nicklaus Oblov raised no objections, demonstrating yet again his confidence in Detty, although the latter was far from sure this was justified.

As they sat in Lawri's emptying restaurant, Mara was a small bundle of silent misery. Detty still wasn't sure whether it was the damage that she had unknowingly caused, the huge blow to her self-esteem or the loss of her betrothed which was crushing her most.

'Now, Frau Gräfin, what do we have to do?'

'For a start, Lawri, it ought to be Detti now and let us give ourselves *du*. You have helped me out of a good many scrapes and I have many reasons to be grateful to you. Formality doesn't seem right.'

Lawri twinkled, 'OK, as I once had occasion to tell the Herr Major,

I don't often order tanks for a lady let alone a *Gräfin*.'

Despite the seriousness of the situation, Detty laughed:

'Sadly, I don't think that this problem will be solved by tanks – not even a Panzer division commanded by my husband. No, it's more delicate than that.'

He got the traditional *Weissbier* for the three of them and lit his huge pipe. She told the story rapidly as she knew it including all the ifs and buts while he listened, puffing. When she had finished, he went on puffing for a few minutes while Detty waited and Mara rolled up on the chair into an even more foetal ball and appeared not to be listening, her beer untouched.

'The first part might not be as difficult as it appears. Then who knows? I have good contacts in Belarus and if we need them in Georgia and the Ukraine, as well. How good is your disabled lady in hacking into computers?'

'Probably as good as anyone in Europe, and better than most. Not my opinion, as you probably know, I don't know a thing about them.'

'We can't all have the same talents. So, if I give you four encrypted computer addresses, the good Frau Hauptmann and her team may be able to get into them?'

'Sure'

'This situation has a trademark. I would guess that your theory up to the present is very close to the mark. The Belarussians have several groups who specialise in this sort of work. They will be the active operators but they will be working for other clients. Hazarding a guess, this smells of people trading with drug cartels who still want to get their claws into Livonia which with its good law and order and incorruptible police stands massively in their way. Weapons are not so prominent these days and anyway the sadly heroic Major Zahnsdorf snuffed most of that out. A not inconsiderable monument to a great lady.'

'Hear, hear!' murmured Detty.

'Can you get Hauptmann Lopokova to fly somebody up here so I can give her the addresses hand to hand. I don't think I'm tapped but with advancing technology you are never sure.'

'I'll ring at once. How about 'load of Marzipan for collection urgently?'

'We will make a Holsteiner of you yet, Frau ……Detti'.

'Don't you think I've got enough troublesome identities already, Lawri?'

*

She drove back to Hamburg for the night with a hunched, catatonic Mara in the back seat. She didn't dare leave her. Not only was she probably suicidal but she had promised Nicklaus that Mara wouldn't be left alone. She had arranged for a message to be faxed for collection at the stage door of the Hamburg State Opera where she was known. She was keen that there was absolutely no possibility of a leak. She called in and collected the envelope. Back at the hotel she read the message. It wasn't in code. It read:

'At least four intruders as well as the apparent resident discovered widely dispersed in the channel and Flunitrazepam in the blood together with another substance hard to identify. Will try to identify but unlikely. May do more with the blood.'

So that was it. A date rape drug then had definitely been used. As far as the semen DNA was concerned, she couldn't believe that a professional team would not have used rubber gloves and probably condoms if they had personally been involved. So, she could only assume that Mara had been violated in some way by casuals whose identity was unimportant. This was a horrifying thought.

They flew back to Königshof in the morning leaving Lawri to continue to ferret for the reasons and the ultimate bosses. Detty left Mara safely and privately at the Hansehaus and went off with Marc to the Intelligence Unit. This time the desk sergeant was different and ushered Detty through without questioning. Tanya swung round from her computer.

'Your Lübeck fisherman is good. Only four possibilities and we struck oil with number two. I have the photos and a couple of videos.

You're not going to like them. The stills are dreadfully good. It's obvious that she's drugged in the videos. I don't know what they used. A sort of *Rohypnol* cocktail I would imagine. Must ask the pharmacos. Anyway, prepare for the worst. Here they are. There are about twenty in all. We start at the mild end.

Detty and Marc sat over the computer screen. Pictures one to five were of Mara and Viktor making love, intrusive but not particularly pornographic. Picture five came up. Mara, easily recognisable and dressed normally in jeans and a sweater, was shooting up with an intravenous syringe into her left forearm. Mara had shown one puncture but that was on the right arm. The left one had been unmarked so it looked as if the photo had been faked with the syringe and the needle in the vein. Picture six showed Mara, still dressed normally, passing a transparent packet of white powder to a young boy about twelve years old while she took recognisable Livonian thalers notes in exchange with the other hand. Picture seven had Mara dressed only in a diaphanous half bra and a cheap Lurex microskirt. It was the sort that covered very little and was favoured by teenage whores or rather by their pimps. She was spreading her thighs to display her crotch covered only partially by a thin thong. In the next she was in the same position but with her knees bent and wide apart and there was no thong. Nine had her naked except for thigh length black boots. She raised a long-plaited whip with her right hand. A man, also nude but unrecognisable apart from his white skin, was on his hands and knees in front of her. Ten consisted of another full frontal in the Lurex skirt but this time it was up round her hips while a large man apparently of mixed race pushed his organ between her thighs, the tip of the penis was out of sight but the message was obvious. Detty noticed that when the photo was taken, the penis was probably touching her but not penetrating her. Eleven had Mara, with her head turned for recognition towards the camera, leaning over a stool while a figure with an Arab head dress but naked from the waist down had his penis with the tip again hidden. This time it was between her buttocks but the base of the engorged organ was clearly in view. If it was a simulation, it was a very realistic one. In the next, she was naked prone over a bed while a nude man, white this time but head out of view, brandished a cane in his right hand, apparently about to strike her while he looked as if he was masturbating over her with his left hand. Thirteen had Mara with a paunchy European's penis deep in her mouth. Again, there was no view of the man's head. In fourteen, she was on the bed in the sixty-nine position, with a dark haired young pre – teenage boy. She faced the camera, he looked away from it. The boy seemed to be about twelve or thirteen. She appeared to have his penis in her mouth. At the other end it wasn't quite clear what was happening but the intention was obvious. Number fifteen came up, Mara naked with a dildo strapped round her loins appeared to be forcing it into the groin of a little girl – no more than ten or eleven. The sixteenth had Mara back in her micro skirt and bra lying between the legs of a dog. She was apparently grasping its penis and drawing it towards her mouth. There were three more. The first was of Mara being carefully given a shower with body shampoo foaming over her and her private parts being washed carefully and almost solicitously by male hands whose owner was again unseen. In the next shot the detached hands were seen drying her body carefully. Her face was in view this time, staring vacantly into space. Her expression reminded Detti of the rather vacant stare on certain religious limewood statues. In the last picture, Mara was again dressed in her own clothes and lying on the same bed that had featured in the earlier pictures. She was apparently fast asleep.

'Thorough, aren't they' Tanya said 'They haven't left much out. How can they possibly think such things up? They probably didn't have to actually put the unconscious Mara through all these contortions. Nowadays you can do quite a lot with forgery impositions but some would be real.'

Detty thought that she was really going to vomit and rushed out to the loo. She retched over the basin then pulled herself together and went back into the office trembling. Tanya looked at her sympathetically:

'It had that effect on me when I first saw them. You've never seen a wheelchair move so quickly. But this, understandable as it is, doesn't take us further forward.'

'There is one thing that is certain. I don't know how they made those pictures but certainly Mara knows nothing and remembers nothing, not even undressing, although she may suspect a lot. In her present state I think she will kill herself in a rage of self-loathing if she sees them. I believe in truth but I think I would kill myself if it was me. They flogged me as a whore but although I was humiliated and my body suffered terribly. I never lost my sense of self-respect entirely. I knew they were wrong and thirsted for revenge but this ......'

'What about Nicklaus? Isn't he entitled to see them?'

'Leave it to me. I will talk to Mara then possibly Nicklaus. I am probably now closer to him than anybody except Mara. Meanwhile can we get on with doing something about it? I think I should go back to Lawri. I suspect that he has knowledge that is denied respectable operators.'

They nodded,

'Right! I suggest that you, Marc and Detty, approach your Holstein fisherman again to try to define more clearly who our opponents are exactly, and what they are after. Then perhaps you can discuss with him whether we can put anything in their way although I confess that I am not very hopeful. There doesn't seem much that we could do to stop the problem at source. This contact of yours, however, seems resourceful and it may be worth asking him.'

They nodded assent. It was extraordinary how this disabled girl, still in her mid-twenties, could assess and command in a way that none of her elders could possibly resent. She had had a good teacher in Liese, Detty thought sadly.

'Our part will be to try and strangle the possible outlets in a more official manner. This will not be easy either and I am not sure how we can set about it. Any ideas?'

This question was addressed to the gathering in general. To all their surprise a small serious voice came from the back of the room:

'As you will probably understand, I have thought about it a lot and I have an idea.

12
THE CHASE

Soon trembling in her soft and chilly nest,
In sort of wakeful swoon perplex'd she lay,
Until the poppied warmth of sleep oppress'd
Her soothed limbs and soul fatigued away;

JOHN KEATS: *ST AGNES EVE*

Detty had wanted to save Mara the pain and go herself to see Nicklaus and explain things. However, it was a very different Mara who arrived that morning at the Intelligence Unit. Detty couldn't believe that she was the same woman that she had left curled and almost comatose the day before. Now Mara would have none of Detty's plan. She had stormed into Tanya's office and before Detty could get a word in, she had demanded to see the pictures. After looking at them, she had tossed her head back defiantly and said venomously:

'I will see my father myself and take them with me. It's my fault and my problem. Can I have a car to take me to the Hansehaus?'

Detty and the others knew that there was to be no argument, no discussion, after that. Detty was secretly pleased. This was the virago she knew and admired. The rest of them were left in the Intelligence Unit office while Mara, thankfully with an army driver, had been driven away to see her father.

When Mara arrived back at the Hansehaus, she went straight to his office. Without saying a word, she flung the photos on his desk and watched him shuffle through the ghastly file. Then he took her in his arms and they cuddled for a long time. After a time, they parted:

'My poor darling' was all he said at first. No reproach, no 'I told you so.' Then he said calmly:

'We have both been through a lot alone and together. We have survived. We will survive this. We need a meeting with everyone who knows about it but nobody else. I will try and arrange it myself for later to-day. Meanwhile you try and get some rest.'

They gathered in the simple drawing room of the Hansehaus penthouse in the afternoon. Marc and Detty had had to carry Tanya's wheelchair up the last narrow flight to the Penthouse. They were early but after only a few minutes, Professor Hoffman and Nicklaus Oblov joined them. Mara's morning fury appeared to have exhausted itself and her. She now looked pale and washed out. She came in very quietly and sat at the back. Detty felt desperate for her friend but didn't know how to comfort her. This meeting to discuss her error, her indiscretion would be so horribly humiliating for her.

If you will allow me, Herr Präsident, I would like to outline the present situation and then discuss possible plans of action.'

Nicklaus nodded his permission to Tanya. She summarised the current situation then:

'We are a bit further forward. We know the material that they have. Thanks to your fisherman, Marc. We also know a bit about who they are or at least we have some electronic information. We don't know how they intend to use it although we can guess. We don't know what they want from this professional, outrage although again we can guess. Is that a fair assessment?'

Mara's voice was firm but very quiet.

'If you will allow me, I would like to hold a press conference – TV, radio, broadsheets, gutter press, foreigners – the lot. I will tell them exactly what happened to me – broad outline – then details if they want it so that it is no longer a dreadful secret. We can tell the world what the shameful ruse used on me involves – it will be hard but afterwards there is no secret – nothing to hide.'

'Mara, you can't!' Nicklaus said aghast, almost in a whisper. There was a long pause whilst Mara's dramatic intervention sank in. Tanya broke the silence:

'Tamara, I think that your idea is brilliant. If you really feel able to do it, I would say go ahead. Tell them all what they did to you and dare them to publish it in a pornographic way. Yes, I think that you may have provided a brave, difficult, but brilliant solution to the most difficult part of the problem.'

*

Lübeck Airport was wet and cold. They kept under cover as long as they could and, fortunately, it didn't take them long to pick up a car. Marc drove grimly through the sheeting rain which almost destroyed all vision. With relief they arrived outside Lawri's extraordinary establishment. From the outside you would have thought he sold second hand tyres but once inside there was that vista of immaculate chilled counters of fresh and smoked fish which led down towards the battery of grills. These stood sentinel over the entrance to the dining hall which formed the base of an L shape with the shop. It was half past three and the place was deserted. Even the buxom, cheerful lady who presided over the herring grills had gone off for a well-earned rest.

Lawri saw them through the glass door of his office and came out, huge pipe in mouth, smiling welcome.

'Welcome, Frau Gräfin – Detti' he corrected himself belatedly recollecting the agreement to share the *du* made at their last meeting 'and you, of course, Herr Major. It's a pleasure to welcome you both together.'

They shook hands then Marc got straight to the point:

'First, thank you for the first class work you have already done. The Livonian intelligence unit has been hugely impressed.'

'Mutual' Lawri said 'Your disabled young lady seems an extremely efficient officer. I am very glad that she has never been on my tail.'

They smiled at Lawri's allusion to his chequered past.

'However, I don't imagine that you have come all the way here just to thank me. I assume that there is something else we need to discuss.'

'We are trying to prevent this material being used. Frau Tamara wants to give a grand press conference to describe exactly what happened to her and so spike the guns of the criminals.'

'Interesting initiative, it's brave and it might work' Lawri said 'but I don't suppose that I can help much there. I am not exactly a chat show host. I imagine that you had something else in mind.'

'No, it's a bit more sensitive and trickier than that. Can you do anything-anything at all – to help gag the perpetrators, at source?'

There was a long pause. Lawri pulled out his leather tobacco pouch and re-filled his pipe slowly all the while staring distantly across the room.

'You said anything at all, Herr Major?' It was a question not a statement. Marc nodded. There was another long pause.

Eventually as the smoke curled up towards the darkened beams, he said:

'It might just be possible to do something. I have a close contact in Minsk – almost a close friend, you might say, but these days, like me, he doesn't go in for the rough stuff. He is now usually only -' he looked at Detty '-as you English would say, a money laundryman.'

Detty, stifling a broad smile, remonstrated,

'Lawri, I'm not English.'

'No, but you speak it.'

'True and usually better than they do.'

'Anyway, I would like to help you and I will certainly try. I am sure that I don't need to say any more. I don't think that you would want to know the details. I am not even sure whether I can do anything at all but I will call in an old favour and we will see. However, I think it would be much better if you left it to me and remained in ignorance yourselves. Informally, I can give you the assurance that any measures will only involve the criminals responsible for this outrage. There will be no nuclear war or civilian atrocity but apart from that you should know nothing, and that as far as the outside world is concerned this conversation did not take place.'

'I understand, but we will be asked back in Königshof whether we were able to arrange anything. We had better agree what to say.'

'I would suggest that you just say that I was very sympathetic to Frau Tamara's situation but that, although I would think about it, I couldn't really see any immediate way to help any further. I would, however, like you to do one thing for me. I would like to know exactly how much of the squalid details of this outrage, Frau Tamara reveals at this press conference. I imagine that she will not reveal more of the personal details than she must but it would be useful to see a DVD of the conference. I will probably see something about it on NDR as it is bound to cause a major stir and will be reported on German TV but it would be helpful to see the complete press conference. Do you know when it will be, by the way?'

'As soon as it can be arranged, I think, possibly to-morrow or the day after and, yes, we will make sure that you get a DVD delivered at once by air courier.'

'Given the difficulty of air connections, motorcycle might be quicker.'

'*Genau*'

*

It was a crisp winter morning. The furrows, new ploughed through the rich loam, shined on their cut surfaces in the morning sun and the occasional copses of trees sparkled in the frost. Detti and Marc had spent the night at Krenek but he had to go back to join his unit at Ingolstadt. She drove to Königshof alone. She was anxious and gave less attention to the beautiful morning scenery than it deserved. What was going to happen later that day? The press conference had been arranged as Mara had ordered. Only the conference hall of the *FreiSender Livonia*s was deemed big enough as Mara, in her most magisterial, had ordered that no press, TV or diplomatic personnel should be excluded. The City Police department had muttered anxiously and long about security and some thought that they had a point, but the leading lady of the day wouldn't listen 'The whole exercise is pointless unless everyone is there' she had said.

Detty put her car in the dilapidated extra car park behind the Hansehaus and walked the seven hundred metres to the *Sender Halle*. Masha, the Outside Broadcast Director of *FreiSender Livonias*, was an old friend from FWL days. She had been terribly treated by the NAS when she had been captured during the Civil War and was lucky to have got away with her life. She greeted Detty with an affectionate kiss. She offered to escort her to the reserved VIP seats. Detty thanked her effusively but said that she would like to stay outside to see Mara arrive.

She felt edgy and being in the frosty open air was much better than sitting in an auditorium perpetually looking over her shoulder. Somehow the day seemed to her like a reckoning, pay-off time for the good things that had happened. Just behind her only a block away was the bulky fly tower of the Hoftheatre, the scene of her emotional performances of *Fidelio* at the end of the civil war and the more recent triumph of *Die Meistersinger*. She felt it was looking on, watching this terrible day and its dreadful ceremony unfold. She had been secretly horrified by Mara's determination to go through with it. She knew that Tanya and the other professionals – even Lawri – had agreed with it. But she saw clearly, with Nicklaus, how this plan of Mara's to publicly describe her ordeal, show the dreadful pictures and publicly curse their perpetrators could, more than probably, harm Mara herself rather than the criminals responsible. How could she survive the world's media seeing her in the most horrible pornographic poses? Would anybody believe and, would the gutter press want to believe, that this material had been posed without her knowledge when she was to all intents and purposes unconscious?

The car drew up. Mara and her father were escorted by Irina Malinowska, who had nearly died in the crash and explosion which had killed Liese and her comrades. Irina had only been back in the Intelligence Unit for a couple of months after a prolonged convalescence. Tanya had wanted to be in the car herself but had decided that her disability made it impracticable. She had 'phoned Detty the night before to let her know that Irina had volunteered.

'Do you think it's OK?'

'No problem with Irina, if she feels up to it but I'm dreading the whole thing.'

'That makes two of us although, as you know, I think Tamara's right if she can do it.'

'Do you have deployed security?'

'Yes – our people and the police will be everywhere but it won't be adequate. It can't be with all those buildings around.'

That comment did not make Detty feel more confident. She had worked out that if their opponents felt threatened by Mara's effort to finesse them some sort of outrage might be the response. With her special clearance badge she stood on the stone terrace right above the steps where the Presidential party were scheduled to enter the building. She watched the car door open and Masha and her welcoming party from the *FreiSender Livonias* greet Nicklaus, Mara and finally Irina. Detty had not seen Irina in person since she left hospital although she had watched her being invested with the Livonia Ehren Medal First Class on TV about a month ago. Promoted after the crash, she was now in the dress uniform of an Oberleutnant with the ribbon of her medal of honour proudly displayed on her chest. Detty thought sadly that she looked very thin and a lot older than when she had so successfully played the voluptuous roadside hooker with Liese in the deserted lay-by before the crash. Not surprising, Detty thought, after all that she's been through.

There was a brief pause while the press photographers snapped the arriving party. Mara had been insistent that the fullest publicity was available. Detty heard one of the press boys asking if Mara would step forward in front of her father to get a better photograph. Mara duly obliged.

At that moment Detty felt a stab in her thigh followed by something warm and sticky. She just had an instant to think that the feeling was somehow familiar then everything then happened in a flash. As she put her hand down to touch her trousers, she saw Mara lying on the ground just below her. She was covered in blood and there was an indescribable whistling noise. She was panting and going a dreadful grey-blue colour. Nicklaus was bleeding and being supported by the people in Masha's party. Suddenly a tall figure burst through the crowd and, kneeling beside her, put his huge hand on Mara's bloody chest. In an instant the whistling stopped and Mara's breathing eased. Just then there was a loud gunshot and everybody except the tall man ducked. The crowd separated to the howling of ambulance and police sirens. The paramedics rapidly realised that Mara was the most critically injured. They produced a field dressing which replaced the man's hand and put up a transfusion. After checking her blood pressure, pulse, and breathing, they put a sensor on her chest and gently moved her onto a stretcher and into the ambulance which screamed off towards the University Hospital. A second ambulance arrived and repeated the assessment on Nicklaus and then, despite her protestations, on Detty. They were then both bundled into the vehicle which set off in hot pursuit of the first ambulance. At the hospital Detty, now in a wheelchair, was pushed through a series of doors and realised she was in a sort of operating theatre. She was lifted onto the operating table. A tall, masked doctor gave her a jab which he said was a local anaesthetic and proceeded, slowly and meticulously to clean her wound then dress it again.

'You should be OK now, Frau von Ritter, the wound was quite superficial but it was messy with bits of cloth from your clothes in it. We will have to leave it open until we are sure it's clean and safe to close. I see that you have a scar on the other thigh too. What caused that, would you mind telling me?'

'A sniper's bullet.'

'What another one?' said the astonished doctor 'if I may say so, for a young lady singer, you do seem to attract macho injuries.'

'Well, I hope this is the last. I was a serving officer in the FWL last time so I suppose it went with the job. I am not sure what happened this time. But first, how are the others? How is Frau Tamara?

'Are you a relative?' he asked sounding official.

'No, but I am her closest friend. She is Godmother to my son and, as I suppose there will be an official press bulletin, I don't see that it would be incorrect to tell me.'

'No, I suppose that you are right but please keep it to yourself. Frau Oblova was shot through the chest. She has what is known as a sucking chest wound- the technical term is a tension pneumothorax. There is some damage to the lung itself but the main short-term problem is that this type of wound collapses the lung or lungs by sucking air either from outside the chest or from inside the lung which then cannot return. The lung is progressively collapsed. It is very dangerous and life threatening. The result is that the injured person finds it more and more difficult to breathe. Very fortunately the man from the crowd knew what to do, put his hand over to close the wound temporarily and almost certainly saved her life. She is in intensive care but is stable and there is a good chance that she will live but there are a number of potential complications. Perhaps you can tell us, she has quite extensive and unusual scarring over her back and shoulders. She obviously has received skilled plastic surgery at some stage but it would be helpful to know about the original problem. She is not fully conscious at the moment and certainly not able to answer detailed questions.'

'You put me, Herr Doctor, in much the same situation as you found yourself in a few moments ago. Yes, I can tell you but Frau Tamara is, as you know, a public figure here and she, herself, has been very keen that some aspects of her history remain entirely private, so I can only urge the strictest confidence. Can I have your guarantee that this information will only be shared by you by word of mouth on a 'need to know' basis and will not appear in written or electronic records?'

'This is unusual – but you don't give me much choice. I agree.'

'Very well. Frau Tamara was extensively tortured at The Farm Camp under Travsky's regime here when we were both prisoners of the NAS. First, she was given electric shocks involving many parts of her body including her back. This was followed by branding with a hot electric needle. Finally, she was confined in a stun belt which was periodically activated causing further injuries. She received extensive plastic surgery in Berlin after she was rescued. If you need further information about this, I am sure the Charité Hospital in Berlin could supply them through the proper channels.'

'Thank you. You have cleared the picture considerably. This is a terrible story but we were concerned that she might have had some lung disease or injury which would complicate our present management. I am glad that that is not so and I will make sure that this information is kept to senior colleagues, an anaesthetist, and a thoracic surgeon, and myself. To return to you, we would like you to stay under observation overnight. I believe your husband is here and he can visit you as soon as you get back to the ward. We will fix up further appointments later for wound treatment.'

'One more important thing, how is the President?'

'Fortunately, he only had a graze on his hip. He's fine but naturally extremely anxious about his daughter.'

Marc was waiting in her side room. He kissed her then for a moment they sat in silence. Then she said:

'I'm sorry.'

'But are you OK?'

She laughed and winced:

'You keep asking me that. Yes, I'm fine, but not to-night, first I am a bit sore and second it might cause another scandal if we were found on the nest in a public hospital' then she added grimly 'and I guess that, after to-day, the media have enough to be going on with. What the hell happened, Marc?'

'While I was waiting, I managed to speak to Tanya on her private scrambled line. I still had the number from Liese's time. Bless her heart she must be tearing her hair out but she found time to fill me in and was relieved to hear that you were OK. But I gather that you have a hole in your other thigh – how does it feel?'

'It's still frozen at present but I imagine that it will be as sore as last time. Still, I'm told that I'll live.'

'You seem to have a propensity for getting shot. It's a bit odd as I'm supposed to be the soldier and I seem to avoid it.'

'Don't even joke like that -you keep doing it and it terrifies me. Don't you realise that every time you go off on an exercise, I'm worried sick. But tell me what you know about today's events?'

'Quite a lot. To start with the assassination attempt seems to have been on Nicklaus not Mara. It looks as if at the last moment she – and you – just got in the way by moving slightly.'

'Come to think of it I remember Mara being asked to move by one of the paparazzi just before it happened but I didn't hear the first shot. I only thought something had hit me on the thigh.'

'That fits. The noise of the shot would have been a fraction later, anyway, but in this case, there was a silencer so there was no sound to hear. The later shot would have been from Tanya's lad. Anyway, fortunately the sniper made a number of mistakes. First, he wasn't a very good shot. He was using an old fashioned Russian SVD – not state of the art- thank God he wasn't using one of our PSG-1s- but, even so, it should have been accurate at five hundred metres and the range was well inside that. Fortunately, too he seems to have panicked. He showed himself after the first shot aiming at Nicklaus again. One of Tanya's boys was quick enough to spot him at a lavatory window from the roof opposite and dropped him, shot through the head. Her marksman did well – it must have been a very small target. Anyway, he's dead which is just as well but doesn't help the investigation. There was no identity on him and we probably don't have a DNA record, although Tanya's already beating hell out of Interpol and several other possible references to trace him.'

'Fortunately, our would-be assassin made another error. He was carrying soft point bullets which presumably he was supposed to use but for some unknown reason he used full metal jacket bullets – otherwise Mara would certainly be dead and possibly one of you as well.'

Detty shuddered.

'But there is more news. I was on to Lawri to-day and he asked if I had heard that the Minsk newsroom had reported the fact that a prominent young Belarussian singer had been hit by a hit and run driver in the city in the early hours of yesterday morning. Yes, you've guessed it – the young celebrity was said to be Viktor Lobchenko.'

*

Mara, still very weak but out of danger was taken by ambulance to Oberdorf to stay with Max and Sophie von Ritter. It was thought that she would be safe and comfortable there. The local medical people had agreed to co-operate and check her progress and if need be her surgeon could fly to Hof.

A few days later Detty and Marc arrived in the afternoon and a celebratory dinner was organised, *Brotzeit* was always early at Oberdorf but this time it was especially organised for the convalescent Mara,

'I never had a daughter' said Max beaming over a glass of *Côte Rotie* 'but now I have two. I can't tell you what pleasure it gives me to have you and Mara here – although of course I wish the circumstances had been different. But tell me,' he said eyeing his daughter–in–law.

'How's the Champion?'

'She's very well' Detty smiled 'I'm going to see her next week.'

'Are you going to do it again next time?'

'I hope so.'

'Can we come and watch or will that bring you bad luck?',

Before she could answer, her *Handy* rang. The words of apology to Max were hardly out of her mouth when she noticed the call came from Lawri.

It was an awkward situation. She had to answer but a presentiment told her that she didn't want to talk in front of Mara in her delicate state. She simply said as placidly as possible, without saying who the call was from:

'Can I call you back in an hour?'

'*Natürlich,* Frau Detti'

'I am sorry, Max, I really should have turned the thing off before dinner. Trouble is that I always forget to turn it on again.'

'*Kein problem!*' smiled Max.

The elaborate ruse didn't avoid Mara's question.

'Anything important?' she asked.

'No, just a sort of agent' Detty tried to keep as near to the truth as possible.

'You're much in demand these days' said Max adding 'I heard your interview on *BR Klassik* about the Königshof '*Die Meistersinger*'.

She disappeared to her room as soon as good manners allowed. She punched in Lawri's number.

'Sorry, Lawri, but I was with Mara and somehow didn't want to talk in front of her.'

'*Genau,* Frau… Detti. What I must tell you will need to be broken to her gently. First the good news – I think my friends have stitched up the hoods in Minsk although it took a turf war to do it. I think that you might need to buy some dubious types a vodka or two if you ever find yourself in Belarus.'

'I don't think it is top of my holiday destinations just at present.'

'*Genau!* Anyway, I don't think Frau Tamara will need to give any interviews to the Press or anyone else. But that isn't the main reason I rang. I asked my friends in Belarus to do a bit of research on Viktor Lobchenko while they were about it. You remember that he was supposed to have been killed in a road accident recently and I wondered about the 'accident' circumstances. However, they came up with something very surprising. Apparently, it seems that he hasn't existed for some time past.'

Detty gasped:

'What do you mean?'

'Viktor Lobchenko or at least the Viktor Lobchenko who exists in the State Records and as a promising tenor at the Minsk Conservatoire died of radiation related leukaemia three years ago. He appears miraculously to have reappeared restored to life about two years ago. Photographic, and dental records of the original Viktor seem to have mysteriously disappeared or at least nobody has seen them.'

'But the voice – you can't suddenly invent a tenor voice of that quality.'

'That's where it gets more interesting. We move to Russia. Apparently, the FSB are known to my contacts to have had an officer of Viktor's age who was an outstanding student at the N.A. Rimsky-Korsakov Saint Petersburg State Conservatory. He had or has a magnificent tenor voice. Strangely, his career seems to have faltered and since about a year ago there is no record of his whereabouts or any musical activity. Odd, isn't it?'

'You mean that he reappeared as our *Walther* and Mara's fiancé having been planted on me in Budapest? It seems a bit farfetched.'

'I think they had a bit of luck in Budapest. I guess that the original plan was to insert him into Königshof musical life more slowly through a normal agent. I don't expect that they could believe their good fortune when you appeared in Budapest to take one principal role and the other one suddenly became vacant but, and you would know this better than I, Russia is a source of very good singers these days and an obvious place to look if you have to fill a role at short notice. So, it wasn't difficult to push the false Viktor forward via an agent.'

'Sure, but I always thought that it was strange that a singer of such talents had such an empty employment diary. He explained it was because of his youth and inexperience but it still seemed odd. Perhaps I should have been more suspicious.'

'I don't think that it was your fault, Detti. Of course, I am no musician but I think that anybody would have done the same in your place. However, the fact that he was actually invited to Königshof rather than having to invite himself certainly allayed any possible suspicions and made it easier for him and them. It is not clear whether the report of the road accident is true or whether it was just another ruse of theirs to "write him out of the plot".'

'Tell me – who exactly are 'them'?

'We can't be certain but the FSD, like its predecessors, has some unsavoury connections which drift off into organised crime. I doubt if latest series of events was an official FSD action if that can be defined. However, we can be reasonably sure that powerful elements in Belarus and Russia itself are willing to go to considerable lengths to suppress a democratic European Livonia and get their useful client state back in one form or another. I think that they are falling for the fallacy of many increasingly autocratic regimes that power in a democracy resides in the hands of a few *prominenti* – in this case the Oblovs and yourself.'

'I am not sure why they should include me but I don't find it a very comforting thought. But thank you for your wisdom, Lawrie. I will chew it all over. Please let us know if you hear anything more – I am sure that you will anyway. *Aufwiederhören!*'

*

Mara felt very lonely when Detty and Marc left. After seeing them off, she settled beside the flower-filled grate where the fire had crackled in winter. The feeling of unreality which had dogged her over the last three weeks made her subside into a doze with the book slipping from her hands and sliding softly down the rug to lodge above her ankles. The book was Keats. The poet had had a fascination for her ever since she had fastened on a dimly remembered quotation in the light of the blazing Winterburg. Then she needed Marc to remind her that the poem which she quoted was indeed by Keats. That scene left an indelible impression on her memory and a thirst to know everything about Keats. Later she had shyly asked Detty to buy her the collected poems. Detty had raised an eyebrow but had ordered the book at once. In a few days it arrived and became her most treasured possession. It was true that her modest English struggled with the Regency verse but she worked hard to understand the sentiments. They seemed so close to her deepest thoughts and when she was lonely and desperate, she always turned to the tragic poet. She even worked hard to improve her English just to understand Keats better. That morning of her convalescence, she had started reading again St Agnes Eve and she had reached;

> *Soon trembling in her soft and chilly nest,*
> *In sort of wakeful swoon perplex'd she lay,*
> *Until the poppied warmth of sleep oppress'd*
> *Her soothed limbs and soul fatigued away;*

It was uncanny that those lines described her state so exactly. The book slipping down woke her from her doze. She started her daily attempt to remember the blanks in her memory. She knew that she had been near death. She didn't remember much about it. She tried to think about the details of setting out for the meeting but could only recall dimly the days before when she had rehearsed endlessly her speech and answers to predicted and predictable questions but the day itself remained hidden. A few days before she was ready to leave hospital, Detty had suggested that she convalesced at Oberdorf. She had accepted the idea. She knew that there would have to be security men, particularly after the latest outrage, but at Oberdorf they could remain low-key. It was very difficult for strangers to get in or out of the remote Franconian village without being noticed and relatively few agents would make the place reasonably secure.

For all her physical recovery and the comfort and peace of her surroundings, she was desperately miserable inside. Her life was a complete mess. She had given herself seriously to three men. The first appeared to be a stooge and turned out to be a hero only when he was killed. She still mourned Stefan but was it right to dedicate her life to a gravestone? Her second major entanglement was with Bill von Ritter. In truth she had never really loved him but she had enjoyed his body and his fun and had been furious at the casual way he had cheated her. She now knew just what an incurable womaniser he was and she had wasted her time with him and had felt scorned and furious.

This however had been nothing to her humiliation that she had felt when she found out that Viktor was a real spy and she had loved only his fictional persona and his cynical cover story. As gently as she could, Detty had told her that Viktor, as she had known him, was a fiction. The whole story of his early life and parents was the adopted story of another man, already dead, and that the 'aunt' whom she had met in Minsk was another security agent planted to confirm 'Viktor's' fabricated life history. For all that, she had been taken in and had loved him and her time with him. What had her short life left her with? A dead hero, a philanderer, and a spy. Were all men like this or was she just a bad chooser? She thought about Detty and, although she loved her dearly and tried not to be jealous, she couldn't help reflecting that Marc was everything that she dreamed about but that it seemed she could never reach.

Detty and Marc would be there again at the weekend which raised her spirits a bit. She sighed then picked up her *Handy* and punched the security number.

'May I go for a walk now?'

'*Ja, natürlich, sofort,*[25] Frau Tamara'

She was sticking to the rules this time and one was that, even round Oberdorf, she knew that she had to have a security guard with her. It

---

25 Of course, at once, Frau Tamara

was tedious but there it was. When the security issue had been discussed, she had pointed out that the bullet that had nearly killed her wasn't intended for her anyway but she knew it was no use arguing.

It was the nearest it got to warm early in the summer, high up in the *Frankenwald* in the afternoon sunshine, but even so the sharp air hurt her wounded lungs. As the warmth faded in face of the oncoming evening, soon she had had enough and turned back to the *Schloss*. She was greeted by a solicitous Hildegard as she changed in preparation for the evening *Brotzeit*.

13
TANNHÄUSER

Love in these labyrinths his slaves detains,
And mighty hearts are held in slender chains

ALEXANDER POPE: *RAPE OF THE LOCK* CANTO 2

Mara stayed at Oberdorf as summer came on. The peace and the scenery added to the maternal care of Hildegard and the stimulating company of Sophie and Max, was healing. She would take long walks through the forests and along the Saale watching the Franconian spring struggle into life. Her detective was there but tactfully kept out of sight. She wished that she knew more about birds and trees but she had always been a city girl. The streets and the port life were her natural habitat. She started to read about wildlife in the books at Oberdorf and even had had a few sent by post herself.

As the weeks passed Detty was spending more and more time at the *Schloss*, rehearsing, and putting the final touches to *Elisabeth* ready for the new *Tannhäuser* at Bayreuth. Sometimes Mara would drive with her to the theatre. The magic of the temple like theatre on the green hill was infectious and she began to feel that she knew *Tannhäuser* pretty well herself. If she wasn't at a rehearsal, she went down into the town to wonder at the jewel-like baroque *Markgräfliches Opernhaus* or walk round the Hofgarten. Her detective was a bright young man from Königshof who was quite good company and they was often chatted a bit. When he had been selected and accredited by the Bavarian police, he had been given a ribbing by his colleagues who reckoned that accompanying the attractive President's daughter was a rather good assignment to have landed.

Once, when Detty was free, they drove together up to Eisenach to visit the real Wartburg. When they left the Wartburg, Detty said that she wanted to go to the Bachhaus and the Reuter Villa's Wagner collection near the town. After paying a reverent visit to honour Bach, Detty told Mara the bit she knew about the Villa before their visit:

'Fritz Reuter should interest you for I believe he is known as a leading, possibly the leading poet, in *platdeutsch*. I read about him at Oxford, but I don't believe there is much about him here. His museum is at Stavenhagen near the border. The Wagner collection, I think, came from a private collector later. I can't remember the exact details.'

It was all interesting but by the time they left, Mara's head was in such a buzz of *Minnesänger*, added to Wagnerian busts, letters, and other memorabilia that she reckoned that she had a severe dose of intellectual indigestion. She had felt this before on a tourist visit with Detty, who seemed to have a voracious appetite and enormous capacity, for such things.

'I don't know how you remember it all' Mara said as they got into the car with the long-suffering detective.

'Oh, that's nothing' laughed Detty 'try learning *Isolde*, if you really want to challenge your memory.'

As soon as she had said it, she wanted to bite her tongue off. Nobody, not even Mara, was supposed to know that she was learning *Isolde*. She hoped, correctly, that Mara had enough to occupy her mind without worrying about Detty's expanding repertory.

They drove in silence until they were well on their way back to Oberdorf. Suddenly Mara asked:

'They told me in hospital that David Sensky saved my life?'

Detty was taken by surprise but tried to give a matter of fact answer:

'Yes – he's trained as an advanced first aider – going for paramedic to have another career after football. He realised what had happened when you were shot and that your breathing would stop unless you were helped and he did absolutely the correct thing. The hospital people were very impressed.'

Mara lapsed into silence again for a long time.

'And I haven't even said thank you to him' she said at last.

'Would you like to?'

'Yes, of course, I could write but it might be better to do it in person.'

'We can ask him down here but it might have to be back in Königshof because of his commitments. I don't know when the season ends. I'll have a word. I like to see how he is getting on. He's been very lonely since Liese was killed.'

'Poor chap. It must be very hard.'

Detty crossed her fingers surreptitiously and wondered if it was just possible that she was about to make it less hard. When they got back, thoughtfully she composed her text message, then she pressed 'send' and prayed a silent prayer.

*

David Sensky heard the text message come through as he came out of the shower after the match. He looked at it on his *Handy* casually and broke into a yell of delight.

'*Per carita!* What on earth's going on, David? I haven't heard a yell like that since you scored against *Bayern*.' shouted Freddi di Luca, the popular and long serving Italian central defender.

'I've just had a text from Bernadette von Ritter,' said David.

'You haven't scored with her, have you?' asked Helge, the striker, overhearing the first exchange 'I know most of Livonia would like to but I always thought she was otherwise engaged.'

'Dirty minded sod!' David replied 'Don't you think of anything except sex? It is just that she has given me a piece of information which has made me very happy.'

'Not football, then, she doesn't do football.'

'Come on. She's watched us a few times. She was even there for the famous goal in Munich' Sigurd the goalkeeper chipped in.

'No – not football' said David 'although…'

He looked suddenly distant remembering something that had puzzled him at the time. The others started talking amongst themselves and the conversation drifted off onto a dubious offside decision which had deprived Königshof of a winning goal.

David walked back to the staff car park on cloud nine. He wouldn't have dreamt of revealing to his teasing colleagues the real reason. The text had just said:

Mara wants 2 thank u. Can u come 2 Oberdorf? Or Königshof – when and where? THX Love Detti x

He wasn't normally dishonest but he reckoned that this time he was going to invent a possible transfer to *FC Nürnberg* to justify his journey south. Detty didn't appear to realise that the domestic season was finishing and despite their good showing in the European competitions they weren't involved in the Cup finals. His time was his own apart from a few school and charity commitments which left plenty of gaps. He sent a message back – no text speak, just a full message as courteous as possible:

Liebe Detti,
Thanks. I would love to come and see you all. I have a longstanding invitation to go to FC Nürnberg for a chat and could come to you first. Perhaps I could come on Thursday around Mittag and go on to a hotel in Nürnberg afterwards?
Viele liebe Grüsse
David

He waited, but not for long, the reply came back:

Thursday will be fine but you must stay the night and we will be very upset if you don't stay the weekend too if you can.
Mit ganz viel Liebe,
Detti

Cloud nine had become cloud ten. What he didn't know was that Detti had at first written 'Mara' instead of 'we' in the text but had decided that it was forcing the pace and substituted the 'we'.

Thank you. I accept and will go to Nürnberg first and back to Oberdorf late afternoon on Friday. Is this OK?
   Mit ganz viel Liebe
   David

Casually Detti announced at *Brotzeit* that David Sensky was coming down for an appointment at *FC Nürnberg* and would come and see them afterwards for the weekend. Mara would be able to thank him in person.

Mara casually said, 'That's nice' and went on to talk about the *Tannhäuser* rehearsals and their plans for the day. It was only at coffee at the *Herrenhaus* after the after the morning walk in the woods that Mara said casually:

'Detti, my hair's in a terrible mess. Can you make an appointment for me with your *Friseur* in Hof? Sometime next week perhaps?'

How transparent can you be? thought Detty but only answered 'Of course, I'll arrange it. I need to get some things for Niki at the same time. Then we will have coffee together. There are splendid *Küchen* at several places in the town.'

She sensed her mother's Joyce Grenfell voice creeping into her German but was secretly pleased with her efforts.

Meanwhile David Sensky, back in Königshof, was furiously working out gifts. He didn't even want to ring his mother or sister for advice. Both were sharp and would realise that their famous son/brother had something very special on his mind. He worked it out for himself and set off. Two things he could get at once, the other, the most important could be ordered but could wait. He set off to the city centre and made *Janis*, a little private shop off the *Seemarkt Boulevarde* his first stop. The little shop had perhaps the finest selection of amber in the Baltic and without difficulty he was able to buy a sweet amber amphora vase for Sophie which was in excellent taste without being ostentatious. Next stop was the *Kaufhaus Lübeck* where he found Detty a silk scarf which was striking and, he thought, classy. Final stop was *Ostenblumen* here he was closeted with the florist for half an hour. He explained how important the recipient of the flowers was but that also he didn't yet know her very well. Eventually, it was decided that he would collect a beautiful but modest arrangement of spring flowers before leaving on Friday.

He arrived back at his flat feeling happier and more excited than he had in the two years since his beloved Liese had been killed. He made himself a coffee and then performed his final task for the day and rang a friend in the *FC Nürnberg* squad.

'Hi David, good to hear from you. What a surprise! It has been quite a time.'

'I want to ask you a favour. If you are free and still in town, could I come and see you next Friday morning? I'd like to see the *Stadion* after its makeover.'

'Sure. Are you thinking of joining us? We could do with you although we are doing OK.'

'Not yet but who knows what might happen in the future. No, I have another reason for being in your neck of the woods and thought that I would like to have a look.'

'OK See you at the ground. About eleven, OK?

'Fine'

Great! That will at least play me onside, he thought as he put the phone down.

*

Detty watched the scene evolving before the Schloss Oberdorf dinner closely. Mara had emerged from the *Friseur* with her cascading fair curls looking immaculate and she wore a stunning Italian draped silk burgundy dress which Detty guessed that she had bought for the occasion. However, she gave no other sign of attaching importance to the evening. Over a glass of champagne, she had very courteously but coolly thanked David for what he had done and for the flowers. She then asked him how the current season had gone. David, who had very obviously been in such a high state of tension that the glass in his hand shook, was relieved to calm down talking about his own subject.

The rest of the David's visit was odd and rather uncomfortable. He was so nervous in Mara's company that it was almost painful to watch him. But it was Mara who was strange. Despite her flirtatious hints before David's arrival, once he was actually there, she seemed cold and detached giving him no help or encouragement. Detty was frankly disappointed and really did not know what was going on but it was obvious that neither the meeting nor the whole weekend could be rated a success.

David left to go back to Königshof on the Monday evidently crestfallen. However, just before he left he summoned up his courage and said to Mara:

'Can I see you again back in Königshof?'

'Of course,' she said with a friendly, if rather distant smile 'I'll write down our direct number and by the way it is scrambled. Better to use a fixed line if you can.'

David left feeling slightly better.

Two silent days later Mara announced that she would like to return to the city. Detty was disappointed with the way things had turned out but felt some relief that she could now get on with preparing *Elisabeth* for *Tannhäuser* without distraction.

*

Mara looked gloomily out over her beloved sea from the Hansehaus penthouse. The sea, calm grey, reflected the setting sun lining the horizon, shading from rose pink through the serried lines of low clouds finishing in bright gold in the clear sky above. It was indescribably beautiful and she was indescribably miserable. She knew that she had behaved like the whore that she knew she was and knew that she had always been. She had set up the meeting with David in love with the romantic idea that he was the hero who had saved her. On the first evening she had realised that he was in love with her in a way that she had never suspected. He had made it obvious that he adored her to a disabling extent. He was hardly able to say anything sensible or stop his hands trembling in her presence while his eyes told her that he loved her from the bottom of his heart.

This was a new and shocking experience for her. It was also strange. She realised now that not since Stefan had she sensed real affection – no – love on the part of a man. Even the fraud that she had been supposedly engaged to marry had never given her the electricity of real love. She had had good sex with him and with a number of others but this was quite different. She was mature enough now to recognise it but she did not know how to handle this real love. She felt deeply, horribly, ashamed. She had only seen in David a splendid male form and fantasised about the physical sexual thrill that he might be able to offer to her receptive body. She had realised at once that he was experiencing something much more profound. She sensed that he worshipped her – her soul, although he didn't know how unworthy of it she was. She, on the other hand, realised that all she was looking for was an orgasm. She knew that she was seeking what men were always supposed to be seeking in women, just sex, only in her case it was a well-furnished manly hand which would turn on her rotten, corrupt body. She knew that she really was, therefore, as she had always half suspected, a shallow, worthless hooker and she hated herself. The scenes of debauchery in the pictures from Belarus, she now realised, were not an act of horrible pornographic abuse. They were the truth; they had uncovered her ghastly true self. She wasn't a victim, rather she was a predator.

Was there any answer? To kill herself would be best. Put a stop to this hopeless putrid existence. But could she really do that to her father? It would destroy not only him but the State that he had devoted his entire life to saving. Could she fake an accident – steal a boat and sail out to give herself to her beloved Baltic Sea? It would be too obvious and the resultant distress for her father and friends would be the same. Besides she was terrified by the prospect of eternal damnation. She was so rotten that she had not even the strength to kill herself. Perhaps a Convent? Go away and become someone else. All of this went through her mind but nothing made any sense.

And what should she do about David, this kind, fine man who she now realised loved her? When he contacted her again, she could hardly refuse to see him but seeing him would drag him further into her putrid life.

Every time the private Hansehaus phone rang in the next days, she jumped with her heart pounding with anxiety. She had been home a week and there had been a good many other calls. She was beginning to think that she had been wrong about David and that he wouldn't call. Perhaps her cold unresponsiveness at Oberdorf had put him off altogether.

Then on a Sunday evening, it happened and the call that she thought would never come arrived:

'Tamara, I just rang to find out how you are. '

'I'm getting on fine. The wound is completely healed. They may do a skin graft to make it look better. I'm breathing much more easily. I still don't like the cold air for too long but the weather's getting warmer and I try to go out for a walk every day.'

She paused. She knew that she had been babbling in her anxiety and was afraid that even over the phone, it was obvious. But she had given him the opening that he needed. He took the plunge.

'Could we go for a walk together one day? I know a place down the coast where it's very quiet. It should be possible to avoid the press.'

It was out before she had had time to think about it.

'I should like that very much.'

'Would Wednesday or Thursday be OK?'

'Thursday would be fine. Father has got a lunch here for businesspeople on Wednesday. I think he wants me too.'

'That's settled then. I'll pick you up at three. There's room for your detective too if that is necessary.'

'He usually takes his own car behind – says it's better.'

*

It was a grey day with a biting east wind. It was painful as she breathed the cold air but she was determined to stick it out. Winter had returned in the midst of summer. The drive passed almost in silence until they turned into the state forest car park. At that point the forest reached almost onto the shoreline but there was a path parallel to the shore about one hundred metres inland. When they got out of the heated car, Mara put on a fur hat and a Delta Russian jacket which, because of her diminutive size, looked almost like an overcoat on her.

'Not very elegant, I'm afraid' she smiled.

'It looks fine and I am relieved because I nearly rang to cancel as the weather was going to be bad. Are you sure you don't mind walking in the cold? You will say straight away if you need to go back?'

They set off down the path in silence.

'I'm glad you didn't,' said Mara suddenly.

David looked quizzically at her.

'Didn't what?'

'Cancel the walk.'

They walked for about an hour making a circle through the forest. Mara's detective kept tactfully out of sight except occasionally showing himself behind them to indicate that he was still around. As they got back to the car it began to sleet which gradually got heavier. It was late enough in the year for the sleet not to settle but it promised a cold unpleasant evening.

David dropped Mara off at the private entrance of the Hansehaus,

'Thank you for coming. I'm sorry about the weather. Can we do it again and try for a better day?'

'Yes, I'd like that.'

'Perhaps the same day and time next week?'

'OK'

She got out of the car and went to the lift thinking hard. There was no doubt he was attractive. Most of the women in Livonia would like to have been in her shoes. He was also kind and sensitive. The problem didn't lie with him; it was buried within herself. She needed someone to talk to. Her first thought was Detty. She could always talk to her but deep down she knew that on this occasion that would not be enough. Her father? No, she had given him enough burdens already. She would not go to him again. Counsellors or the like might be the answer but she couldn't see herself going down that path. She needed a grandfather. Somehow, she felt it had to be a man, an old wise man but she didn't know why?

She slept little that night, wondering and wondering. In the morning she waited until after breakfast and then, trembling, picked up the phone. She had decided what to do. A female voice answered.

'Is it possible to make an appointment with Bishop Majorowski, please?'

'His Excellency doesn't normally give interviews now. Can I give you an appointment with Bishop Höfer instead?'

Mara knew and admired Dieter Höfer from Oberdorf days but emphatically this dedicated and pleasant young man did not fit her current needs. She felt rather panicky and stuttered:

'I was hoping very much to see Bishop Majorowski, would not even a short interview be possible?'

There was hesitation at the end of the phone:

'Who is enquiring, please?'

Mara had considered using an alias. She often called herself Anna Nicklaus or Anna Weber on such occasions but any such ruse now would, she felt end the conversation. She took a deep breath:

'Tamara Nickolaevna Oblova' she said firmly at last and waited for the audible intake of breath which she knew would follow.

'One moment, Frau Oblova, please.'

There was five minutes pause then a high-pitched male voice came over the phone.

'Tamara, you need to see me?'

Mara immediately noticed that he had said *du hast nötig* rather than using the *brauchst* or *willst* – he understood.

'Yes, Father' she said simply.

'Would tomorrow do? Say at eleven.'

'Thank you, Father. I will be there.'

*

She had to leave very early to be sure to be there. She had told her father that she needed to go to Bialovsk on charitable business which she reckoned, in a sense, was hardly a lie. It got light early now and there was a streak of sunlight through the trees, penetrating through the pines and sparkling off the birches. After a couple of hours, she came to the river and crossed the temporary bridge. She paused for a moment on the bank of the Fojn to look at the new permanent bridge a few hundred metres upstream. It was nearly finished and would be formally opened soon.

After a moment she drove on and parked her car by the Cathedral. She grabbed her Russian jacket and walked the few hundred metres to the modest town house which served as the makeshift Bishop's palace.

'Frau Oblova?' she didn't wait for an answer 'His Excellency is expecting you.'

'Thank you'

The passage from the front door was cold even in June and Mara wondered how a sick old man managed in such temperatures. However, the drawing room was small but well heated by a wood burning stove which had conquered the pervasive unseasonable cold at least there.

The large armchair seemed to engulf the shrunken figure sitting in it. There seemed almost nothing of him and that a sudden puff of wind might blow him rapidly from this world into the next. The almost transparent skin taught over his face was so wasted that the bones of the skull were clearly outlined. Mara was shocked. She had seen him before quite recently at Bishop Dieter's Enthronement but in the intervening months he had obviously slid nearer to his end. Mara wished she had not troubled him with her sorrows.

'Thank you for coming to see me, Tamara. I am always glad to see friends and those whom I have had the privilege of baptising are particularly special. I have read about your troubles and am sorry for them. Is your wound healing well? Are they the reason you need to talk with me now?'

His voice was surprisingly firm and seemed much stronger than the one that she had heard on the telephone.

'Only indirectly, Father, and yes, thank you my bodily wound is healing very well.'

'But your spiritual wound is not?' he paused 'Suppose you start at the beginning and tell me about it?'

She started slowly but the story had its own momentum and, as the old priest just sat and listened, it all poured out. She told the whole of her life story from the Fascist coup onwards until her recent wound and her uncertain relationship with David. At last, she paused.

'Tell me how you feel about yourself?'

She then told him how she felt cheap, superficial and dirty. She had been driven by physical lust and although she had never had sex for money, she had made herself no better than a common street walker. If David really knew what she was like he would never want to see her again let alone love her.

The old priest looked at her for a long time. In a way it was a penetrating stare but she never felt it was reproachful. Then he spoke:

'Tamara, how have you ever injured others?'

'Never, Father, as far as I know.'

'Remember that'

'Have most young people in their twenties been tortured and shot?'

'No, Father'

'Have most young people had their mother taken from them, their best friend brutally hanged and two lovers killed?'

'No, Father'

'I could go on but I don't think that I need to. Now tell me about David Sensky.'

Mara began to describe David, his life, his abilities, his personality. His tragic loss of Liese. Without realising it she became more and more animated as she talked about him. When she had finished, the bishop began to speak firmly but very quietly.

'Tamara, it is clear to me that not only does this young man love you but you love him. Or at least you would if you were not now afraid of love. As for you, you have lived in the present age and suffered in it terribly. You are not a whore and you never will be. Perhaps you have tried to compensate for the awful world you have experienced by seeking physical love but that should not make you fear the total love which is now, perhaps, within your grasp. You think a lot about Stefan but it is clear that he would wish you to have life after him. As for the others, you have suffered more than they have. Some were worthy but unfortunate, some less so, for none of this were you to blame.'

'Remember, Tamara, that the *Magdalene*, perhaps the greatest saint of Christianity after the Mother of God, was accused unjustly of being a prostitute. She comforted our tortured Lord at the foot of the Cross and was the first to announce his Resurrection. She had a troubled life and was strong in adversity, so have you been. Keep that strength and go to your David and love him. If it goes as I hope and sense that it will, I would dearly like to marry you as I baptized you. I fear though that this is selfish of me and I will not last to perform that office – it will fall to bless another.'

Mara burst into uncontrollable sobs as he finished and, as she wept, she felt as if a great weight had fallen from her. It had not been a proper Confession; he had not formally absolved her or given her a penance. It was however the greatest Confession she had ever experienced or probably ever would. She sat crying for some minutes then she dried her eyes. She kissed the old man's ring. Thanks seemed inadequate and she left silently.

She walked by the battle-scarred river front for over an hour until she felt composed enough to drive back to Königshof. Two days later she walked again through the forest with David. She was still quite quiet. Superficially nothing had changed but gradually David sensed that the tiny figure beside his giant frame was now different. There was a lightness in her voice when she did speak and a bounce in her step which made him dare to hope. The alacrity with which she accepted his invitation for the next walk to end with a snack in the country confirmed his hope.

14
TIRESIAS

"He sets this wizard on me, this scheming quack,
this fortune-teller peddling lies,
eyes peeled for his own profit--seerblind in his craft!"

SOPHOCLES: *OEDIPUS REX*

Sergei Mikhailovich Zanedin gazed gloomily down the Neva which seemed intent on re-butting summer weather; he was reflecting that life was unfair. Other people seemed to have everything fall into place for them. They seemed to have reliable staff who got things done, missions completed and plans working out.

'Fucking women' he said to himself 'First the Irish whore ruined our Moltravian agreement, then the soldier dyke rubbed out the useful travelling priest and, when we thought that at last, we could remove Oblov, his bloody daughter got in the way and the useless Alexei couldn't even kill her. He had not been in favour of the attempt to 'delegitimise,' the daughter. It seemed to him clumsy and complicated but the FSD hierarchy approved of it and the people in Minsk liked it so, although he was now the boss, he had to tread carefully and for once he had given way.

The cretins organising the 'delegitimisation' hadn't told him fully what was going on and the result had been a thundering muddle and instead of getting the daughter on the front pages of Europe's press as a perverted nymphomaniac, she had appeared as a brave heroine – useless! Thank God that imbecile, the incompetent Alexei didn't survive to blab and at least they had dealt with the singer once he was suspected of turning native.

He sighed to himself 'I don't want to but I suppose I must get involved again myself. What a mess! I must go to the pathetic little state that blocks us. They will feel the fearful hooves of the pursuit by the bronze horseman. He smiled to himself. He had been dubbed the Bronze Horseman by his admiring friends and fearful enemies – the relentless pursuer. He was powerful. He had controlled the trade in arms, the trade in drugs and the trade in women. He had the ear of people in very high places in several countries but they were getting restive now. A call from Moscow a few days before had been blunt and to the point:

'How many attempts do you need, Sergei Mikhailovich? You and your thugs have already lost Moltravia and made a hash of two attempts to get it back- it's not a difficult job. We only need to blow away Oblov, a few ministers and a couple of service chiefs and we will be able to put in place a sympathetic regime and get back to work. It shouldn't be a problem.'

'There have been problems, Mikhail Borisovich, but I am going to handle the next stage in person. I need a favour though, a particular sort of cover. Can you remind me who is the cultural attaché of Belarus in Königshof?'

'There isn't one – anything like that is handled by Foreign Trade.'

'They'll do. Can you do me a favour and ask them to get me a list of public events involving the President, ministers, and service chiefs etcetera? I would like the net cast wide and I would like it soon – yesterday in fact. Probably better to get them to do it – we don't want to involve Moscow with anything traceable.'

'That shouldn't be a problem. They don't have much to do in that one horse place. It will do them good to get off their fat arses for once.'

Mikhail Borisovich was as good as his word and the list had been scrambled through that morning. Sergei got it out of his briefcase and studied it while absentmindedly stirring his coffee. He then pulled out his ball point and underlined several items; one he underlined twice. He felt better but would have liked some support. How he missed Pueblo. He could work with the priest and his ideas had always been original and helpful. The technique for exchanging payments by means of calligraphic scripts via Pic Noix had been brilliant. The final attempt to get rid of the CIA and their hangers on by blowing them up hadn't quite worked out. It would have done little harm if Pueblo hadn't been killed himself later by an incompetent helicopter pilot.

As he thought about his colleague, an idea was beginning to form in his mind. The Nunnery was still there, perhaps he should go and inspect the ruins of Pic Noix and introduce himself to the Reverend Mother.

*

Golabki at least in the back alcoves, was warm against the evening chill and private. An open bottle of champagne was on the table in front of them.

'I'm not sure how to say this. You see I'm only a footballer – you know my only brains are in my feet – as I'm always being told.'

'I'm – I was – when I was little – a bit of footballer too.'

'I think that I always knew that. You once said something…'

'But never like you – never ever…'

'Rubbish – but not let's have an argument about skill versus strength in football. It needs to be different this evening and now I shall blurt out why. He paused, shocked by his own impetuousness at last, but the die was cast,

'Tamara, I love you more than I can say. Is it possible that you could be my wife?'

'Of course, I will. I thought that you would never ask.'

Mara curled up on his broad lap and their kiss lasted until they were disturbed by a tactful but embarrassed waiter.

After a long silent time, they collected their coats and, pausing at the door relished the fine but chilly late summer night. Not a word was said as they walked back to the Hansehaus. The goodnight kiss in the atrium was witnessed by Falk doing his turn on the main reception.

Slyly from the reception desk, he murmured to himself:

'At last, she's got the right one – thank goodness for that.'

And then, very properly, as the small pink faced figure emerged from the security gate.

'Had a good evening, Frau Tamara?'

'Yes, thank you Falk.'

'Good night. Sleep well.'

'Yes Falk. I think that I will.'

*

The following morning David, uncomfortable in his best suit, collar and tie, asked to see the President.

'Have you an appointment?'

'No' he stammered awkwardly he realised that he should have telephoned.

'I'll try but his diary is very full. Who shall I say it is?'

She clearly wasn't a football fan but she picked up the phone all the same.

'He asks if you can wait for ten minutes and then he will be free and happy to see you.'

It was the longest ten minutes of David's life but after the seeming endless wait he was in the lift to the Penthouse.

Nicklaus came out of his private study wearing a dark red open neck shirt and twill trousers. He smiled broadly as he greeted David.

'What a relief to see you. I've just had a torrid hour with the finance minister. Basically, he came to tell me good news but he is such a nitpicker you would think that the country was on the verge of bankruptcy. Still, I shouldn't grumble – meticulousness is an asset when it comes to finance and we are lucky to have him. What can I do for you?

'I have come to ask you if I may be allowed to have Tamara's hand in marriage.'

He said it very formally.

'I assume that she has agreed' smiled the President.

'Yes, Sir,' said David.

'Well then —welcome to the family. It is small enough in all conscience and could do with a strong re-enforcement in mid-field. She's a good girl but she's had a bad time. I think she needs you and I'm glad you feel that you need her. Congratulations.'

'They shook hands. The following morning the *Osthansa Kurier* bore the formal notice:

The President of the Republic, Nicklaus Alexandrovitz Oblov, has great happiness in announcing the betrothal of his daughter, Tamara Nickolaevna, to David Mario Sensky.

Mara had already made a phone call to Detty on her *Handy*. The signal at Krenek was infuriatingly poor but eventually she got through. You always knew when Detty was really excited because she spoke English and her Irish accent came through strongly:

'Oh, how wonderful! It is the greatest thing. Oh Mara, he will make you so happy. He's a wonderful man.'

This time Mara knew that her friend meant it.

'I know – I don't deserve him but he seems to like me.'

Detty remembered the trembling figure at the disturbing Oberdorf weekend and whispered.

'I'll say'

'What on earth do you mean?'

'I mean that you must be blind if you don't see that he adores you.'

It was a very contented Detty who walked up from the Lodge to the *Schloss* at Krenek to discuss plans for the *Nicklausfest* with her deputy. She felt so relieved, so pleased for Mara, and so sure that somehow this time it really would work.

It had been a suddenly cold morning as she set out to walk the four hundred metres from the Lodge to the *Schloss*. She thought there might have been an early frost or perhaps was just heavy early autumn dew on the grass. She heard a clicking and snipping sound as she walked along followed by a muttering in dialect *platdeutsch*. Then an old man in an ancient sealskin coat emerged from the dense yew hedge, she smiled and asked.

'Frost last night, Ludis?'

'I don't think so, *Fräulein*, but there will be soon, indeed there will be soon'.

Detty grinned to herself. She was always *Fräulein* to Ludis. He had been one of the first outside staff to be taken on when they bought the *Schloss* for the College. He always cycled the seven kilometres from his timber cottage in the village every day at dawn, rain or shine. Only massive falling snow would stop him. He remained very old fashioned in all ways and took no account of political correctness, Detty's marital status or her position as effectively his boss. But she loved it.

'The hedge looks great. *Vielen dank*.'

'*Bitte schön, Fräulein*'

The fire had been lit in the great hall of Krenek for the first time. A sure sign that summer was nearly over.

Helga von Grunstrand was warming himself with his back to it.

This year there was no massive *Die Meistersinger* to prepare but the programme was longer and it was time to get the arrangements in place for the great patriotic festival. It would start in the second week of November although the Saint's Day itself wasn't until December 6th. They had got the main items in place but details had to be finished. Rehearsals for *Der Freischutz* were well underway. Hank was coming shortly to do some masterclasses at the College then he had to go back to the Met but would return to sing Schubert's *Winterreise* twice at the Festival. Then there was *Totti*. Maria Angela Spinelli, always known to her friends as *Totti*, had agreed to come for a week to this year's Nicklausfest and sing *Serpina* in both the Pergolesi and Paisiello versions of *La Serva Padrona*. However, there were problems. *Totti* had agreed to come informally on Detty's last visit to Florence and, in her usual, casual debonair manner had said that there was no need to discuss contracts with her agent. She would fix all that and she would give any fee to the College as a gift anyway. This was very generous but the casual way it had all been said had worried Detty, who was only too well aware that upsetting agents, even if you were the most promising lyric soprano in Italy, was unwise.

'Do you think that I had better track down *Totti* and get her to firm up the arrangements? She's hard to get on the 'phone. She leaves it turned off then always forgets to ring back. Also, we must ask Walter Liebig if he can sing one *Uberto*. Could we ask Max Hieren to do the other one?'

'Good idea. I think that he would like to be asked. I saw him last week and morale has recovered after the *Die Meistersinger* debacle. However, I think that you should try to see Madame Spinelli in person. From what you say we need to know that she is definitely coming, she's a very popular young lady nowadays and we can't just leave it in the air. By the way, I know that she is singing *Violetta* at the Fenice soon. Perhaps you could treat yourself to a Venetian fix and kill two birds with one stone?'

'I wouldn't take much persuading but it would have to be a short trip – there's a lot to do here. How's the work on the students' concert going?'

'They want to do the whole of Rossini's *Stabat Mater* and Olaf Svenden and the voice department are backing them up. I don't see why they shouldn't do it although it's not very festive but after all advent is supposed to be a fast time– unless you think it makes the programme too heavy weight. Apparently, they can do it in the Cathedral- the Cardinal has already agreed.'

'No, it's not too heavy weight. I think it would go OK – after all we don't have to be seasonal – there's time for Christmas later. Rossini, Weber, Schubert, and Paisiello/Pergolesi seems the right balance apart from the addition, perhaps, of a new piece or something early.'

'I'll have a think about it – nothing springs to mind.'

'Oh, and one other thing – I told Hank that Trudi had offered to accompany him for the *Winterreise*, if he agreed, and he said that he would be honoured.

*

The rehearsals had gone well. Detty was beginning to feel that the *Festspielhaus* was like home –or at least her second musical home after Königshof. This year was different, however. The strange circumstances of her singing the *Siegfried* Awakening had allowed no time for rumination and not much even for anxiety. But in the last few years she had done all the *Woglindes* apart from her pregnant year and was completely familiar with the theatre and the organisation. But this time she was billed for the first time in a major role. She knew her performance was eagerly anticipated by the press and the VIP audience alike. She had a new exciting Scottish tenor, Andrew Mann, to partner her which helped to spread the publicity a bit but there could be no excuses this time. As she flew onto the stage to greet the *Sängerhalle* the wall of sound coming back at her from the pit was almost a comfort. In *Siegfried*, of course, the orchestral arpeggios had been subdued before her entry, this time she had the full force of the orchestra surging over her before the sound diminished for her entry. As soon as her cue came she forgot everything except that she was *Elisabeth* about, trembling, to greet her lost love.

They were a good team and there was a glow of satisfaction as the audience thumped the floor and booed the production. A standard good start for any new show at the *Festspielhaus*, in fact. At their individual curtain calls, she had had an equal share of rapturous stamping and cheering with Andrew but imagined that the critics were sharpening their pencils before going back to their computers. They would bring them down to earth and tear the performance apart. It had already been christened in the press The Celtic *Tannhäuser*.

Excited, content and beginning to be very tired she finally freed herself from the last of the backstage well-wishers and allowed Marc to shepherd her back to the *Anker.*

She went up to the theatre a couple of days later to have a chat and deal with messages. As she left the *Festspielhaus*, her phone pinged with a text message. It was from Eileen Vaughan. 'Get to-day's Times- u r in it'.

Marc, propping himself up on the edge of the comfortable double bed of the *Goldner Anker*, had got a copy of *The Times* and riffled through it.

'Have you found it? Has the old ogre given me beans at last? He was at the first night and the *Die Meistersinger.*'

Marc found the page.

'There's a feature article and a picture of you taken from your wrong side.

She tried to grab the paper but he jumped up and held it out of reach. They were both tall but his extra five centimetres were decisive.

'Vanity will not work' he triumphed.

She gave up and made a rude gesture. He tutted with false propriety, settled, and keeping a poker face, read:

'Visiting Bayreuth after a year's absence should be refreshing and inspirational but the current production of Die Meistersinger, new last year, seems designed to dampen any nascent enthusiasm. The producer and designer do not seem to know whether they are on Mars or Earth. They are certainly not in Nuremberg. The stage is cluttered with meaningless projected images and the cast caper like circus performers from a second-class touring tent show. Sadly, the general confusion seems to have affected the direction and a talented cast of singers, Maestro ....

'Come on' interrupted Detty impatiently 'we get the message about *Die Meistersinger*. Has he ignored the new *Tannhäuser* altogether or do we get a dose of the same medicine?'

Marc read on:

'Things improved with the new Tannhäuser. The established team of Martin Johannsen producing, with Olaf Beckmann's sets arrived at a twentieth century setting, highlighting the battle between lust and the human spirit. It has all been said before and the message of Tannhäuser can seem prudish in the twenty first century. With this production, however, there were appropriate new slants and a refreshing beauty in some, at least, of the stage pictures. Although it was received with the standard torrent of disapproval on the first night, it is the sort of production that the audience will come to understand and appreciate after a little time.'

'Pompous bugger!' broke in Detty in English

'Really Bernadette your convent would not like its star *alumna* using language like that!'

'Well, he is, isn't he?'

'I will ignore that and go on:

'It was the music, however, which was triumphant. Anton Meilin can always conjure the best out of this orchestra and he was supported by a strong cast, anchored by a sturdy Landgraf from Manfred Erfult and promising, forceful, performance from the debutant Andrew Mann in the demanding name part. His commitment made up for the errors, which he should be able to correct with practice and confidence.'

'That's almost a rave review from Henry Knight.'

'Wait a minute – I haven't finished' Marc read on:

'We have come to expect extraordinary things from the Elisabeth, Bernadette O'Neill, in her short career, and we were not disappointed. This performance is truly remarkable. Her 'Dich teure Halle, grüss' ich wieder', is bright, true, and powerful. The thoughtful wonder of 'Ich preise dieses wunder' shows us another polished facet of her diamond voice. 'Lass ihn zu dir ihn wallen du Gott der Gnad' und Huld' shines through the other soloists, not by unbalanced power, but by sheer penetrating vocal beauty. There is a conviction there that suspends disbelief and almost makes you think that Saint Elisabeth of Thuringia is, herself, before your eyes. Before we have stopped being astonished, this truly talented artist goes on to give us an 'Allmächt'ge Jungfrau, hör mein Flehen', so tender that nobody could doubt that this was a real prayer sung by a devout young woman and, at this time, one cannot help remembering her own astonishing background. Those of us privileged to hear her impromptu Brünnhilde in Siegfried two years ago had no doubt that here was an artist of exceptional potential. That potential is now being realised beyond our most optimistic hopes.'

'I'll need a new size of hats for the press conference' shouted Detty from the bathroom. 'By the way, which is my best side?'

'The right in the daylight, the left in the evening' Marc employed a Teutonic seriousness that left his wife wondering if she was being teased or not.

The press conference at the *Bayerische Hof* passed off with the usual inane questions, mainly from foreigners, mixed with serious enquiries from German would-be music critics.

*

David, still on cloud nine, went back to his flat and changed into track suit and fleece. He headed out, not towards the training ground but turned his elderly Land Rover south. He made a point of having his own car and had infuriated local importers by turning down their ever more pressing offers of glitzy sports models. As he drove towards the southern suburbs, he reflected that as the husband of the President's daughter, he might have to partially abandon his principles and get something smarter and more comfortable. For the moment the Land Rover served him well enough. He glanced anxiously at his watch and headed out through the still deprived southern streets. There were groups of young people hanging about looking bored but at least nobody now looked afraid. He parked in the last serviceable street, got out of the car and gazed over the desolate expanse of rubble which stretched for a considerable distance towards the *Zehnheiligenweg*. The whole immense area was surrounded by a red and white security fence. Across the expanse of muddy rubbish scattered with puddles not yet turned to snow, there were three intersecting lines of ruined roofless houses. Travsky had evicted the residents then half demolished the houses to give a clear field of fire in his last-ditch defence of the *Zehnheiligenweg*. David knew that, thank God, it hadn't worked. Marc aided by the partisans to say nothing of his extraordinary wife had crossed the *Wilhelm's Kanal* and breached the *Zehnheiligenweg* bastion.

David had been gazing across the expanse of ruined buildings, puddles, abandoned vehicles and iron girders for some minutes when a voice at his shoulder said;

'What do you think, David, will it do?'

He turned to see Dmitri Zahnsdorf dressed in jeans and a padded Polish jacket standing at his shoulder. David had seen him many times but even so in the cold Baltic autumn with that smile on his face and his hair ruffling in the wind, he was disturbingly like his dead cousin, Liese, and for a moment it took David's breath away.

He stammered 'It's going to need a lot of work but I do want to do something quickly.'

'It's going to need a lot of money too but I've had a bit of a start there. I have been able to talk to Sergei Malinov and he is very keen that the FWL can make it safe and at the same time clear the rubbish. He wants to meet you to-morrow and discuss the first stage. He thinks that he can decontaminate and make safe enough for two football pitches, four hard tennis courts and a tartan running track by next autumn and by the way, he is going to ask the Haupt Bürgermeister if it can be called the *Liese Zahnsdorf Sport Platz*. I didn't think you would object.'

Dmitri was startled that David had pulled out a handkerchief and was wiping wet eyes, muttering as he did so.

'It's the wind'.

Dmitri went on quickly:

'It is sharp to-day. General Malinov wants to know if you can raise the money for the facilities, if they clear the site of hazards.'

'I'll bust in the attempt if I don't' said David with a watery smile 'These kids deserve it and it would be a wonderful living memorial to Liese. I have half an agreement for a charity match in Nuremberg and we can do one in the *Hansestadion* here. There might also be the chance of a fund-raising Ball and a Charity Concert. I think that it can be organised. I'll ask General Malinov to go ahead when I talk about it with him to-morrow.'

15
THE LETTER

How long willt thou forget me, O Lord, for ever:
How long will thou hide thy face from me?

Psalms *13v1*

She walked over to the theatre from the Hansehaus car park enjoying the feeble autumn sunshine and the misty Baltic morning. She just needed to settle a few details of the future programme with Gerhard Staufen, the Administrator.

'Frau O'Neill, there are several letters for you – arrived to-day. I didn't send them to Krenek because Dr Staufen said you were coming over this morning.'

Paul, at the stage door fished in his stack of pigeonholes. Fan mail, she thought. It always trickled in even between productions. She stuffed them into her briefcase and thanking Paul took the lift up to Gerhard Staufen.

'We have settled the dates and are quite well on with the casting for *Armide* for two years' time but Maestro Helge thought that you should have a look at them at this stage.'

Detty read the production outline carefully.

'Sounds fine. As usual we need to find a lyric tenor.'

'Yes, I think Helge has some ideas but he will probably talk to you about them at Krenek.'

'We mustn't wait too long.'

There was an hour before her scheduled *Der Freischutz* rehearsal. She needed a coffee. After waving to Paul as she left then crossed the road to the Café Daina. It was beginning to fill up in mid-morning but her usual table in the window was still free. She ordered a croissant and a long espresso and pulled the letters out of her briefcase. The first four were fan letters which she read with a smile and put them back in her bag for a reply and an autographed photo of *Leonore* when she got to Krenek. She opened the fifth letter absent-mindedly, still thinking about casting *Renaud* and the *Danish Knight*. It was a much longer letter than the others and as she scanned the first page she came to with a shock and turned back to begin to read it carefully:

Dear Frau O'Neill,

I am writing to ask you if you could possibly help us. You will not remember me but I was at school at the Sacred Heart and, briefly, you taught me English. I was in the same house as Tamara Oblova but left when I was seventeen to go to technical college to get the preliminary qualifications for my physiotherapy course.

I know that you run a charity to help victims of the war and the previous regime. I also believe that you had some personal contact with the Frauendienst in the years gone by and that perhaps, for that reason, you would be inclined to help us, if you can.

As you probably know it is now possible to consult the registers of the two branches of the Frauendienst, if you think you might be in them or have another good reason to do so. I, myself, was taken into the Fortphlanzung Züchtung Weiblich at the age of eighteen (FZW 1641). I looked for you in the Sozial Rassenhygiene Dienst as I had read an article by you about your experience of going there but you did not appear in the list, so I have taken the liberty of writing to you at the theatre.

My father and mother were both arrested and disappeared during the fascist coup. I was very active and interested in sport and at that time I had left The Sacred Heart and was at college in Königshof studying to become a physiotherapist and living at home. When my parents were arrested, I was also detained and taken to the central school which had been converted into a suspects' interrogation centre. From there I was taken to the Frauendienst. Without explanation I was examined and had several scans and blood tests. Eventually a supervisor took me out of the group of terrified, waiting people to her bare office. She told me that I was a physically healthy and welstructured girl, despite my 'tainted' parentage. I was therefore very lucky and had been selected to help to breed the future elite of the state. Although virtually nobody knew anything about the recently formed Frauendienst at that time, one did not have to be a genius to know that some form of enforced prostitution would be involved in my 'luck'.

When we got to the Frauendienst, there was a lot of effort with charts of periods, temperature, and blood tests, presumably to determine when my companions and I would ovulate. That was the time that, as they put it, 'we should be put to the male'. They used farm expressions and, come to think of it, it was a sort of stud farm although unlike your Farm it didn't have the name. We were instructed how to behave as we were being 'serviced,' raped might have been a better word. Our 'partners' would be selected fit young soldiers but we would have our heads covered by a mask so that we couldn't recognise the man nor him us. We were not on any account to speak to our partner but we should relax and make it easy for him and never resist in any way.

The first problem that the staff faced was that many of the selected women were so shocked that they had no periods and no sign of ovulation for some time after their arrest and Travsky, who took a personal interest in this initiative, was keen to get results. For some reason I had a regular period soon after I was admitted and had always had a regular cycle. So, I was in one of the first batches to go for insemination. We were put in cubicles and left alone with the man. The staff felt that an audience would inhibit the male. It was the worst experience of my life. I couldn't see the man who was trying to rape me but he was clumsy and vicious. In addition, he stank of sweat, tobacco, and cheap vodka. He hurt me so much even before he entered me. I could stand it no longer and kneed him hard in the groin. He shrieked satisfactorily and the severe beating that I was given afterwards almost seemed worth it. I was beaten by the worst guard of all who was a man with cropped hair and an always expressionless face but the most striking thing about him was his startlingly blue eyes which seemed dead, lifeless. He was terrifying because he seemed bored and emotionless but was still coldly cruel and devoid of human feeling. He was a foreigner but we never knew where he came from. He spoke Russian most of the time and only German when he had to and then with a strong accent. But his Russian wasn't like ours – it sounded different. The girls called him 'Seryozhka der Schlauch- the hosepipe' after the thing he used to punish us but we never knew his real name. He appeared almost an automaton. He didn't even seem to be a sadist. It wasn't pornographic as there seemed no sex about it. He didn't appear to enjoy punishing offenders; but he just did it because it was his job, but he certainly punished us severely. He even looked bored, frustrated while he beat us. In fact, none of the guards, male or female, ever abused us sexually. They knew that was forbidden because it would interfere with our job which was breeding. Travsky himself, it was said, was very firm about this. I was told that some time before I arrived at FZW the only guard who had broken the rules had himself been sacked and then taken to the men's unit and castrated. None of the others tried it on again after that.

When I attacked my 'partner' I had the strange and stupid idea that, as I had stopped him before he got to me, I might be considered 'unsuitable' and transferred to the Farm or other institution. I knew I ran the risk of being 'spayed' – their term- next door or even executed but I was so desperate that I didn't really care.

Strangely my periods carried on as usual despite the vicious beating that I had had and I realised quickly that I was wrong about being thought unsuitable. Oh no! A month later I was on the list again but this time, together with two other 'difficult' women, I was marked not only for Befruchtung but mit Gewahrsam. They had considered the problem of the uncooperative and now they had three cubicle cells where we could be restrained so we were unable to offer resistance. It was to one of these that I was led blind-folded to receive my second partner. I don't need to tell you that I was helpless, terrified, and really wanted to die.

Then a miracle happened. As usual I was locked in with a man. I could not see the man but instead of attacking me, he whispered to me gently. He told me that I had a beautiful body and how he wished that he could see my face. He went on about how he would do as he had to but could I try and think of him as a lover not a criminal. He kissed me softly on the neck and caressed me. When he entered me, it was gently and carefully like a real lover and he kissed me again almost reverently on my breasts murmuring:

'This could have been so different.'

After that I broke the rules again and whispered

'I know and perhaps it could be some day – if we both survive.'

The miracle didn't end there, however. I was spared another beating for the 'crime' of talking to my 'partner – the cells were all bugged – because in a few days I realised that I was pregnant and the tests confirmed it. Pregnant women weren't beaten. I felt almost proud that my unknown hero had given me a baby. When we were pregnant, we were treated reasonably well with good food, exercise on the grass compound and light work. The time passed slowly but I day-dreamed about the father of my child. Nine months later I gave birth to a baby girl. The screws were disappointed as the top brass wanted boys. I was made to feed my daughter for six weeks then she was taken away and I haven't seen her since. Like the others I went through agony from my full breasts but eventually it stopped. Two months later I was tested again and found to be ovulating and I was given to another man. He wasn't as bad as the first one but it was still horrible. Fortunately, I didn't conceive and within weeks the FWL over-ran the Frauendienst and we were freed.

I was desperate to find out about my parents. It was not good news. Although I am still not completely sure, I am almost certain that they were both amongst those shot and buried in a mass grave in the Ostwald. Perhaps one day we will find out for sure. But with my other preoccupation I was luckier. I wanted more than anything to find my lover but I had never seen him and didn't even know his name. However, I knew that our number was always put on a sticker on the door of our cells or cubicles. If he really cared about me I thought that he would have remembered my number FZW1641. I put an advertisement on several missing persons and social network websites and in the Osthanse Kurier – three insertions – it read:

'If you have Umgang (knowledge) of FZW 1641 please contact the following e-mail address…'

The newspaper was very helpful in setting up a special e-m address to use only for replies. I hoped that my hero would interpret the Umgang as meaning the biblical knowledge and know that it was from me. I hoped that at the same time the real meaning of my message wouldn't be obvious to others It was a very long shot as I didn't really know if 'he' remembered me or really wanted to see me again.

I was glad that I took these precautions. I had a load of junk mail offering to sell me everything from condoms to Viagra as well as nauseating offers of young women from several countries. These respondents clearly hadn't understood anything about my advert, even my sex, and I was glad. I also had two invitations to join FZW survivors' groups – one suggested that the only solution for ex FZW girls was to join their female-companionship gay group. Despite all my troubles, the last solution that I wanted was to become a Lesbian. I began to get very depressed and started to think that I was playing out my fantasies and it was all useless and stupid. Then one morning as I, once again, checked the e-mails, rather hopelessly, there was this one:

"Gnädige Fräulein, I think that I might be the person that you are seeking. Was the date the 3rd May four years ago? If you think that I am right please reply to my e-m. I attach a photo. Do not be put off by the uniform – after I met you-if it was you – I changed my allegiance, deserted, and joined the partisans. From there I joined the FWL and the picture was taken of our platoon with the burning Winterburg in the background. I have circled me. I yearn to think that I have found the right person.

With much respect, Jurgen Holberg"

The picture was of a dark very good-looking young man in FWL uniform. I was thrilled – only he could have known the date of our encounter. It had to be right and it was. We are now together and very much in love. We hope to get married later this year.

However, we have one further wish and this is the reason for this letter. We are trying to find our daughter who was taken from me at six weeks old. It is difficult as, although there were records, I understand that they were burnt in the Winterburg explosions and fire. I know that you have a charity organisation helping people who suffered under the fascists and the war and that you have many contacts. Can you possibly help us find her as we have had no success so far?

With best wishes and profound admiration,
Alexandra Kulanova (soon to be Holberg!)
PS I attach a recent photo of us both.

Detty sat for some minutes ignoring her very cold coffee. In a country where extraordinary things happened, this had to be the one of most extraordinary. She looked at the photo. Alexandra was a tall girl with fine strong features and lovely almond shaped eyes. Dressed simply in jeans and a tee shirt it was obvious that she had a beautiful figure and Detty could understand why Jurgen had fallen for her even without seeing her face. Jurgen was about the same height as his partner and dressed almost identically; he had his arm round her and smiled warmly and broadly at the camera. In the background there was a beach and a calm sea. Detty couldn't identify the place but the letter head had an address in a village, Seesovils, north of Sovils in the east of the country, so she assumed the beach was near there. The letter also had an e-mail address and *Handy* number. She read the letter again still thoughtfully.

She had heard about the much smaller, breeding side of the dreadful *Frauendienst* but until this moment had never really come into direct contact with anybody from it. She tried to recall how it was organised. She thought that the babies were taken off to a communal nursery to start their life as brain washed servants of Travsky's state. Because the regime was overthrown rapidly none of the children were more than a year or two old at the end of the civil war – but what had happened to them?

She pulled out her *Handy* and punched in the number on the top of the letter. A soft female voice answered.

'Frau Kulanova?'

'Yes, who is that?'

'Bernadette O'Neill, you wrote to me.'

There was an audible indrawing of breath at the other end.

'Where are you and when can we meet – with Herr Holberg, if possible?'

'We both live in Seesovils. Jurgen works for a building firm and is studying quantity surveying and I work at the local gym – I have restarted my physiotherapy training but must combine it with a job but they do let me have time off for college but I don't like to ask for too much. We are only really free at some weekends but we could get time off to see you.'

'I don't think that is necessary. Are you free next Saturday?'

'Of course. I'll make sure we are.'

'We could meet at Krenek but that's a long journey. Could you come to the Hansehaus in Königshof?'

There was another gasp.

'Yes – of course.'

'Right. I'll begin to make some enquiries on your behalf and arrange for you to be sent the necessary security passes. Would you mind if Tamara Oblova was with me when we meet you?'

There was a third longer gasp.

'Of course not… But…'

'That's settled then – let's say about eleven thirty. This is my *Handy* number. If there is any problem, we will phone each other. See you on Saturday.'

'Thank you so much.'

'No thanks – I haven't done anything yet and may not be able to. Don't expect too much.'

She punched the red button and ended the call.

*

Saskia gripped Jurgen's hand tightly as they approached the massive, forbidding military figure at the reception desk of the Hansehaus. They had felt rather important going to the main front entrance with a large, polished brass plate marked *Präsident Hanseatic Republic Livonias* rather than going round to the everyday offices for Visas etc clustered around the ground floor, but now they were feeling very nervous. Were they really going to the private residence of the Head of State or was it all a joke?

'Alexandra Kulanova and Jurgen Holberg for Frau O'Neill – we have an appointment.'

The rugged face broke into a broad, welcoming smile:

'Ah yes, Frau Kulanova, Welcome to the Hansehaus. Frau Bernadette is with Frau Tamara upstairs and they are expecting you. Use this key to the lift and it will take you straight to the floor below the Penthouse. I am sorry but there is no lift for the final flight but it isn't very long. I'll take the key back once you have gone up. There is a doorbell in the Atrium just ring it.'

The door was opened by a diminutive figure with the most famous female face in Livonia.

'I'm Tamara but of course we were at school together so you may remember' she said unnecessarily 'Come in. Leave your coats out here. It's quite warm as long as the heating doesn't pack up again. Detti's already here. Would you like coffee?'

They both said yes. Tamara poked her head round another door which was presumably the kitchen and asked for coffee for them all to an unseen presence inside. She then led them both into the drawing room. It was simply but comfortably furnished and a number of toy trucks and cars were scattered over the floor.

'Sorry about the mess. I didn't have a chance to clear up after Niki's morning romp.'

The speaker was as startlingly tall as Tamara had been short. Saskia had, of course, seen her at The Sacred Heart and later on television in the famous '*Fidelio*' but she had forgotten just how impressive Bernadette O'Neill was. Saskia herself was over one metre eighty but the other woman was three or four centimetres taller. She was wearing a dark red woollen sweater and light brown trousers which only partly disguised her enviably athletic figure. There was an immediate friendly, open smile from her generous mouth. The famous red gold mane of hair was gathered into a slightly careless ponytail. Despite her friendly manner and smile, Saskia thought to herself that she wouldn't like to be on the wrong side of this woman. She then remembered her country's history and that the Fascist regime had learnt the hard way that you didn't mess with Bernadette O'Neill. With a professional eye, Saskia also noted that she appeared extremely fit and gave the lie to the popular image of overweight singers.

A small dark girl, who looked foreign, appeared with the coffee.

'One thing about this place' said Mara 'the coffee is both made in a proper machine operated by an expert Italian coffee maker. Meet Gianna.'

'*Molto gentile, Signora*' grinned Gianna with a slightly overdone Italianate gesture.

They sat and talked over coffee for some time. Then Detti came to the point:

'I have tried to call in a favour from the Intelligence Unit of the Swans on your behalf. The national intelligence service might be able to help you. In fact,' she smiled 'the director of national intelligence is about to go on maternity leave which could be a problem.'

Saskia didn't know what to say at this new and unexpected turn of events but Jurgen burst in:

'But can they do anything, Frau Komturin?'

'I don't know – nobody can know. Please call me Detti. We are going to see a bit of each other in the next few weeks and I think that we would both like you to think of us as friends and in that way, we can face the good and the bad together as it happens. Perhaps this is the right time to say that Mara and I admire you and the way you have got past your misfortunes. If we can do anything to help you find the final reward that you are wanting then we will do it and so will Tanya.'

'Sorry, I should explain she is Hauptmann Tanya Lopokova, director of the Livonian intelligence service, which she has commanded with huge skill from a wheelchair having lost her legs in an early revolt against the Fascists. She took over when her predecessor was killed on active service, Major Zahnsdorf, you will have read about it. Tanya is currently nearly at term with her first baby hence she has the spare time to try and find yours.'

There was a pause for some minutes. Mara broke it.

'Suppose we all have dinner together at Golabki, then we can talk some more and you can meet my fiancé.'

'But we have nowhere to stay in town.'

'No problem. You can stay here. I assume that you only need one room.'

Detty laughed.

'Sorry, Jurgen, it's beginning to sound like an old girls' reunion from The Sacred Heart.'

'You can't be part of an old girls' reunion, Frau Bernadette' said Mara with mock seriousness 'You were the fearsome foreign English teacher who taught the seniors about Alexander Pope and Twickenham, terrifying all of us.'

'I didn't make a very good job of terrifying you, Tamara Nickolaevna.'

Saskia and Jurgen could hardly believe that they were sitting in the private quarters of the revered President of the Republic laughing and joking with his daughter and the author of the Livonian National Anthem and arranging to have dinner together.

*

The back room of Golabki was candle lit and romantic. David appeared from training. He kissed Detty then Mara, who then did the introductions. Jurgen was less wonderstruck than Saskia and joined quickly in the spirit of things, saying:

'Today has been amazing. We are being entertained by the First Lady of Livonia, the Komturin of the Order of Sankt Nicklaus and now I have met my sporting hero.'

He stopped. They all waited for him to go on.

'Just before my discharge from the FWL we were down on the Fojn. It was muddy, very wet and not much fun. But we did have a television and we saw the match – we saw the goal against *Bayern* and now I am talking to the man who scored it.'

'Team effort' said David, but he smiled all the same.

'One day I will ask you how you managed that turn.'

'Not tonight. It'll bore the girls.'

'Rubbish' chipped in Mara 'I asked you the same thing once and you still haven't told me.'

'You knew without me telling you.' said David 'in spite of your act as an undercover *Fachfrau.*'

Despite the badinage, the adoration from David was obvious.

*

At the Hansehaus, Nicklaus was drinking coffee over the fire, reading papers from a dispatch box. Mara introduced the newcomers. Nicklaus courteously offered to get them coffee but everybody agreed that it was time for bed.

Before they separated for the night, Detty asked casually: 'Would you be our guests at The Sacred Heart celebration? I can't think of anyone more suitable. Don't answer now, think about it overnight and let me know at breakfast.

16
THE LONG PILGRIMAGE

Yesterday upon the stair
I met a man who wasn't there.
He wasn't there again today.
Oh, how I wish he'd go away.

WILLIAM HUGHES MEARNS – *ANTIGONISH*

The morning was bright and very cold with a pale blue sky. It was a sharp cold with a cutting edge that her Irish soul had learnt to recognise in the Baltic. During the night the temperature had been down to minus sixteen and by the early morning it hadn't recovered much. She ran round the lake to try and clear her head but she wasn't sure what she should do next. She had promised Tanya's help but hadn't even consulted her yet. Detty certainly had no idea how you found a missing baby – correction – toddler and she wasn't sure how Tanya was going to do it either. The first thing was to have a detailed chat with her. She then realised that she had forgotten her notebook with Tanya's personal mobile number. She cursed – then thought – that will cost me ten Hail

Marys and guiltily realised that she hadn't been to Confession for far too long. Nothing for it, she would have to ring the Security Corps switch board number.

'May I speak to Frau Hauptmann Lobokova, please?'

'I think she is free. Who shall I say it is?'

'Bernadette von Ritter'

'A moment, Frau von Ritter.'

'Detti, hi – why didn't you ring the private line?'

'I left the number at the Hansehaus – anyway it didn't matter. Your young lady was very courteous and put me through quickly. How are you?'

'I'm fine and swelling nicely. I go on Maternity leave this week. It worries me a bit. We are a bit short at senior level but fortunately Irina has recovered and is brilliant. She will be in charge. It is quite a task for a twenty-two-year-old who was three parts dead not so long ago but she is capable and I think she'll cope. But you didn't ring just to enquire after my health – what can I do for you?'

'Could I come round and find out what you know about missing toddlers?'

'Sure – it's routine for them to be reported to Military Intelligence – What are you up to? Come clean, will you?'

'When are you free? It might be better, and possibly safer, face to face.'

'Here at eleven for coffee?'

'Fine I'll be there.'

As soon as they had got coffee it was down to business.

'OK, it's not quite the usual pram-outside-the supermarket thing. You know that one of Travsky's more unpleasant tricks was selecting young women for insemination by anonymous rape in order to build his master race. Well, I am anxious to know what happened to the children who were born from this programme – and one in particular.'

She went on to describe to Tanya the contents of the letter.

'I'll have a go. At least it's something different. It'll keep me occupied during my maternity leave.'

*

He grabbed his rucksack and sticks and got off the morning bus casually. Nobody took any notice as in late summer when the weather got cooler, the region had many hikers. They came from the four corners of the globe and were of all ages, both male and female. Nobody looked at the spare man whose temples now showed more grey than fair. He was wearing cotton shirt and casual trousers, wide lens dark glasses and a light khaki broad-brimmed hat. If anybody had looked at him, they would have put him down as a casual hiker anxious to explore a little of the *Via Frances*. Obviously, he was not a formal pilgrim, as pilgrims wouldn't be on a bus at that part of the route to Compostella and, anyway, he had no scallop shell.

Off the bus, he adjusted his rucksack, put his sticks under his elbows and headed out of the village towards the pilgrim route. Once amongst the trees, he paused for a few minutes to check his watch and drew a map out of the side pocket of his rucksack. Timing was important; he knew that he had to arrive during the business hours of the afternoon and well before the Office of *Vespers* which, from Monsignor Jose Maria Pueblo's old diaries, he knew would be at the summer time of six pm. He had, of course, phoned Reverend Mother Immaculata to ask whether he could visit. He was Dr Ivanov, an old friend of the sadly late Monsignor Pueblo. He was about to begin an informal pilgrim's visit to *Compostela* and wondered whether, on the way, he could visit the site of the great Monastery where his friend had done so much of his wonderful work. Yes, sadly, he knew that the Monastery had been blown up by terrorists. But he still thought that he would like to make a visit. It was a separate pilgrimage really, but as a courtesy he thought that he should ask Reverend Mother first, as he knew the Nunnery continued to do its fine work. Perhaps he might even visit her?

In response he had been promised a warm invitation. Did he know the times of the Office so that he could come at the right time? He assured her that he did and anyway he would be in no hurry so he could always wait until the service was finished.

He had to stride out, but he was fit despite his sixty plus years and he barely panted as he walked up the steep slopes to the Monastery site. It still took him a couple of hours, passing beside the wild thyme, the cork oaks and the pines while the cicadas paused, then resumed, their incessant song.

After about two hours walking, he rounded the final massive rock and gazed at his objective. The recent ruins of the ancient Monastery looked back at him, almost reproachfully as if they knew about his role in their destruction. He gazed at fallen masonry and dismembered statues without emotion. The gatehouse had been demolished, presumably because it was unsafe, after the explosion. The left side of the Courtyard beyond was still relatively intact although windowless and abandoned. The right side which had housed the famous library and scriptorium was just a pile of rubble. He wasn't surprised that the two CIA agents had been killed. It was just amazing that he knew the two women had survived. The hand of God, perhaps, he said to himself with a chuckle. He adjusted the dark glasses, which he was careful to wear to hide his pale blue eyes, which had seen so much but gave so little.

After some minutes looking at the rubble, he turned to the left and walked slowly down to the modest buildings of the Nunnery and rang the visitors' bell.

The young black novice looked a bit anxious and uncertain as, after some moments, she opened the wide oak door in response to the deeply clanging bell.

'*Buenos dias*' he said and continuing in acceptable Spanish. 'I am Dr Ivanov, the friend of Monsignor Pueblo and I wrote to Reverend Mother. She is expecting me, I think.'

'Please wait in here. I will tell Reverend Mother that you are here.'

The Mother Superior was a worn, troubled figure. Her community was diminishing as the older sisters went, one by one, to the Mother House infirmary to be looked after, leaving too few able-bodied nuns to run the house and gardens. Money was short and they had to rely on home grown produce. In the old days, much of the work and victualling had been done in conjunction with the much larger and wealthier adjoining Monastery which was now a ruin. Sadly, the Mother Superior realised that their days were numbered and that soon they would have to close. It would be so sad to leave the place where some of them had lived in faith and contemplation for many years. Her major worry however concerned the small number of novices and very young sisters, mainly from Africa, who were her special concern. Even within the same order they might find it difficult to fit into another House. However, for the moment, she must concentrate on her unusual visitor.

She shook hands with Dr Ivanov and, very courteously, he said how grateful he was that she had agreed to see him.

'It was the least I could do. We don't have many visitors here and any friend of dear Monsignor Pueblo's is doubly welcome. His death was a terrible blow, coming so soon after the destruction of the Monastery. God sends us many trials. Would you like to leave your rucksack and sticks in the Atrium?'

'I will leave the rucksack but I like to keep the sticks as sometimes I get giddy attacks and need them for support. The attacks pass quite quickly.'

'As you wish. You have seen the ruins, already?'

'Yes, I looked at them as I came up. I felt so distressed that I could look no longer. Such a wonderful place and all gone so suddenly! I shall of course go back to pray after I leave you. It is a place where I will be near to God and my dead friend.'

'Of course, I understand, I will ask two of the sisters to go with you if you wish.'

'Many thanks, but that won't be necessary. I just want to spend the time with God and the spirit of my dear friend. Now tell me, how is it for you here now the great House has gone?'

That opened the flood gates. Mother Immaculata could not discuss her worries with her juniors, but this was a sympathetic academic from a faraway country and a friend of the late Monsignor – well – he was almost a confessor, wasn't he?

He listened in silence for many minutes whilst the troubles of the Convent poured into his ear. When, at last, there was a pause, he leant forward to touch Mother Immaculata's hand in a gesture of sympathy. His left stick got caught in her robe and she gave a soft cry as it pushed against her ankle.

'Oh, I'm so sorry' he said 'how clumsy of me. I do hope that I didn't hurt you. There must have been a thorn stuck on the stick. It happens sometimes.'

'It didn't really hurt. I'm sorry I made a fuss – it's nothing.'

'Please go on with telling me about the future.'

Gradually her speech got slower and her lids drooped. When she seemed finally to sleep, he reached out towards her desk and deftly took two or three pieces of paper with the Pic Noix insignia and letter head '*Deo gratias, La Madre Superiora, Abadia de Pic Noix*. Quickly, he got out his miniature camera and photographed the Abbess's signature on a daily order of work. The signature was probably unnecessary but it was a further safeguard. As an old KGB hand, he took the motto 'we never make mistakes' seriously. Contented, he waited until Mother Immaculata came back to a fluttering consciousness, then he rang the bell. The black novice appeared followed by an older sister.

'La Abadesa seems unwell. I am so sorry if I have disturbed her. We talked of sad things, the fate of the Abbey, the death of Monsignor Pueblo perhaps it was too much. She had a short seizure. I am so sorry if I had any part in causing it. She seems to be recovering but perhaps she should have a physician. Unfortunately, I am a theological historian and I know nothing of medicine. Perhaps I can call a doctor before I leave?'

The older nun took charge.

'Thank you, Dr Pavlov, but that won't be necessary. We have our own physician who will readily come up from the valley. I am so sorry that your welcome visit has ended in anxiety.'

'Then I shall go to the ruins and pray for the health of your wonderful Mother and the soul of my friend. Then I shall go on my way towards the shrine of the blessed St James. Sadly, my bad legs prevent me doing the pilgrimage but I shall do what I can and pray for salvation.'

He chuckled as he left the Convent. Now he was fully equipped. The laboratory had done well. The abbess had lost consciousness quickly and had awoken with no idea of what had happened to her. He had had his habit made by a tailor who specialised in providing forged police and military uniforms when they were needed for foreign operations. Making a nun's habit to measure was different but the tailor had done it well and he was sure that it would pass muster. Now he had the Abbess's signature and the letter heads that should be all he would need. He could get back to Minsk satisfied and arrange the final part of the operation. He took the complicated journey from Toulon to Berlin. At the changing of flights in Berlin, an elderly academic entered the airport hotel; a blind nun left it. He wanted to put in a bit of practice in his new persona.

*

Marc was away in England. She had a teaching appointment at eleven and should have spent the available two hours working on *Agathe* and *Isolde*. This morning, however, she was uncharacteristically lethargic and, after writing to the Mother Katerina at the Sacred Heart, confirming their appointment, she sat in her dressing gown in the Lodge Flat at Krenek drinking coffee and glancing idly at the *Ost Hanse Kurier*. Not that the news was up to much. In common with most of Europe and the rest of the world, the economic situation was deteriorating. The Russians had pulled out of a joint venture for gas exploration. A local popular soap opera actress has been admitted to hospital with a strange illness after suffering an insect bite in a crowded metro station. There was speculation about David Sensky's possible transfer to *Nürnberg FC*. The last item was the only one that really interested Detty. She wondered if David would really be able to leave Livonia, even if it was to his professional advantage, now his engagement to Mara had been announced publicly.

*

Shrove Tuesday – *Fastnacht* – eight hundred years since the foundation of *Frauen Kloster* – *Herz-Jesu* – the forerunner of The Sacred Heart Convent and school. The most prestigious girls' school in Livonia had been suppressed by the Fascist revolution although the community at the Convent had survived with a struggle. The school had been re-founded after the civil war. The usually rigidly aesthetic nuns were allowing themselves a festival.

Detty had been back to The Sacred Heart once or twice since she had been bundled into a bus on that terrible day when the Convent and school had been raided by Travsky's NAS. It still all came back to her as she nervously she climbed the stairs to the Abtissin's office. Halfway up, she moved to one side to allow a thin old nun in dark glasses using two white sticks who was struggling down the stairs, to pass her. They exchanged greetings and Detty offered to help her. The nun croaked a courteous 'Danke' but said that she liked to do these things independently even if it took some time. 'I am old and have no need to hurry'. Detty felt some admiration for the old woman as she finished her climb to the Superiors's office.

'I am so grateful to you for coming to help us, Frau Komturin,'

Detty couldn't get used to being addressed formally by the aristocratic lady who had been her boss when she was a student teacher. When Detty had been at the school the Abbess had always been kind and considerate but, none the less, rather distantly Olympian.

'I am very happy to try to help on such a prestigious occasion.'

'Well, it's not only celebrating the eight hundred years of the Foundation; it is also in a sense celebrating a renewal. As you know only too well, the school was closed by the Fascists and the Community suffered abuse, and, but for the Grace of God, would have collapsed absolutely. This is therefore a time to be joyful and thankful. The Cardinal Archbishop has agreed to celebrate a Choral Mass in the Cathedral which will be followed by a reception in the Great Hall Refectory here. That is the bare outline and this is where I would like your advice and, if possible, help. We have a quite good girls' choir again here now – not perhaps quite as it was when you were here, but, considering, they do very well. We would of course like them to be involved but an occasion like this needs professional help. Do you have any ideas?'

'After your 'phone call, I had some thoughts about a few suggestions. May I go ahead?'

'Of course – gladly'.

'Well, I thought that we could do the Schubert Mass in C Major, do you know it?'

'Yes, a bit. It's a joyful piece and would be entirely right but how about performers?'

I took the liberty of consulting Helge von Grunstrand and he has said he would be happy to ask the Philharmonica to play.'

'It would be wonderful for the girls to sing with the country's leading orchestra. They would be amazed. But what about fees – I saw a Swedish paper had called the orchestra one of the finest ensembles in Europe the other day. We can hardly afford those sorts of fees.'

'I don't think that will arise. It is a very special occasion and Helge has remarkable powers of persuasion with the Ministry of Culture.'

'And obviously so do you, Frau Bernadette.

Detty noticed that the title had become slightly less formal.

'I haven't finished yet' she laughed 'Henry Schliessen will be here for a Board Meeting of the Conservatoire. I rang him last night and, if you wish, he said he would sing the tenor solo. Walter Liebig is here for rehearsals of *Der Freischutz*. I haven't asked him yet but I am pretty sure he will sing bass. And we have a splendid young contralto from the Conservatoire, Julia Kitze, for the alto part. I hope they can provide some men from the Cathedral choir and that should set us up.'

'You haven't mentioned the soprano part' said the Abtissin with a twinkling smile.

Two can play at that game thought Detty:

'Well, we could ask Martina Schlerova. She has a lovely voice.'

'I think that would be entirely inappropriate, although I know Frau Schlerova artistry is superb. I think that it would be much better if the soprano part was sung by a former member of staff.'

'If you say so, Reverend Mother, I will do it. I assume that we would sing the *Agnus Dei* at the Elevation with the congregation taking the Communion afterwards. I think that we should ask Dr Georg, the Cathedral Organist to play after the Blessing and Dismissal.'

'Agreed'.

'I will go away and fix up rehearsals but, first, I would like to ask two favours from you.'

'Please'

'I am sure that none of the choir or soloists will want to charge fees but, if His Eminence agrees, we would like to have a Collection for the

Committee we have set up for the victims of the war and the previous regime.'

'I am sure we can do that. I will ask His Eminence how he would like it staged.'

'The other is a more personal favour. I am at the moment helping a young former pupil of The Sacred Heart who has a strange and appalling story to tell. Briefly it is this…'

She went on to describe Saskia's ordeal and its aftermath.

'If you agree we would like Saskia and Jurgen Holberg to come as our personal guests. My husband will look after them as I am singing. She is, after all, a former pupil.'

'And triple jump champion – I remember her – a good brain and a formidable athlete. I am so sorry that she has had such a dreadful time. Of course, you should ask her. We want to spread the guest list as wide as possible. We currently have a visiting sister from a Spanish house. She is elderly and almost blind but has come to look for a family sister of hers here who disappeared during the war.'

'Please tell her to contact me if I can be of any help. I will keep in touch over the arrangements and please let me know if you need to discuss anything further.'

'*In nomine Christi*'

*

She flung herself, exhausted, on the sofa in the Krenek flat and mindlessly turned on the TV. There was bloodshed in North Africa, the Spanish economy was presenting a problem. Nearer home there was good news about the boom in Baltic timber. David Sensky had changed his agent and turned down all offers to leave Königshof. Then, right at the end was an item saying that the soap opera actress had died in hospital after a week's mystery illness and that the doctors were all puzzled. It was thought to have been an unknown infection from the insect bite but nobody was sure and further tests were being done. She turned off the TV and, hoping Marc would make it back on the morrow, went to bed.

The day was important. The dress, apple green and black silk with a cream silk shirt, had arrived from Lanoure in Paris by special courier. Marc, her severest critic, had stood back when she tried it on, gazing at his wife with undisguised admiration and not a little awe.

'Is it all right?' she asked.

'It's stupendous' he said for once seeming to abandon his teasing then reverting to form:

'All the fourth form will have a crush on you.'

'It will make a change from the brutal and licentious military. I shan't ever ask you to look at me again' she pouted 'you might be generous for once. It's in the Cathedral and it's important.'

*

Hank had arrived already in the Sacristy and was chatting to Julia Kitze who obviously was enjoying her flirtation with a living legend.

'I see that I've got another rival' said Detty as she took off her winter coat displaying her Lanoure model.

'That's a fine way to greet me after I've flown the Atlantic just to see you. Still, you look gorgeous as ever, come here and give me a kiss.'

'Can't – it will spoil my special make up. This will have to do' she held out her hand upon which Hank dutifully bent low and kissed.

Helge poked his head round the door.

'If you have quite finished the Conservatoire Directors meeting, it's time we started. The chorus want their coffee.'

They had only a quick rehearsal and then it was almost time for the main performance.

Helge ushered Julia and Detty in front of him and then the two male soloists. After taking up her position at the side of the High Altar, Detty had a chance to take a quick glance at the Congregation. Mara was accompanying her father and the government guests, to do honour to the famous house. After the announcement of the engagement, for the first time, David was formally included in the front row beside Mara. Detty saw Marc, Jurgen and Saskia behind in the second row opposite the Convent community and their guests on the other side of the nave. She saw the old blind nun that she had passed at The Sacred Heart, sitting at the end of the row opposite Marc and the others. She had her two sticks but no longer wore her dark glasses. Detty presumed that the subdued winter light in the Cathedral made them unnecessary. She only gave her a passing glance before returning to the matter in hand.

As always Helge wasted no time, and they were into the *Kyrie*. The bright lively music sounded just right and as they moved through the six sections everybody, artists, clergy and congregation were enjoying themselves. Detty had persuaded Helge to grant her a little indulgence and to include the soprano solo original of the *Benedictus* as an additional part.

'It will make up for my back seat in *Die Meistersinger'* she had pleaded 'I need to persuade people here that I'm still a soprano.'

'I don't think anyone doubts that, Detti, after your *Elisabeth* at Bayreuth and your London Times review.'

She never knew whether he was serious or not.

The mixed forces sounded great in the short lively mass. The soprano music was quite challenging, but Detty loved it and really enjoyed herself. It was music making as it should be with young and old, amateur, and professional, sharing the same pleasure in the experience. Detty was sorry that it had gone so quickly as she started the final part, the *Agnus Dei*, and was joined by the other three in the varying combinations. The Cardinal Archbishop had raised the Host and Chalice. The congregation started to file forward for the Communion. The front row with the President, Mara and David, Catholic ministers and official guests moved up first.

The second row began to move and the old nun stepped out from the end of the row with surprising agility, holding her two white sticks in front of her. For a second, she faced Saskia, two back in on the row opposite. In an instant, Saskia was back, whimpering with terror on the cold concrete, with that face and worst of all, those eyes, expressionless and remorseless, staring down at her. The nun saw the girl's horrified expression of recognition. For a moment her composure was lost and she glanced back over her shoulder at Saskia with pure hatred mixed with fear. Saskia didn't wait. She pushed past Jurgen and flung herself at the habit covered legs of the old nun with a fierce Rugby tackle. Detty said later that she had not seen the like of it since Ireland beat the Australians at Lansdowne Road. But, for now, it was a shocking scene and no time for jokes. The old nun crashed to the ground with her habit in disarray and her white sticks flailing. In the process she dug one white stick into her own leg and banged her head hard on the marble floor. She lay still with a small trickle of blood creeping over her habit from her leg.

Plain clothes police leapt from their covert positions behind pillars, drawing their pistols from their shoulder holsters. They grabbed Saskia roughly, handcuffed her and dragged her down the Nave and through the West Door, presumably to a waiting police car. Somebody sent for an ambulance. There must have been one outside because in a few minutes, the unconscious nun was lifted onto a stretcher and carried off in the same direction as her assailant.

There followed a shocked silence. In a low trembling voice, the Cardinal then spoke:

'We have just witnessed a terrible act of sacrilege in the middle of the Holy Mass. It is difficult for us all to recover from such a shock. However, I shall now ask you to join me in a prayer for our poor Sister who has been so viciously assaulted and for the soul of the demented young woman who perpetrated this dreadful, sacrilegious act. After we have prayed, we will complete the Mass, as it would not be proper to abandon it.'

After the Blessing and Dismissal, a subdued congregation began to file out of the Cathedral. Marc rapidly picked up the nun's two abandoned white sticks. Something about them caught his eye and he remained behind for some minutes examining them carefully. Then following the rest of the congregation, he left the Cathedral. Irina Malinowska was waiting just outside the tympanum of the west door with its famous supplication to the Virgin. It had been thought that there was less risk once the VIPs were inside the Cathedral and security there had been left to the police. Irina's special force had therefore been deployed outside to counter the danger inherent in the arriving and departing. Marc spoke quietly to her.

'Frau Oberleutnant, could I have a private word?'

'Of course, but could it wait until we have seen the cars off? After last time, we need to be particularly careful.'

'I understand. I'll stand back and use my eyes too.'

'Thank you'

Marc stood watching as the official cars left without mishap. Shortly afterwards two coaches carrying the chorus, orchestra and, he hoped, the soloists, left too. Everybody was supposed to be going back to The Sacred Heart for the reception and, although it now hardly seemed appropriate, this had not been cancelled. It appeared that the drivers were carrying out their original orders. As the last of Irina's motorcycle escort streamed away from the cathedral after the cars, she turned to Marc and said anxiously:

'I'm so sorry keeping you waiting. I've got a nerve doing that to a senior officer.'

'You had an important duty to perform. As a fellow soldier, I would have been shocked if you had allowed me to distract you. Anyway, I'm only a guest here.'

'Some guest! But what was it you wanted to say?'

'Have a look at these' he showed her the two sticks, demonstrating the complicated miniature mechanism in both the shafts.

'My God' she said 'the Bulgarian umbrella! A bit before my time, I wasn't born then, but we learnt about it in training. They made a film, didn't they?'

He nodded.

'Exactly, but I think these are multi-chamber and much more sophisticated' he said as she took a closer look 'be very careful. They are almost certainly still loaded and I haven't worked out how the trigger or triggers work exactly. It has the benchmark of the KGB stamped all over it. We must presume that it's loaded with ricin or another analogue. Can you get them off to your ballistic department as soon as possible to get a proper inspection and the tiny shells, which presumably are still in it, sent for analysis?'

'At once and thank you.'

'Don't thank me. I just noticed the sticks looked odd when I picked them up. However, I think we have a lot to thank our young assailant for. How on earth did she know?'

'Search me' said Irina 'but she must have known something. You don't assault a nun in the middle of a Cathedral High Mass for no reason, do you?'

'I've done some pretty strange things in my time in the line of duty, including dumping my future wife in a garbage truck, but never that.'

'So, the myth about the garbage truck, is true?'

'Yes, Detti or I will tell you the whole story sometime over a beer, but I think we need to get on with other things at present.'

'Sure, I'll send a couple of senior NCOs round to the hospital and tell them to make sure that they don't let the 'nun' out of their sight and shoot if they must.'

'Agreed, but I hope they won't have to as I guess you would like that lady to do some explaining.'

'Sure would – but almost equally important is to let our friends in the police know that they are holding a national heroine rather than a demented virago. I'll go round myself. We might be quicker cutting through the red tape and getting her released if an officer goes.'

'OK and I'll go to The Sacred Heart and put the people there in the picture as far as I can.'

'Thanks. I must also spread a net to catch any accomplices.'

'You're right. My guess would be that, at least inside this country, she was acting alone but you are quite right. You should make sure if you can.'

'I will. Ferry ports, border crossings, airports and the usual suspects. Anything else you can think of?'

'Not for the moment – if I do, I'll let you know.'

He entered her mobile number on his phone then he hailed a taxi and asked to go to The Sacred Heart.

*

He was ushered in through the impressive doors of the Great Hall Refectory where desultory groups of people were standing round looking rather lost. Nicklaus Oblov had been as good as his word and had gone to the reception with Mara and David, despite the changed circumstances. They were talking quietly to the Mother Superior, backed by several anxious looking security guards. Detty, he saw with relief, was there talking with a group of the musicians further down the hall. He went straight to the President's group and told Nicklaus in as low a voice as possible what they had discovered.

'Would you like me to make an announcement, Herr Präsident, or should we leave it until we know more?'

'It's a serious matter when you call me Herr Präsident, Marc. But I think that you should do it and do it now. I think that, if we don't explain things, there will be a lot of rumour and we should try to avoid that.'

'Very good, here goes' he had a twinkle in his eye as he repeated the 'Herr Präsident.'

'Herr Präsident, Frau Abtissin, *meine Damen und Herren*, you will all know what happened in the Cathedral at Holy Mass this afternoon. You will all have been very shocked, as I was, by the apparently sacrilegious and vicious assault which took place. I now must tell you that what happened there was nothing short of a miracle and that several people, including some in this hall, almost certainly, owe their lives to the swift and courageous action of Frau Alexandra Kulanova.'

He waited for the murmur to subside.

'" Sister Barbara" – we shall continue to call her that for the moment – entered this country, this community, and the Cathedral this afternoon fraudulently. She appears to have been on a mission to assassinate one or more of the leaders of this country. This would seem to be the latest and, we hope very much, the last of a number of outrages directed at destabilising the new Livonia.'

'The intended method was sophisticated. Many of you will have heard of the murder in London in 1978 of the Bulgarian dissident Georgi Markov. It seems that this was an attempt to use an updated version of the same method. What is known for certain is that when 'Sister Barbara' entered the Cathedral this afternoon, she was intent upon pricking a number of this country's leaders with her lethal weapons. This was designed so it would appear to inflict only an accidental prick or minor insect bite which might go almost unnoticed even by the victim. It would, however, result in the death of all the victims after an interval of a few days. She was prevented from carrying out this plan by the very brave and prompt action of Frau Kulanova. At present we do not know how this very ordinary, extraordinary, young woman managed to realise what was afoot, but clearly, she did, and for that we must be very grateful.'

'Obviously, there is much more that will emerge about this event but The President thought that it would be right to inform you straight away of what we know so far, as obviously the media will know soon.'

A babble of conversation broke out again.

The President called for silence and began to speak.

'Thank you, Marc. Not for the first time in the history of this country, I think that we must be grateful to you, too. However, as you have said the major credit for our safety belongs to Alexandra Kulanova. I think that you will agree, Reverend Mother, that our extraordinary deliverance smacks of the miraculous and I would ask you to begin the Celebration that you had planned, which can now both honour your House and give thanks for our safety.'

The Abbess said a short prayer. Then the members of the Community left and reappeared with food and drink. The chatter resumed.

The Great Door of the Hall opened and Irina Malinowska, still in uniform, entered leading Saskia Kulanova by the hand. Irina, who had a driver, had used the jeep ride from the police Headquarters to help Saskia tidy her hair and do something with her make-up but she still looked a little bemused and bedraggled.

There was a spontaneous burst of applause as she entered which obviously startled the young woman further who now looked rather scared. Marc wasn't surprised. To risk your life, be arrested, thrown into prison, and then be released and greeted as a heroine all in one day, would have been capable of confusing most people. He walked over to the new arrivals:

'Saskia, come over to the President. He would like to thank you personally'.

Still looking bemused he led her over to Nicklaus and his group which now included Mara and Detty. Nicklaus simply shook Saskia's hand vigorously and said his thanks. She smiled but said nothing.

'What we would all like to know' said Marc 'is, how did you know?'

Saskia suddenly pulled her shoulders back regained her poise and looked quite fierce and very serious. She turned towards Detty and Mara.

'Some of you already know that when I was just eighteen, I was put in the FZW of the *Frauendienst*. If you will excuse me, I don't want to repeat most of my experiences there now. You asked, 'how I knew'. Let me just say that when you have been made to lie naked on a wet, very cold, concrete floor in winter with a man staring at you holding a thick loop of rubber hose. When you know that, when he has finished staring at you, coldly, he will use the hose to beat you unconscious, you do not easily forget the face or the lifeless staring blue eyes. I saw that face and those eyes in the Cathedral this afternoon.'

'But she is a woman and how did you know what she intended?'

'" She" is not a woman although he was well disguised. You will find that out. What was he going to do? I didn't know exactly – how could I? But I did know that there was great evil there and that I had to stop him. I never knew his proper name. We knew him as *"Seryozhka der Schlauch-* the hosepipe' and we were terrified of him. It was his job to beat us when we made a fuss about being raped or broke the rules in some other way. You see we were supposed to think of being raped as a privilege. In reality, we were quite anxious to get pregnant after being raped because it saved us from the hose. Odd –isn't it to want to be pregnant after being violated? He was pure evil but not even sadistic. He took no pleasure in what he did. He just did it as a boring office job like an inhuman automaton. I think we would have preferred a proper sadist – someone who got a sexual kick out of torturing us – it would have been perverted but more human. I was lucky. I only had the hose once but I could never, ever forget him – or it.'

Once she had started, the words had poured from her in a torrent like a dam bursting. It was now the turn of the group around her to be silent. After a long pause, Nicklaus took her hand and said:

'Even in a country with the benighted past of this land, that is a terrible story. How extraordinary it is that by chance you were there in the Cathedral this afternoon.'

'The hand of Providence' the Abbess said almost to herself.

One of the sisters came up quietly and whispered in the ear of the Abbess:

'Reverend Mother, there is a Feldwebel Müller on the telephone who wants to speak to Frau Oberleutnant Malinowska.'

'Very well. Please take her out to the telephone. I don't suppose that she knows the way – not being one of ours.'

The Abbess smiled and the little comment had broken the aghast silence. She knew quite well that Irina was the daughter of a protestant minister, the principal, in fact, of the Lutheran theological college in Königshof.

After some minutes she came back from the telephone.

'Some news from the hospital. "Sister Barbara" is indeed a man and the first thing he did when he came round from the blow on his head was to try and escape out of a window. They had put him in a womens' emergency assessment ward on the ground floor. He is now in a men's ward five floors up and handcuffed to the bed with two of our men on guard – one inside and one outside the room. Excuse me, Reverend Mother, but can you tell me how he/she arrived here? Please don't think that I trying to make a sectarian point.'

Irina couldn't help responding with a gentle dig to the Superior's allusion to her 'not being one of theirs.'

'I wouldn't dream of thinking that, Frau Oberleutnant' she smiled, good humouredly 'I was wondering about that myself. It happened like this. We got a letter purporting to be from the Abbess of Pic Noix in the Pyrenees.'

At this Detty interjected with surprise 'Pic Noix?'

'Yes – it is not of our Order but the letter said that the blind Sister Barbara was trying to trace her blood sister who had disappeared in Livonia during the Fascist regime. Could she stay with us while she tried to find out what had happened to her sister? Of course, I said that we would welcome her and, particularly in view if her disability, that we would do everything we could to assist her. When she arrived, she had another letter from her Superior, thanking us for having her. 'Sister Barbara' herself was quiet and withdrawn and went out a lot.

She refused an escort despite her blindness which was, I suppose, odd. She said she had a number of leads to follow in trying to find her sister. I shall ring Pic Noix tomorrow and find out about 'Sister Barbara' I probably should have done so earlier but the letters were on a proper letter head and I really had no reason to doubt their bona fides. Also, it seemed an innocent enough request at the time.'

*

After a pause while they digested this terrible story, the Präsident then said: 'If you would allow me, Reverend Mother, I would like to propose a toast to the eight hundred years of your community and also a toast and a vote of heartfelt thanks to Saskia here.'

'Please do. Then Bernadette, if you could, perhaps you would sing something appropriate for us? I remember your beautiful voice so well from when you were here before and of course it has been heard all over the world since.'

'I would be honoured, Reverent Mother, and, by chance, I have my favourite accompanist here with me.'

She indicated Marc and they laughed.

'Perhaps somebody could prepare the piano for him?'

Nicklaus gave his toast and the vote of thanks to Saskia who looked dead on her feet with tiredness.

'Of course, we will continue the celebration afterwards informally but, understandably enough, Alexandra, you look very tired so perhaps you would like me to get you a taxi?'

'No need for that, thank you' said the Präsident. 'Saskia is staying with us and I'll get one of our cars to take her back to the Hansehaus, when she is ready.'

'I'd like to stay and hear Detti sing but I will go, if I may after that, as I am very tired. Please can somebody find out what's happened to Jurgen? I haven't seen him since he left me in prison with all our dreams in tatters. He went to try and get me a lawyer to defend me.'

'I'll get onto it' said the indefatigable Irina 'as soon as I've heard Bernadette.'

Marc ushered Detti over to the piano.

'I hope that I can remember it' he whispered, 'The score is still in Henley.'

'That you should worry' his wife whispered back 'I haven't sung it since Henley. Perhaps we should do the *Liebestod* instead?'

Marc, note perfect despite his doubts, played the introduction and Detty's voice started, '*I know that my redeemer liveth*'. It was right for the occasion, as they had seen a miracle that day. It hardly mattered that only a minority of the gathering understood the English words, they were moved by the familiar music. Many of the overwrought guests were wet eyed by the end.

One person who obviously did understand the language, however, was Irina who, before she turned to go, whispered to Detty with a wicked smile twitching round her mouth.

'I imagine that you chose a Protestant text just for my benefit.'

'Be careful, Frau Oberleutnant' Detty smiled back 'You know that I am a good Catholic too- no- perhaps not a very good one. But we've had enough violence to-day. Don't start the Thirty Years War all over again.'

17
SEARCHING

Grief fills the room up of my absent child.

SHAKESPEARE: *KING JOHN* ACT 3 SC 4

The penthouse of the Hansehaus was distinctly overcrowded. Mara who was rather relishing her chatelaine role, had ordered Detti, Marc, Gianna and Niki junior down into the seldom used state bedrooms on the floor below. These were a private suite of rooms reserved for state visitors and only used on special occasions. Everybody was determined that Saskia should be allowed to sleep until she woke. Jurgen had been found late in the evening. He was still engaged in chasing possible defence lawyers who seemed to have all disappeared at sundown. When he was approached by a stopping police patrol car in the street and asked if he was Herr Holberg, he had feared the worst. However, when told that lawyers were no longer needed and that his partner was sleeping comfortably in the President's flat, he looked surprised but mightily relieved. The police took him to the Hansehaus where he got the story to date. He then agreed to spend the night in a room at the Hansehof Hotel booked by the President rather than disturbing Saskia. He looked anxiously at Mara as if he didn't really believe what had happened:

'No, I tell you she really is OK but she is very, very tired. Tomorrow she will be on the front page of all the papers as a national heroine. I have had to fight off Masha from the *FreiSender Livonias* already this evening who wanted an immediate interview.'

'You can understand why I'm worried, Mara, I have been through so much to get to her, I don't want to lose her now.'

'You won't lose her; she is quite safe here.' Mara was at her most maternal.

Detty and Marc had gone for a run along the harbour at seven o'clock and weren't back when Mara, who didn't like early mornings, had struggled up at eight. Shortly afterwards when everyone else was still asleep, Mara was consulting with Leyla, the Turkish girl who had arrived to clean the flat, as to how to cope with breakfast for a large and possibly varying number of guests. They had just decided that Leyla should go out to the early morning *Bäckerei* to stock up with rolls and *Viennoiserie*, when the phone rang:

'I have Frau Oberleutnant Malinowska here, Frau Oblova, shall I send her up?'

'Of course, I expect that we can find some coffee.'

'Oh, and by the way, the visitors in the State Apartments locked the doors when they went for their run. I think that they didn't work the exit properly. The young Italian lady and the baby are still locked in. Should I go up and unlock them?'

'Have they tried to get out?'

'Fortunately – no.'

'Well please unlock them at once. We can't have the heir of the von Ritters locked up with an Italiana in the State Apartments, can we? It would look like a Mafia coup.'

'*Genau*, Frau Oblova, that wouldn't do at all. I'll see to it at once.'

She had only just had time to switch on the coffee maker when the entry phone bleeped.

'Irina' said the voice and a moment later Irina Malinowska bounced in. She was resplendent in her uniform. From the green and white cockade to her beautifully polished black leather shoes, she looked like an officer just returned from a week's leave and prepared for a full-dress parade. Nobody would have guessed that she had not been to bed the night before.

'I have some news, Frau Oblova'.

'Before you go any further start calling me Mara—I'm getting old quickly enough without being made to sound like my mother.'

'Perhaps we should get used to calling you Frau Sensky?'

'Get on with the news, will you.'

Privately, it gave Mara a thrill to be called, even in fun, by her not-yet-acquired married name but she wasn't letting on.

'Hadn't we better wait until the others are up?'

'OK, then have some coffee and a brioche and I'll see if there are any signs of life from the sleeping beauties.'

*

Tanya was fretting. She had taken her maternity leave as late as possible but even so inactivity was getting to her. Oddly, she thought, that it was these times when she was on holiday or off duty that she resented her handicap. When she was working, she didn't really miss having normal legs. Her office was so organised that she could reach everything from her wheelchair and the computer was a great leveller.

She had brought the problem of Saskia's daughter home to her apartment overlooking the old Hanseatic harbour. It was a serious sort of holiday task. She had started by getting a list of all the FZW babies and where they had been placed after the liberation. There were just over thirteen hundred in all. As a result of the Winterburg destruction there wasn't much documentation. She had the approximate dates of birth from maturity estimates after the FZW nursery had come into Livonian hands. There were about one hundred and ten babies probably born during the months on either side of the date of Saskia's confinement. Unfortunately, it was the most productive period of the whole ghastly enterprise but even so it was easy to do the first part of narrowing down the possibilities. Excluding the boys, that left just fifty-two girls. Working through these wasn't very straightforward. Because of the racial prejudices of the regime all the mothers had been tall, healthy white girls. The soldier fathers were of similar stereotypes, so there was not much to go on physically. She knew from fragments of surviving records that some of the men had 'serviced' more than one girl. She tried to trace these but, not surprisingly, there was little response. Even if the rapes were carried out under military discipline, the men in question, who probably had other relationships now, would not wish to come forward. In any case, they certainly wouldn't be proud of their role in the FZW.

She then called in a few favours with the media and published announcements to the effect that she wanted to trace one particular girl baby born at the FZW whose natural mother was desperate to find her. Could anybody looking after children born at the FZW between… and… contact her? She set up a special e-mail address, an outline of the reason for the enquiry and a potted biography of herself to establish her good faith. To her surprise, no less than twenty people contacted her and produced their little girls for a DNA check but none was positive.

She was left with thirty-two. She went through their records and those of the institutions who had care of the children, individually and very carefully. She was able to do DNA checks on fifteen. Of the remainder, four of the babies had apparently died, although the evidence was circumstantial. Several of the detainees had also died in uncertain circumstances. Thirteen were left; there was simply no record at all of five and eight had been, or were being, adopted abroad. She was able to contact the adopting parents of some of these but none agreed to have their children DNA tested. She could find no way of checking these thirteen. It was messy and she wasn't used to messy conclusions. She then contacted over fifty adoption agencies in Germany, Poland, the USA and several other possible countries outlining her enquiry. She got frosty or unhelpful responses from most. She wasn't surprised.

She sat frustrated and unhappy over her laptop staring out at the Harbour, wondering how she should tell Detti and Saskia that she had drawn a complete blank. She had just one more thought but it was a long shot. Easing her large bump into her outside wheelchair, she went round to her office in Military Intelligence. She answered all the enquiries about how she was getting on from her colleagues, and fetched Liese's laptop from the strong room. She felt rather guilty but she knew the entry code from her dead colleague. There was just a chance that there might be something useful about the FZW in her private files. When she got into Liese's files, to her disappointment, she found that there wasn't a great deal and most of what there was consisted of war crimes evidence which might possibly be needed in future investigations. There was a file of letters written by Liese informing relatives of the girl detainees who were known to have died. Most of these were recorded on a word processor for posting. One or two had been sent by e-mail presumably because Liese had no postal address. They were sensitive, compassionate and very human. Tanya would have expected no less.

Feeling very sad, she was just about to close the folder when an odd address suddenly struck her. What were relatives of FZW girls doing in Washington DC?

Curiosity alone made her look at the letter. It had nothing to do with FZW and was headed 'TOP SECRET For dispatch and onward transfer via CIA Washington' with the relevant security coding following. The letter was written in English and she read it with mounting curiosity:

Military Intelligence
Freiwehr Livonias

Dear Ms. Klonsky,

Bernadette O'Neill and I heard from your brother, Jeff, of your engagement to Craig. We gather that his fate was still uncertain up until recently. However, when we met Jeff here Bernadette was able to confirm that she had met your fiancé shortly before his death. She also found his body, by accident, shortly after his death. Unfortunately, we can also confirm to you that he had been murdered in Spain. Bernadette only met Craig very briefly but found him an extremely interesting and friendly person.

For reasons that you will understand, we cannot include more details even in a secure letter at present but we both felt that we would like to send our sincerest sympathy for your tragic loss. If you felt that it would be helpful to visit us here in Königshof, we could give you more of the information which we cannot unfortunately include here. It is of course entirely up to you.

I am transmitting this letter on behalf of us both as, in my military position, I have the relevant secure facility.

With kindest regards,
Liese Zahnsdorf
(Major, Freiwehr Livonias)

Attached to the file was a scanned copy of a letter in reply. At the top was a Washington DC address and telephone number. It read:

Dear Major Zahnsdorf,

I was greatly touched by your letter and would like to thank you and Ms. O'Neill for taking the trouble to write to me. I think that I understand, at least in a general way, the reasons for your precautions.

I would very much like to come to Königshof to learn more about Craig's death but Jeff will, I am sure, tell me more when he gets back.

In addition, I have a rather demanding job supervising adoption procedures in the Office of Children's Issues attached to the US State Department which would make it difficult for me to come to Europe at this time.

If I may, I will be in touch again,
With gratitude,
Gail Klonsky

Tanya sat staring at the letters for a long time. Then she looked at her watch. It was just after twelve thirty. It would be seven forty-five in the morning in Washington. Americans get up and start work early. Better at home than at the office. Anyway, she didn't have an office number and she would have to get through the bureaucracy. The thoughts rushed through her head. Nothing ventured …… She dialled the number remembering to insert the 001 before it. She held her breath and prepared her English. A pleasant female voice answered:

'May I speak to Ms Klonsky, please?'

'That's me.'

'I am Tanya Lobokova. I am speaking to you from Königshof, Livonia. I am a Captain in the army here and have taken over the command of military intelligence from Liese Zahnsdorf who wrote to you after your fiancé's death.'

She went on to explain the reason for her call, in detail.

'I am sympathetic and would like to help. There are however serious ethical and professional issues in your request. Also, excuse me, but how can I be sure that you are not a private detective or a spy.'

'If you are willing to take the trouble, go to the Livonian State Information Service which you will find on the web. Give them this number... They will confirm that it is the number of the Military Intelligence Centre. If you ring the number, call collect, you will get through to the front office of my unit. The officer on duty will confirm that I am who I say I am and put you through to me. I am sorry to give you so much trouble but this is the most secure way.'

'OK. Your colleague was very kind writing to me. How is she by the way? You said that you are doing her job. Has she retired? I thought that she was quite young.'

'Liese was killed on active service shortly after your brother was killed. That is why she never wrote to you again. Bernadette O'Neill wanted to write but had no security clearance with your people so, under the circumstances, she decided it was better not to.'

Tanya heard Gail's stifled cry over the 'phone.

'Oh my God! It gets worse and worse. From what you say it seems impossible that you are not genuine but we had better go through the motions. How long will it take you to get to your office?'

'Say an hour. Should be less but it depends a bit on the traffic.'

'Tell me about it! I'll ring in one and a half hours. Are you usually in the office?'

'Not at present, you see I'm on maternity leave but I can go in now.'

'OK'

When she arrived for the second time at the Unit, Jurgen had taken over on the Desk. He adopted partner role more than subordinate.

'What on earth are you doing here? I have been told that you've been in once already this morning. Can't you keep away from the place or don't you trust the rest of us?'

'If I didn't trust you, Feldwebel Müller, I wouldn't be in this state.'

She patted her increasing bump.

'No, it's just a little holiday job that I'm doing and shortly a nice American lady will ring you wanting to know if I am who I say I am.'

'I hope you are or that will put me in a fix' her partner grinned.

'How's your English, by the way? I don't think she speaks German or Russian.'

'It's just dynamite, Ma'am' said Jurgen in a passing attempt at an American accent.

'OK' still laughing Tanya headed for the lift and her office.

Dead on time the phone rang:

'Tanya, it's Gail. Your main man downstairs seems to know you.'

'He sure does.'

Tanya was tempted to add that his knowledge was Biblical as well as professional but decided that it was none of Gail's business and that it would complicate the matter further. Don't joke with foreigners – even nice sympathetic ones – she said to herself.

'Do you have the parents' DNA?'

Tanya was about to ask the same question about the children.

'Yes, we do'.

'We can you send the details to me because I think that I might have solved your problem. At least as far as the identity of the child goes. We have one little girl in the process of being adopted from Livonia with a developmental age which is spot on. We have DNA as part of the adoption medical so if it's a match, we have your couple's daughter.'

'I'll send it to you under security cover straight away.'

'I'll get back as soon as I can. To-day or to-morrow, do you want me to ring you at home?'

'That would be kind and save me sitting here.'

As good as her word, she rang late that evening.'

'Bull's-eye! We have a match. However, the next bit is very tricky but I am prepared to contact the adopting family and see if I can negotiate the child's voluntary release. I shall probably lose my job but I'll try. I would like to give something back in memory of my boyfriend and my brother. Obviously, I can't identify the child or the family to you yet but very fortunately the child is being fostered prior to adoption and it hasn't gone through. I haven't got a legal opinion but I am almost certain that under US law the natural parents have the right to re-possess the child – particularly as she was taken from them by force which would legally constitute abduction, albeit not by the prospective adopters. I'll get back to you as soon as I can.'

*

The von Ritters returned looking muddy but virtuous from their run. Marc, normally sure-footed, had slipped on the wet surface of the narrow wooden bridge over one of the disused sluices to the old docks and taken Detty with him into a foul-smelling icy mud bath at the bottom of the sodden, cold bank.

'*Totti* tells me that they pay money for this sort of thing in Tuscany' she said ruefully before they both went for a quick shower and change.

The others assembled slowly. Saskia still looked as if she was dreaming but perked up considerably once Jurgen arrived. He was bearing several morning papers with, as predicted, pictures of his girlfriend as the heroine of the moment. Irina asked the President's permission to begin:

'Well, I'll start with our nun. Surprise, surprise there is no sister Barbara at Pic Noix and nobody has sought leave of absence to come to Livonia looking for a lost sister. However, there was a rather strange visitor, a Dr Ivanov, who claimed to be a friend of the late Monsignor Pueblo. He had an appointment and had visited the Abbess. She had a 'minor seizure' during the interview and she doesn't remember much of their conversation. It seems an odd coincidence.'

'Can't we get some information out of our friend?' asked Detty 'At least when he's fit enough.'

'Well, that's the second problem. He is ill and getting worse. The doctors seem reasonably sure that he is suffering from *ricin*, or whatever, poisoning from his own white stick. This should be confirmed when all the tests are back. It certainly looks as if he injected himself accidentally in the mêlée. His behaviour would seem to support this as he is refusing to say anything. As he is probably dying and knows it, there is not much we can hold over him to bargain with.'

'I had a word with my boss this morning' said Marc 'he thought that our nun was probably a top man in the old KGB who has now transferred to its namesake in Belarus and the shadowy Lev. He is called Sergei Mikhailovitc Zanedin and, interestingly, he was known to be once very close to Travsky. He used to be purely a puller of puppet strings but we think he may have been in Moltravia in person before the Civil War. It was never known exactly what he was up to but it seems he may have been Saskia's charming torturer, *Seryozhka,* although it is difficult to see what he was doing there. The Pic Noix connection certainly fits, as does Saskia's description. I also spoke to Lawri in Lübeck and he agreed independently with Brigadegeneral Kramm's view.'

'So, we have gamekeeper and poacher in agreement' said Detty.

*

The plain grey Audi drew into the Cathedral close at Bialovsk before the autumn dawn. A well-preserved man who might have been in his late seventies got out. He put on his overcoat, scarf and black Trilby hat as a precaution against the piercing cold and walked towards the West Door. There were lights beginning to show, one by one, in the Cathedral in preparation for the seven-thirty workers' Mass. Reaching the atrium, the newcomer carefully removed his hat, and went into the Cathedral. He took a seat in the back and knelt in prayer for some minutes. Finishing his prayer, he sat back on the seat deep in thought, his head held in his hands. The Sacristan crossed the Nave and spoke quietly to the stranger.

'If you are here for the Mass, *mein Herr*, it is in the Lady Chapel at the East End.'

'Thank you' said the man turning towards the Sacristan 'but I only came in for a private prayer.'

'I'm so sorry that I disturbed you, Your Eminence, I didn't recognise you in the poor light and your plain...'

'You were doing your job, being welcoming to visitors for prayer. Thank you for taking the trouble.'

The Cardinal raised his hand in blessing, moved into the Aisle, genuflected, turned and left the Cathedral. He put on his hat and walked across to the line of houses a couple of hundred metres away. He went up to one door and rang. A woman opened it.

'Good morning, Your Eminence, thank you for coming.'

'You said it was best to be early and I have taken you at your word. How is he?'

'Very weak, I'm afraid. I think that he is sinking quite fast. But his mind is clear and he will be pleased to see you. He is at his best in the early morning that's why I said to come early.'

She led him into the dining room of the house re-arranged as a makeshift bedroom. Bishop Majorowski's fragile head barely indented the neatly pumped-up pillows. On seeing the Cardinal his face broke into a smile.

'Very good of you to come, Cardinal. Please forgive me for not standing. It is always a pleasure but I think this time it's a special privilege. I know that you are pre-occupied and troubled by recent events.'

'I felt that I wanted to see you again very much, Andrei, we have been through so much together. But perhaps also I needed to see you now anyway.'

'Can you tell me about it?'

For some minutes the Cardinal described recent events. The he outlined what he proposed to do.

'I want to offer Alexandra Kulanova and Jurgen Holberg marriage and Nuptial Mass in the Cathedral. I am told that they wish sincerely for a Catholic wedding. There is talk of a joint wedding with Tamara Oblova and David Sensky. I am troubled that I want so much to do this to make amends to my conscience after the scene in the Cathedral.

However, whether it's joint or separate, I wonder about the past history of the brides – unusually the grooms hardly present any problem. What do you think?'

The old man smiled gently.

'I think it is a wonderful idea. From what I hear Saskia is very devout and has performed a miracle saving the innocent in the Cathedral and I know Mara well. She is a good honest girl and she has been through a lot. But if your position and theirs is troubling you, go to The Office. You know the Cardinal well, get his view and if possible, support, but I'm sure it will be allowed.'

'Very well. Thank you. One more question. If it goes ahead, I would like to ask your auxiliary, Bishop Höfer, if he would act as my Deacon for the Mass. He knows Tamara well and I think that he would like to be involved. Would you have any objection?'

'Of course not, but I don't think that he will be my auxiliary for very long, if, of course, the Holy Father confirms the appointment.'

After a prayer, the Cardinal sadly departed.

The following morning the Chaplain brought a message to the archbishop to say that Bishop Majorowski had died peacefully in his sleep during the night.

When he heard it, a moist eyed Cardinal whispered to himself: *'Nunc dimittis servum tuum, Domine, secundum verbum tuum in pace*[26]

Rest well, old friend.'

*

It was good to be back at Oberdorf. Somehow Detty could always relax with Gianna and Niki in the Herrenhaus and the peace made study easy. At the moment, however, despite the increasing cold of late autumn, she was working on the summer house. It was nearly finished. The foundation was firm and double panels lined the walls. The floor was of sound new boards and the glazier had been while she was in Königshof to double glaze the windows. Detty looked with

---

[26] Lord, now lettest thou thy servant depart in peace according to thy word.

some regret at the beautiful work which had been done by Viktor in happier days. Why did a bastard with so much talent, vocal and practical, have to become a spy and a crook? She got on with oiling the oak floor. She was still wondering whether a piano would survive in the summerhouse. The suspended floor and double glazing and panelling had been done with this in mind and heating was to be installed but she still wasn't sure. She enjoyed going to the *Schloss* to practise but she was conscious that she effectively kept Sophie and Max out of their living room. They had never objected but it would still be convenient to have a modest piano nearer the Herrenhaus. Her *Handy* rang interrupting her reverie.

'Detty, it's Tanya. Very good news. We've got Jurgen and Saskia's daughter. Well, not exactly but she is being fostered by an American couple in South Carolina. I haven't told them yet – I wanted to have a word with you first. How's your fund for victims of the war doing?'

'Pretty well – we have some money left after the current applicants are accommodated – why?'

'I'll explain. The foster parents had hoped to adopt the little girl but fortunately the process hadn't gone very far and they acknowledge that it is only right that she should return to her natural parents here. They probably have no right to retain her under US law anyway but it will be better if it's done voluntarily. Problem is, however, that Jurgen and Saskia will need two very expensive triple air fares plus transits and help with formalities. I would try and do it but I'm very near term and the quacks are muttering about induction. I don't want to leave them in the lurch.'

'Leave it to me. I'm not sure how to fix it all but it certainly seems a reasonable, if unusual, call on the fund. I will also try and get them some help with the formalities at this end. Meanwhile get on with the job in hand and I don't mean Military Intelligence.'

A very unmilitary giggle came from the end of the line.

'I should be terrified, particularly with my disability, but I'm hugely excited.'

'All the very best.'

She rang off and sat and thought. She should have been working at

'*Und ob die Wolke*[27]' but somehow getting Jurgen and Saskia to America took precedence.

She asked Saskia to meet her in Königshof the following day. On her way she called at the Hoftheatre to collect her post. Coming out of the theatre she passed Julia Kitze on her way to a rehearsal of the Mozart Mass for next Sunday's concert.

'Hi, Julia, I haven't yet had a chance to thank you for a splendid performance in the Schubert Mass. I am sorry that it was overshadowed by other events.'

'It was still quite something to sing with the Philharmonica and Hank Schliessen, in spite of the interruptions.'

'I bet it was' said Detty, smiling, remembering the flirtation in the Sacristy.

'I'm glad it didn't spoil it completely. One more thing – have you ever thought about learning *Brangäne?*'

The youngster went rather pale and eyed Detty curiously:

'No, not yet. Surely, it's a bit early. Do you really think I could?'

'Just might be worth seeing if it lies comfortably for you. Talk it over with Edit, she's normally game to try anything. You could start with the second act passage.'

A puzzled and somewhat elated young Julia headed into the shopping streets with no idea of where she was going. Detty headed for the Café Daina to meet Saskia. Saskia had come in for an interview for a job which she had applied for, anticipating her qualification. The physio job would be at Sovils but the interviews were done in the capital. Saskia seemed very positive about the interview which had gone well. Casually over a second coffee, Detty explained, 'purely hypothetically of course' that if there was any expense involved in finding the little girl -the War Fund would be glad to help if needed.

'It hasn't arisen yet. We are still just hoping – but thank you.'

*

They had become friends – close friends, but even so Saskia never expected this.

---

27 'And over the clouds' aria from Der Freischutz

'I want to get married very soon' said Mara out of the blue 'So do you. You don't have to agree to this and I won't be offended, if you don't but would you consider our getting married on the same day and sharing our nuptial mass? I mean I had it in mind that perhaps it could be quite quiet perhaps in the Commanderie chapel or your own parish church.'

Saskia looked staggered.

'But… but you're the first lady of Livonia – there will be all the VIPs –you won't be allowed to have a quiet wedding and surely we can't be a part of that?'

'Hang that. Livonia is a Republic. The President's daughter is a citizen, so are you. Your practical service to the country has been more than mine.'

'But I've had a baby.'

'As a result of abduction and rape. OK, it turned out well but it can hardly have been lust on your part. I suppose we'd better ask the men but are you prepared to give it a go? I'll have a word with *Vati* but I usually get what I want as long as it isn't treason and doesn't breach the Constitution or the Bill of Rights. Are you on?'

'I am not sure. I am not sure about a church wedding either. I want one very much but I went to Confession at home last week. We have a young priest and given my unusual situation he seemed unsure of what to do.'

There was uncertainty about the weddings and both the girls were worried that their very public misfortunes would prevent them from having the church wedding which they dearly wanted. There was a awkward pause for several weeks into the autumn. Then one day Nicklaus appeared from his study grinning from ear to ear. Mara looked quizzically at her father.

'Can you get in touch with Saskia, David and Jurgen? There is something that I would like to share with all of you.'

'Saskia's at College working hard before her final physiotherapy exams but I am sure that they could come down this evening, particularly if you asked them to. David is picking me up at seven anyway.'

*

The four gathered, mystified, in the penthouse drawing room.
Nicklaus came in carrying a letter.

'This is from Cardinal Kunz. I would like to read it to you all;

Dear President,

Thank you for your letter concerning the forthcoming marriage of your daughter, Tamara Nicolaevna to David Sensky and also mentioning the possibility of a joint ceremony to include the forthcoming marriage of Alexandra Kulanova to Jurgen Holberg.

As you say in your letter both the young ladies in question have very unusual histories which you have described to me in detail. You ask whether under the circumstances they would be eligible for the Sacrament of Marriage in Holy Church.

I have given the matter much thought, and as you will know, I was personally involved at one point. Because of this and because the circumstances in each case are so unusual, I felt it necessary to consult my friend and colleague The Prefect for the Congregation of the Doctrine of the Faith. He gave a very detailed ruling on the theological aspects of these young peoples' unique situation. I may say that I was very relieved that in the end he entirely agreed with my conclusions and plan. I will not recap the entire ruling but just give you the conclusions.

Both the ladies in this case were victims of abduction and assault. The perpetration of abduction does of course rule out Roman Catholic marriage but these two were sinned against, not sinning. The previous birth of a child out of wedlock would normally be a serious sin and impediment but the circumstances surrounding the birth of Frau Kulanova's child left her entirely innocent and she is now to marry the child's father. We have therefore obtained a dispensation from the Holy Father that both these marriages may take place, jointly if they so wish, with the full Sacramental Rite of the Church. There is a provision that all four parties are baptised Roman Catholics, that they have attended regular confession and the normal pre-marital instruction. These latter provisions are, of course, entirely usual.

Finally, I would like to add a personal request. I committed a grave injustice towards Frau Kulanova in the Cathedral when I publicly accused her of sacrilege. I now freely confess my error and recant. I would like to try to make some amends if she will permit me to do so.

If the two couples are willing, I would like to celebrate their marriage and Nuptial High Mass with myself as Celebrant in the Cathedral of Santa Maria Regina Coeli, Königshof on a date of mutual convenience to be arranged. I sincerely hope this is acceptable to them. Unless I hear to the contrary, my chaplain will be pleased to conduct the normal pre-marital instruction privately when mutually convenient. I have asked him to contact Frau Oblova to arrange this.

+ Martin Kunz Primate

'Poor man! How could he have known?'

Saskia had broken the silence.

Mara smiled:

'So much for our quiet wedding! High Mass in the Mother Cathedral of the country with the Cardinal Archbishop as celebrant! I'm relieved and delighted that some of my private life seems to have passed on the nod.'

'It's a wonderful gesture and of course a great thrill' said Saskia 'but it scares me a lot and there are problems.

She looked worried and thoughtful.

'Can I have a bit of time to think about it?'

'Of course,' Mara looked crestfallen.

'Just wait a bit and we need to discuss it together.'

'We need to be too busy to get scared. Do you write the acceptance and thanks, *Vati*, or should we?'

'I think that you should both write and accept and thank him, if, of course you decide that is what you wish. Meanwhile I will get hold of Horst Miklov, the Archbishop's Chaplain, I know him, and we will start on the practicalities.'

*

Back in the Hansehaus drawing room, Mara felt flat. Her huge elation at the high absolution that had been freely given, gave way to worry. She loved Saskia but knew that she was fretting but couldn't discuss it. If she really thought that they must have a quiet ceremony apart from David and her then of course she would understand. But was that it? It could be all sorts of things –safety for instance. Not surprising- but it did appear that at least for the present, the security threats had been dealt with. It might be the media but Saskia had dealt with her sudden celebrity status well and handled the press and television like a practised pro. Money – yes- that could well be the problem. How could she unravel the conundrum?

There was an obvious answer. She reached for the telephone and dialled Detty's private Krenek number. To her relief she got straight through.

'Detty, I've got another favour to ask' she explained the problem,

'Sure, I'll talk to her again. The problem is that I have already, in a vague sort of way, offered her money from the War Fund. I am not quite sure how we can dress up something for the wedding without offending or patronising them but I think that I can help. Marc's getting back from Ingolstadt on Wednesday and Jurgen kindly offered to bring him down here when he comes to look at the leak in the attic at the *Schloss*. They could do with the work even though it's a long way from Seesovils. I think that they are meeting for a snack and a coffee first in town. I said Jurgen can stay the night if they are late. If I can penetrate the *Bundeswehr*, I will tip Marc the wink and see if he can get to the bottom of Saskia's problem via Jurgen.'

'That's wonderful' Mara felt mightily relieved.

*

Jurgen realised that Saskia was very concerned and guessed what was troubling her.

As they got into the lift he said:

'It's money, isn't?'

She nodded miserably.

'Nothing must get in the way of the possibility that we might get our baby back but I realise that it may cost a fortune. We can get help from Detty's fund but we can't spend that on our wedding. There is not much work for you and I'm earning virtually nothing yet. We can't spend money on a fashionable wedding as well, it just wouldn't be right. We just don't know what any of this is going to cost.'

They got into the car in silence. As they left the western suburbs of the city, Jurgen said:

'As you know I am going down to Krenek to look at some work this afternoon. I agreed to meet Marc von Ritter at the airport and give him a lift. If you agree I might talk to him.'

'I don't like to land our problems on him but I suppose it might help. He's kind and sensible.'

When they got home to Seesovils, it was blowing an icy gale off the Baltic bringing flurries of snow down the village street to their apartment over the builder's storehouse. Jurgen lit the wood stove to aid the creaking, struggling central heating and then fired up his computer. There were two advertisements for trips to the Caribbean and then underneath there it was.

'Found – ring me. Tanya' and her home number

He rushed over to Saskia, hugged her off the floor and swung her round to see the message. In an instant the gloom was forgotten. He looked at his watch, decided that it was a reasonable time to call and picked up the phone.

Tanya confirmed the news and gave them the details. Like lottery winners, and this was far more important than any lottery, they couldn't really believe it until Tanya had confirmed it. But it was true, really true; their daughter had been found in America.

18
A STONY PATH

America is God's crucible, the great Melting-Pot

Zangwill: The Melting Pot

'This is kind of you- you have saved Detty the double journey.'

'Not a bit. I hope that we can give the College a good quote for the work and, I don't know whether you have spoken to Frau Bernadette but we had some good news yesterday. We think that we have traced our daughter.'

'That's great. What happens next?'

'We shall have to go to America.'

'It sounds as if you're in for a busy time – and a lot of expense.'

'I'll say – that's a bit of a problem although Frau Bernadette has said the War Fund can help but now there is the Wedding. Saskia would love to do it with Mara. She adores her and would revel in the pageantry but the expense is a problem. We would have to share the cost and then there is a dress for her. She would have to have something half decent to go to the Altar alongside Mara. There is all this as well as America.'

'Hang on a bit. Let's tackle America first. The Fund is for people who have suffered under the Fascists and that certainly includes you both.

'Oh yes, but that should be for the homeless and the starving, we can't really claim on that and certainly not for a wedding.'

'Isn't losing your daughter comparable to being homeless or starving? And anyway, thank God, there aren't so many as there were destitute in Livonia now. I am sure that under completely normal rules you could have a grant towards the cost of getting your daughter back.'

Jurgen was silent. They stopped at the *Chakta*, an old Polish cabin on the road out to Krenek and ordered coffee and *sernek*, the Polish cheesecake. Then Jurgen returned to the problem:

'But if we get money from the War Fund, how do we justify appearing later in a society wedding – unless Saskia wears rags and I would hate that and so would she.'

'Look, Detty says that we have many families here in Livonia who are not destitute but still have great needs and who are too proud to take advantage of the Fund. What better role models could they have than you and Saskia? She is a national heroine, you abandoned the bastards and faced great danger for what you believed was right.'

He thought for a long time.

'I see what you mean but it still could be misrepresented.'

'I think that we can see that it isn't. Let's get back and talk to Detty. I have some excellent *Zwetschgenwasser* at Krenek and I would like you to try it.'

*

The fire was blazing in the Krenek apartment and steaming *spaghetti alla carbonara* was served by a proud Gianna. Detty stretched back in her chair and took her son on her knee.

'You're a true von Ritter. It won't be long before you are tucking into the pasta. Gianna, it was marvellous. Will you do it again when *Totti* comes in a few weeks?'

'*Prego, Signora, voluntieri!*'

They sat contentedly over coffee and plum brandy.

'I have arranged a grant of €15,000 from the Fund if your American trip comes off and I'm sure it will now, Jurgen. It may not be enough but we can settle that later. Can you get Saskia down here in the next few days – after work would be fine? There is something I want to put to her'.

'But you didn't even know about the problem' said the astonished Jurgen,

'Marc and I are telepathic' laughed Detty 'we had to be when I was in The Farm.'

Two days later they sat again by the fire. Saskia had driven down after work. This time they had eaten wild boar from the Krenek estate and Marc was serving Jameson Reserve after dinner.

After a suitable relaxed pause, Detty said, 'Now I want to ask you both a favour. We need to give a wedding present to Mara and David. And we would like to give one to you both too. I have a relationship with the fashion house of Lanoure in Paris. I am mainly well known to them because I write off their models in several difficult situations. They seem to forgive me and even think that it adds a little *je ne sais quoi* to their distinguished enterprise. If you agree, I would like to give you both Lanoure dresses, to your taste of course, for your wedding. How about it?'

Saskia rose to the occasion:

'Frau Bernadette, I am not often speechless but every time you do something incredible, I am struck dumb. What can I say? Your suggestion is amazing, amazingly kind, amazingly generous and amazingly surprising. Jurgen will probably say that I shouldn't dream of accepting but I will. Thank you.'

Jurgen bemused said nothing. Detty went on: 'There are two more things that you need to know. The first is that Mara has received a very large gift from an anonymous donor which will meet the costs of the weddings and a reception in the Commanderie. The donor made it clear that it was intended for all four of you. It would obviously be improper to make the weddings a charge on the public coffers. The second thing is very tiresome. Lanoure will not produce model gowns of any sort without a personal fitting. Therefore, tediously, the six of us will need to spend a few days in Paris to get things sorted out. We can arrange a date after you have been to America. This also is, of course, part of your Wedding Presents. Now I must fly rapidly to Ireland as a certain other, very important lady is engaged at Newcastle in the Fighting Fifth Hurdle. Wish her luck, it would be great to lift a race named after a English regiment. I shall be home in Kildare with my family for a week first. We can sort everything out when you are back and I am back.'

*

They had wanted it so much but now it seemed unreal. At first Saskia was excited: 'I've always wanted to see America' she said to Jurgen 'But is the money enough?'

They had all met for dinner at Golabki.

'Do you know your daughter's name?'

'Not yet – we were going to talk about it when we get to the States.'

'Well, I thought we might set up a special fund for her and all the children who suffered from the regime and war. Would you mind her being used as a symbol, a sort of poster girl?'

Jurgen looked at Saskia who answered with decision.

'Not at all, if it helps. Our story is public now anyway.'

*

It had been raining in Washington when they made their way to Gail's office and more heavy rain down the east coast was forecast. Gail and her Secretary were warm and welcoming, getting them to shed their wet clothes and warm up with a hot coffee and muffins before sitting them down to talk.

'It's an unusual situation. Almost all the cases that I deal with involve people wanting to adopt into the USA. You, of course, want to take a child out of America and an additional unusual feature is that she is not currently a US citizen. The last part may help but it does make it all rather complicated. However, you have absolute proof of biological parenthood and I have got hold of the best adoption attorney in Washington who will sort out the legal side. With any luck it should be plain sailing. Leah should be here soon to meet you.'

Gail then guided them through some of the paperwork until the door opened and the secretary announced:

'Mrs Hayward-Thompson is here, Gail.'

'Ah Leah. That's great.'

Leah Hayward-Thompson filled the doorway. The huge African American attorney had an ear-to-ear smile and a rather incongruous Bronx Hispanic accent. She wasn't Saskia's idea of a lawyer. Physically she seemed more like a Blues singer than an advocate. However, after a few minutes, Saskia knew why Gail had asked for her help. She was friendliness itself and explained the legal complications of the situation in plain language and how she had been able to resolve them. She would come with them to the small township near the Texas Louisiana state line where the foster family lived not as they had at first thought South Carolina. They were to fly to Alexandria then hire a car for the rest of the journey. The family were expecting them.

The meeting with the sadly reluctant family was short but friendly enough. Maureen, the wife agreed, readily enough, that Holly should have her real Mom and Dad, although they loved her and had looked forward to her growing up with them.

'I have explained to her that she will be going to live with her real Mom and Dad but I'm not sure that she really understands. She is a bit clingy. But you want to see her. She's lovely but you two are very handsome so I suppose that's natural.'

'You have been so generous and it must be a great disappointment for you. I wish that we could express how much we appreciate your sacrifice. Thank you.'

Maureen wept a little and then murmured: 'It is only right. We have a conscience.'

'Just one question – has Holly been baptised?'

'No, we were going to arrange it once the papers were through.'

Saskia couldn't believe that the little girl who shyly peeped round the door really was, her – their- daughter. However, she had the look of Jurgen about her. Leah was the only dry-eyed person in the room as they loaded the car with Holly's toys and possessions and drove away. Holly didn't cry but she looked bewildered and forlorn. Saskia talked to her in English but added the occasional German endearment. The little girl gazed at the strange woman wide-eyed until she dozed off against Saskia's thigh.

The rain that had been threatening all day under a leaden sky had started in earnest as they began the journey back to Alexandria. At last it became so heavy that it formed a grey impenetrable blanket. Jurgen peered into the gloom with the wipers losing their battle against the water sluicing like a weir over the windshield. After about an hour the terrible weather cleared slightly – enough at least to see the red and blue strobe light bar of the police car pulling them over.

'Perhaps they've got some advice about the state of the roads' Jurgen said to Leah who was beside him. Saskia was in the back with Holly who was sleeping soundly. Leah didn't have time to reply before the police car door opened and a gorilla figure in uniform weather clothes and gun emerged.

'Out! Hands on the roof' came the order.

Saskia started to protest that the child was asleep only to have the gun prodded in her face. This time Holly did begin to howl.

'ID?'

They produced passports, visas and Jurgen his driving licence. The gorilla studied them for some minutes before declaring:

'These don't mean nothing to me.'

'We have a US visas here – look'.

The gorilla grunted: 'What about the kid? She isn't yours-right? You kidnapped her.'

Leah explained that she was an attorney and that Jurgen and Saskia were legally in charge of Holly.

'Ma'am' he said sarcastically 'Do you expect me to believe the word of some *schvartze* and two *heinies* who've obviously kidnapped an American kid. I'm taking you to the Police Department.'

The next few hours were a nightmare. At the police station, gorilla sent for the captain and there was hope that the senior law officer would set things straight. Not a bit of it: 'I am arresting you all on a charge of kidnapping and unlawfully abducting an American juvenile. There are further indictments of issuing false papers and falsely impersonating a lawyer. Hand over all your valuables and possessions.'

They protested loudly but had no option but to give everything they had to the Deputies. Worst of all, Holly screaming was taken away. They were then handcuffed.

'Strip search the man,' ordered the captain.

'I will get a woman in to strip search the women. Take them to the jail.'

Saskia lay alone in her cell anxiously waiting the humiliation which she knew too well from the past. At least they were looking for a woman to do it. Nobody came except to rattle the corridor spyholes at regular intervals. She dropped into a fitful sleep. She woke terrified but still fully dressed in the damp cold refrigerator of a cell. Her experiences in the FZW of the *Frauendienst* came flooding back to her. She screamed. Nobody came – not even to rattle the spy hole. After hours of shivering dozing a new Officer unlocked the door and, wordlessly, shoved in a bowl of cold glutinous spaghetti. Saskia was getting hungry but felt nauseated by the grey formless dollop which had been put deliberately on the foul-smelling stainless-steel WC top. She tipped it into the bowl.

She had no idea of the time. She seemed to have escaped the strip searching – perhaps it had been forgotten. Her watch had been taken with the rest of her possessions. It could be morning, midday. Time had passed slowly and the only light in the cell, a dim lamp in the ceiling under a grid had been on since she arrived. She didn't know whether the dreadful meal was intended to be breakfast or something later.

She worried what they had done with little Holly and the worry made her think that she would go mad. She wondered if she could beat her brains out on the mud-coloured plastic wall. Probably not and that wouldn't help Holly. It was all her fault. If they hadn't come Holly would be at home happy with her loving foster family. Saskia felt so guilty.

It seemed ages then there was a rattle and the door swung back. A new unfamiliar Officer motioned to her to hold out her hands and snapped handcuffs on them. He dragged her back along the corridor to the main building. The captain was standing by the door of his office. To her amazement he just said: 'You're lucky. You can go.'

'But…' she muttered 'my daughter, my man, Leah … my things. How…?

'Look, lady, you're lucky. If you don't want to spend 15 years for kidnapping and child trafficking in the State Pen, you won't chance your luck and you'll get out of town fast. If you hang around here, I'll arrange an indictment so long that it will reach the next state.'

Dazed, Saskia found herself pitch-forked out of the door into the bright Texas sunshine, cool after the storm. She tried to take control of the situation. She had to get help but she had no money, no phone, no possessions and, worst of all, no daughter and no partner. She stood by the side of the road trying to think. They had let her go – but why? Presumably because as a foreigner with no money, limited English and no papers, they must have felt that she couldn't be a threat to them. How could she do anything – turn this round?

She stood for a long time at the roadside amidst the drenched scrubby sand. Suddenly she decided. Reluctant as she was, she must use the only asset that she had left. She must hitch a lift away from this place and get help. She thought that she had seen a main highway about two miles to her left as they were taken in the police van. She cursed herself for not paying more attention. She turned left and started to walk. To her great relief after about twenty minutes, she saw the cars. Not the procession of slow vehicles that characterised many US states but fast traffic, fast almost by European standards. This had to be the road.

She was out of breath as she arrived at the junction and started thumbing. She knew that she didn't look great but she had tried to tidy her hair and knew that her tall leggy athlete's figure would stand out at the side of the freeway. Cars speeded pass with boring regularity. The road was flat and straight and nobody slowed down. She started to walk westwards. She didn't really think that she could walk nearly two hundred miles to Alexandria but it seemed better than walking deeper into Texas. Two hours passed as she trudged on and she was now really tired and horribly hungry. She felt desperate. She was alone in a hostile land and had lost everything dear to her. Then in her misery she saw in front of her a sign that there was a commercial rest area. At first it didn't mean much. She trudged on helplessly but as she got close, she realised that here there were people there that she could talk to and she might even get help. She rehearsed her story in English until she thought it sounded as good as she could get it. She wondered which truck to choose. At the first one she said very politely: 'I need to get out of town. Can you help me please?'

'I don't need no foreign hooker – get home.'

She went round the corner to a large red tanker. The driver was leaning against the truck step eating an obscenely large hot dog. Saskia felt her empty stomach turn over. Shaking she repeated her polite request. He burst into a smile to die for: 'Where are you from, Ma'am?' he asked.

'Livonia' she replied expecting the inevitable "Where the heck is that?"

But no:

'My Granddad came from Danzig or Gdansk I guess you have to call it now.'

'What's it like in Livonia now?'

'Much better' she stammered.

'I guess so- but what are you doing here?'

Then it all flooded out – every detail.

'I've heard about that sort of trick. I'm from Philadelphia myself but they have some funny goings-on down here – usually they go for blacks and spics but I guess that they felt that you, as foreigners, were fair game. What do you want to do?'

'Get away, find a number, make a phone call.'

'Uncle Sam ought to be ashamed of this – I'll help you.'

'But I've got no money, no ID, no 'phone numbers.'

'You've got a contact in Washington?'

She nodded: 'Gail Klonsky'

'Can you remember her department?'

'She looks after adoptions in the State Department – Office of Children? Something like that.'

He sat over his smart phone clicking away for several minutes.

'How about State Department –Office of Children's Issues?'
'Sounds right.'
'I'll call it.'
Saskia sat, tense, while he punched in the number.
'I want to speak to Ms. Klonsky.'
There was hope after all then:
'When will she be out of the meeting?'
'This is very urgent. A child is in grave danger.'
That did it, he turned to Saskia, 'They are getting her out of the meeting – apparently it is very important so I had to come a bit heavy.'
'You are a saint – I can't thank you enough.'
'Here she is- take the phone.'
'Gail, it's Saskia. Something dreadful has happened – now listen.'
She told the whole story breathlessly.
Gail only said, 'Where are you?'
Saskia turned to him and asked: 'Where are we?'
'Mason Truck Rest Area – Interstate 11 interchange1011.'
Saskia duly repeated the location.
'Stay right there. I'll get the FBI.'
'Will they be quick?'
'Sure – after what you have told me but they have to come from Alexandria'.

She felt relieved and very hungry. Her guardian angel, Brett, offered to get her a hot dog and she accepted and munched gratefully.

Gail had been as good as her word in and in just under an hour, two FBI cars, sirens blasting, turned into the rest area beside them. The Special Agent, the senior cop, was wide without being fat, short but with huge presence. She reckoned that it was good to have him on your team. She had never seen the famous shield which he flashed at her before except in films. *Fidelity, Bravery Integrity* –she sure needed all of them. Despite the dreadful situation, she felt a Hollywood thrill of unreality. But these were the real people, they were as courteous as the local police had been brutal. They asked her to describe what had happened to herself and her companions. As they listened to Saskia's story their faces became more and more grave.

At the end, the Special Agent, the senior cop, said: 'We know that your presence in the US is entirely legal, that Advocate Hayward-Thompson is truly a genuine attorney accompanying you and that you are fit and proper people to have charge of the little girl, Holly. Mrs Klonsky copied all the relevant papers to us by e-mail at Alexandria. So, what the heck is going on? It sounds, Ma'am, as if the County Police have committed several felonies and that the Captain and these Deputies will be the ones facing an "indictment sheet long enough to reach into the next State". Come with us.'

The expression on the captain's face, when Saskia reappeared at the Police Department and Jail in the company of a group of FBI agents almost, but not quite, made the whole experience worth –while. At least she knew now that the USA was not a re-incarnation of Travsky's Moltravia.

Fidelio had become part of the Livonian national mythology after the nation-wide broadcasts of Detty's production after the Liberation. When Leah and Jurgen, who had still been locked in their cells, appeared rapidly in the front hall without handcuffs, it made Saskia think of the equally rapid appearance of the prisoners in *Fidelio* after the arrival of Don Fernando aka the Special Agent in Charge. Equally quickly the captain was convinced that his best bet in a sticky situation was to co-operate fully. The seized property was returned to them, first their passports, then their money, their personal possessions, and the car. After a longer wait, another car drew up and a pale and tearful Holly appeared in the charge of a woman in civilian clothes.

The drive back to Alexandria was accomplished with the comforting presence of an FBI police car escorting them front and back. It was too late for a flight to Washington and the Police took them to the Cherish Hotel where they were given, true to its name, the best suite. Saskia, as always anxious about money, protested that they couldn't possibly afford such luxury but the Charge Agent only smiled:

'There will be no cost, Ma'am, this is the least Uncle Sam can do after what has happened to you.'

Feeling calm at last, Saskia checked Holly's clothes and found everything provided by the foster family was still there. Then she borrowed a swimsuit for herself and holding Holly's hand, they went down to the Spa Tub and together got in the water. This worked as Holly gradually lost her terrified expression and started giggling. It was the best sound that Saskia had heard since she had arrived in the USA.

They got out of the tub and holding hands went into the changing cubicle. Saskia had nearly finished dressing Holly when there was a rap at the door. A woman's voice cried hysterically, 'Can you help? I think he's drowning – round in the swimming pool.'

Saskia remembered her English and said quickly to Holly: 'Wait here, darling, I will be back in a moment.'

When she got through the changing room to the swimming pool, it was empty. There was clearly nobody drowning but when she returned there was no Holly. Saskia, exhausted, cried out in anguish then dashed from the pool complex desperately looking for her daughter. She was nowhere.

Frantic, she dashed round the hotel.

'My little girl – she's gone. Have you seen her?'

Receptionists and managers looked sceptical and then concerned. They scanned the closed-circuit TV screens. The cameras in the pool complex had gone blank. They had been expertly covered. This confirmed Saskia's worst fears. The duty hotel manager was a very young man but calm and efficient.

'This looks like a professional snatch. I will ring Jackson Street at once. The FBI are already involved. We will go to them at the Resident Agency not the police.'

*

Saskia lost the next two days. She was going out of her mind. She had fleeting images of being whirled from place to place. Snatches of grim urgent phrases from agent Willy Navarro. Something about Washington, Haiti and the trade. Then there was a flight. Jurgen was there. They were bundled onto the aircraft. She just held Jurgen's hand. They landed flashing up to the buildings of a huge airport – much larger than Alexandria.

She was brought back to reality by Agent Navarro. 'Washington are involved and it will be a big raid. I'm sorry, Ma'am, but you can't come with us. It's not right for a lady. Mr Holberg can come if he wants —we may need him if we find Holly.'

She suddenly became determined: 'If my daughter is there, I'm coming too and please remember, that I alone am her legal guardian – at least until we are married'.

'OK then perhaps you should come – if we find her your comforting may be needed – but it won't be a candy party. Perhaps Mr Holberg should wait in your place? There might be a message which he can respond to.'

Inside the large courtyard were trucks and men so heavily equipped with machine pistols, body armour and numerous unidentified weapons that Saskia wondered how they could move. She also wondered how all this was about finding her daughter. Probably not and that wouldn't help Holly, her poor little lost girl.

As they waited for everything to be ready, Agent Navarro explained some of the mystery.

'For some time now, we have been investigating disappearing children. It just so happens that your daughter has been added to the list just at the moment that we were ready to pounce. I am afraid it is a terrible story. They steal children in Mexico, the Caribbean and in the USA. Mostly they are from the poorer parts but foreigners have also been targeted. I suspect that your friends in the State Police may have tipped them off about you – for money or revenge or both.'

Saskia could hardly dare ask but steeled herself: 'What happens to them when they are stolen?'

'We don't know everything but it appears that they are 'sorted' here in Miami. Most are the sent to Haiti. From there some go for illegal adoption in other countries and some are used to make films.'

Saskia knew the answer before she croaked the question: 'What sort of films?'

'Paedophilic pornography,' Navarro said flatly.

'What happens to the ones who stay here?'

Navarro didn't answer and turned his attention to stare intently at the preparations for the raid.

The equipment and FBI SWAT men had disappeared completely into anonymous looking trucks purporting to be delivering office furnishings. The sign writing on the trucks gave the name 'Dolson Inc.' and underneath 'Out of hours service a specialty' – that at least was true, thought Saskia. She was encouraged to sit in the cab of the second truck. Navarro hinted that her perplexed expression would help the disguise. With her stomach cramped in fear, she hardly focussed on the trip. They arrived in front of huge gates with a dark mass of a sort of warehouse behind. The deployment for the raid was silent. She was hardly aware of the SWAT agents noiselessly disembarking as she waited in the half-light in the darkened cab.

The climax was short. There was a crash as the steel gates were forced.

'That's done by the breachers – they are trained to get through anything'.

Just after that was the huge flash and bang from inside the building. Saskia was terrified that the building had exploded. Novarro reassured her.

'That's just the stun grenades – they don't hurt –just turn off the muscles.'

There were a few shots and a short burst of machine gun far from the building.

Saskia was in a whirl. Her English couldn't follow what she was being told and she wasn't sure that she would have understood even in Russian or German. It seemed though that Navarro, who remained sitting beside her, apparently calm and confident, as the SWATs had gone in, was still quite relaxed. After a seeming hour which was probably only a few minutes, Navarro turned to her.

'I must go in now. I'll be back and let you know what we find.'

'Is Holly in there?'

'We can't be sure but she may be.'

'I must come too then.'

'But, but – we don't know what we will find inside. '

The macho Special Agent seemed nonplussed.

'I must come if my daughter is – could be – in there.'

He paused then spoke on his phone: 'I see, I see but the lady wants to come. Are any of them alive?'

Cold fear gripped Saskia.

'Some are then. OK I'll tell her'.

'Ma'am, you can come but I warn you, you will see terrible things.'

'I don't care. I must see if Holly is there.'

They followed the SWATs route in. The first part was an office that had been turned over by the raid but seemed much like any other. The desk drawers and filing cabinets and their contents were sprawled across the floor. They went through a door. On the other side of the door, it was like a butcher's shop or rather an abattoir. All around lay buckets with pieces of meat, carcasses lay on slabs split open. Organs were in solution perfused with bubbles rising to the surface of glass containers. The horror took a moment to sink in. The body parts were human – worse- they were childrens. Saskia wanted to scream and then she vomited. She was grabbed by Novaro who dragged her to a second door. This time there was noise, terrified crying. The SWATs with horrified faces above their weaponry were standing by doors closed with steel wire grids. The agents were waiting for orders. Inside the steel grids were children of all ages and all colours. Usually, there were three or four to a cage – their clothing soiled –their faces distraught.

Without waiting Saskia began searching the cages. She had gone down the first line in vain. Then at the far end of the second she found her – sitting on the floor sobbing quietly.

Saskia was a devout Catholic but, up to that point, she had not really believed in miracles. The agent standing at the door of the cells said quietly: 'Is she yours, Ma'am? I'm really glad but the others… We are just waiting for the gear to get the gates open without frightening them. It won't be long.'

*

She slept and slept and slept and the nightmares came and went. Holly woke her at last – she must have slept long too.

Gail had arranged it all. Saskia remembered almost nothing except Gail saying the best way was via London as now Ryanair were trying out a direct flight from London to Königshof. Unfortunately, they found out, it was only twice a week and not on the right day. London was still best then Frankfurt. They would stay in England for the night and Marc von Ritter would meet them and arrange it all. They must have got to Washington and Dulles International somehow but, as the British Airways flight took off, Saskia, shell shocked and exhausted sprawled out across Jurgen. On the other side Holly stared into a bemused space. Gail had whispered something to the authorities and somehow got them through security and the formalities with a minimum of disturbance.

Heathrow was enormous. They waited for ages in the Border Control queue. No special favours here. Eventually they were passed through and they fumbled their way to the arrivals gate. Waiting at the gate was the tall figure of Marc von Ritter. With him contrastingly was the tiny Tamara Oblova. Marc seized their minimal luggage, paid the car park charge and shepherded them into a military looking Landrover which, incongruously announced that it belonged to a mountain rescue team. How Marc had got hold of this vehicle remained a mystery.

By the time they turned out of the Airport complex onto the Motorway in the driving rain, the three travellers were asleep. Marc and Mara talked quietly together and in no time, they pulled up outside an old white panelled front door. Saskia turned down the offer of food and drink and Holly had hardly woken up. Marc bundled them upstairs into a low-ceilinged bedroom where miraculously a small bed had been prepared alongside the great four- poster. Both were immaculate with fresh linen. Somebody had been working hard.

Saskia woke in the morning, trying to remember where she was. The rain had stopped and pale winter sunshine streamed through a small gap in the curtains. She climbed out of bed, went to the bathroom and then looked through the crack in the curtains. Outside to the left the sun glinted on an expanse of water with barely a ripple. On the far side grassy meadows stretched away to scattered houses on the slopes of a gentle hill. Further ahead still on the other side of the water, lay a pontoon in front of a large sprawling house with a bare flagpole. Four young women were stretching their muscles. As she watched they climbed into the thin boat. The road below her looked clean and wet after the rain. There was not a soul about. She wondered why the road was empty. She looked at her watch. Nine o'clock. Then she worked it out. It was Sunday. There were noises downstairs. Saskia, now fully awake, put on her dressing gown, left the door open so she could watch in case Holly woke and then crept down the stairs. The kettle was singing its way to the boil. Marc was doubled into the fridge liberating diverse ingredients.

He looked round: 'Hello, have you slept?'

On being assured that she had, he added by way of explanation: 'Here you must have the full Irish breakfast, otherwise Detty would never forgive me. We have time, it's not far to the airport and the flight is later.'

Sausages, white pudding, eggs and bacon were duly produced and eaten with relish. Miraculously hot chocolate and strawberry cream appeared for Holly who began to look a little less lost.

Frankfurt Airport was also vast and they could have got lost but Mara had pulled diplomatic rank and called in a few favours to get them rapidly transferred to Hahn and into the departure lounge for the onward flight.

'Detty sends her apologies – she's in Venice, talking to the Mafia or something.'

Mara spluttered: 'Marc, you should respect your wife's professional activities and, anyway, the Mafia aren't in Venice.'

'I sit corrected' he said in English smiling.

It broke the tension and they all laughed.

At Königshof Airport they were bundled into a waiting car. They didn't even ask where they were going as the black limousine swished them through the city to the back entrance of the Hansehaus and up to the guest suite.

Saskia with Holly at her side went straight to bed. Jurgen accepted Marc's suggestion that they might go up to the Penthouse and have a *Zwetschgenwasser* before retiring. They sat for some minutes in silence.

'You have had a life of nightmares' Marc said after a pause.

Jurgen thought a moment: 'It has had its miracles too, but what about you? You say that I have had a life of nightmares but you experienced the full horror of Moltravia then you got Bernadette out and led the tanks across the Fojn and much else.'

'I always could be myself. Yes, I could well have been tortured and killed. My wife was tortured but somehow, we always knew what we wanted – where we were going. You didn't have that comfort – yet from the depths you emerged strong and brave.'

'To be here with Saskia and Holly is wonderful and extraordinary but somehow, when you have experienced so much, your confidence is shaken and you always wonder what is round the next corner.'

Marc just nodded.

19
FESTSPIELE

Stadtpfeifer, spielt! Dass 's lustigwied!

WAGNER *DIE MEISTERSINGER* ACT 3[28]

Detty stepped out of the stage door of the Fenice groping in the Venetian half-light for her *Handy* to turn it back on. She was pleased with herself – *Totti* had not only confirmed her agreement to come to Königshof but had fixed the date. *Totti*, had rushed back into her dressing room after her curtain calls following her death bed scene in *Traviata*. She was bubbling on a high after her rapturous reception. Was this a good moment, Detty had thought, to remind her of the promise, hastily given the summer before to sing *La Serva Padrona* at the *Nicklausfest*? *Totti* had remembered and had booked the date in her increasingly crowded diary. No, she hadn't told her agent but that didn't matter. She had blanked out that week. She then had thrown herself, breathlessly, into the organisation of her visit to Königshof. Her very senior *vestiarista* was good humouredly struggling to organise her bouncing young prima donna who, in her death scene, had moved the theatre to tears a few

---

28 Town pipers play and make us joyful.

minutes before. The dresser must have been frustrated but she didn't let the frustration show. Rather different, thought Detty, from her own first experience at Bayreuth with the efficient but fierce and gloomy Norn. *Totti* had said rather airily that she would sort out her agent but she had definitely booked the dates of the three performances and left ten days clear to allow for rehearsals and a bit of sight-seeing. Detty was left wondering if she would remember to square her agent. *Totti's* parting shot was that she wanted to meet Detty at Quadri for a snack when she had disposed of the rest of her adoring fans.

'You won't get any of this in Königshof,' warned Detty.

'Ah, no, but the fish, *mi sono appassionata dei pesci!*[29]' *Totti* called after her.

Detty made her way along the dripping narrow *Calle* from the theatre then realised that she had turned the wrong way. She turned back. The damp Venetian autumn had started in earnest. As soon as there was a signal her phone rang, she was miles away thinking about *Totti's* visit and wondering how her Tuscan soul would get on in a Baltic winter. Then she remembered something *Totti* had said about sub-zero temperatures being common in winter in the Tuscan hills. She had to grope in the pocket of her leather jacket to find the phone again. As she did so, she slipped sideways on the wet stone nearly losing her balance. She steadied herself against the damp wall, grateful that there was no canal alongside. At last, she answered the call.

'We've got them back.'

Marc's voice sounded relieved and pleased.

'And Holly?'

'She has had an awful time but she seems tough and to have taken to Saskia.'

'Where are you?'

'Henley. We got in late to Heathrow and the direct flight is from Stansted tomorrow afternoon, so I thought that we would stay at the house.'

'Oh God – what sort of state is the house in?'

---

29 I am a huge fan of fish.

'Don't worry – I rang Grace from America – she did a great job.'

'So, I'll see you in Königshof tomorrow evening?'

'We'll be there. One more thing – Saskia is very devout and she made a promise that if she ever got her daughter back, the first thing she would do was to have her baptised. She wants me to be a Godparent with Tanya but it must happen the day after tomorrow to get it in before Advent. All arranged by phone! Are you free?'

'Where is it to be?'

'Seesovils'

'Oh Lord – right out there. OK I'll have to do a bit of re-arranging so I can make it. If I can't manage it, can you go by yourself?'

'Of course, I still have leave, but they would love you to be there. Jurgen worships you.'

'You could set him right about that.'

She chuckled down the phone.

She knew that *Totti* would be at least an hour so she sauntered back to *San Marco* and down the *Piazzetta*. She gazed across at the floodlit splendour of the *Redentore*. She thought that it looked even more splendid, lit in the autumn darkness than with the summer sunshine. She remembered how she had looked at it for the first time in morning light on her honeymoon out from the window of the Danieli. So much had happened since then – some terrible things but good ones too. She felt contented; Venice always had that effect on her. She turned quickly and crossed the Piazza to the Café Quadri.

Totti was already there and greeted her with two highly coloured cocktails whose ingredients were beyond imagination. Detty thought that she detected Campari somewhere but the rest remained hidden. *Totti* laughed at her puzzlement and said: 'I don't know what is in them either, Fabio said they were on the 'ouse but would make my voice even more beautiful.'

'Change you into a dramatic soprano as like as not. I'd better mind my reputation.'

'*A proposito*, can we sing the Rossini *Stabat Mater* in Königshof later. As an extra I mean, I'd love to sing it with you.'

'You're trying to turn me into a mezzo now. I detect Italian cunning in all this. Sir Henry in London has already ticked me off for singing mezzo in *Die Meistersinger.*'

'What is a tick-off- some sort of illness?'

'Could be – a career threatening one.'

'Now you are being *furba*, I read sir Knight's notice of your Bayreuth *Elisabeth* – she is hardly a mezzo-no? And he said it was so wonderful that you were like a living saint.'

Detty laughed: 'You're serious about the Rossini?'

'*Certo, cara, perche no?*'

'OK, I'll ring Helga and see if the orchestra and chorus can fit it in this time on Sunday in the Cathedral. If not, we will try for Easter if you let me know any of your free dates and, this time we will get you a proper contract with your agents – if you tell them that we are not the Met.'

*

Detty left Niki with Gianna at Krenek and flew for a week in Ireland and on to Manchester to spend a couple of days with Eileen working on *Sieglinde* and the *Farberin*. Then she hired a car and went to Newcastle on the last day of November. It had been frosty in the morning on day of the meeting but the weather had turned into a cold, misty rain sodden day as she reached the racecourse at mid-morning for The Fighting Fifth Hurdle. She collected her Owners and Trainers badge. She bought a *Racing Post* to check the going and was somewhat relieved to find it was still rated 'Firm soft in places' despite the rain. She found Christy at the stables.

'How is she?'

'She's great. The pundits think that Boscastle will give her a race but they still don't really know her. How many Champion Hurdles does she have to win to convince them? However, she's only a shade of odds on, so you can make some money if you want to.'

'Thanks, but no – I'll just watch this time.'

There were only ten runners and only two others with any sort of a chance against the Champion. Boscastle had won the Triumph Hurdle at the last Festival in March in fine style. She came from a famous, in form, Somerset yard and was strongly fancied. Boots be Gone had won a couple of decent hurdles as a novice and had run well to come third in the Cesarewitch on the flat at that back end. He was known to have an excellent turn of foot. The others were really making up the numbers and running for a possible place in a valuable race. The pace was very steady from the start with no obvious front runner or pacemaker. It worried Detty and even Christy muttered 'Get on with it' to himself.

Normally Firebrand liked to be handy and to track the leaders but Christy and Jess had realised that a false pace was possible and dangerous for their genuine mare. Firebrand jumped the fourth hurdle behind a moderate leader with the two fancied horses tracking her. As soon as Jess had rounded the turn into the back straight and jumped the next hurdle, he let out a notch and the Champion flew the next two, leaving the rest standing and turning for home twelve lengths in front. There was a murmur from the crowd. The gap just increased over the next three hurdles as Firebrand raced up the hill with her fancied opponents struggling fruitlessly to close the gap. She was better than ever. Detty smiled joyfully as she talked to the TV interviewers. She was photographed with the bookmaker sponsors and collected the statuette with Christy and Jess. Too easy she thought as she thanked Christy and his head lad and said an affectionate farewell to her mare.

'See you at Leopardstown if not before' she shouted as she drove out of the owners' car park and back to Manchester Airport. Leading bookmakers, she heard on the radio, had made Firebrand the seven to four favourite for the next year's Champion Hurdle. They knew how good she was at last.

*

The four nights of *Der Freischutz* which opened the Festival, went smoothly and were enthusiastically received. In between, sold out weeks in advance, were Hank's two performances of *Der Wintereise*. After the second the President had arranged a reception for Hank and Trudi Meyer, his accompanist, in the newly restored grand circle bar. After a short speech, Nicklaus presented Hank with a scroll conferring upon him the title of *Kammersänger* of Livonia. Nicklaus commented that he was the first recipient of the honour and he couldn't imagine a more distinguished one. Hank courteous, as ever, replied that this was an honour that he would treasure most particularly.

As the reception ended, Hank took her on one side.

'You've sure arranged this year's operas without a part for me.'

The smile twitching round Hank's mouth gave him away.

'I thought that I was supposed to be the prima donna. And anyway, if doing two public workshops and singing two *Winterreisen* to packed houses isn't enough for you we will see what we can do. Anyway, I have another thrill for you – you could sing the *Cujus animam* in the cathedral with us on Sunday evening. Your pin-up, Dottoressa Spinelli, wants us to do the Rossini as an extra. I have arranged the orchestra, choir and bass but not the tenor yet. There will be a collection for the cathedral restoration. Are you on?

'Hold me back.'

'Then if you are still not fully occupied – how about *'O sink hernieder'* together for the final concert?'

She had said it as a joke but he looked at her with his mouth still twitching with a smile:

'If you are up to speed learning it, I love a challenge. We will do it. I need to go to Berlin for a couple of days to-morrow but when I get back how about a rehearsal in the flat at Krenek?'

'Marc wouldn't approve. We will rehearse it in the Music Room at the *Schloss* with Helge as accompanist/chaperone.'

'Spoil sport – you can't have *Tristan* without passion.'

'That's what you tell Annaliese Seiling, I suppose.'

Detty could be mischievous in her turn and the exact relationship between the great tenor and the leading dramatic soprano of the day was the frequent subject of speculation both public and private.

'Jealous?'

'Arrogant bastard! But shall we really do it? Keep it under wraps. We must ask Helge and I'll see if I can get a score from Bayreuth and if possible, parts with the concert ending. I don't even know if parts still exist. If we announce it, we will have half the world's musical press here.'

'We need a *Brangäne* for the *Zinne*.'

'I have suggested Julia Kitze learns it. I think that she would jump at it. She's been working at it for some time – in secret of course.'

'Fine – see you in a couple of days.'

'Give my respects to Annaliese.'

Hank playfully motioned to smack Detty's bottom.

'Hey, I'll sue you for sexual harassment – I bet you don't dare do that to Anneliese.'

He just smiled.

But the seed was sown. Traditionally the programme for the final concert was an impromptu affair with snippets from the other artists and works that had been performed earlier. There was also a contribution from the winning school choir and anything else that fitted in. It was traditionally quite an informal occasion.

Only Marc and Helge were let into the secret. Marc just said 'You cannot be serious,' with a fair American accent. Helge sighed and said: 'You must both be mad; we've only got a week. Fortunately, everything else is in place. But I will probably finish up with an orchestra strike – hugely difficult score at short notice – you know. However, they did do the orchestral version of the Prelude and Liebestod at Hamburg in the spring so it won't be entirely fresh ground. I'll accompany you at the piano if they won't play ball.'

But Helge used his usual magic and the orchestra agreed and threw themselves into rehearsing secretly and with meticulous enthusiasm.

*

The following morning, it was raining hard as Detty drove to Krenek. She had the radio on to try and hear the weather forecast. She had missed it and the news had started. She was concentrating on the road not the announcer but, with a start, she started listening:

'Henry Schliessen, the famous singer and benefactor of the new republic of Livonia, was involved in a road accident last night in the outskirts of Berlin when his Ferrari was hit by a lorry. Mr Schliessen was admitted to hospital in Berlin. We have no further details about his condition.'

Detty swung into the gates of Krenek, not concentrating and far too fast, she missed one of the massive brick pillars by a coat of paint. She was using Marc's Mercedes for ease of carrying Niki around and she wasn't quite used to its generous dimensions. Leaping out of the car, she dashed up to the flat and rang the office at the *Schloss*.

'Regina, can you ring the Berlin police and try to find out which hospital Hank Schliessen is in? I don't know if you have heard the news but he has had a car accident and has been taken to hospital in Berlin.'

She changed her shoes and grabbed her bike, flung her handbag in the pannier, and rode up to the *Schloss*. She never took the car unless she had a lot to carry. Up in her studio she tried to concentrate on a few administrative papers. The score of *Tristan* lay reproachfully on the piano. She couldn't bear to look at it.

There was a knock at the door.

'Irina has come for her tutorial, Frau Bernadette, she's in the Reading Room.'

'Send her up,'

Hurriedly, she took the *Tristan* score off the piano and turned it over to hide it. She picked up the phone again. There was no answer from Regina, the secretary. Impatiently she dialled the internal number; it was engaged.

She went to speak to the Librarian: 'Daina, can you ring Regina and say that I've got a tutorial and will 'phone her as soon as I have finished but I can't answer the 'phone for an hour'.

Detty found it hard to concentrate during her class with a junior budding mezzo soprano and hoped that she hadn't upset the youngster with her distracted air. At last, they got to the end and agreed the practice for the next week.

Feverously, she picked up the phone again and dialled the college office. 'Any luck, Regina?'

'So, so I rang *LuftBrücke Präsidium* direct. They were very helpful but didn't know which hospital. They said that they were going to contact

Direktion 6 – apparently the accident happened to the east of the city – and get some details. They will ring me back.'

'OK, Ring me on the mobile as soon as you get any news.'

She had to go back to Königshof to the theatre. She had arranged a meeting with all the people involved in the final concert. She couldn't let them down. She ran straight into Helge von Grunstrand coming out of the library. Breathlessly she gave him the news of Hank. His face said it all.

After a pause, he said: 'What are you doing now?'

She explained that she had to go to Königshof.

'I'll give you a lift if you like. I must go to the theatre for an orchestra rehearsal. The car's by the door.'

'Bless you but I must take the car in case I need it later. You could give me a lift back to the Lodge though it would save a few minutes.'

'OK Hop in'

She grabbed her rucksack opened it and checked that she had the schedule for the final concert. It would have to be altered now with no Hank and the paperwork was vital. She put it over on the back seat.

It only took a couple of minutes to get back to the Lodge. She grabbed her rucksack and got out.

As Helge drove off, he called out of the window: 'Let me know when you hear anything more definite.'

'Will do – leave your *Handy* on as much as you can.'

Detty knew that Helge turned his phone off when he was working and often forgot to turn it back on. She turned to the parked Mercedes and dived into her rucksack for the keys. She groped round then opened the bag fully – no keys. Thinking back, she remembered that in her haste she noticed that she had left a small opening in the main compartment when shutting the bag in haste at the *Schloss*. The keys must have fallen out in Helge's car. She punched in his number on her *Handy* – the cool voice informed her that the number she was trying to reach was either switched off or unobtainable. She stood swearing to herself – today of all days!

She rang Helge again – the same cool voice. Heaven knows when Helge would think to turn his phone back on despite her parting exhortation. She stopped to think. Marc certainly had another set of keys but he was in Ingoldstadt, training a new detachment, and almost certainly on an exercise where civilian mobile phones were forbidden. She couldn't think of anything else to do and automatically punched in his number.

The relief swept over her as a warm voice said: *'Schatzi?'*

There was no reproach, no 'why are you calling me at work?' He knew that it must be important.

She tumbled it all out. 'I know that you have another set of keys but have you got them with you?'

'No, they are two spare sets and one is in the flat at Krenek, in my new 'junk' drawer in the sitting room. You will find a heap of stuff from my misspent youth on top of them – photos of old flames etc but none of it's a secret from you and if you rummage around you will find them – I try to hide them a bit in case of a break-in.'

'Thanks, darling, you are wonderful.'

'See you Monday'.

She tore up to the flat and opened the 'junk' drawer. Marc had brought a load of personal stuff back from Oberdorf a month before as Sophie was organising a Christmas party and needed to use his room. There was a lot of old certificates and photographs but only a few of girls. Detty grinned – he had been taking the Micky, as he often did. Even in her haste she paused for a moment over one official looking letter dated a few years before they met. It was headed *Deutsche Kanu Verband* and read 'as a result of the recent trials *Oberleutnant Marc von Ritter* is selected for the *Deutsche Olympische SportBund* in *Wildwasserkanufahren.*' No wonder he was so capable in a canoe at their escape. She found the keys and ran back to the car.

She had just got into the loneliest forested part of the road when her phone signalled an SMS.

'Hospital is *Unfallkrankenhaus*, Berlin. The department direct telephone 030 xx xx xx xx.'

She drew to the side of the road onto a track into the forest and played the message again scribbling the number down on a used car park ticket. There was a signal on her mobile but weak and variable. She got out of the car and it was slightly better. She rang the number. The first time she forgot the 0049, cursed and started again but reception was diabolical and there was some breaking up.

'Should have waited until I got to the city' she thought as an official sounding voice answered. But it was too late now.

'My name is Bernadette von Ritter and I am ringing for information about Henry Schliessen who I believe was admitted to your unit after a road traffic accident.'

'Are you a relative?'

'No, a close friend and colleague.'

'Wait one moment.'

After a pause, the voice crackled back:

'Can you repeat the name?'

'Heinrich – Henry in English –Schliessen. '

She spelt it amidst the signal break-up.

'Ah Heinrich' the voice broke up a bit but she could just hear Schliessen'.

'*Genau!*' she said anxiously.

'He is critical. He has multiple serious injuries.'

'Is he going to be all right?'

'We will do everything that we can for him but he is very gravely injured. The outcome cannot be certain.'

Cold with fear, foolishly she asked again: 'But is he going to survive?'

The voice was still cool and patient but now even more broken up: 'We cannot say. It is too early as I said he is very gravely injured.'

She murmured a strangled '*Danke*' and finished the call. Then she rested on a felled log and burst into tears. All her long memories of Hank flooded by – the schoolgirl who wrote from Ireland and got the precious signed photo, Bayreuth and the miraculous *Siegfried*, his generosity in Livonia, the real live knight errant coming to the rescue in Florence and much, much more. She must go to him but she knew that she couldn't. The whole final concert had to be cancelled or at least rearranged. If he dies, we must cancel but if he is still in hospital, we must do something. She had to go on to Königshof and find Helga and the others. They were supposed to be having an orchestra rehearsal at the theatre as soon as Hank got back the following day.

It was a very gloomy meeting at the theatre. Everybody now knew about the accident to Hank. Detty as chair had to explain that they must make a contingency plan although if Hank died the concert would of course be cancelled as a mark of respect. The second half of the programme had been left blank at Detty's request to allow for the *Tristan* duets. The committee had a vague idea that Hank and Detty were up to something but miraculously the security had held even with the orchestra involved.

'I can see no reason to keep you in the dark any longer,' she explained and told them about the planned *Tristan* duets as a preview for the possible production the following year.

'We now need to fill this gap if we are able to go ahead.'

'Why not take the Rossini out of the Cathedral and give that instead. I am sure one of the other tenors will sing – particularly given the circumstances.'

'It won't please the Cardinal after he has graciously given permission but I am sure he will appreciate the difficulties we find ourselves in.'

'If you need something else, I will do *'Che farò'* said Julia 'if I am no longer needed for the other.'

The 'other' was *Brangäne* but even now Julia thought that she shouldn't mention it in public.

'Thanks, that would be very helpful.'

At that moment Helge entered, apologised for being unavoidably late but incongruously was grinning broadly. Detty was conscious of a moving shadow which became larger and more substantial in the dark theatre corridor behind the Bar.

There was a gasp as a broad unmistakeable American voice said: 'Helge tells me that you have been arranging my funeral service. I am rather sorry, in one way, to have to give you a rain-check – the musical programme sounded rather good.'

Hank smiled broadly and appeared in excellent health apart from a collar and cuff sling on his left arm.

'I don't think this will get in the way – in fact if we were doing the whole act, it would save *Melot* a job and might fit in rather well. Perhaps I will have to settle for you kissing it better, Detty.'

Detty, mouth open, said: 'What on earth…?'

'I think that I can explain' said Helge 'My secretary had a phone call to ask whether she could arrange a taxi to collect Herr Schliessen from the Berlin train. As Detty had told me that he was probably dying, this seemed rather an odd message so I rang the hospital. They told me that Yes, Herr Schliessen had been involved in an accident but that he had been discharged that morning as he only had a fracture of his left elbow. He had left his contact address with the Berlin police. I was astonished and explained that this flew in the face of the information that one of my colleagues had been given. They said that they would look up Frau von Ritter's earlier call, check and ring me back.'

'When the call came there was some embarrassment. The details given to Detty had referred to a Herr Heinrich Thiessen who was indeed on a life support machine from a severe accident in the east of the city the night before. The official who had given the misinformation would be disciplined for not having carried out the complete and proper identification protocol.'

'That seems rather unfair' broke in Detty 'she tried to do the right thing but I was in the depths of the forest and the line kept breaking up. She was very helpful and anyway it was probably my fault for explaining that Henry was the English version of Heinrich. I had better ring them and try and get the unfortunate girl off the hook.'

'Next time, Bernadette, that you appear in *Siegfried* it had better be as the *Waldvogel* – she is pretty clear even in the depths of the forest.'

'You are insufferable, Hank, particularly as your alter ego is on a life support machine.'

'Yes, poor chap, I stand corrected, Frau Komturin. But I have got one thing right. I have located the parts for the concert ending. Annaliese knew somebody who had a copy and they are being sent from Munich by express courier. I will give them to you Helge and you, Detty, as soon as I get them. There are thirteen extra bars with voice and eight more for orchestra which come dovetailed from the close of Act 3'.

The weekend was frantic. Detty spent all Thursday night alone at the keyboard rehearsing herself. She finished tired, dissatisfied, disheartened and miserable with herself despite the joy of Hank's miraculous re-appearance. She needed a proper *repetiteur* and she needed a proper coach.

She had promised to rehearse with Hank and Helge on the Tuesday but she didn't feel that she could possibly be ready. She roused herself from her thoughts of looming professional disaster. Get help. She rang Eileen in Manchester only to be told that she was judging a vocal competition in Sydney. She then rang Haydn Roberts. To her relief a rich Welsh baritone answered the phone. After the usual pleasantries she asked in trepidation:

'What are you doing at present?'

'Why not much, my love, digging leeks, just a few private lessons and a bit of judging.'

'How do you fancy an immediate trip to Livonia? I need help – Act two of *Tristan*. I have learnt it but we have just a week and it's going badly. By the way, it's the missing concert ending – Hank has found a copy.'

'All I've sung was the rather ineffective instruction to our hero to "Save yourself" but I have taught it and know the score backwards. Yes, I think that I can help. Yours to command. I can postpone one pupil.'

'Can you get to Stansted by to-morrow morning. There's a direct Saturday flight. I'll meet you. Should I ask Trudi Meyer if she will accompany us? Helge is swamped but Trudi has stayed on after accompanying Hank in *Winterreise* to play the Chopin Opus 27 Nocturnes at the final concert. She offered to help me when I panicked.'

'Good idea. I would like to work with her. I heard her play Chopin in London – marvellous. As we are short of time we will run through with her tomorrow. I haven't sung tenor for a bit' he chuckled 'but I dare say I can mark it for you until you get the real one.'

She felt better immediately and arranged for rooms in the village at Krenek for Haydn and Trudi the following evening.

*

They started that evening. Notwithstanding his years, Haydn had lost none of his phenomenal energy. For their first run through he just marked the soprano cues and listened hard. At the end he looked pensively for a moment at an anxious Detty.

'Well?' she said.

'There's nothing wrong with the voice. The sound is fantastic.'

'But?'

'But you're not in the role. I know that it is difficult without a partner and for a concert. But you're giving it a real concert rendering – correct – vocally secure – but no drama. Let's go back a bit – Act 1 – you are a furious Irish princess, deeply in love with the man who killed your fiancé. You hate him and love him and hate yourself for loving him and to cap it all he has betrayed you. Inside you is turmoil. You know it will, must, end in death – eternal night – you want it to. But this is the one earthly night you have with him before the longed-for abyss swallows you both up. You are enough of a human woman to need this man and to muse on the word *und*. This one night you are in a human union and hope, uselessly, that it will never end. It is almost a truism that *Tristan* is entirely Schopenhauer's metaphysics. Of course it is, but it is more, there is real humanity in it. Both the principals are real human beings expressing love and suffering as only human beings can.'

Detty was silent for a long time staring into space. Trudi kept her head in her score. Haydn wondered if he had got it wrong and destroyed Detty's self-confidence rather than helping her.

She smiled at Haydn and said quietly in English: 'Thank you for that. I need a few hours to re-think. How about to-morrow morning at eleven? Can you both make it?'

'*Morgen Mittag am Elf*' Haydn laughed 'now that's a role that would really suit you, Frau Gräfin. I would love to hear you in *Capriccio*.'

'Let's get *Isolde* right first.'

Fortunately, Gianna and Niki had gone to Oberdorf for a few days and the Lodge was empty. She worked feverishly until the small hours with Haydn's dramatic picture always before her. At two in the morning, she felt that she had got it right bar some fine tuning on phrasing.

The following day it was a different performance with Haydn making a fair stab at the tenor part. Then on the Tuesday she really enjoyed the full piano rehearsal of the three duets with Hank, complete with Julia's solo from the tower. Helge had asked Trudi if she would play so that he could listen and, ever willing, she agreed.

The final concert started with the winning school choir. To Detty's surprise and delight the girls of The Sacred Heart had won the competition for the first time since the Convent had been overrun. They received a well merited ovation and she made a mental note to go and give her personal congratulations after the concert was over.

Moving onto the professionals, *Totti* thrilled the audience with her signature '*E strano*' straight from La Fenice and a good contrast with the Pergolesi and Paisiello of *La Serva Padrona* which she had done earlier in the Festival.

Detty was pleased with the high standard of the programme. Hank had insisted that, despite his welcome re-appearance, Julia Kitze should give her rendering of the immortal '*Che faro*' even though it lengthened the programme. Then it was the turn of Trudi who through high talent and hard work had now achieved international stature. Detty felt a swell of patriotic pride as she listened to her heartfelt playing of the Chopin Nocturnes. After all, John Field the originator of the Nocturne had been born in Dublin and was honoured in the National Concert Hall where Detty's career had begun. As she listened to Trudi's magical timing, she was conscious of the adage 'don't concentrate on the notes just listen to the silences.' It all passed far too quickly but she was grateful for the chance to relax for a moment in the magic that Chopin conjured by way of Trudi's fingers, before her own great test. The thunderous applause demanded an encore and Trudi, tactful as ever and conscious of time constraints played the miniature B flat minor Mazurka. Detty kept to herself in the interval, getting into role as Haydn had directed. There would be time for socialising afterwards.

The second part of the concert was merely referred to as an 'additional musical offering from local musicians.' Nobody knew quite what to expect but there was an air of anticipation which burst into thunderous applause as Helge ushered the three soloists onto the platform. She was very anxious singing the great '*O sink hernieder*' duet from cold but once started the music took over and in a seeming instant, they were pausing for Julia who was placed at the back of the orchestra for her upstage warning. Hank sang *Tristan*'s musing monologue on love delicately and then she questioned the *und* with her eyes on him and eternity. On to '*So stürben wir um ungetrennt*' and finally the climax of '*O ew'ge Nacht*' fading into the gentle Liebestod inspired concert ending.

It was not what the audience had expected and for some moments they seemed stunned. Then gradually the applause started and swelled. Detty, apprehensive, was looking down. Then she looked up at the huge grinning figure of Hank, smiled at last and remembered to bow. The dressing rooms were pandemonium. Excited, the Sacred Heart students coming to collect their neatly pressed concert clothes, milled round Hank, Detty and Julia trying to fight their way through to a modicum of privacy. One of the students realised that they were literally bumping into two of the living legends of Livonia. She whispered to her companions and they all stood back respectfully. Detty paused and smiled at all of them:

'You sang superbly' she said, 'I was so, so proud of you all.'

Then they rushed forward with their concert programmes pleading

'Please, Fräulein O'Neill, please!' as they begged for her autograph thrusting their programmes forward. Detty, happy, began to think that she would never be able to get to her dressing room but she didn't really mind.

20
NO LAWS BUT HIS OWN

What fools are they that have not known,
That love likes no laws but his own,
Away with these self-loving lads.

JOHN DOWLAND

The sea fog was thick. The nearer that they got to the coast the thicker it got. Marc, guiding the family Mercedes with unaccustomed care, swore softly in the Franconian patois of his schooldays. To Detty's relief, the fine brick spire of the Seesovils church finally appeared over the top of the fog. It reminded her of Cleeve Hill miraculously surfacing from the mist of Cheltenham on the day of the Champion Hurdle. The church itself was a wonder. The ancient brick building, whose spire had once guided the cobs of the Hanse, had miraculously survived the wars of the twentieth century and the civil war. In an admirable ecucmenical moment the Lutheran pastor had agreed to make his church regularly available to the tiny Catholic section of the population of small coastal village. The Sunday service was still in progress as they arrived and it was a strange feeling to stand listening to a Lutheran service while they all tried to keep warm. Detty was taken back to Oxford when she had sung John Keble's words 'Blest are the pure in heart' to the melody that she now listened to from inside the church. She had not heard it for years but dimly remembered that the tune was called 'Franconia'. She must look it up and find out the German words. Saskia and Jurgen arrived with a rosy cheeked Holly, the leading lady of the day. With them were Jurgen's father and mother who farmed on the rich coastal soil just inland from the village. Shortly afterwards the portly local Father Kampe bustled up the path. Saskia did the introductions. Tanya, who had had to go to an antenatal visit and who had come separately was the last to arrive, rapidly driving up to the church door and swinging her heavily pregnant, disabled body expertly out of the adapted vehicle onto her crutches. She remarked with a smile that soon she would need one of Marc's tanks.

They listened to the blessing at the end of the service. Jurgen and Father Kampe courteously thanked the Minister at the door for the use of his church and he, in turn, welcomed them. The ceremony was short and Holly was duly baptised as 'Holly Liese' with Tanya and Marc as Godparents. Saskia had had to be restrained from making it 'Holly, Liese, Bernadette, Tatiana, Gail' but eventually agreed that it would overload the little girl and that it was best to honour only her dead benefactor.

They went back to Jurgen's parents' farm. A large gathering of friends, neighbours and more distant relatives of Jurgen's all arrived bearing parcels which they presented to a wide-eyed Holly. The table laden with steaming soups, salads, piragi and cheeses accompanied by copious quantities of beer and honey liqueur. Marc and Tanya, sober for their different reasons, teased the others about their prospect of sore heads while Jurgen's father bounced his newly found granddaughter on his knee and tried to teach her to call him *dyevachka* which made her giggle.

They headed back to the city in the early winter dusk – mission number one accomplished.

*

The President looked at the formal request for an audience and was puzzled. It was not that its contents were puzzling; he got all sorts of requests for meetings or interventions daily and normally they were sifted by the office downstairs. This time, however, the request had been sent straight up to him and he knew why when he saw who the signatories were. He stared at the list at the bottom of the page –Max Schäfer – First Minister, Sergei Malinov –Defence Minister, Ulrich Zahnsdorf – Commander-in-Chief Armed Forces and Bernadette O'Neill-Komturin Order of Sankt Nicklaus. What on earth was going on? Any of these people could have had immediate access to him by a simple phone call, so why the sudden formality? It sounded like a palace revolution except that the list contained his staunchest allies and none of them would be likely to interfere with the democratic process which had been so hard won. Better find out. He rang Petra.

'Arrange for this meeting as soon as they all can make it and my diary is clear, Petra. I have no idea what is going on.'

'Neither have I, Herr Präsident, I will do it at once.'

He busied himself with the other papers. After an hour he looked at his watch and went for a coffee with his mind still on the strange request. The internal phone rang.

'I have fixed the meeting for seven this evening, Herr Präsident. You have the Engineering Conference to open in town this afternoon but that should allow you plenty of time.'

'Thanks, Petra.'

He was unaccountably anxious as the clock approached seven. He couldn't think why. These people were some of his oldest friends and colleagues. He wished that Mara was around but she had gone to Bialovsk to open a college and was staying overnight at Bishop Dieter's house, Petra announced very formally: 'The Herr Ministerpräsident, Frau Komturin O'Neill, Herr Komtur General Malinov. Herr General Zahnsdorf for you, Herr Präsident.'

'Thank you, Petra. Come in Detty and friends. What can I do for you?'

He deliberately used Bernadette's nick name. He wasn't going to join in this charade whatever its purpose might be.

'We are here to present a petition to you, Herr Präsident' said the Prime Minister handing an important looking scroll to Nicklaus. He took it and read:

'We the undersigned formally petition the Hochmeister of the Hanseatic Order of Sankt Nicklaus that the Rank and Honour of Ritterin of the Order of be conferred on Frau Tamara Nickolaevna Oblova in recognition of her gallantry and distinguished service to the people and freedoms of the Hanseatic Republik of Livonia.'

Below were the signatures and ranks of each of the petitioning party.

Nicklaus paused for some time gazing at the paper then he looked up. This time he was formal.

'Frau Komturin, gentlemen' he said 'you know very well that I have always disapproved strongly of marks of distinction conferred on myself or my family. I have in fact turned down several requests made less formally for an honour for my daughter. However, as you also well know, it would be arrogant and unconstitutional of me not to approve an official request from the Minister Präsident, the two *Komture* and the father of a late heroic *Ritterin* of the Order. Under protest, your petition is granted. As you all know the order is limited to thirty-six members and after the sad events of last year there are now two unfilled vacancies. I propose that Frau Oberleutnant Malinowska is awarded the second vacancy in recognition of her distinguished service at the time of the outrage and since. As you know we already have protestant members and the Chaplain has no objection to her admission as long as she can swear the oath. I instruct you Frau Komturin to approach the candidates and secure their willingness to serve. The Ceremony of Initiation can take place at the Commanderie on 27th December, the Feast of St John the Apostle, and a symbol of steadfastness.'

'As you are all gathered here may I also make a request' said Nicklaus 'May I ask this company if we may use the Hall of the Commanderie for the Wedding Breakfast after the forthcoming marriage of my daughter and David Sensky and Alexandra Kulanova and Jurgen Holberg?'

Detty spoke as first Komturin: 'It seems entirely appropriate if one bride is to become one of the junior members of the Order. Is there any objection?'

A shaking of the heads and it was settled.

The men left. Detty stayed behind.

'I have a very undiplomatic title for you, young lady' the President said when they were alone 'you fixed this – didn't you?'

'If you think so, Herr Präsident' said Detty demurely.

Then suddenly they both laughed.

'But I couldn't have done it myself, could I?'

Nicklaus didn't wait for an answer: 'But I have one piece of revenge, you will preside and Sergei will take the Komtur's role at their initiation. Of course, I will be there. I would not miss it for the world but I will stand with the regular members for Mara and only resume my place for Irina. I am glad everybody agreed to her initiation. It will honour the Unit –the dead and the survivors.'

'They thoroughly deserve it but, for me, it will be a particular privilege to honour your family and my dearest friend.'

'You always have the last word!'

Smiling at her sucessful gambit, she left closing the office door quietly.

*

The preparations were complete for the morrow and Mara was sitting in the half-light by the window looking out over the darkening sea. Detty crept in, pulled up another chair and sat beside her in the unlit salon. As the light seeped away and the lights of the city below shone more brightly, Mara broke the silence.

'I can only say it to you. After everything, after all the horrors, I cannot believe that it is happening to me. Last week there was a crowd cheering when I got out of the car here coming back from the Initiation. I felt so proud of my sash. For years I suppose that I have slightly resented being a sort of also-ran public figure although, of course, I have done my best to support *Vati* – he is so lonely poor thing. But this time it was different; it was for me, I felt, and not just for the President's daughter and I loved it. I blushed scarlet with pleasure and excitement – not very *ritterlich* – I suppose but not the worst of my sins. I am so lucky. To love and be loved by David, to be welcomed by the people, it is too good to be real. I am so glad the wedding tomorrow is to be with Jurgen and Saskia – somehow, they hold me down to reality and make me realise that it isn't a fairy tale after all.'

*

The twenty first of January dawned sunny but bitterly cold. Saskia woke early in the large simply furnished guest bedroom of the formal downstairs apartment of the Hansehaus. She got up, shivered and realised the heating was not yet fully on. She swept the curtains back, looked at the sparse morning traffic in the road below and then jumped back into bed and lay thinking. She had chosen the date. It had been deliberate and she thought it would go unnoticed. She did not realise that her fellow bride, Mara, had a passion for the English poet Keats. She had smiled when Saskia suggested the day over coffee together. It was practical – clear of New Year and Epiphany and before Lent, Saskia had explained.

'Very true' to her surprise Mara had answered 'I think it will suit very well. It is also the feast of St Agnes patron saint of chastity, engaged couples and rape victims. I feel a bit left out but I suppose I qualify under the second one.'

Saskia had felt angry and blushed. Then she had realised that Mara was obviously embarrassed at what she had said: 'All right. You think that I qualify under all three. Wrong, hardly the first and, well, I cannot now really plead the third – given the outcome. But how did you know? I have never thought of you as a hagiographical encyclopaedia.'

'The English poem of Keats – *St Agnes Eve* – I looked up all the details of the Saint and the day. I had struggled with a poem of his at school when my English was even worse than it is now but I liked it and somehow it stuck with me. Then later my English got better and when I was wounded and convalescing at Oberdorf, Detty got me a copy of his complete works and I read all the poems and really loved them. He is so sad and so romantic – to think that he died so young.'

*

As the Procession gathered under the tympanum of the west door with its famous supplication *'Mater Dei Ora pro Nobis'*,[30] snow began to fall again. The choir entered singing the great chorale which opens the *Wachet auf* cantata. Then came the lectors and servers, all glad to be out of the cold. The Cardinal Archbishop processed in with Bishop Dieter behind. The two couples followed. They had argued about the procession order. Mara had declared that it should be strictly alphabetical and as Kulanova and Holberg both came before Oblova and Sensky there could be no argument.

'But you…' Saskia had started:

'I am a citizen of the Hanseatic Republic of Livonia – like you, like all of us – you remember. There is to be no argument.'

There was a determination in Mara's eyes that made Saskia think that it was better not to argue. Then she had found the answer.

'We go up first, you come down first – nothing could be fairer than that.'

To her relief, Mara had nodded. 'All right then – you minx!' she knew that for once Saskia had outsmarted her.

'I've been called worse things than that in my time.'

*

Saskia tall and elegant in her burgundy silk dress with its embroidered bodice walked up alongside Jurgen, smart in his black suit and sneaking frequent glances at his beautiful bride. Mara's dress was of old gold silk in a Romani style. It set off her cascading golden curls splendidly. David from his great height reached down to hold her hand and kept looking at her unbelievingly.

Detty was pleased with herself. Her wedding presents to the brides looked gorgeous and had increased her already high standing with Lanoure. It had also given them the chance of a riotous few days as a

---

30 Mother of God pray for us

sixsome in Paris culminating in lunch at *Le Grand Vefour* before flying home.

For her own dress she had reverted to olive green silk with a matching cloak. She had insisted that she paid for it all but even with her healthy finances, she had shuddered at the size of the bill. It had taken the prize money from the Fighting Fifth Hurdle and a bit more besides. It was worth it as, after all, this was a special event.

Nicklaus Oblov and Jurgen's parents followed the couples and last in the procession came the two witnesses; Marc pushed the wheelchair of Tanya. To avoid crowding the ceremony the two couples had decided to have the same witnesses.

Hank had gone straight to the choir section to sing the tenor solo in *Zion hört die Wächter singen* over the grand old tune of the *Wachet auf* cantata.

The Cardinal greeted the congregation and led them in the Penitential Rite then the combined choirs sang the *Gloria* from Schubert's German Mass. The Cardinal asked everybody to join his prayers for the two couples.

Marc gave the first reading from Proverbs 31 dwelling on the incomparable value of a worthy wife. The resonance with the final chorus of *Fidelio* was clear and the choice had pleased them all. The choir sang Waldhuter's setting of Psalm 103. Nicklaus gave the second reading from the Book of Revelation Chapter 19. After the Alleluia, Bishop Dieter read the Gospel, the moving exhortation by Christ on love from St John chapter nineteen. The Cardinal's homily was short. He took the opportunity to publicly ask forgiveness for his past error and then praised the courage and fortitude of both couples which had brought them to the altar. Then he stressed the power of marriage and the nuptial sacrament before asking them if they would bring up children in the love of God. First Saskia and Jurgen gave their vows followed by the exchange of rings then Mara and David.

Detty and Walther Liebig went forward to sing the cheerful duet *'Mein Freund is mein!'* from *Wachet auf* and then led the whole congregation in the final chorale *'Gloria sei dir gesungen'*.

Detty whispered to Walter as the sopranos soared 'that's not a bad sound for a load of amateurs.'.

'Arrogance doesn't suite you, Signora Contessa'.

'No, I should be ashamed of myself. Confession next Sunday!'

The Cardinal offered a special intercession for the soul of Bishop Majorowski and Mara groped into David's pocket and surreptitiously wiped away a tear. The *Sanctus* rang out from the choir and Detty sang the *Benedictus*.

The Lord's Prayer followed and the blessing of the couples. After the sign of peace, the Cardinal broke the host as the choir sang Schubert's *Zum Agnus Dei*.

Then with them all kneeling except the singer, Detty again stepped forward to sing Mozart's '*O Gotteslamm*' as the Cardinal took the bread and wine giving the Host to the two couples then to the rest of the congregation as they came forward. This time there was no hitch. Detty joined the back of the queue feeling like the student teacher she had been at The Sacred Heart all those years before. The Blessing and Dismissal followed quickly and the recessional procession move to the West door with the choir singing '*Jesus bleibet meine Freunde*'.

At the door, the Cardinal Archbishop greeted the guests. He stepped forward as Detty and Marc arrived.

'Frau Bernadette, I cannot tell you how much I was moved by the service and particularly your singing to-day. This has been a wonderful start for the young people. I trust that they are not overwhelmed by it and are able to build on it.'

'Your Eminence, I think that there is one virtue in the horrors that they have overcome and that is that they have come to be strong and to know themselves. I think they will be OK.'

'That is wise, my daughter; may it be as you predict! *Pax vobiscum!*'

ACKNOWLEDGEMENTS

To Elizabeth and Malcom Ecclestone for their comforting and expert musical help and text editing, Janet and Dick Turpin for reading the texts and helpful suggestions, Lauren Bailey and Holly Porter of Troubador for putting up with me, Kirsti Neumueller for helpful Bayreuth advice.

Also encouragement and advice from: The late Jennifer France, Diana du Luart, Ted Edmondson, Peter Pearson, Jo Cummins, Steve Robson and many others.